AFRICAN COVENANT SERIES

1

THE PRIDE

AND THE

PASSION

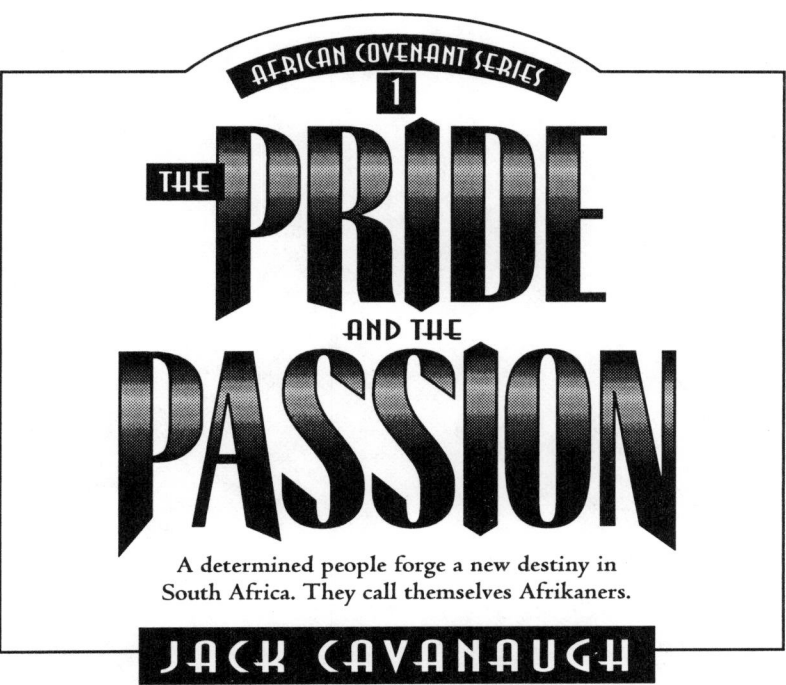

AFRICAN COVENANT SERIES

1

THE PRIDE AND THE PASSION

A determined people forge a new destiny in
South Africa. They call themselves Afrikaners.

JACK CAVANAUGH

MOODY PRESS

CHICAGO

ISBN: 0-8024-0862-1

1 3 5 7 9 10 8 6 4 2

Printed in the United States of America

This story about a young woman is dedicated to my two daughters, Elizabeth and Keri—both young women now—and their friends:

Nolina Beauchamp
Crister DeGuzman
Summer Hellewell
Lindsay Howard
Cindy Knight
Danielle Leming
Cari Lowery
Meghan McClure
Jaimme Pascua
Djuna Passman
Ariane Porras
Deana Shifter
Caroline Travis

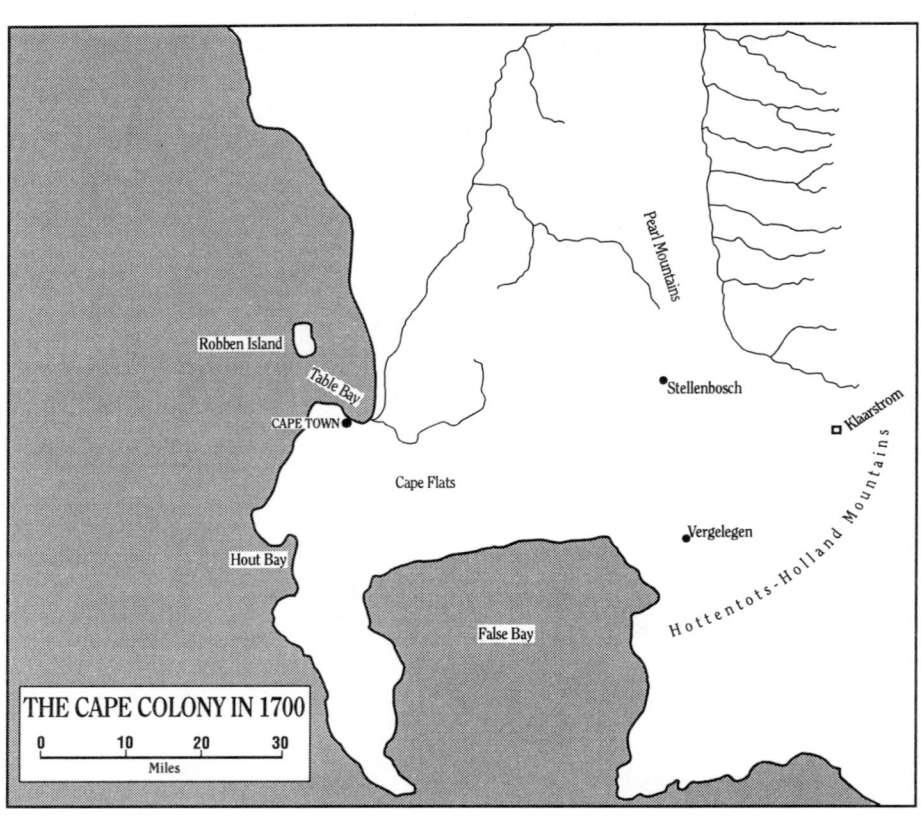

Robben Island

Table Bay

CAPE TOWN

Hout Bay

Cape Flats

Stellenbosch

Pearl Mountains

Klaarstrom

Vergelegen

Hottentots-Holland Mountains

False Bay

THE CAPE COLONY IN 1700

0   10   20   30

Miles

Acknowledgments

To Kim Garrison, John Mueller, Barbara Ring, and Karen Stoffell—my faithful readers. We have been to England, New England, Canada, France, and now the Netherlands and South Africa together—all through the manuscripts I've written and you've read. The journey has been grand. I couldn't have better readers. Thank you again.

To Linda Holland—this is the second historical fiction series we have started together. From the beginning you believed in me. I hope this effort is worthy of your trust.

To Ella Lindvall and the staff at Moody Press—you have entrusted me with a once-in-a-lifetime opportunity with this series. I have enjoyed getting to know you and working with you. May God bless all your publishing efforts.

1

Margot lovingly closed the nutshell and whispered a prayer.

She heard a muffled thump downstairs. The front door? Hiding the shell in the folds of her dress, she held her breath and stared at the closed bedroom door. Four candles on the far side of the bed were the room's only light. Her heart pounded in her ears.

Then she heard the muffled cry of a coachman on the cobblestone street followed by the *clop, clop, clop* of horses' hooves. Margot breathed again. It was not Monsieur Fabarez.

She pulled the nutshell from its hiding place. Was it worth the risk? With slender, nimble fingers she made a necklace of it by tying a delicate string around the two halves of the shell.

A moan from the bed pulled Margot's attention away from the nutshell. She glanced worriedly at the plump woman lying there. A checkered quilt formed a mound, its edge tucked beneath the woman's chin. Her eyes were closed. She was perspiring heavily.

Knotting the two ends of the string together to complete the nutshell necklace, Margot spoke pleadingly, "Don't leave me, Mother—don't leave me here alone."

A restless moan was the woman's response.

Margot set the nutshell aside and wrung the cloth that had been floating in a basin beside her. The swish of the water introduced the earthy scent of aniseed to the room. Margot wrinkled her nose. It was an unwelcome odor, a scent she associated with illness and fever. She preferred the more familiar aromas of frying oil, tobacco, and soap that were common to the Dutch household.

The bed upon which the sick woman lay was high. Though Margot was tall, she still had to use a footstool to reach her. Shoulder-length light brown hair fell forward as she bent over the patient. Two quick motions hooked the hair over her ears to keep it from getting in her way.

With tender strokes Margot dabbed the woman's forehead, her round red cheeks, and the folds under her chin. Margot winced as she felt the woman's fever penetrating the damp cloth.

"Mother?"

The woman's breathing was labored.

"Mother, can you hear me?" Margot said louder. Hasty strokes pushed back a few stray hairs that clung to the woman's wet temples.

The sick woman responded to the cool cloth. Her head moved slightly from side to side. She moaned faintly.

Margot gently laid her own head against the quilt mound. "Please God," she said, "let her live. Let her live. I've watched one mother die—must I witness the untimely death of my precious Sylvie too?"

In 1685 Margot's parents, Philipe and Aimee de Campion, fled Paris along with thousands of other Protestants of noble birth. The Edict of Nantes, which had protected the liberties of France's Protestant minority for eighty-seven years, had been revoked. Their predicament was reminiscent of France before the edict, when, on August 24, 1572, the bell of the Palace of Justice signaled the wholesale slaughter of Protestants by Catholics. Ten thousand Huguenots, as the French Protestants were called, were slain on that day.

Now the same thing was happening all over again. Louis XIV was on the throne. Believing that the ideal state was one of complete uniformity, he embarked on a crusade to rid France of the Huguenots. Churches were destroyed. Certain professions were put out of reach of the Huguenots. Protestant children were taken away from their parents and brought up as Catholics. The notorious practice of dragonnades—the billeting of soldiers with Protestant families with permission to behave as brutally as they wished—was introduced.

Then came the final blow—the revocation of the Edict of Nantes. As the slaughter of Huguenots began anew, thousands of industrious noblemen and their families—among them the de Campions—fled to remote corners of France, some to other lands, taking with them skills and knowledge that would ultimately enrich France's enemies.

Philipe and Aimee de Campion found refuge in Asile, an obscure hamlet situated on the Somme River in northern France. Its thatched cottages and patchwork fields resembled those of any other French village. Secretly, it was a haven for Huguenot fugitives.

To safeguard the village's secret, the townspeople limited their contact with the outside world. They depended upon one another, each contributing to the needs of the community as he was able. Noblemen who had formerly advised the king's court in international matters now carried rocks from fields and layered thatch on rooftops and pounded fiery orange metal into useful tools. Ladies who were

10

accustomed to having servants attend to their needs now baked their own bread and scrubbed their own floors and sewed their own clothes. At night, behind shuttered windows, the refugees taught their children to worship God in the Protestant tradition.

It was into this uncertain world that Aimee de Campion delivered baby Marguerite.

Margot—her parents called her by her nickname—had sketchy but graphic memories of Asile. She remembered the furrows in the field behind their house. Little Margot would have to negotiate each furrow separately as she carried her father's water cup to him. She recalled how he would wipe his dirty hands on his pant legs, then lift her high over his head while he twirled around. She remembered his big teeth and whiskery chin as the earth spun beneath him.

Of the house in Asile, Margot could recall the cool wooden planks of the floor. They were smooth and smelled of soap. She also remembered how her mother hummed as she scrubbed them with a hand brush and how her mother talked softly to her while they shared Margot's plane of existence close to the floor.

Then one scrub day the humming abruptly stopped.

Margot was six years old then. Using her own brush, she was sharing a bucket of soapy water with her mother. Margot remembered the door bursting open. Her father yelled something. She couldn't remember the words, but she would never forget the twisted look on his face. She'd never seen her father look that way before. His familiar features were distorted, ugly with fear. Margot remembered looking to her mother for reassurance. Instead of comfort, she saw that the twisted distortion of her father's face was contagious, for it had infected her mother's face too.

Then everything happened quickly. Hands that had so often caressed her, cuddled her, soothed her, loved her, now yanked her up from the floor. The next thing she knew she was being jostled roughly in her father's arms as her parents bolted from the house. They splashed through the river—the river that Margot had been expressly warned to stay away from—and ran into the forest.

All around them were people from the village—running, splashing, crying, shouting. All with twisted faces.

Her father gripped her so tightly it hurt. Her mother kept glancing her direction, reaching out and touching her and crying, "No, no, no! No, God, no!"

Margot remembered their crouching in a cluster of large bushes, her father's head comically crowned with leaves. But there was no laughter. Father fought to quiet his heaving chest as the three of them huddled together. Mother's hot, wet cheeks pressed against Margot's arm in the silence.

Then beyond the leaves came the sound of horses galloping. Margot remembered seeing people and horses running everywhere. The forest was no longer silent. Shrieks and moans echoed through the trees. The men on horses chased people from bushes and from behind trees. Guns spit fire and belched smoke with thunderous booms. Twice, horses passed close to their bush, and swords were thrust randomly among the leaves, both times narrowly missing them.

After the second pass, Margot remembered her father's cupping her face in his callused, dirty, farmer's hands. He made her promise to hug the ground and not make a sound, no matter what she heard, no matter what she saw.

Then, miraculously, the twistedness in his face disappeared, and once again she saw the familiar gentleness and love in his eyes. Tenderly he pulled her face close to his until their noses touched. He said, "God protect you, my little Marguerite."

Her mother hugged her fiercely and wept, seemingly unable to form words. Rocking Margot back and forth, she hummed the same tune they had hummed while the two of them scrubbed the floor.

Margot remembered being laid on the ground, her cheek against the dirt. Her father reminded her to stay low, to keep her eyes closed, to remain silent until God told her it was safe to get up. So she lay there and listened for the voice of God.

It wasn't long before Margot realized she was alone in the thicket. She opened one eye.

Beyond the trunk of the bush, Margot saw a circle of sweating horses, some of them rearing. Mounted upon them, terrible men shouted ugly things. They swung angry swords and clubs. She saw her father and mother standing in the middle of the circle. The terrible men struck her father with their swords. Red appeared all around his face and neck. He fell to his knees. More terrible men swung clubs that hit her mother, knocking her to the ground.

Two of the terrible men got off the horses and hit them again. And again. And again. Mother begged them to stop hitting Father, but they wouldn't stop. Father called out God's name, but the terrible men wouldn't stop. Even when Mother and Father lay still, the terrible men kept hitting them over and over and over.

Margot bit her fingers to keep from crying out. She bit them even when they bled. Clamping shut her eyes, she pressed hard against the dirt and waited for the voice of God to tell her it was safe to get up.

With one hand Margot scooped up the sick woman's drenched head, looping the nutshell necklace over it with the other hand. Gently she lowered the head to the pillow.

The woman's eyes fluttered, opening halfway. "Margot?"

"I'm here, Mother."

Weary eyes strained to pull the room into focus. "Monsieur Fabarez?"

Margot mopped the woman's forehead. "He's not home yet."

For as long as Margot could remember, Sylvie called her husband "Monsieur Fabarez." Never once had she heard her call him by his given name, Marc. Around the house he was always Monsieur Fabarez.

And though for thirteen years Margot regarded Sylvie Fabarez as her mother, she never felt comfortable thinking of Marc Fabarez as her father. Nor did she think Monsieur Fabarez would want her to think that way of him.

The physical differences between Margot and Marc and Sylvie Fabarez were striking, almost comical. It came as no surprise to anyone to learn that Margot was not the couple's natural offspring. She was taller than both of them by almost half a foot. She was lean to the point of gauntness, whereas they were both stocky and heavy from a lifetime diet of dairy products, meat, and fried foods.

Sylvie would joke about the physical differences between Margot and her as if Margot were her natural daughter. She'd say, "When God designed us, He withheld my portion of beauty and gave it to Margot. She looks like a beauty from Dordrecht, don't you agree?" At this point, the red balls on Sylvie's cheeks would bounce wide apart in a proud grin.

Monsieur Fabarez did not share his wife's humor. Nor did he share her love for Margot.

A fleshy arm worked its way from under the quilt. Sylvie tested her temperature by placing the back of her hand against her forehead. "Why is it so hot in here?" she asked. Then, as though the effort drained her of all remaining energy, the hand plopped onto her chest, landing atop the nutshell. A puzzled look crossed her face. She lifted the shell and looked at it. It took her several moments to recognize what it was.

13

"Spiders' heads inside?" she asked.

Margot shook her head. "No, Mother."

The sick woman's eyes grew wider, charged with fear. "Monsieur Fabarez must not see this!" She pulled her other hand from under the quilt and attempted to open the nutshell.

Margot stopped her, gently but firmly. "I'll make sure he doesn't see what's inside," she said soothingly. "It will remain our secret."

The two women's eyes met.

Sylvie let her hands go limp; Margot laid them on the quilt.

The sick woman closed her eyes. A thin smile stretched between her ample red cheeks. "God was smiling down on me the day I found you," she said.

"He was smiling down on both of us," Margot replied.

Little Marguerite remained in the bushes for days, waiting to hear the voice of God. When carts came and hauled away the bodies of her parents and the other dead Huguenots, she remained hidden and silent. When darkness fell and she shivered in the cold, she remained hidden. When her stomach pained her terribly and sounds in the night frightened her, she remained true to her promise and did not move from the thicket.

Early one morning while the gruesome scene of her parents' death played itself out in a dream, the rustling of leaves awoke her. Startled, she sat upright, blinking back the brightness of the sun, her heart pounding with fear.

The bush parted. A round head appeared and hovered over her, the sun forming a halo around it.

"Dear God! What have we here?"

As Margot's eyes adjusted to the light, she saw kindly eyes and cheeks so round and red they looked like balls glued on both sides of a nose. Margot was sure it was the face of one of God's angels.

"In the name of all that is holy, my child, what are you doing in this bush? Come here!" Plump arms reached toward her.

It wasn't the voice of God, but Margot reasoned that God must have been busy that day so He sent an angel in His place.

As it turned out, Sylvie Fabarez was indeed one of God's special creations, though not an actual angel. However, from that moment and forever Margot was convinced God had sent Sylvie Fabarez to rescue her.

To hear Sylvie's side of the story, she and her husband, carrying everything they owned on their backs, were returning to Amsterdam from Rouen, following a brief, unsuccessful business partnership with Fabarez's brother, who owned a tailor shop there.

As they walked, Sylvie endured a constant barrage of verbal attacks from her husband. It was all her fault. They never should have left Holland. What made her think anything good would come of a venture with his brother? The two brothers had never gotten along! What made her think they would get along now?

Marc Fabarez accused his wife of being just like his brother—both of them always thought they were right, that they knew the will of God. Well, what was God's will for them now? To starve to death? And if she was so favored by God, why had God shut up her womb? Weren't children a sign of God's favor? So then why did she not bear him children? Did she have an answer for that?

It was in the midst of this tirade that Sylvie heard a whimpering.

Fabarez scoffed at her. That wasn't a whimpering sound she heard, he claimed. It was wood sprites laughing at them for the miserable condition of their lives.

She heard it again. Coming from a bush.

Fabarez cursed at her and walked on ahead.

Sylvie cocked her head and listened. When she heard the sound again, she peeked into the bush from which the sound had come and, instead of wood sprites, saw a little girl, curled up in a ball.

While Fabarez whined and murmured that daylight was fast passing them by and that Amsterdam would not come to them—they would have to go to it—Sylvie Fabarez patiently coaxed the story of Margot's parents from the frightened girl. Sylvie then concluded that God had hidden the child from everyone's eyes until she came along and that the little girl was God's gift to her. And so Margot de Campion traveled to the seven provinces of the Netherlands and the city of Amsterdam in the tender care of Sylvie Fabarez.

The Dutch soil upon which Margot was raised yielded only two exploitable products, sand and peat. Sand proved to be an irony for the Bible-quoting people of Holland, for they were literally a country built upon sand; but instead of being its downfall, sand was its salvation. Dikes, ramparts, and foundations were all made of sand. And it was these man-made fortifications that kept the sea from swallowing up the land.

As for peat, this was the standard fuel rather than wood. The peat was removed in slabs, cut into brick shape, dried, then stored in lofts, where it hardened. These bricks were used in fireplaces to warm the houses, in ovens for baking, and in boxes about six inches square made of hard wood and pierced with holes—to be used as foot warmers.

Other than peat and sand, everything else in Holland had to be imported—wheat, rye, coal, leather, metals, wool, hemp, ship timber, and dyes. This poverty of natural resources forced the Dutch people to carry on extensive trading. This they did readily, becoming a world distribution center, a role for which they were ideally suited. Situated on the maritime routes that linked northeast and southwest in Europe, they built a large merchant fleet that soon dominated world trade.

As one observer said, "Never any country traded so much, and consumed so little; the Dutch buy infinitely, but 'tis to sell again, either upon improvement of the commodity, or at a better market. They are the great masters of the Indian spices, and of the Persian silks; but wear plain woolen, and feed upon their own fish and roots. Nay, they sell the finest of their own cloth to France, and buy coarse out of England for their own wear!"

Marc Fabarez's position in this grand Dutch economy was an insignificant one. He was a peasant fisherman.

Fishing had provided the original base for Holland's economic system, and, even though now overshadowed by the lucrative trading companies, it was still a fruitful business. The Netherlands overflowed with fish and boasted one of the largest and most powerful fishing guilds. In the markets, fishermen and dealers stood among barrels of fresh fish daily and bargained and drank brandy.

However, Marc Fabarez was at the lowest end of the guild hierarchy, not because he lacked experience but because he lacked good sense. He was a brawler; and if he was not fighting with someone, he was provoking others to fight. Consequently, his skill as an ambassador of discord landed him the lowest of jobs aboard whichever herring boat he happened to serve. It was his task, as soon as the herring were taken from the net, to gut the fish, remove gills and entrails from the milt, and discard them. The herring were then barreled in brine for storing.

He was often gone from home for weeks at a time, which suited Margot immensely. For the difference in the household between the times he was home and the times he was absent was the difference between misery and joy.

When Monsieur Fabarez was home, the household revolved around his every demand and whim. He was a petty dictator in a peasant's castle. Not only did his presence disrupt the daily household schedule, but it cast a pall over everything and everyone, especially Margot.

She could do nothing to please him. Everything that went wrong was her fault. And whenever Sylvie intervened on Margot's behalf, Fabarez responded with the back of his hand across his wife's face.

When they were alone, Margot pleaded with Sylvie to refrain from defending her; she could take the verbal jabs, but she could not bear to see Sylvie hurt on her account.

Once, while Fabarez drank ale and watched Margot clean the front doorstep, he berated her for not working fast enough. This went on for an hour. Then he dragged her down to the *Heiligeweg*, the Holy Way, to the House of Correction so that she might see what happens to slothful children.

A forbidding assembly of stone figures adorned the gateway of the House of Correction. The female personification of Amsterdam dished out discipline to heavily manacled and fettered delinquents. A single word adorned the step upon which the stone figure of a woman sat. It said "CASTIGATIO"—punishment.

For a copper coin each, Fabarez and Margot were admitted with others to gawk at the unfortunates. Fabarez dragged her to one room in particular—the drowning cell. It was here that idle children were taught the value of work. They were placed in a large cistern that housed a pump. Then the cistern was filled with water. It was a simple lesson. To keep from drowning, the delinquents were forced to work the pump.

Fabarez watched with glee as one lad stood with his arms folded in stubborn defiance until the water reached his neck. Only then did he place his hand to the pump—and then quite vigorously. Fabarez yelled and hooted at the sputtering boy, thinking the spectacle to be great fun.

Margot found the whole experience revolting.

Whenever Fabarez was home, the house was a prison. Neither Sylvie nor Margot was allowed out except for some purpose that directly served him. Neither were visitors welcome at such times. Margot noticed how the neighbors altered their perception of the house whenever Fabarez's fishing fleet was in port.

But if life with Monsieur Fabarez was unpleasant, life without him was heavenly. Margot came to summarize her life with Sylvie Fabarez as disciplined joy.

The day began early, about half past five every morning. Upon waking, the two women rose and exchanged a kiss, as was the Dutch custom. They opened the shutters to let the day into the house, then walked outside to greet their neighbors.

They would converse to the sounds of the milkman and bakery man starting their rounds. Carrying a pail, the milkman would cry, "Beautiful milk! Sweet milk! Warm milk!" The baker pushed a hand-cart and cried, "Hot white bread! Rye bread! Barley biscuits! All hot! All hot! Fresh bread rolls!"

Breakfast was eaten at 6:00 every morning. It was a simple meal of bread and butter or cheese with milk to drink. This was followed by a time of prayer.

Then the cleaning began, something for which the Dutch developed a world-renowned reputation. Sylvie Fabarez, like all Dutch women of her generation, prided herself on the cleanliness of her house and furniture to an unbelievable degree. She was forever washing and scrubbing all the wooden furniture and fittings, even the benches and floorboards, as well as the stairs. She was so fastidious about her floors that whenever visitors came, she provided them straw slippers in which to encase their feet, shoes and all. And hers was a conservative approach compared to others.

According to one story, a burgomaster knocked at the door of a house and told the servant, a sturdy peasant woman, that he wished to speak to the woman's mistress. He made a move to enter, but the servant noticed that a little mud was clinging to the soles of his shoes. Without saying a word, she seized the burgomaster by the wrists, hoisted him onto her back like a sack, and carried him across two rooms before depositing him on the stairs. She removed his shoes, fitted him with a pair of slippers, and only then did she allow the man to visit her mistress.

The cleaner any surface appeared, the more mercilessly Sylvie scoured it. Twice a week the house was stripped of its furniture, and things were scrubbed with copious applications of water, or scoured with sand, or polished. It was not uncommon for her to use thirty or forty buckets of water a day simply for cleaning purposes.

On a typical day, the midday meal broke up this cleaning frenzy. This was the principal meal of the day and usually comprised two or three courses and concluded with a salad or fruit. Sometimes it even included dessert: pancakes or waffles or, most often, rice pudding. *Hutsepot*—made of finely chopped mutton or beef, green vegetables, and parsnips or prunes, sprinkled with lemon or orange juice and moistened with strong vinegar—was the most frequent course of the midday meal.

Errands, the daily shopping, and more cleaning followed the noon meal. Then, at about three o'clock, a snack was enjoyed—bread and cheese accompanied by almonds, raisins, or other delicacies.

Between five and seven o'clock, activities began to wind down. The usual activity, if it was not too cold, was for Sylvie and Margot to sit on the bench in front of the house. Here, between the houses and the canal, they watched children play and young people flirt, while sharing their experiences with the other women on the street. This outdoor relaxation lasted until dusk, at which time they prepared dinner.

That was unless Fabarez was home. Then the women were not allowed to go outside at all.

Dinner was served at eight or nine in the evening. It generally consisted of the remains of the day's previous meals, complemented with butter or cheese or a porridge of stale bread soaked in milk.

The time between dinner and bedtime was Margot's favorite time of the day. When Fabarez was home, the women would sew or embroider. But when he was at sea, the time was magical.

The magic began one night when Margot was eight years old.

Sylvie pulled two chairs together so that she and Margot were sitting knee to knee. In a hushed voice, as though Monsieur Fabarez might hear her at sea, Sylvie said, "What I am about to tell you is a secret. It has been a family secret for generations, passed down from my grandmother to my mother to me and now to you. You must never tell Monsieur Fabarez what you are about to hear. Do you understand?"

Margot nodded eagerly, perhaps a little too eagerly. She took special delight in the fact that she was about to enter into a pact that would in some way displease Monsieur Fabarez.

Sylvie rose and went to her cupboard. Along with her table and chairs, a Dutch woman's cupboard was one of three basic units of furniture. Sylvie's cupboard was an old-fashioned medieval chest that sat on the floor. It opened with a lid that was painted red and green and decorated with drawings of daily life.

She dug deep into the chest, past her towels and blankets and sheets. Her eyebrows lifted when she found what she was looking for. She drew them out one at a time—one, two, three books—and balanced them on the corner of the open cupboard. After using the side of the chest to push herself up, she took her seat opposite Margot, setting the books on her lap.

"These are my treasure," Sylvie whispered.

19

"Books?"

"Of course, books!" Sylvie cried.

"But what good are books if you can't—" Suddenly Margot realized the secret. A hand flew to her mouth. "You can read!" she squealed.

Sylvie's eyes lit up brightly as she nodded her head.

"But how? I thought you were raised a peasant. Have you been to school?"

"You are looking at one peasant woman who can read—and write too!" Sylvie said with pride. "And soon there will be two of us. Just as my mother taught me to read and write, so I will teach you. But I must warn you—" All signs of humor drained from Sylvie's face. A rigid, pudgy index finger punctuated the warning. "Being able to read is a barbed blessing, not unlike a rose with thorns. You must be careful how you use it and when. Otherwise it will rise up and prick you."

"But being able to read and write must be a wonderful thing!" Margot exclaimed. "Why must we keep it a secret?"

With a sober expression Sylvie asked, "How do you think Monsieur Fabarez would react if he knew his wife could read and write better than him?"

An image formed in Margot's mind. She recalled the times she had watched Fabarez agonize over a gazette or a simple note. Laboriously he pointed to each word as he worked through a document. Every line was as much work for him as hoeing a long row in the garden. At the end of each sentence he would straighten up with a superior look in his eyes as though he'd accomplished some great feat.

"I understand what you mean," Margot said. Still, a part of her would have loved nothing better than to see Monsieur Fabarez's delusion of superiority punctured.

"This book—" Sylvie held up a thick, leather-bound black volume "—is the Bible in Dutch." Picking up the second book, similar in appearance, she said, "And this book is the Bible too. In Latin."

Margot's mouth fell open. "You can read Latin?"

A nod and a smile answered the question.

"And this book"—a red volume—"is a book of stories, some historical, others Dutch folklore, and still others of Greek and Roman origin from long ago."

"How is it that your grandmother first learned to read?" Margot asked.

Stacking the books on her lap, Sylvie rested plump hands atop them as she spoke. "Long ago, my grandmother—Claertje van Os— was the servant maid for a prosperous family in Leiden, the Blankaarts. She was the personal servant to the youngest Blankaart daughter. Well, Willem Blankaart insisted that all his children receive an education in the arts. He hired personal tutors for each child. Catalyn, his youngest, cared for none of the things her tutor taught her. She had eyes for the burgomaster's son and wanted only to marry him when she came of age.

"So while the tutor drilled the disinterested daughter in languages and music and art, day after day, my grandmother—a woman of quick mind and wit—learned even though Catalyn did not. The way the story was passed along to me, my grandmother knew Greek as well as French and Dutch and Latin. However, she died before passing along her knowledge of Greek to my mother."

"What did Claertje do with her knowledge, besides passing it along to her daughter?"

A sparkle appeared in Sylvie's eyes. "She would read documents in secret—business documents in Latin that were left lying around her master's study. In subtle ways she would pass along this information to the peasant man who was courting her. With this knowledge he eventually earned enough money to buy his freedom and marry Claertje. They purchased a loom and produced exquisite tapestries in Leiden for years. Your grandfather became an important man in his guild."

Margot's eyes fell on the books. She saw them as her keys to a happy future. "Read to me!" she pleaded.

Sylvie looked pleased at Margot's eagerness. They moved to the table and sat side by side.

Opening the first book as if it were the gateway to a city of great wealth, Sylvie read, "A good name is rather to be chosen than great riches, and loving favor rather than silver and gold. The rich and poor meet together: the Lord is the maker of them all. A prudent man foreseeth the evil, and hideth himself: but the simple pass on, and are punished. By humility and the fear of the Lord are riches, and honor, and life."

For the remainder of the evening Margot listened rapturously as Sylvie read from the Bible and then from the book of stories. And from that night on, the evenings when Fabarez was absent, the downstairs table became Margot's classroom.

Little did Margot realize how painful it would be to keep Sylvie's secret. During the day, while she scrubbed, she reviewed her lessons

21

in her mind. It was all she could do to keep from blurting out a question. A couple of times she had to bite her tongue lest she say something that would reveal the secret in the hearing of Monsieur Fabarez.

The evenings when Monsieur Fabarez was home became more torturous than ever. While he propped his chair in the corner and snored loudly, it took every ounce of self-restraint she had to sit quietly and embroider, knowing that the three magical books were a few feet away in the cupboard. Even harder still were the nights when he was out to a tavern. Sylvie refused to get out the books lest he happen to come home early and catch them reading.

But the tortures of the evenings when Monsieur Fabarez was home were more than compensated for by the evenings when the two were alone. Sylvie took great pride in her student, and Margot loved her Sylvie more than ever. By the time Margot reached her nineteenth birthday, she was her teacher's equal in reading and writing Dutch and French and Latin.

Sylvie tried to push off the quilt that covered her. Normally, this was a task that could be done without thought. In her weakened condition it was proving to be more than she could manage.

"What are you doing?" Margot cried.

"My pots," Sylvie said, "I must scrub my pots."

Margot blocked the side of the bed.

The sick woman began shivering uncontrollably. Her shaking was so violent that the whole bed trembled.

Margot pushed her back under the covers. "Now see what you've done," she kindly scolded.

"But my pots! My kitchen!"

"They're clean," Margot said. "I cleaned the pots and the kitchen myself, just like you like them."

"Is Monsieur Fabarez home?" Sylvie asked again.

"He's not home yet." Margot tucked the quilt around her mother's neck and did her best to hold the woman steady.

Soon the shaking stopped. Her eyes closed, Sylvie took to moaning. Her head flopped back and forth on the drenched pillow. "Marc . . . Marc . . . please, Marc . . . take me with you, Marc."

Margot felt a jab of anguish as Sylvie cried out her husband's given name. She tried to shake it off. The man was her husband. Why wouldn't she call his name? Still, it was *she* who loved Sylvie, not Marc Fabarez, and each cry of his name pained her.

Sylvie calmed down, and Margot stepped off the footstool and collapsed into a chair. She had been at Sylvie's side since early morning, and she was exhausted. A short distance from the four candles, the room fell quickly to darkness. She could hear the ticking of the clock in the next room. She closed her eyes and prayed for her mother.

Her prayer was interrupted by the slamming of the downstairs door, then the tramp of heavy boots coming up the stairs. Monsieur Fabarez was home.

Margot could almost hear Sylvie's voice. *Monsieur Fabarez! How many times must I tell you to remove your boots before entering my clean house? Go outside and take them off! Now! Go!* But there would be no wifely outburst tonight. Margot glanced sadly at the woman on the bed.

The door to the bedroom flew open, banging loudly as it hit the wall. One of the candles in the four-branched candlestick went out.

"What is going on here?" Fabarez thundered. "Where is my dinner? Where is everyone?"

The strong odors of herring and brine and beer barged into the room with him. There wasn't a stitch of clothing on Fabarez that wasn't soiled or torn, from his felt cap to his short sailor's doublet to the trousers that billowed around his legs. His face and arms were filthy with dirt and sweat. He'd been brawling again.

Margot placed a finger to her lips to signal quiet. "Mother is ill," she said softly. "She took sick shortly after you left four days ago."

"What kind of sick?" Fabarez boomed. He kept his distance from the bed, straining his eyes as though to see if it was really his wife under the quilt.

"She has a fever and chills," Margot answered him softly.

"Did you call a doctor?"

Margot hesitated. No matter how she answered, she knew Monsieur Fabarez would find fault.

"Are you deaf, girl?" he roared.

"The doctor examined her yesterday."

Fabarez stomped in a circle and cursed. "Stupid, stupid girl!" he ranted. "And where am I going to get two *stuivers* to pay him? Answer me that!"

He's more concerned about two stuivers *than he is about Sylvie!* Margot thought. Struggling to ignore his blatant pettiness, she replied in a condescending tone, "The doctor said all we can do for now is keep her cool with aniseed water. I've been doing that. If she gets worse, the doctor said he would return and bleed her."

"And how much is that going to cost me?" Fabarez threw up his hands. "This is all your fault! Your fault!"

"My fault?"

"Yes, your fault! We have been cursed since the day Sylvie found you! If I'd had my way, we would have left you in that forest to die like God intended!"

Monsieur Fabarez's revelation stunned Margot. In Sylvie's rendition of the event, she had always implied that rescuing Margot from the bushes was as much Fabarez's idea as it was hers. Margot attempted to shrug off the effects of this verbal mauling but found it difficult to do so. To think, all this time she had lived under the roof of a man who wished her dead.

She edged closer to Sylvie's side. So did Fabarez. They both stepped up on the footstools, facing one another on opposite sides of the bed. The stale odor of fish and beer crept over the sick woman like an encroaching fog.

"What's that?" Fabarez's face wore a perverse grin. He pointed to the nutshell necklace around Sylvie's neck. He reached for it before Margot could react. Turning the shell over in his hands, he said, "Spiders' heads? I thought you weren't superstitious, *Marguerite*." He spoke her name as if it were a filthy word.

Margot's heart was pounding. Monsieur Fabarez must not see inside, Sylvie had said. As calmly as she could, Margot reached for the aniseed cloth and proceeded to dab her mother's beaded brow.

Fabarez snatched the cloth from her hand. "I'll do that!" he yelled. "Go fix my dinner."

Sylvie lay between them breathing shallowly, mercifully unaware of what was taking place over her.

Margot didn't move. She didn't want to leave her mother's bedside.

"Fix me dinner!" Fabarez roared again. Yellow eyes bulged threateningly.

Margot stepped from the stool and went downstairs.

In the kitchen, she tossed a piece of stale bread into a bowl and splashed milk over it. On a separate plate she cut some cheese flavored with cumin. Beside the cheese she added a few slices of cucumber. She carried the bowl and plate to the table and plopped them onto the tabletop none too gently. Some of the milk sloshed over the side of the bowl; one of the cucumbers jumped from the plate and rolled halfway across the table. Margot retrieved it and wiped up the spilled milk.

She didn't want to give Monsieur Fabarez the satisfaction of knowing he'd made her angry.

After pouring a mug of beer for him, she climbed the steps to the upper bedroom, hoping that the meal would put Monsieur Fabarez to sleep so that he would leave them alone for the rest of the night.

When she entered the bedroom, she found him seated on the footstool beside the bed. The aniseed cloth lay next to him on the floor. He didn't look up when she entered, but he knew she was there.

"You've killed her," he said. His voice was low and threatening.

Margot's gaze bolted to the bed. The checkered quilt was still. She clutched her chest. Her heart felt as if it had been struck by lightning. Racing to the far side of the bed, she stood over her mother. She reached tentatively toward Sylvie's face.

The woman's cheeks—which had always looked like red balls— were colorless. The sweating had stopped.

Margot touched her mother's cheek. It was moist and cool. "Mother?" She shook Sylvie by the shoulder. She got no response. There was no sign of life. No breathing. No moans. Everything was still.

Like a specter rising from the grave, Fabarez appeared on the far side of the checkered quilt. He was dark and menacing. "You killed her!" he shouted. "We took you in, and this is how you repay us! You killed my wife!" His face quivered with rage, sending drops of sweat flying from the ragged ends of his hair.

Margot stood there, numb. Grief, like a heavy blanket, descended upon her. Her precious Sylvie dead? No! It couldn't be! She refused to believe it! Surely God would not allow this to happen! She had prayed so hard for Sylvie's recovery; she had . . .

The nutshell. Sylvie's warning echoed in her mind. Monsieur Fabarez must not see what was inside! Momentarily pushing aside her grief, Margot looked for the shell. The quilt was high around Sylvie's neck. It must be underneath. Under the pretense of covering her dead mother's head, Margot lifted the bedcover.

"Looking for this?" Fabarez held the nutshell in his hand. It was opened. In his other hand he dangled a small piece of paper, the one that Margot had folded and placed inside.

Fabarez lifted the paper to his eyes and scrutinized the writing. Struggling with the vocabulary, he read: "Fear thou not; for I am with thee: be not . . . be not . . ."

"Dismayed," Margot said.

"Dismayed; for I am thy God: I will strengthen thee; yea, I will help thee; yea, I will uphold thee with the right hand of my . . ."

"Righteousness." Margot completed the verse for him.

"Who was here?" Fabarez shook the paper as though it were a document in a criminal trial. "Who wrote this? Who was in my house?"

It would have been easy for Margot to lie, to lead him to believe the doctor had written the verse. But something inside her wouldn't let her do that.

"And these words—" Fabarez studied the paper again, holding it close to his eyes. "I can't even read them! What are they? An incantation?"

Margot placed a loving hand on Sylvie's shoulder. She gazed calmly with admiration and love upon her teacher. "The words are Latin," she said without looking up. "They say, 'God give you strength, my beloved.'"

Fabarez cocked his head sideways. Squinting yellow eyes scrutinized her. Like a demonic spirit, his anger was now controlling him. "'Beloved'? Beloved!" he fumed. "Who wrote this? I demand you tell me who wrote this right now!"

Lifting her head proudly, Margot said, "I did. I wrote those words."

2

Yellow eyes quivered as they glared at Margot from across the bed. Monsieur Fabarez shook his sweaty head slowly from side to side. Clearly he did not want to believe that Margot had penned the Scripture and the Latin phrases he'd found in the nutshell.

She understood his dilemma: even though he hated her, he knew she was not one to lie or stretch the truth.

His eyes bulged with fright as his superstitious nature provided him with an answer. "Witchcraft!" he croaked.

Watching the transformation of his expression from bewilderment to fear, Margot now knew what demonic terror looked like.

Fabarez stumbled backward and fell off the footstool, crashing to the floor.

Margot had to rise up on her toes to see him over the bed. The nutshell and paper lay beside him.

Steadying himself against the table that held the four-branched candlestick, Fabarez struggled to get up. He had gotten as far as his knees when he noticed that only three of the candles were still burning. He caught his breath loudly.

"Three candles! An omen of death," he muttered. He stared wildly at Margot and pointed an accusing finger. "Witch! Witch! Witch!"

"Don't be ridiculous!" Margot replied. "I'm not a—"

"Witch! Witch!" Fabarez wasn't listening. He stared at the three candles, then at Margot, then at the candles again. "Witchcraft!" he said in a hoarse voice. "That explains it! That explains a lot of things that have been happening around here ever since—"

"Nonsense!" Margot cried. "Witchcraft had nothing to do with Sylvie's death or my ability to read. I've been learning how to read for years."

Fabarez rose slowly to his feet, inching his way up the wall, careful not to turn his back on Margot. "I've been harboring a witch in my house," he murmured. He glanced at the nutshell and the paper on the floor. "An incantation! That's what it is! An incantation. You killed my Sylvie with an incantation!"

"This is absurd!" Margot cried. "It's a Scripture passage!"

"The devil in the wilderness with Jesus—quoting Scripture for his own evil purpose!" Fabarez was trembling. Sweat poured down both sides of his face and dripped from his chin. His speech was increasingly incoherent.

"It is a common practice to place verses of Scripture in a nutshell and place it around the neck of a sick person!" Margot said. "And the words following the Scripture are not a spell! It's a prayer written in Latin! That's all it is!" Her words were having no effect on Fabarez. "It's not evil!" she cried.

Fabarez rolled his eyes heavenward and began praying frantically. "God, our Father, protect me from the evil one in this room!"

Margot's eyes rolled upward too; hers did so in frustration. "Will you listen to me?"

"Bind her with the power of Your Holy Spirit—"

"Will you stop praying like that? I'm not a witch just because I can read!"

"And deliver her soul to hell, which is its rightful place for all eternity."

"I have known how to read for eleven years!"

"And deliver me from her evil powers!"

"Sylvie taught me!" Margot screamed. "Sylvie taught me to read!"

Marc Fabarez stopped in mid-prayer. He shot a clawed hand toward her. "Get away from my wife, you she-devil!" he cried. "Get away from her! Get away from her with your black magic." He lunged at Margot over his dead wife.

Instinctively Margot pulled back. She lost her balance and fell from her footstool.

Before she could regain her feet, Fabarez had circled the end of the bed and was standing within a few feet of her. Both hands were in front of him now, bent and rigid like claws. He began chanting in a frightening singsong voice, "Witch! Witch! Witch! Witch! Witch! Witch!"

Margot retreated from the claws into the dark corner. "I'm not a witch!" she cried. "O God, help me! I'm not a witch!"

Fabarez wasn't listening. "Witch! Witch! Witch! Witch!" He clawed down at her with quick, striking motions.

Margot had worked her way as far into the corner as she could. Her feet were pulled up close. She wrapped her arms around her legs so that she was in a tight ball.

The clawlike hands of Fabarez swung wildly. Closer. Closer.

"Witch! Witch! Witch!"

Margot buried her head against her legs. "In the name of God, leave me alone!" she screamed. "Leave me alone!"

The chanting stopped.

"We'll see if you're telling the truth," came Fabarez's voice, raspy from his screaming and chanting. "The test of water will prove your guilt!"

The next thing Margot knew, he had slammed the bedroom door and locked it. Hurried footsteps descended the stairs, followed by the muffled sound of the downstairs door banging shut.

All was silent again. Margot shook uncontrollably in the corner. She rested her forehead against her knees and wept.

Fabarez undoubtedly was going to retrieve the burgomaster and the town crier. It was their duty to verify charges of witchcraft. He had mentioned trial by water. The familiar tests for witchcraft played out in Margot's mind.

One popular method of unmasking witches was to tie the suspected witch's thumbs to her toes. She was then thrown into deep water. If she drowned, she was pronounced innocent of the charges; if she floated, she was judged guilty of being a witch and burned at the stake.

Another method was to plunge the suspect's arms into boiling water up to her elbows. If the water scalded her arms, her innocence was proved.

Another method—this one waterless—was to weigh the suspect. This method was based on the idea that sorcerers and witches weighed less than their height and size warranted. If the suspected witch's weight was considered normal, she was released after paying a fine; otherwise she was convicted of witchcraft and burned alive.

Margot brushed away tears. She shook her head in disbelief. It was as though her head were stuffed with clouds; her thoughts wandered blindly in search of some semblance of reality. Surely the burgomaster would be a reasonable man. She could convince him this was all a mistake, couldn't she? What evidence was there against her? The contents of a nutshell. A fisherman's ranting accusations. The officials would recognize the writing on the nutshell paper as Latin, not an incantation.

But how would she explain her ability to read?

The explanation was innocent enough, but who would believe it? The suddenness of the revelation made it appear magical. One day she couldn't read, the next day she could. There was no one who could affirm that she had been studying for years. No one else knew that *Sylvie* could read! It had been such a carefully guarded secret! Who then would believe that one peasant woman taught another peasant woman to read and write Latin?

Lifting her head, Margot stared at her beloved Sylvie lying so still on the bed. She arose from the corner and mounted the footstool once more.

"Dear, dear Sylvie," she whispered, tenderly arranging thin strands of hair on the woman's cool forehead. "My teacher—my friend—my mother."

Tears filled Margot's eyes as she gazed for the last time at her Sylvie. Dead such a short time, yet already the body looked unnatural. Gone was the life that had animated the shell of flesh. There was no color in the woman's cheeks; they hung limp and gray. Her mouth was a humorless, thin line. The body remained. Sylvie was gone.

"Where are you right now, my dear?" Margot wept. "Are you at this moment experiencing the things we've read? 'For if we believe that Jesus died and rose again, even so them also which sleep in Jesus will God bring with him.'

"Did Jesus greet you when you arrived? Was He glad to see you? Are you happy there, Sylvie? Already I miss you so much my insides ache. Will you do something for me? Will you visit my mother and father? You can find them by listening for my mother. She'll be humming. Like this . . ."

Closing her eyes, Margot hummed the melody her mother had hummed the day she was killed.

"Will you tell them I still remember them?" she whispered. She laid her head against Sylvie's still chest. Her tears splattered on the quilt like raindrops.

"Thank you, my dearest. Thank you for taking me in—for teaching me—for loving me. I'll never forget you—never."

A distant commotion could be heard coming down the street, the noise carried along by the watery surface of the canal. Margot raised her head to hear better. She thought she heard the raspy sound of Fabarez's voice in the midst of the clamor.

What should she do? What could she say to persuade the burgomaster that she was not a witch? Margot's eyes wandered aimlessly around the room as her mind jumped from one explanation to another in search of a convincing argument.

Then her head snapped still as an idea lodged in place. Why make a defense at all? What was she fighting for? The right to live in a house where she wasn't wanted? There was nothing here for her. There was nothing here she wanted. Now that Sylvie was gone, there was no reason to stay.

The street noises were directly in front of the house now. In the next few moments the downstairs door would open, and she would hear a parade of boots trudging up the stairway.

She took one last loving glimpse at Sylvie. "You will forever be in my heart," she whispered. "Good-bye, my dear Sylvie. Good-bye."

Tearing herself from the bedside, Margot raced to the bedroom cupboard. Throwing up the lid, she grabbed several items of bedclothes, unfurling them like flags. Then, tying the corner of one bedcover to another, she fashioned a rope, which she anchored to the foot of the massive wooden bedframe. Gathering up the length of covering, she ran to the window.

Hastily she unlatched the window and peeked out into the alley. At the canal end, a number of men with torches straggled by. Downstairs the door slammed open.

"Up here!" Fabarez's voice yelled.

Margot checked the alley again. The last of the men cleared the end of the passage. She threw open the window and tossed out the bedding.

Footsteps were starting up the stairway.

She remembered the nutshell and the note.

As the footsteps pounded on the stairs, Margot ran around the bed and snatched up the piece of paper from the floor.

Outside the door, the footsteps came to a halt.

"Well, go on, man!" an unfamiliar high-pitched voice cried. "Unlock the door!"

Fabarez's shaky voice replied, "What if the witch has conjured up a grievous spell? Or changed herself into a ferocious beast? Shouldn't someone else go first?"

Margot ran back to the open window.

"Nonsense, man! Unlock the door!"

"You don't know the power of this witch like I do!" Fabarez defended his failing courage.

Margot poked her head out. The alley was clear. Lifting her skirt, she swung one leg over the sill.

"Let me have the key then!" demanded the high-pitched voice.

There was a rattle of keys, then a jangle and clank as if they had been dropped.

"Imbecile!" the high-pitched voice shouted. "Wait—don't—you almost knocked me down the stairs! Stand back, man. I'll get the keys!"

Margot swung her other leg over the sill. She gripped the bedding rope and slid down. She reached the end. It was short. She was still four feet above the alley.

In the room above, the bedroom door banged open.

Margot let loose of the bedding and dropped the rest of the way. She hit the ground hard, falling backward. She found herself staring up at the bedroom window.

From inside came a voice: "Look! Over there!"

Scrambling to her feet, Margot leaped into the shadows close to the building and ran down the alley away from the canal. Then, hearing her footsteps echo, she stopped and squeezed into the shadow that ran the length of the alley wall. Trembling flesh pressed against cold, rough bricks.

High above, she saw three heads at the open bedroom window, each trying to see around the others as they searched up and down the alley. One of the heads belonged to Fabarez.

"Looks like she lowered herself with this bedding," said the high-pitched voice, stating the obvious. The voice belonged to a round-faced, bearded man wearing a black cloak and black hat.

"Don't be deceived, noble and austere *Seigneur*," Fabarez cried. "Maybe she just wants us to *think* she lowered herself into the alley."

"What do you mean?"

"She's a witch!" Fabarez cried. "She could have turned herself into a bat or a raven and flown away!"

The man with the high-pitched voice snorted loudly. He pulled his head back into the room. The two other heads followed.

Noiselessly Margot tiptoed the length of the shadow. Reaching the end, she stepped into the street and did her best to appear casual as she strolled toward the heart of Amsterdam.

Margot hadn't gone far when she was startled by the roll of a drum. It was ten o'clock. The city's night patrol was being called to convene. With lanterns, hand rattles, and pikes they would guard the streets and keep a vigilant eye open for fires. Should they encounter any trouble they couldn't handle themselves, the twirling of the rat-chet-style rattle would alert the townspeople and summon assistance. Margot would have to stick close to the shadows to avoid their watch-ful eyes.

It wasn't unlawful for her to be on the street at night, but neither was it wise. A young woman alone looked suspicious and invited trouble. Should a night patrolman find her, he would insist on escorting her back to Monsieur Fabarez's house. And that was the last place she wanted to be right now.

She hurried along the paved, convex street that curved continu-ously to her left, staying close to the gutter on the building side. The shadows were thickest here. Besides, the opposite side of the street now bordered a canal, and there was no railing to keep her from fall-ing in should she stumble in the darkness.

Reaching a corner, she stopped. A few moments ago, fleeing the Fabarez house seemed the right thing to do. Now, at a crossroads, she realized she had no idea where she was going. Fear swept over her like a fever. Indecisive, she began to shake again.

The curved street she had been traveling was one of a series of parallel streets, each bordering a canal. These paved and watery pas-sageways spread out like a fan around Amsterdam's harbor, stock exchange, and town hall. The cross street was one of several that radi-ated from the harbor like the spokes of a wheel.

Margot looked up and down both streets. The darkness made it difficult for her to choose which way to go. Although oil lamps were positioned at regular intervals, they were inadequate for the task on a dark night such as this one. Each provided no more than a few feet of illumination.

Coming toward her, fog crept up the canal, leaping against the sides as it approached as though it were trying to climb out of the canal to run along the streets. Down the other way, approaching from the direction of the harbor, came a whiny, drunken voice. Two sailors, arm in arm, stepped into the light of a corner lamp. It was difficult to tell which of them was supporting the other.

They didn't see Margot yet. Quickly she jumped beyond the range of the light, choosing the way of the fog over the way of the sailors. The farther she traveled, the thicker was the fog until she was feeling her way along the street from one porch step to another.

The absurdity of her predicament prompted an ever-so-brief chuckle. Which was the greater dilemma? Not being able to see where she was going or having no place to go? Her levity dissipated when she came to another corner.

She knew it was a corner because she ran out of houses. However, the stew of fog and darkness was so thick now that she could see but a foot in any direction. The corner oil lamp was nothing more than a dull yellow ball hung high against the building. Margot clung to the corner, too frightened to move.

Then suddenly another yellow ball appeared. This one swung from side to side. It was accompanied by whistling. The night patrol! He was headed straight toward her.

Margot swallowed a whimper and felt her way around the corner. Moving hand over hand, she crept along the edge of the building as the street descended toward the wharf.

She did her best to stifle her breathing, realizing how well the fog carried sound. The night patrolman's whistle sounded as if he were standing next to her, yet his light hadn't appeared around the corner yet.

Margot continued feeling her way along the wall, casting quick glances back toward the corner.

Just then the patrolman's ball of light emerged from the mist. The whistling stopped. So did Margot. The light held still, barely illuminating the figure behind it, making the man appear more like an apparition than a person.

Had he heard her?

Placing a hand against her chest, Margot swallowed each breath. She could feel her heart pounding madly.

The whistling started up again. A carefree tune. The light began bobbing again. He was coming her direction!

Tossing caution aside, she turned and proceeded down the street, running her fingers along the wall. Her feet quietly tested each step in the same manner as a blind man's walking stick.

Then, without warning, the wall next to her disappeared. An entryway? Margot took a cautious step, then another, feeling for the resumption of the wall. Her hands hit nothing but fog.

Behind her, the whistling and the bobbing light closed the distance between them.

Panic struck her in the chest with the impact of a physical blow. Should she go forward? What was to keep her from walking into a canal? She took a cautious step, waving both hands wildly in front of her. Nothing but air and darkness.

The whistling grew louder. Now it seemed the man was whistling directly into her ear.

Margot took another cautious step. Her toe stubbed something. A step? She leaned over. Stairs of some sort. Where there are stairs, there's a wall, she thought. Her hands on one step, her feet at the foot of the stairs, she worked her way sideways, searching for it. She kept going and going.

How wide can these stairs be?

Another step, then another. Still no wall. Then it dawned on her. What kind of building had wide stairs? A church! She knew where she was! She'd passed this church before. It was a large Catholic cathedral, converted by Protestants following the defeat of Spain's Philip II. The sandstone steps were gnawed round by the bite of the salt sea elements.

Margot felt her way up the stone steps, still on all fours. Just as the bobbing yellow ball was passing in front of the church, she reached the top. In her haste to find a place to hide, she stumbled.

The whistling stopped again. So did the bobbing yellow ball.

"Hulloa?" The voice was deep, challenging. "Someone there? This here's the night patrol. Answer, if you're there!"

Lying against the top step of the church, Margot did her best to blend into the stones.

Beneath her, the light bobbed this way and that, indicating that the night patrolman was uncertain of the sound's direction. Several moments passed. The corner of the top step pressed painfully against Margot's rib cage.

There was a shuffle of feet as the phantom figure performed a clumsy pirouette. Then, slowly, the light began to bob again down the street. This time it was not accompanied by whistling.

Margot did not move until the light was out of sight. Then she picked herself up and felt her way to the church's massive wooden doors. Finding a large iron ring, she lifted and pulled. The doors creaked—too loudly—but did not swing open. So Margot felt her way along the wall to a dark corner and collapsed into it.

To keep herself from shaking uncontrollably, she pulled her legs up to her chest, wrapped her skirt around her, and snuggled up tightly. The chill of the stone penetrated her clothing; the fog nipped her exposed skin with its damp kiss.

Like a frightened child, Margot squirmed and fidgeted and shivered, arranging and wrapping and rewrapping her clothes. She had done nothing wrong! So why did she feel like a criminal? How had her life come to this? Just this morning she was safe and warm. Sylvie was alive. Everything was as it should be.

In spite of her best efforts to hold back her tears, Margot began to weep. Her entire life had been intertwined with Sylvie's. Where would she go now? How would she eat? Where would she live?

Laying her forehead against her knees, she prayed, *O Lord, show me the way. Keep me strong like my Sylvie.* Following her prayer, however, Margot felt no infusion of courage. All she felt was cold and miserable and all alone.

After a while, exhaustion caught up with her. She drifted in and out of conscious thought. Her mind conjured up images of possible courses of action. One thing was clear. She had to flee. She could not stay in Amsterdam. Monsieur Fabarez would find her. And the burgomaster and town crier would not be far behind. But where could she go? Back to France?

Half awake, half dreaming, she envisioned herself traveling the road that led out of Amsterdam, passing beneath one of the innumerable arches in the brick wall that guarded the city on its land side.

Along the base of that wall lived hundreds of destitute, homeless men, women, and children in the most miserable of conditions. In her dream, the rotting smells and the filth and the swarms of flies sickened her. She found herself surrounded by empty-eyed children, hands stretched toward her, begging for a coin or a morsel of food. She reached into her pocket to get them something. It was empty. All her pockets were empty. She had nothing to give. Still they came. Begging her. She tried to explain, but they wouldn't listen. A sea of waving hands reached up to her for help.

Then, to her horror, the open, outstretched hands turned into grabbing hands. They clamped onto her arms. They clutched her skirt, her sleeves. Pulling her down, down. She fought to break free. There were too many of them. Too many hands. All of them pulling on her. Her knees gave way. She found herself on the ground. In rags. Flies swarming around her. And why not? She owned nothing. She lived nowhere. She was one of them. Without a home. Without food. Without hope.

Margot's head popped up with a start. She was sitting again amid darkness and fog and stone. However, the effects of the dream lingered, along with a question. If not France, then where?

There was the sea. The idea intrigued her.

One of Sylvie's books was a collection of stories, many of them sea stories that portrayed the providence of God. One story was of the siege of Leiden in 1574.

From May to September the Spanish laid siege to the city, cutting it off from assistance and supplies. Although Leiden's armed militia fought bravely, the city was gradually succumbing to desperate hunger and disease. Then, miraculously, God sent a formidable storm that swept across country and ocean and scuttled the Spanish ships. The deliverance of Leiden became a national epic of God's providential care. With their stories the survivors kept alive that day when the sea, the wind, and the polders rose up and fought on the side of the righteous.

Margot's favorite sea story, however, was "The Memorable Account of the Voyage of the *Nieuw Hoorn.*" It had all the ingredients of a great story—disaster, virtue, and a heroic escape.

The story began on the *Nieuw Hoorn,* a gigantic East India vessel. The crew and passengers numbered 206 persons. Since the average Dutch ship maintained a crew of 12 men, this large ship carried with it an equally large capacity for loss on a grand scale. According to the tale, the ship caught fire in the Sunda Straits in the East Indies, causing a dramatic explosion of the powder kegs. The skipper himself was blown high into the sky before dropping into the ocean and miraculously surviving.

Seventy-two people managed to survive the explosion only to find themselves helplessly drifting in small boats. During this time, their faith in God and obedience to the divine will were put to severe tests. To ward off starvation, they were tempted to practice cannibalism. After much argument, the majority agreed that the boys among them should be eaten first. When all the boys were gone, lots would be drawn to see who was to be eaten next.

The godly skipper was shocked that the people would abandon hope in God and even consider such a thing. He prayed that God would not let them come to this gruesome, desperate act. He finally succeeded in dissuading them from their plan for three days, thus giving God three days to rescue them by other means.

After two days had passed, the skipper himself began to doubt the providence of God. Then, on the third day, land was sighted.

However, their troubles were not yet over. Upon their reaching shore, murderous natives fell upon them with poisoned spears, killing many. The Christians among them—those who had been opposed to eating the boys—escaped. Finally the survivors were rescued by a passing ship and brought home to safety. A great banquet was held in their honor. Following a toast, the godly captain praised God for His watchful care over the godly among them.

The eleventh hour escape. Trial by water. Stories that confirmed that the Dutch were the people of God. These were the stories that thrilled Margot's soul night after night as Sylvie had read to her. And now, in the late-night shadows of the church, the remembrance of these stirred her hopes anew.

"God was preparing me for this moment with those stories," she whispered, as she fought the weight of her eyelids, heavy with sleep. "Through my beloved Sylvie, God was foretelling that my salvation would come from the sea."

As the night breeze chilled her cheeks, Margot huddled against the church building, dreaming of God's deliverance the next morning.

The next time Margot looked up, the sky was lightening. The fog and the darkness were gone. Wiping her face with her sleeve, she arched her back. It complained painfully about the night's accommodations. Her joints echoed the sentiment. They were stiff. And her flesh was chilled.

For the moment the street was silent. Margot knew it would not be that way for long. In a short time the streets of all Amsterdam would come alive, giving testimony to the city's commercial vitality.

From her vantage point she watched as now the sun peeked over a row of warehouses. Its light struck the windows of a three-story house, causing them to shine like gold. Margot smiled. The golden windows reminded her of an incident when she was a child.

It was this same time of morning. Monsieur Fabarez had gone to sea on his first fishing excursion since returning to Holland. Margot was sitting on the bench in front of the house. Sylvie had gone inside for something. Then, as now, the sun appeared and struck the windows across the canal, causing them to shine with golden splendor.

When Sylvie came out again, she found little Margot staring in wonder at the golden windows and vowing that someday she would live in a house with golden windows. Sylvie did her best to explain that the windows in that house were no different from their own, but Margot insisted that the windows were truly made of gold.

When Margot was older, she and Sylvie laughed about the golden windows. But this morning, as Margot prodded her aching muscles to get her to her feet, the golden windows didn't seem childish. They were more like a sign from God. A confirmation that God was watching over her—that everything was going to work itself out according to His good will.

Without anything to call her own except the clothes she was wearing, Margot de Campion strode down the steps of the church toward the wharf, confident that God was leading her. She was soon joined on the street by bakers and milkmen hawking their wares.

Then, reaching a street that led to the wharf, Margot gasped. *Every* house had golden windows! God was leading her to the sea. She was sure of it. With a confident stride, she set off down the street, smiling.

She reached the end of the street. Unfolding before her was the early morning beehive of Amsterdam harbor. Sailors swarmed everywhere, loading cargo, hauling crates, tarring lines. Sitting proudly at the docks was a huge East India ship, its green, ornamented stern jutting majestically high. And there, on the stern, were the windows of the great cabin. They too looked as if they were made of gold.

Margot straightened her skirt and sleeves in an unsuccessful attempt to brush out the wrinkles. She ran fingers through her hair, wishing she had a comb.

As she stepped onto the wharf, the briny smell of the harbor greeted her. The salt air made her skin tingle. Seagulls squawked overhead. Already the dock was crowded, and more people were emerging from every street that served as an outlet to the harbor.

Margot wove her way between towering stacks of cheese, barrels of various sizes, and mountains of stuffed brown sacks. Horse-drawn wagons crowded close to the ship while workers scurried around them, transferring loads from the wagons to the vessel.

"Move it, Miss!" The shout came from behind Margot, right in her ear.

Startled, she jumped out of the way to keep from being knocked over by a bearded sailor carrying a sack that drooped over his shoulder.

"Look out!"

Margot pulled up short. Two sailors rolling a barrel nearly knocked her down. No matter where she stood, she was in somebody's way.

For a long moment she stood on a patch of wharf that seemed to be safe. Then, "Excuse me," she said to a brown-skinned man hauling two small barrels, one on each shoulder. "I'd like to speak to the—"

"Outta me way, Miss," the man growled, pushing past her.

Margot threw up her hands. "All I want to do is talk to the captain!" she shouted to no one in particular. And no one in particular paid any attention to her. "Then I'll just find him myself!" she said to the air.

Whirling around, she came face to face with a horse. Huge brown nostrils flared inches from her nose. Margot jumped backward, lost her balance, and fell to the side onto a mound of grain sacks. From atop the driver's seat, the man holding the horses' reins looked down at her and shook his head in disbelief.

"This is no place for you, Miss," he said.

Margot blinked. She was looking directly into the sun. Shielding her eyes with one hand, she tried to push herself up with the other. "I'm not hurt," she said. "Thank you so much for your concern."

The driver muttered a derogatory comment about females as he slapped the horses' backsides with the reins.

"The least you can do after knocking me down is tell me where I might find the captain of that ship!" Margot yelled after him.

Either the driver didn't hear, or he ignored her, for he continued on his way without looking back.

Carefully navigating the wharf traffic, Margot made her way to the ship's gangway. No sooner had she set foot on the plank than someone grabbed her arm.

"And where do you think you might be goin', Miss?"

Margot turned to the man who had a grip on her arm. He was tall—she had to look up to him—and skinny. His cheeks were more than hollow—they were cavernous. He had a thin, flat beak for a nose. A green felt cap lay back on his head.

"I must speak to the captain," Margot said.

"Is he expecting you?" The way he said it, his words were more a challenge than a question.

"Not exactly," Margot replied.

"Not exactly," the gangwayman repeated, staring at her. "Are you on the passenger list?"

"No."

"No," he repeated. "Then you're a relative of the captain's—or his mistress?" A sly wink accompanied the question.

"Of course not!" Margot cried.

"Of course not," the gangwayman said.

Margot frowned. With a firm yank, she attempted to pull her arm free. But his thin, long fingers formed a shackle that encompassed her arm. It was strong as iron. "Sir, release me!" she said firmly.

Without relaxing his grip, the sailor studied her face, then moved her an arm's distance away while he looked her up and down with undisguised desire.

"If you will please inform the captain that I would like to speak with him—"

"Not likely," drawled the man. "We're about to get under way. The captain doesn't have time for socializing."

Margot's dislike for this man was matched by a growing sense of fear. His cold tone and crude glances caused her to shiver.

"I really must insist," she said, struggling harder to free her arm. It did her no good. The man's grip was unyielding.

"And I must insist—" He stopped his mimicking mid-sentence. He took another long, vulgar look at her. "You know," he said, "I just might be able to put you to good use myself."

"Let me go, you boorish louse!" Margot cried.

The folds of leathery skin that were the man's cheeks pulled back like curtains to reveal stained and blackened teeth. "That's the way I like my women—with good fight in 'em," he drawled.

"For the last time, unhand me!"

The sailor wrinkled his beak nose. One eye squinted shut. "I have a mind," he said, "to let you on board . . ."

Margot stopped struggling for the moment.

"If we can come to some mutually beneficial arrangements," he said. "I do something for you—you do something for me."

Margot stood stone still.

The man with the hollow cheeks leaned into her. She closed her eyes and pulled back. Still, she couldn't escape him. His breath smelled like that of a sea lion after having feasted on herring.

"Well, Missy?" he whispered.

She shrank back from the odor. The only thing keeping her from falling backward into the water was his grip on her arm.

"What say you to my little proposition?"

Another wave of herring breath crashed upon her. The odor twisted her empty stomach into a knot. What should she do? Scream? Kick him? But what if he let loose? She'd surely fall into the water between the ship and the dock.

Now he was so near to her she could feel the heat of his breath on her face. *Dear God, help me,* she prayed silently.

Then she had an inspiration.

Margot let her head fall backward, limp. She moaned and let her knees go weak.

41

The man had to catch her, lest she drag them both over the side of the gangplank and into the water.

Margot let out another moan. With half-opened eyes, she rolled her pupils upward toward the back of her head. Spittle drooled out the corners of her mouth. She began to shake, then jerk violently, making doglike growling sounds. "What are you doing?" the startled gangwayman cried. "Are you sick? What's wrong with you?" He looked frantically around him, obviously not sure what to do with a woman who was slumping down to his knees, jerking and growling.

"Timmons! Wainwright! Get over here!" he screamed. "Help me with this woman! She's got the plague or something!"

Margot felt two pairs of hands support her under her arms.

"What do we do with her?" a voice asked.

Margot drooled and jerked and growled.

The next thing she knew she was being dragged away, her shoes scraping the gangplank. After about ten steps, she planted her feet under her, pulled herself up, and stood tall.

Startled at her sudden strength and composure, the two sailors released her. "Thank you, gentlemen," she said to them. "I can take care of myself from here."

Their faces were portraits of comical puzzlement.

Margot turned back to the hollow-cheeked gangwayman. "If you were more familiar with your Bible, sir," she said in a superior tone, "you would have recognized that ploy. David used it to escape Achish, king of Gath. First Samuel, chapter twenty-one."

She straightened her skirt and strutted down the wharf.

Sitting alone on a chair-high stack of grain sacks, Margot let the emotions of her encounter with the hollow-cheeked sailor catch up with her. She was trembling, truly this time, and fighting back tears. This whole morning had overwhelmed her—the bustling wharf; feeling as if she didn't belong here—or anyplace, for that matter; the sailor's crude advances. If this was God's will for her, why was it so difficult to get on board that ship?

Margot suddenly laughed aloud at the absurdity of it all. She didn't even know where the ship was going! But then, what did it matter if she ended up in India, or the Caribbean islands, or the American colonies, or England? She had to get away!

She couldn't have been wrong about the ship, could she? It had golden windows!

Margot drooped forward and hung her head dejectedly. Her limbs felt heavy and tired. Tears spilled onto her cheeks. She wanted to give up, to go home, to feel Sylvie's fleshy arms around her, to hear Sylvie's soothing voice telling her everything—

She bolted upright with a sudden realization. Sylvie wouldn't coddle her. "Who ever told you life would be easy?" Sylvie had said to her one particularly bad day. "And if they said it, you shouldn't have believed them! You've got to work hard for everything, and if you get to keep half of what you work for, count yourself blessed. Remember Job. Everything he'd worked for all his life was taken from him in one day. And when he refused to be unfaithful to God, the good Lord gave him back everything he'd lost and more. But don't think it was easy for him!"

Margot jumped off the grain sacks. She scanned the wharf for a man who looked like a captain. One way or another, she was going to get on that ship! She knew that if she could just speak to the captain, she could convince him to let her work—

A small cry escaped her mouth. Fabarez was walking in her direction!

She looked for someplace to hide.

Too late. He'd already spotted her.

3

Fabarez came barreling toward Margot as fast as his stocky legs would carry him. He raised a fist and shouted. His words were lost in the clamor of the docks. Half the length of the wharf separated him from her, but that distance was diminishing rapidly.

Margot instinctively backed away. Her head swiveled this way and that as she looked for a place to run, a place to hide. There! Those barrels. She ducked behind a wall of casks stacked three high. She was out of his sight but not out of danger.

Should she try to outrun him? Directly behind her, the street that brought her to the wharf was one possible avenue of escape. To her left, another street led to the warehouses. The harbor blocked any escape to her right.

A large coach caught her attention. It was black, polished, with gold trim and was parked beside the waterfront. The driver sat like a statue, reins in hand. Leaning against the coach next to its open door was a tall, striking young man with blond hair. He was staring at Margot with an amused grin. At least, she thought he was staring at her. The man glanced in the direction of Fabarez, then looked at Margot. He covered his mouth with his hand and chuckled!

The man's glance up the wharf brought Margot's attention back to Fabarez. She pressed her face between two of the barrels, using the crack between them as an eyepiece. He was almost upon her! She shot a look at the man standing by the coach. His arms were crossed. A toothy grin stretched wide across his face. She looked between the barrels again and monitored Fabarez's approach. She placed her hands against the barrels, waited a moment, then pushed with all her might. Empty casks tumbled down upon an unsuspecting Fabarez, sending him sprawling.

"Witch! Stop her! She's a witch!" Fabarez cried from the ground, cursing, his arms and legs jumbled up with the barrels.

Margot bolted down the street. Racing through a broad alley between two towering brick warehouses, Margot entered a district of canals, streets, and footbridges. Unlike the busy wharf, this section of the warehouse district was nearly deserted. She bounded across a canal by way of a footbridge and, once on the other side, raised the bridge to keep Fabarez from following.

Moments later he appeared between the warehouses, puffing and cursing. Catching sight of her, he slowed and moved toward her like a cat stalking a bird. He perched on the far side of the canal.

"Leave me alone!" Margot cried.

A panting Fabarez pointed an accusing finger. "Witch! Witch! Witch! Witch!" he chanted.

Margot rested against the brick warehouse, fighting to catch her breath. "I'm not a witch," she cried wearily.

Scanning the length of the canal in both directions, Fabarez looked for a way to cross. One hundred yards in each direction were other footbridges. He moved toward the one on his left.

Margot countered by moving to her left, increasing the distance between them.

Fabarez stopped. So did Margot.

"Lower the footbridge," he ordered.

"Jump across!" she retorted.

They stared at each other across the waterway. Fabarez bent over to catch his breath. He wiped sweat from his brow with a soiled shirt sleeve.

Margot seized the moment of inattention to begin creeping to her right. Fabarez's head jerked up. He mirrored her movement. Margot stopped.

Farther down the canal on Margot's side, two workers emerged from a warehouse. Like bookends, they were at opposite ends of a huge trunk. One was stepping backwards, looking over his shoulder, ready to negotiate the crossing of the footbridge.

"Mates!" Fabarez called to them. "Mates! I've cornered a witch! There's a reward in it for you if you help me catch her!"

The trunk-carrying sailors looked at Margot.

"I'm not a witch!" she cried.

"I swear it's the truth!" Fabarez yelled. "She done killed me missus last night with an incantation, then escaped through a locked door when I went to fetch the authorities."

The sailors exchanged glances, then set down the trunk. Fabarez was already moving toward the far footbridge. Since there were no alleys between the warehouses on Margot's side, he was cutting off her only avenue of escape. From their end, the sailors moved cautiously toward her.

Margot waited until Fabarez was halfway to the next bridge, then she began to lower the footbridge in front of her.

Fabarez saw what she was doing and ran back.

Margot had to pull the bridge up again.

"Might as well lower it." He motioned with his hand. "You can't escape."

The sailors were closing in.

Leaving the footbridge, Margot ran away from them.

On the opposite side of the canal, Fabarez paralleled her movement, remaining slightly ahead of her to prevent her raising the next footbridge.

But Margot had something else in mind. The doors to the warehouses.

Each warehouse had two doors, a large one for loading and unloading goods, and a normal-sized door for pedestrian entry. Figuring the loading doors were too heavy for her, Margot concentrated on the smaller ones.

She ran to the first door and leaned on the latch.

Locked!

Fabarez saw what she was doing. "Grab her, mates! Grab her!" he screamed.

Margot ran to the next warehouse and tried the latch.

Locked. She bit her lower lip in exasperation.

The third warehouse had a massive wooden beam and two external padlocks securing it. Skipping that one, she ran to the fourth warehouse, the one by the next footbridge. Fabarez already had his foot on the bridge. This door was her last hope.

It swung open.

Margot glanced over her shoulder at Fabarez. His wide-eyed astonishment pleased her. She stepped inside the warehouse and slammed the door behind her. Darkness engulfed her. The only light came from small, filthy windows high overhead. She searched the blackness around the door for a lock or bar. There was none. The good fortune that had provided her a way of escape quickly soured to misfortune. Without a lock, how would she keep Fabarez and the two sailors from getting in?

From the other side of the door came the sound of hurried footsteps and the wheezing of a man unaccustomed to running. She swung around and leaned her back against the door even though she knew there was no way she could stop three men from forcing their way in. She squinted her eyes in an attempt to hasten their adjustment to the dim light. Gradually, rows of crates and barrels and casks stretching nearly to the ceiling came into view.

Leaving the door unattended, Margot ran past several rows of these, looking for something to use as a weapon. A tool. A bottle. Anything. But all the goods were sealed in crates or barrels. She could find nothing with which to defend herself.

The warehouse door flew open with a crash that rattled its hinges. A shaft of light poured through the opening, followed by three dark figures. They entered cautiously. One at a time.

"Is she really a witch?" one of the sailors asked.

Fabarez, who was leading them—Margot could tell by the familiar stooped shape of the first silhouette—replied, "Believe me, mates, she is. I've never seen anything like it. She cut out the very heart of me missus, she did! Was about to burn it in sacrifice to the dark devil of the underworld when I caught her!"

Margot stifled a gasp of disbelief. How could he say those things?

"She's in league with Satan," Fabarez explained as he probed forward with his hands, his eyes still not accustomed to the darkness. "I knew it. Knew it all along."

One of the sailors behind him said a quick prayer for protection from the witch's dark powers.

Margot slipped silently down the third row. She found a meager space between a stack of barrels and piled-up grain sacks. Backing into it and crouching low, she pulled a couple of sacks of grain in front of her.

"Each of you take a row," she heard Fabarez say. "Yell if you see her."

After that, all was silent. She waited, straining to hear some sound that would give away their location. But she heard nothing.

When she thought she'd waited long enough, Margot decided to push aside one corner of a grain sack just enough to peek around. She caught her breath. A baggy pair of sailor's trousers were less than a foot away. She froze.

The grain sack prevented her seeing in which direction the fellow was looking. For all she knew, he was staring down at her!

Then the sailor's feet shuffled, and he continued on.

Margot breathed again. After she'd given him time to move well down the row, she quietly pushed aside the grain sack and checked the sailor's progress. He was more than halfway down the aisle. His back was to her.

Careful not to make a sound, Margot emerged from her hiding place. She backtracked toward the door, checking each row before crossing it. She slid undetected past the second sailor's row. Fabarez must have taken the first, the one closest to the doorway. When she reached it, she saw him stretching high and bending low as he worked his way down the aisle. Somewhere he'd found a stick. He was poking it into every crevice.

Margot moved noiselessly toward the open door. She checked Fabarez one more time. He was on his knees prodding between two barrels.

She stepped into the shaft of light, and a long shadow leaped across the warehouse floor like a black flag, signaling her location.

"Mates! She's at the door!" Fabarez's raspy voice screamed.

Margot sprang through the doorway. Shielding her eyes against the bright morning sunlight, she ran to the footbridge.

Behind her, her three pursuers exploded through the warehouse door. They hesitated because of the sunlight, but only slightly. Once again, the race was on.

Margot's lungs burned, her legs were drained of strength. *I can't run anymore! There's no place for me to hide. It's no use. They're going to catch me.* She envisioned herself being led to a huge black cauldron of boiling water and being forced to thrust her hands into it.

She forced her complaining legs down the alley that led back to the wharf. A glance over her shoulder revealed that Fabarez was lagging behind, but the two sailors were gaining on her.

Just as she was about to come out onto the wharf, a black carriage pulled in front of her, cutting off her only avenue of escape. Margot drew up abruptly. It was over. Even if she could run farther, there was no place to go!

The door of the carriage flew open.

"Get in!" a voice cried.

Margot hesitated.

"Get in! They're right behind you!"

Margot leaped into the carriage.

The door whipped shut behind her. The coachman barked orders to the horses. The carriage bounded forward, sending Margot crashing into the lap of the carriage's sole occupant—the blond man who had been laughing at her predicament.

"My, my, my. Isn't this a fine introduction?" the man said merrily.

Margot's cheek was pressed against his nose. She scrambled to the far side of the carriage.

Her rescuer, smiling that wide smile she'd seen earlier, smoothed his trousers and doublet and adjusted the rapier that hung at his side.

Margot smiled cautiously back at him. Then she took a quick glance out the window.

In the distance, the two sailors had stopped running. Fabarez emerged from between the buildings with an upraised fist. He appeared to be screaming at the top of his lungs.

"Don't worry," said the smiling young man. "You're safe from them."

Struggling to catch her breath, Margot settled into the carriage seat. She didn't relax, though. What the man had said was true. She was safe from Fabarez, at least for the moment. But she wasn't about to let down her guard until she was sure she was also safe from the handsome man sitting across from her.

The man reclining casually on the opposite seat introduced himself as Uys van Jaarsveld. Everything about him gave testimony to his wealth, from his slashed white sleeves with their frequent bursts of purple underlinen, to his close-fitting black trousers decorated with French ribbons, to his sparkling rapier, to his polished sentences.

Even the steady clopping of the horses testified to his high position. Common people in Amsterdam walked or rode the canals. Only the wealthy had carriages such as the one Margot found herself riding in.

As for the man, he was as smooth and refined as his clothing. Long blond hair, which he frequently primped with delicate white fingers, framed a confident, even dashing, face. He had a soft, almost feminine quality about him. A thin nose separated lazy blue eyes. In keeping with the fashion of the day, he wore no facial hair.

He would look even more handsome if he did, Margot thought. *A beard would give strength to his rather weak chin.*

"Do I amuse you?" van Jaarsveld asked. He was still smiling.

Margot blushed. "Please forgive me, sir. I didn't mean to—" She lowered her gaze. Nervous hands comforted one another in her lap.

"No, please don't run from me." Van Jaarsveld reached across the carriage and placed a hand on hers.

Margot had never felt a hand so smooth. "I can hardly run away, sir," she said without looking up.

"Your eyes did," van Jaarsveld said softly. "Look at me."

Though his hand was gentle, still it made Margot feel uncomfortable. He was too close too soon.

When she didn't look up, the hand rose to her chin. Tenderly he raised her head.

Margot's eyes remained downcast.

"There is nothing to be afraid of," he said soothingly. "Look at me."

Slowly Margot raised her eyes. An arm's length away, pale blue eyes were locked on hers. Her first instinct was to turn away. She resisted it and matched his steady gaze with one of her own.

Amused wrinkles formed in the corners of his eyes. "Much better," he said. "Yes, much better."

To Margot's relief, van Jaarsveld retreated to his side of the carriage.

"Now then. What is your name?"

Margot wasn't sure she wanted to reveal her name.

He waited patiently.

"Margot de Campion."

"A lovely name. Truly lovely. And tell me, Mademoiselle de Campion, why was that ruffian chasing you?"

Again she hesitated, not wanting to say too much to a man she didn't know. But she felt she owed him something. After all, he did rescue her. So without mentioning the nutshell, Margot briefly described her relationship to Monsieur Fabarez and narrated the events of the last couple of days up to the point when she jumped into the carriage. She made no mention of Fabarez's charge of witchcraft—only that he had convinced himself that Margot was somehow responsible for Sylvie's death.

"You poor child," van Jaarsveld lamented. With a look of concern, he added, "And this illness from which this good woman died—you have not felt any similar effects?"

Margot shook her head.

"We must thank God for that," he said, obviously relieved.

Whether from exhaustion, or weakness from lack of food, or possibly just from the steady, reassuring beat of the horse's hooves, Margot felt herself sinking back into the cushioned seat. Her fears were melting away in the warmth of his concern.

A couple of times she caught him staring at her figure—or was he just looking at her clothing? Hadn't she looked at *his* clothing in an attempt to learn something of him?

"And how did you come to be at the docks?" van Jaarsveld inquired.

"I was hoping to get passage aboard a ship. The green one."

"The *Eagle?* And what business might you have in Cape Town? That is, if you are debarking at Cape Town. You just don't look like a person who would have business in India."

Cape Town. Margot had read the name in Sylvie's book of sea stories. She knew it was located on the southern tip of the African continent and that it was a halfway station for the long voyages to India. But that was all she knew about it.

"A new start," she replied. "I hope to find a new start there."

A rakish grin crossed van Jaarsveld's face. "You're not one of the King's Nieces, are you?"

"King's Nieces? I don't understand. Surely, dressed like this, you don't think I'm royalty."

He laughed and shook his head. "No, no. The King's Nieces is a term used to describe women who go to Cape Town to become wives for the settlers. They are orphans who have no dowry of their own. So in exchange for a modest dowry and passage to the colony, they agree to marry one of the colonists."

"A man they've never met?"

Van Jaarsveld seemed entertained by her astonished reaction.

"I most certainly am not one of the King's Nieces!" she cried. "I would never consent to marry a man I'd never met!"

Her passionate dissent prompted a wide smile with plenty of teeth. He held up both hands in surrender. "Don't attack me!" He laughed. "It was an innocent inquiry!"

Margot felt her rising blood color her cheeks. She was embarrassed by her overreaction.

"Would you be equally offended," van Jaarsveld said teasingly, "if I were to ask if you were able to book passage aboard the *Eagle?*"

Speaking softly, Margot replied, "I would not be offended. And it would be misleading for me to imply that I was attempting to book passage since I have no funds. It was my intention to secure passage aboard the ship by offering my services to the captain."

"So you're a sailor then?" he said with a grin.

Margot turned away. "You're laughing at me."

"Forgive me." Van Jaarsveld's hands shot up again. "That was ungallant of me." He cleared his throat in an attempt to recover from his failed jest. "So then, tell me, Mademoiselle de Campion, were you able to secure a position with the captain?"

Margot related her rather odious confrontation with the gang-wayman and her subsequent failure to locate the captain.

"An unfortunate encounter," van Jaarsveld replied pensively.

For several moments they rode in silence. Until now, Margot had given no thought as to where he was taking her, so relieved was she that he had snatched her from the clutches of Monsieur Fabarez. However, this momentary pause in the conversation gave her mind opportunity to raise the question. She leaned forward and looked out the window. When she recognized where they were, her heart began to race with renewed fear.

The carriage was completing one of the city's loops. They were re-entering the wharf from the opposite side! A gasp escaped her lips.

"Don't be alarmed," van Jaarsveld said hastily. "I'm sailing aboard the *Eagle* myself."

Margot jumped to the window and scanned the docks for any sign of Monsieur Fabarez. Anyone watching the coach pass by would have seen her perfectly framed in the window.

For a second time van Jaarsveld reached across the carriage. He touched her arm gently. In soothing tones he said, "Monsieur What-ever-His-Name-Is can't harm you. You have my word. I can protect you. You see, I own the *Eagle.*"

Margot stared at him in disbelief.

Van Jaarsveld shrugged modestly. "Well, actually, the Dutch East India Company owns her. But I'm one of the Lords XVII." When the reference failed to register an impact, he explained, "I'm one of the directors of the company."

"So then, having rescued me, are you now just going to dump me out on the wharf again?" Margot asked.

"My dear lady, no! You wound me!" He acted as though he'd been skewered with a sword thrust to the heart.

Margot fought back a smile.

Straightening himself, he said, "Originally, my intentions were to instruct the driver to take you wherever you wished to go."

"And now?" Margot asked.

"Come with me to South Africa!"

The suddenness of his offer caught her off guard. She lowered her eyes. "Monsieur van Jaarsveld, I couldn't—it wouldn't be right."

"Oh, no, I did that all wrong," he said apologetically. "I assure you, Mademoiselle de Campion, my intentions are honorable."

Margot looked at him.

He looked genuinely sincere. "You must understand, I have a lovely fiancée eagerly awaiting my return to Amsterdam. We've known each other since we were children, and we've been planning our wedding since the age of five! I would do nothing to imperil her love!"

A smile slipped through to Margot's lips before she could catch it.

"No, my dear lady—as lovely as you are, I have no designs on you. What I am offering you is work in return for passage to Cape Town."

"What kind of work?"

"It was the worst possible timing," van Jaarsveld explained, "but just as I was preparing for this trip, the dear woman who serves as my chambermaid took ill. She has been with the family since before I was born and has cared for me for as long as I can remember. I just didn't trust any of our other servants to take her place."

"But you're willing to trust *me?* Someone you met a short time ago?"

Van Jaarsveld grinned a toothy grin. He hooked a stray lock of hair behind his ear. "It seems ordained, does it not? You are looking for passage aboard the *Eagle,* and I need a chambermaid. But I must confess, when it comes to orderliness, I am a barbarian of the lowest sort."

Margot shook her head slowly. "I'm not sure—"

"You can clean, can't you?" he asked.

"If there is one thing I learned from Sylvie Fabarez, it is how to clean."

"So what is stopping you from accepting my offer? We'll have separate quarters, if that's what is concerning you. I'll pay you for your services, in addition to passage to Cape Town. And once we arrive, I'll give you references which will help you find a position in the colony."

Margot wrinkled her nose in thought. It was everything she wanted —in fact, it was more than she could have hoped for. So what was stopping her? Something just didn't seem right.

"Let me ask you this," van Jaarsveld said. "If you had found the captain and he had offered you a position—let's say, serving and scrubbing in the ship's galley for passage to Cape Town—would you have taken it?"

"Of course I would," Margot replied.

"Then why do you hesitate to accept my offer? It serves your purpose, does it not? Does it make that much difference to you that it is I and not the captain who is offering you employment?"

Margot had to admit that at best the difference was trifling. So what was stopping her? She was being offered passage aboard the ship with golden windows.

"Monsieur van Jaarsveld," she said bowing slightly, "meet your new chambermaid."

It wasn't long until they were ready to board. Margot watched as van Jaarsveld's trunks were hoisted aboard, and she suddenly realized that she had no change of clothes or any personal effects. When she expressed her dismay to van Jaarsveld, he patted her reassuringly on the hand and told her that, given her current relationship with Monsieur Fabarez, it would be disastrous for her to attempt to retrieve them now.

He called the driver of his coach aside and rattled off a set of orders that launched the servant into action. As the coach sped off, van Jaarsveld informed Margot that the driver had been given instructions to purchase all the necessary garments and personal items she would need. He assured her they would be delivered to the ship before departure.

Margot followed him to the gangway.

The man with the herring breath was still on watch. He hailed van Jaarsveld elegantly, at the same time casting a cautious, if not suspicious, glance at Margot. Though the man assured van Jaarsveld that his cabin was ready, van Jaarsveld refused to board until he had discussed something of great import with the captain.

The sailor instructed a common tar to fetch the shipmaster. Meanwhile, the three of them stood and waited for the captain to join them.

Van Jaarsveld assumed a posture of regal impatience. His nose in the air, he did not look at anyone directly. He never spoke. And he shifted his weight with annoying frequency from one foot to the other.

Meanwhile, the gangwayman scratched his beaklike nose with filthy fingers, sniffed a lot, and cast covert, crude glances at Margot.

Of the three of them, Margot was probably the most uncomfortable. She found the public van Jaarsveld to be more distant and formal than he had been in private. His aloofness fostered twin concerns.

First, he seemed to take no notice of the gangwayman's vulgar glances at her. She was beginning to wonder if van Jaarsveld would indeed honor his promise to protect her. Then there was Fabarez. She had not forgotten him. In fact, she expected him to appear at any moment. She had positioned herself on the dock in such a way that she could not only keep an eye on the gangwayman but also watch for Fabarez. She couldn't help but wonder what Fabarez would do if he spotted her—or what she would do if she were spotted. Would van Jaarsveld still rush to her aid if Monsieur Fabarez began chanting, "Witch! Witch! Witch"?

"Ah! Monsieur van Jaarsveld!" The voice boomed from atop the gangway.

Van Jaarsveld's response was a diplomatic smile, nothing more. He did not greet the captain until the officer joined them on the dock side of the gangplank.

The captain was a short, stocky man who looked and walked like a bulldog. His reddish brown complexion, which was all the more evident because it stretched unhindered across the top of a bald head, was testimony to a lifetime at sea. He smiled as he descended the gangway, but it looked as if it pained him to do so.

"It seems we have a problem, Captain," van Jaarsveld said.

"Oh?" The bulldog face wrinkled up. He was instantly ready for a scrap.

"My problem is this man here!" Van Jaarsveld pointed to the gangwayman, whose face registered immediate shock. "Earlier today he assaulted my chambermaid in a crude and boorish way." He indicated Margot. "Is this the kind of behavior we can expect from your men on this voyage?"

The captain turned his bulldog face toward Margot. "Is this true, miss? Did van Wyk assault you?"

Margot looked at the sailor.

There was murder in his eyes.

She nodded anyway. "I had to feign illness to get him to release me," she said.

The bulldog tore into van Wyk. "Get your things and get off my ship!" he barked.

"But, Cap'n—" the gangwayman protested.

"But nothing!" The captain cut him off. "Consider yourself lucky. Had you done this at sea, I'd have personally thrown you overboard! You have five minutes to get off my ship!"

Van Wyk bared his teeth for a fight, then backed down. He was no match for the bulldog. Like a whipped pup, he scuttled up the gangway to collect his belongings.

"My apologies, mademoiselle," said the captain to Margot. "It won't happen again."

"Thank you, Captain. I'm sure it won't," Margot replied.

"Are we ready to get under way, Captain?" van Jaarsveld asked.

"With the tide, Monsieur van Jaarsveld," said the captain. "With the tide."

The two men made their way up the gangplank, van Jaarsveld first, then the captain. Margot followed them.

Van Jaarsveld's cabin was spacious—larger than the captain's cabin, van Jaarsveld was quick to point out. Certainly the three windows on the ship's ornate stern added to the cabin's expansive feeling. But considering the common complaint of sailors regarding cramped quarters, the cabin was immense. It was larger than the entire downstairs room of the Fabarez house.

Three large trunks occupied the center of the room. "I'll get right to work unpacking them," Margot said.

"Fine," replied van Jaarsveld, preening his hair. "I have to go over the manifest with the captain."

"Do you have a preference as to where things go?" she asked.

"Use your best judgment. You can acquaint me with your decisions after we've gotten under way."

Margot turned her attention to the trunks. The cabin door closed, and she was alone. It wasn't until after van Jaarsveld had left that she remembered she'd not asked about her own quarters. *There will be plenty of time for that,* she reasoned. *I had better earn my keep.*

For the next hour she unpacked van Jaarsveld's finery. She had never seen so many clothes in her life. Leather gloves. Silk gloves. Embroidered handkerchiefs. Leather belts. Nearly two dozen ruffs of various shapes. Forty pairs of trousers. One hundred fifty shirts and as many collars and ruffled cuffs. Over a dozen hats—though van Jaarsveld had gone all day without wearing one. Margot thought it unlikely he wore many hats, the way he loved to constantly smooth his blond hair.

She put away a dozen nightcaps, two dozen nightshirts, and even a variety of ornamented daggers. One trunk held papers, ledgers, and stationery supplies. She put these neatly atop the elegant French-style wooden desk.

After everything was stowed, Margot made up van Jaarsveld's bed. Then she found a cleaning cloth and went around the cabin polishing wood and brass surfaces until she could see her reflection in them.

She finished just as the ship was getting under way. Standing at the windows, she stared out at the wharf in fascination as lines were thrown off and the vessel began to distance itself from the dock.

She could hear what sounded like an all-male chorus on deck. The captain was the chorus leader, sounding one order after another. In response, a different sailor's voice rang out each time, some loud and near, others faint and distant. They were singing words that, to Margot, sounded like a different language. And like most languages, their language was uniquely suited to their world.

"All hands, up anchor, ahoy!"

"Haul out into the stream."

"Trim the yards!"

"Tumble up there and take the sheet!"

Margot steadied herself against a post as the deck beneath her moved. The ship pulled farther away from the dock. That's when she saw him.

Monsieur Fabarez was standing on the wharf. He happened to glance her direction and saw her in the window of the East India merchant ship. The look of shock on his face was quickly supplanted by rage. He ran along the docks, shouting at the ship, pointing at Margot. The *Eagle* did not heed his cries. She continued to pull away, leaving him behind.

Margot felt faint. Watching Monsieur Fabarez grow smaller and smaller on the Amsterdam wharf seemed to bring all the emotions of the last two days crashing down upon her at once. She was tired and hungry. She had not eaten anything since yesterday, when she prepared a few wedges of cheese and some fruit for herself and Sylvie.

Sylvie.

The thought of her beloved Sylvie brought tears to her eyes. She wondered if Sylvie could see her now. If she knew that Margot was about to add one more story to all the sea stories they had read together. Salvation stories. Just as the sea had risen up at various times to defend the people who occupied these lowlands, so now it was rescuing her from the clutches of Monsieur Fabarez, carrying her to a distant land where she would begin a whole new life.

The figures on the dock were indistinguishable now. Like a vanishing jewel, Amsterdam was fading in the distance. The *Eagle* had caught the current flowing from the River Ij. It carried the ship on watery wings toward the North Sea.

"But they that wait upon the Lord shall renew their strength; they shall mount up with wings as eagles; they shall run, and not be weary; and they shall walk, and not faint." Margot whispered the verse from Isaiah as she caught her last glimpse of the city in which she'd been reared.

Just a few hours before, she had trembled as the light of the early morning sun turned the windows of the *Eagle* to gold. Now she stood in safety in one of those golden windows. God had indeed heard her and answered her prayer.

4

Thank you, Lord!"

Margot twirled merrily around and around in the center of van Jaarsveld's spacious cabin. Her hands waved over her head in a carefree manner.

For the last several moments, her emotions had teetered between two extremes. On the one hand, she felt like weeping over her loss of Sylvie; on the other hand, God had brought blessing out of her loss. He had rescued her and placed her in luxurious surroundings—like the biblical Ruth, who one day was poor and hungry, gleaning barley in the fields, and the next day was forever secure in wealthy Boaz's arms. The thing that tipped Margot's teetering emotions to joy was the thought that Sylvie, had she lived, would be the first to rejoice with her. Once that thought occurred to her, Margot could suppress her emotions no longer. They bubbled up inside her and overflowed in an expression of thanksgiving.

Suddenly the floor swayed beneath her. She stumbled to her left, catching herself on the corner of the desk. She giggled. This new world of hers had an undulating surface. It would take her a while to grow accustomed to it, but she was eager to learn and explore every facet.

"No time like the present," she said to herself. She swung wide the cabin door. A burst of salt air greeted her. Fresh. Cool. Invigorating. Unlike the stagnant and defiled canals of the city. She stepped onto the sunlit deck.

Against a clear sky, sailors scurried about the rigging, scampering among the spars like chipmunks in a tree while the first mate snapped crisp orders. Scrunched squares of canvas fluttered in the sailors' grasp. Then, with a distinctive *whomp*, which only canvas and wind together can make, the canvas blossomed magnificently. In full glory, the huge sails overhead looked like harnessed white clouds.

The ship leaned dramatically to the left and picked up speed. On uncertain legs Margot made her way to the rail to steady herself. Small choppy swells, spangled with sunlight, raced against the hull. She turned her head into the wind. Her long brown hair fluttered like a flag. It was a glorious feeling.

Beyond the railing, land was still visible. Across the deck, on the starboard side, a large island loomed in the distance. At least Margot thought it was an island—she couldn't tell for sure if it was connected to anything. Though they hadn't journeyed far enough to escape civilization, it wasn't hard for her to imagine that the island was a distant land, occupied by natives with strange customs, who talked in an unknown tongue.

"What's that dame doing on deck?"

The shout came from behind her. Margot swung around. The first mate was pointing at her. "Yeah, you! Get off my deck!" he bellowed.

Margot glanced about her. It seemed that the entire crew had stopped what they were doing to look at her.

"Get off! Off! Off!" the first mate screamed.

Margot couldn't understand why he was irate. She wasn't doing anything wrong, neither was she in anyone's way.

Still he screamed. "Are you deaf? Get off my deck!"

Snatching up her dress angrily, Margot turned toward the cabin. As she took her first step, the ship hit a downward swell. The deck sank beneath her. Her foot searched frantically for something that was no longer there, and she tumbled in a very unladylike manner.

All around her and overhead, sailors whistled and laughed. This earned them the first mate's profane ire. He cursed first at them, then at Margot—all the way back to the cabin.

She slammed the door behind her and leaned against it. Her heart pounded in furious humiliation. Angry tears warmed her cheeks. So much for exploring her new world. Did that first mate really think he owned the deck? The question gave her pause. Maybe he did own it. She was in a new world, and every world had its own set of laws.

Margot decided she would say nothing of the incident until she learned a few of the ship's laws. And the first law she was going to look into had to do with the first mate's right to the deck.

Suddenly, as the cabin interior came into focus, she realized she had a new problem.

"What happened here?" she cried.

It looked as if someone had completely dismantled the room. Everything was on the floor! Books, papers, writing instruments—everything she had stacked so neatly on the desk was now scattered all over the place. Mementos and small paintings she had found in the trunk and carefully set around the cabin to give it a feeling of home were strewn carelessly about.

Who had done this? She hadn't been gone that long! Had Monsieur van Jaarsveld come in, looking for something? Was this any way for a civilized person to search for something? He'd told her that when it came to orderliness he was a barbarian, but this was beyond what she'd imagined! From the condition of the cabin, he must have been furious.

"At least I hope he found what he was looking for," she muttered. She picked up some scattered papers and books and replaced them on the desk.

She was midway through her reordering of the mess when the ship hit a couple of large swells. The papers on the desk spilled over the edge, followed by the books and everything else. Margot stared at them dumbfoundedly. Then she burst out laughing.

So it hadn't been Monsieur van Jaarsveld after all!

"Somebody needs to warn people about the strange ways of this new world of mine!"

Two quick raps sounded on the cabin door. It swung open. In walked van Jaarsveld, followed by two sailors carrying a trunk. The three of them were halted by the mess on the floor. The sailors looked first at the chaos, then uncertainly at Margot, then at van Jaarsveld as if to see what his reaction would be.

Van Jaarsveld placed his hands on his hips.

Margot stood defenselessly in the middle of the cabin with papers and books and pictures strewn at her feet.

"I was just tidying up," she said.

The trunk the sailors had carried in contained dresses and personal items for Margot. With one leg draped casually over the arm of the desk chair, van Jaarsveld watched as she sorted through them. He seemed to take delight in her surprised expressions as she lifted one dress after the other from the trunk.

"Some of them will undoubtedly be too large or too small," he said.

"These are breathtaking!" she exclaimed, holding a yellow dress up to her neck to see if it fit. It was of French design, tastefully accentuated with lace and little satin bows. "I've never worn anything this extravagant!" She turned toward van Jaarsveld for his opinion.

He nodded approvingly, but his facial expression was less than enthusiastic.

"Is something wrong?" Margot asked.

He waved her off. "Nothing of consequence."

Margot was not convinced.

His hair was windblown, and, as fussy as he was about his hair, he made no attempt to smooth it. When he spoke, his sentences were clipped short, and he had a sour look on his face. "There should be a blue one in there," he said, pointing to the nearly empty trunk. "I told Willem to look for it specifically. I hope it fits."

Margot sorted through the remaining dresses. She found a robin-egg blue dress and pulled it out. It had a close-fitting bodice with matching waist scarf. A frown formed on Margot's forehead.

"Don't you like it?" Van Jaarsveld sat up. He appeared genuinely displeased at her reaction.

"It's gorgeous!" Margot cried.

"Then why the frown?"

"These are not the dresses of a chambermaid."

Relaxing again in the chair, he said, "Oh, but they are! Have you ever been to the van Jaarsveld mansion to see what the maids wear?"

"But these are too elegant to be practical!" Margot cried. She held up the blue dress as evidence to prove her point.

"Mademoiselle de Campion," he said in a mock condescending tone, "you have a lot to learn about wealth and position. So much depends on appearances. If you were to dress in anything less than this while in my employ, my position as one of the Lords XVII would be called into question."

Margot studied the dress. "I suppose so."

He wasn't listening. His face was twisted in a wince.

"Monsieur van Jaarsveld, are you sure you're all right? You don't look well."

With another wave of his hand, this one less enthusiastic, he said, "Try it on." He indicated the blue dress but made no attempt to get up from his chair. "I will be glad to," Margot said, "once you leave."

A weak smile curled the edges of his mouth. He pushed himself out of the chair with a groan. "While you change, I'll speak to the captain about your quarters." He crossed the room, bent over like an old man.

Margot started to say something, then caught herself. Twice already he had dismissed her spoken concern.

The blue dress and three others fit her. She was concerned about their length, however. When she walked, her ankles could be seen. *It may be the latest fashion,* she mused, *but Sylvie would have had an attack if she'd ever caught me wearing something this short!*

The sun set, and van Jaarsveld had not returned. From the windows in the stern, Margot marveled at the sea at sundown. Never before had she seen such an exquisite blending of nature's colors.

After lighting the cabin lamps, she sat and waited. And waited.

Then three sharp raps came from the direction of the cabin door. Giving van Jaarsveld credit for being a gentleman, though he must have known she would be dressed by now, she opened the door with a smile.

A short sailor with a sunburned boyish face stood at the doorstep with a tray of food in his hands. "Dinner," he said.

Margot swung wide the door, and the sailor placed the tray on the desk. He was in and out of the cabin in short order. Never once did he look at her. In fact, he worked hard to avoid looking at her.

Margot couldn't help but wonder if the gangwayman's fate had anything to do with the young sailor's behavior.

The tray bore a single china plate with enough food on it for two people—mutton, green beans, cheese, bread, accompanied by a bowl of rice pudding. Was this her dinner or van Jaarsveld's dinner? The boy hadn't said, and she hadn't thought to ask. Maybe there was a scarcity of china on board, and they were supposed to share what was on the plate.

She waited for van Jaarsveld to return. He would know.

For nearly an hour Margot sat in front of the food without touching it. The odor of the meat was driving her to distraction. The excitement of the day had revived her sagging spirits earlier, even in the absence of food. But the smell of the mutton reminded her stomach that it had not received any sustenance since yesterday. She was beyond famished, and food was within her reach.

Margot came to a point when she could wait no longer. Precisely and fairly she divided the food in half, even going so far as to count the beans. There was an odd number. She shoved the extra bean onto van Jaarsveld's side before devouring her half of the food.

When it was gone, she sat back in the chair and did her best to convince her stomach she was satisfied. Despite her efforts, she couldn't keep her eyes from wandering back to the plate.

She ate the extra bean. She felt guilty about eating it, but she ate it anyway.

Still, she failed to keep her eyes from returning to the remainder of the food on the plate. So she ate it. All of it. When van Jaarsveld returned she would tell him only one plate of food had been delivered to the cabin.

He stumbled into the compartment several hours later. He was doubled over and clutching his stomach; the last thing on his mind was food. He'd spent the day hanging over the side of the ship, he said. Having emptied himself hours earlier, all he could manage now were dry heaves.

"I think it's worse in here," he said, falling onto the bed. "What's that *smell?*"

"Roast mutton."

Van Jaarsveld clutched his stomach and moaned at the thought. "At least I'm not alone," he said. "Half the crew is bent over the rail." He raised his head; his face screwed up in puzzlement. "Why aren't you sick? Have you sailed before?"

"I've never sailed before," Margot replied innocently. "But I feel fine."

He gave her a look of pure disgust before his head flopped onto the pillow. "This is my second trip to Cape Town," he said. "On the last trip, for the first two days out of Amsterdam I thought I was going to die. This being my second trip, I was hoping I wouldn't have to go through this again."

Margot found a cloth and mopped his face, which was lolling from side to side, dripping with sweat. Her mind flashed to another sickbed. Higher than this one. But it was Sylvie's face she had mopped. Only yesterday morning. It seemed so long ago.

"Does this ship have a doctor?" Margot asked. "Do you want me to get him?"

"Already seen him. Nothing he can do."

"Can I get you anything? Do anything to make you comfortable?"

With a grimace, van Jaarsveld fought back another wave of nausea. In answer to Margot's question, he shook his head.

She pressed the cloth to his forehead. "If there's nothing I can do for you, I'll retire to my quarters for the night." She stood. "Should I ask someone to direct me?"

"Oh . . . that," van Jaarsveld said. "They're not ready yet."

Margot's eyebrows raised suspiciously.

"They weren't exactly expecting you," he explained. "The room that was to be the chambermaid's quarters—" he winced and moaned "—is packed floor to ceiling with sails. Captain said—" he fought back another cramp "—it may be two to three days before they can clear it out."

"And where am I to stay until then?" Margot asked indignantly. "I certainly can't stay in here with you."

"Until those sails are moved, there is no other place."

"Then I'll move the sails myself!" Margot cried. "Just tell me where to put them!"

"Have you seen the size of those sails?" He fought back yet another wave. "It takes three or four strong men to carry them."

Margot crossed her arms. She was determined to figure out a suitable solution to this problem.

While she was pondering, van Jaarsveld struggled to the edge of the bed and swung his legs over.

"What are you doing?" Margot asked.

"This is my fault," he said. "You sleep here. I'll stay on deck all night." Bent over, he shuffled his way to the door.

"It's not your fault," Margot insisted. "You didn't cause your chambermaid's illness. I'm sorry. I shouldn't have been abrupt with you when you have been nothing but kind to me."

He continued toward the door.

"Wait," she said. "You're sick. You sleep in the bed. I'll go out on deck."

"Thanks, but women aren't allowed on deck. It distracts the sailors." He reached for the door latch.

"You're in no condition to spend the night on the deck!" Margot insisted. She took him by the hand and led him back to the bed. "Lie down," she ordered. "I'll make up a bed on the floor in a corner someplace."

Van Jaarsveld didn't resist.

"Aren't you afraid to be alone with me at night?" he said with a weak smile.

"In your condition, I could pin you to the floor until someone came to rescue me," she replied, also with a smile. "Get some rest. Maybe you'll feel stronger in the morning."

She turned away, looking for a suitable place to build herself a floor nest.

"Stay with me until I'm asleep." His eyes closed, van Jaarsveld held out a weak hand toward her.

Margot took it. It felt cold and clammy. "Just until you're asleep," she said, patting his hand and sitting on the edge of the bed.

"By the way," he said, his eyes still closed, "you look nice in that dress."

On the second night, Uys van Jaarsveld was no better, having spent all day in bed, moaning.

Margot tended to him. The smell of food only made him worse, he said, so she gulped her meals hurriedly.

When he finally fell asleep, she was sitting on the edge of the bed. Van Jaarsveld's blond hair, normally thick and full, was plastered to his head. His complexion was pasty white. Colorless lips were parted slightly as he breathed through his mouth.

Margot reached into her pocket and felt a piece of paper. It was the paper with the Scripture verse and Latin phrase she'd placed in the nutshell and hung around Sylvie's neck. She had kept it with her since that night and had found it in her pocket when she changed clothes.

She spoke the words softly: "Fear thou not; for I am with thee: be not dismayed; for I am thy God: I will strengthen thee; yea, I will help thee; yea, I will uphold thee with the right hand of my righteousness." The Latin phrase followed—"God give you strength, my beloved"—but she didn't read it aloud. It was too personal, expressly for Sylvie.

"Did you say something?" Half asleep, van Jaarsveld lifted his head.

Margot hastily thrust the paper into her pocket. It had already gotten her into trouble once. "Go back to sleep," she said soothingly.

He was breathing rhythmically the moment his head touched the pillow. Margot doubted he was ever really awake.

She brushed back a few stray strands of hair from his forehead. In the short time she had known Uys van Jaarsveld, he had made her forget her youthful boast that she would never wed because wives were nothing more than men's personal slaves. This man was different. He thought of others. He'd rescued her—not once, but twice—while an entire wharf of other men ignored her plight. First from Monsieur Fabarez, then from that gangway wretch, van Wyk. In the carriage, he listened to her, sympathized with her, and then offered her a position to help her get aboard ship.

Margot remembered his comment that he would wed upon his return to Amsterdam. But things could change before then. Who was to say that God hadn't brought them together?

Her feelings were alien to her, but she found herself thinking that maybe this would be a two-way trip for Margot de Campion, and the next time she sailed into Amsterdam she would no longer be the chambermaid for Uys van Jaarsveld. She would be his intended.

On the third day out of Amsterdam, van Jaarsveld was feeling well enough to get out of bed. In the afternoon he took a stroll to the captain's cabin to inquire about Margot's quarters. And by evening he was eating safe food—crackers.

A portion of the afternoon had been spent at his desk writing letters and catching up with his journal.

"Margot, did you attend school?" Van Jaarsveld peered over his reading spectacles at her as she was changing the bedding.

The question gave Margot pause. Her hand wandered casually into her pocket. The small piece of paper was still there. *Was he more awake than I thought? Did he see me reading it?*

"No. I never attended school," she said. "Why do you ask?"

Taking off his spectacles, he rubbed his eyes. "I was just thinking that, if you could write, I'd make you my personal secretary and let you write these letters for me. I hate doing it!"

Margot laughed. "Do you think the world is ready for a woman secretary?"

Van Jaarsveld laughed with her. "It would be rather shocking, wouldn't it?"

"By the way," she said, changing the subject, "what did the captain say?"

"Captain?"

"When you talked with him about my quarters. Are they ready?"

"Oh . . . yes . . . yes," van Jaarsveld said, still rubbing his eyes. "Well, actually, no. They're not ready yet. It seems he's having a difficult time finding a place for all those sails. Can't exactly dump them overboard, you know. He said not to worry. The room will be cleared out in a day or two at the latest."

He pushed away from the desk. "Think I'll go on deck and stretch my legs." In quick order, van Jaarsveld was out the door.

Margot stared after him. *How long does it take to clear out one small cabin? Surely on a ship this size there ought to be room to stow sails!* Completing her thought, a salient realization popped into her head. *Without using passenger quarters!* As if to confirm her emerging suspicion, a ridiculous image came to mind—that of sailors hoisting a sail through a cabin door. *No! They bring it up from the hold! Don't they?*

Another thought came to her. An unpleasant one. Wadding up the bedding, she threw it against the wall. *Has Monsieur van Jaarsveld been lying to me? Surely not!* But the more she thought about it, the more unsure she became. She paced back and forth. The longer she paced, the angrier she got. *What should I do? What should I do?*

She stopped in the middle of the cabin. "What am I doing?" she cried aloud. "What do I know about ships? Is it so inconceivable that they *might* use a passenger cabin for storage?" For the moment, Uys van Jaarsveld was vindicated. At least until Margot could talk to the captain. "Which I will do at my earliest . . ."

Her gaze fell upon the writing on the desk. Several recently penned letters lay atop one another in fanlike fashion. Reports of some kind. Written in Latin. But the item that caught her attention was a large ledger-type book. Van Jaarsveld was using it as a journal. At the top of the page, written in Dutch, was the date October 12, 1715. Below the date he had penned:

> *For the last two days I have suffered an illness most grievous and of the strangest sort. At times I was almost certain I would pass from this mortal life into eternity. God forbid! However, with a firm constitution and resolute will I managed to pull myself from the brink of extinction. At this writing, my strength is returning. I have little doubt that as a result of this mysterious ailment—which completely baffled the ship's doctors, who had given up all hope of my recovery —I will emerge more vital than ever.*
>
> *As for the matters at hand, I find myself on a ship of buffoons, the captain being chief in this regard. He is churlish, ignorant, and crude. If the Company were to staff this ship with chimpanzees from Africa it would be more efficiently run.*
>
> *However, the trip to Cape Town will not be without its pleasant diversions. I managed to acquire a lovely little tulip on the Amsterdam wharf just moments before we set sail. In all modesty, I must congratulate myself for the ingenuity it took to lure her aboard. Upon my return, I must remember to tell Jurgen of my brilliant variation on his engagement gambit. It was a stroke of genius! I claimed that I*

had a childhood sweetheart anxiously awaiting my return. This ruse achieved two astonishing results. First, it put my sweet morsel at ease to think that I was wholly committed to another. Second, it made her desire me all the more. As Jurgen so accurately postulated: There is nothing more enticing to a woman than a fish on another woman's hook.

As for the tulip who now shares my cabin, I shall pluck her tonight. Such a lovely thing is she that I doubt I will tire of her until we reach our destination. But then discard her I must, for there is an exotic African flower waiting for me there—the lovely Rachel van der Kemp.

It was during my first trip to Cape Town that I cultivated this wilderness beauty. Now it is time to reap the harvest of earlier effort. It is with reluctance that I admit that I had to resort to the unwise tactic of proposing marriage to get this one. But I was younger at the time, and foolish. Since then I have learned I can get what I want without having to resort to such drastic measures . . .

The ledger sailed across the room and crashed against the cabin door. Margot's hands shook with rage. Her teeth clenched so tightly her jaw ached. It was all she could do to keep from ripping apart every piece of paper on the desk, overturning the desk, throwing everything in the cabin out the door onto the deck. Or, better yet, throwing everything overboard so that van Jaarsveld would have to sit in an empty cabin and wear the same clothes all the way to South Africa!

To think that he had penned those words boldly while she was just a few feet away making his bed! Another book sailed across the room and crashed against the cabin door.

"How could I have been so blind?" Margot screamed at herself. Abuse and selfish demands she understood and had even come to expect from men. But let a man show a shred of sympathy and understanding, and she thought she was in love! In fact, they were nothing but bait to hook her and land her in his bed!

"How could I have been so stupid?"

A third book sailed across the room.

Fully dressed, Margot curled up on her blanket on the far side of the cabin. Shafts of bright moonlight pierced the cabin's windows, highlighting the empty desktop. Her eyes were open wide. She listened to the creaking of the ship and watched for any sign of movement. In her hand she clutched one of van Jaarsveld's silver-handled daggers. She was ready for him.

A creak alerted her—this one short and high-pitched, not like the low moaning creaks of the ship. Her heart began to beat wildly. She watched as a figure with a sheet wrapped about its waist stepped into the moonlight. Van Jaarsveld's long blond hair took on a luminous glow. His bare shoulders had a bluish white cast to them.

He had returned shortly after Margot picked up the journal and the other books she had hurled across the cabin. He remained with her the remainder of the day, making it impossible for her to slip out to talk to the captain. Once the sun set, Margot concluded she would have to wait until morning to make the necessary inquiries regarding her quarters.

All evening the wretch had played the role of suitor. They dined on fine china plates. He poured her wine and complimented her repeatedly on the way she looked in the robin-egg blue dress. His smile never dimmed. His words were sugary to the point of being sickening. He laughed at everything. He allowed himself to be caught staring at her. He created opportunities to catch her eye, or touch her hand, or caress her cheek. It was a masterful performance of the male mating ritual.

Margot was immune to it. Knowledge of van Jaarsveld's true motives robbed his tenderness of all romance.

Her goal for the night was simple: prevent van Jaarsveld from plucking her. Her plan was twofold: assume a surly attitude to nip off any buds of romance the moment they appeared and get him to drink a lot of wine. She was hoping that his physical condition was still weak and that he would succumb to the slumbering power of the grape. If that didn't work, she took one more precaution. She snatched one of his ornamented daggers from the trunk and took it to bed with her.

"Margot? Are you asleep?"

Van Jaarsveld tiptoed across the brightly moonlit cabin.

"What do you want?" Her words were loud and sharp. They bounced around the room, almost startling herself.

"I fear this illness may be overtaking me again," he said weakly.

"It's probably just the wine. You drank a lot of it."

"No, it's not the wine. It's the sickness, I'm sure of it."

What to do? He kept coming toward her. She knew she had to do something quickly. She bolted up from the floor. She held the dagger in the folds of her dress with her left hand.

Van Jaarsveld jumped back at the suddenness of her movement. Still, he blocked her path to the door. He stared quizzically at her dress.

"You lie down," Margot said. "I'll fetch the doctor."

"Don't you recall?" he protested. "The doctor said there's nothing he can do. It was you who nursed me back to health. All I need to make me feel better is your gentle hand on my forehead."

He looked ridiculous standing in the middle of the cabin with a sheet wrapped around his waist. Without shirt and coat, his skinny shoulders sloped noticeably; a white paunch below his chest was accentuated by the night shadows.

"What if this is a different disease?" Margot spoke with alarm. "An entirely new disease altogether, more grievous and deadly than the last! I would never forgive myself if I sat idly by while you succumbed to some strange oceanic fever. No, for your sake, I'll fetch the doctor!"

With his free hand, van Jaarsveld caught her by the arm. The strength of his grip was not that of a sick man. "I assure you," he said with equal strength, "it's the same illness. Now come, help me to bed."

He led her to the bed. Margot's instincts told her to fight, to kick and scream before it was too late, but the strength of his grip cautioned her to wait for a more opportune moment. He reminded her of the gangwayman. Van Jaarsveld had taken hold of the same arm in the same place with the same intensity. Was she going to have feign insanity again to get away? But that trick wouldn't work with van Jaarsveld. He had heard her tell the captain how she pretended illness to escape from the sailor.

Still gripping her arm, van Jaarsveld reclined on the bed.

Margot sat on the edge as before.

Taking her hand in his, he placed it on his forehead. Closing his eyes, he moaned contentedly. "That feels good," he said. He moved her hand to his cheek, then to his lips. Tenderly he pressed his lips against the palm of her hand, then the heel, then the wrist.

"And how does this feel?" she asked. The tip of the dagger pressed against his throat.

Van Jaarsveld's eyes flew open with alarm. "What—what kind of treatment is this?" he sputtered.

"The treatment you deserve," Margot replied.

He forced a chuckle. "You surprise me, Mademoiselle de Campion. But I don't find your humor amusing."

"Do you see me laughing?" Margot asked. "This is my remedy for your illness. And it seems to be working. I see no trace of illness. And look! You no longer have a fever."

"Is—is this the way you repay my kindness? With a dagger at my throat?"

"I will forever be grateful to you for rescuing me from Monsieur Fabarez. However, I fear your motives were not completely selfless. When I agreed to be your chambermaid, I was not agreeing to be your whore."

Glancing nervously at the dagger, he gulped. "You have made your point quite clearly, my dear. Now would you be so kind as to remove that thing from my neck?"

Margot had him at bay and was reluctant to give up her advantage. But what was she going to do—sit at his bedside until morning with a dagger at his throat?

Without removing the knife, she said, "In the morning, we will both talk to the captain and arrange for my quarters to be readied immediately. Understood?"

"Understood," he said eagerly.

"And you must promise me that tonight you will stay on this side of the cabin."

"My dear lady, after what has just happened I am hardly in the mood to—"

She pressed the knife point against his neck. "Promise me!"

"I promise! I promise! Just don't puncture me!"

Margot could think of nothing else to do other than to retreat to her side of the cabin and stand guard until morning. Slowly she pulled back the blade but only an inch or two, fully expecting him to make an attempt to disarm her.

He made no such attempt.

She stood, the dagger still pointed at him.

He raised a forearm to his forehead and sighed heavily. His chest rose and fell in panting fashion as though he'd just completed a race— and lost. She doubted he would give her any more trouble tonight.

Her mistake was in turning her back.

The moment she did, she heard the rustle of his sheet. Before she could recover, he dove at her, catching her by the hips, hauling her to the floor. The dagger flew from her grasp and skidded out of reach.

He was all over her. The next thing Margot knew, she was staring at the ceiling beams. Van Jaarsveld was on top of her. He buried his head against her neck.

"You will make payment for this voyage, willingly or unwillingly," he said. His breath was hot and wet.

The weight of his body pinned Margot to the floor. She landed a flurry of blows on his back and shoulders. They had no effect. She tried to worm her arms between them, to shove him away. He warded them off with his forearms while his hands tore at the neckline of the robin-egg blue dress.

"No! Don't do this! Please, don't do this!" Tears ran down her temples. She was angry with her futile exertion. She couldn't stop him. No matter how hard she tried, she couldn't stop him.

Other than his labored breathing, he made no sound at all, so obsessed was he to disrobe her. He yanked on her dress, unable to get it over her shoulder. He pulled harder. It held. He lifted his head to investigate the problem. As he did, his ear hovered inches in front of her.

Margot bit the ear with all her strength.

Van Jaarsveld wailed in pain. He tried to push away. Like a dog hanging onto a strip of leather, Margot clenched tighter. He tried to shake free. Margot bit harder.

"Let go! Let go! Let go!" he shrieked, trying to pull away.

Now there was some distance between them. Margot worked a leg free. Not until she was ready did she release his ear.

Van Jaarsveld's head snapped back. He grabbed his injured ear with both hands. Before he had time to recover, she planted a foot on his chest and launched him across the cabin like a catapult. He crashed against the bed.

For a moment Margot hesitated. The dagger or the door?

Still clutching his ear, an enraged van Jaarsveld scrambled to his feet.

Margot reached the dagger the same instant he reached her. She swung toward him. The tip of the dagger was inches from his face.

"Don't touch me!" she screamed.

He backed away but stayed within reach.

They both breathed heavily. Margot glanced at the door.

"You're not going anywhere," van Jaarsveld wheezed between breaths. He touched his injured ear and winced. It was sticky and red. "You'll pay for this," he threatened. He moved toward her.

Margot jabbed at him with the dagger.

He backed away again.

Realizing that she had the advantage, she jabbed again. He backed away more. Another jab. Another step. In this fashion, she worked her way toward the door. Van Jaarsveld's eyes darted from

73

side to side, looking for some way to regain the advantage. He lunged toward the dagger.

Margot was ready for him. She slashed at his forearm. A red streak appeared. Van Jaarsveld howled, grabbed the wound, and jumped back. "Look what you're doing to me!" he screamed.

"Unless you want more of the same, stay away from me!" she cried, waving the bloody dagger.

Her free hand fumbled for the door latch. She didn't want to risk looking away from him as she had the last time. Latch in hand, she swung open the door and stepped sideways. It was a mistake.

The moment the hand with the knife passed on the other side of the door, van Jaarsveld pounced. He crushed her between the door and the jamb.

The move was completely unexpected. The edge of the door smacked her in the chest. Her head slammed against the corner of the doorjamb. She tried to cry out, but the breath was knocked out of her. The dagger clattered to the deck.

Van Jaarsveld pressed with his full weight against the door. "I said you're not going anywhere!" he snarled.

He was too strong. She couldn't budge. The door pressed harder against her chest, making breathing difficult. Her only salvation lay in that, with the door pushed against her, van Jaarsveld couldn't pull her back into the cabin.

"I can't breathe!" she gasped.

He didn't let up.

She looked about the deck for help. It was late at night. There was a minimal watch. No one was in sight. Besides, would anyone come to her aid if there was? How many sailors had been on the wharf? Yet not one of them made an attempt to apprehend Monsieur Fabarez. What made her think these sailors would now side with her against a powerful director of the company?

She was growing faint from lack of air. "I—I—can't—breathe!" she gasped again. "How will you—explain my—death?"

Her comment registered a visible reaction on van Jaarsveld's face. Her death would indeed bring ugly and unwanted attention to him. He released the pressure on the door slightly.

It was all Margot needed. She took a deep breath.

"Fire! Fire! Fire!" she screamed.

Van Jaarsveld clamped the door down on her hard. The pressure cut off her cry.

But it was too late. One of the sailors on watch took up her cry. "Fire on deck! Fire on deck!"

Sailors instantly appeared from everywhere, carrying buckets and blankets. The captain himself was not far behind. Van Jaarsveld had no choice but to free Margot from the door.

"Where's the fire?" the bulldog captain bellowed.

Van Jaarsveld yanked Margot inside, where she sprawled on the floor. He spoke to the captain through a crack in the door. "It's all a mistake, Captain," he said. "There is no fire."

Margot screamed, "Fire! Fire! Fire!"

"Let me in there," the captain said.

"I assure you, Captain," van Jaarsveld replied huffily, "there is no fire in my cabin!"

From behind him, Margot yelled again. "There will be unless I talk to the captain immediately!"

"Open the door!" the captain ordered.

"Captain, take my word for it—"

"I said open the door!" The thunder of the captain's voice echoed across the deck.

Reluctantly, van Jaarsveld opened the door.

The captain pushed past him. The ornamented dagger was in his hand. Turning the blade over and over, he examined it. One eyebrow arched suspiciously. Then placing his hands on his hips, he stepped between Margot, still on the floor, and van Jaarsveld, who had grabbed a bedsheet to cover himself.

A sea of sailors' faces crowded the doorway.

"Now, will someone tell me what is going on in here?" the captain roared.

5

Look, Mademoiselle—"

"De Campion."

The captain sat on the edge of his desk. He addressed Margot in a fatherly tone. The cabin in which they sat was less than a fourth the size of van Jaarsveld's. It contained a simple bunk, a heavily scarred small desk and chair, and space to store a trunk. These items were packed so closely together there was barely room for two adult bodies besides.

Margot sat on the trunk, looking up at the captain, her hands in her lap.

The captain had taken her to his cabin following a lengthy, frustrating, nonproductive exchange in van Jaarsveld's cabin. The company official accused Margot of trying to murder him while he slept. He displayed the teeth marks on his ear and the slice on his arm as evidence that she had nearly succeeded. Mademoiselle de Campion insisted she was merely defending herself against his perverted advances.

Had the two combatants been sailors, the captain would have put them both in chains for the night and sorted things out in the morning at his leisure. The fact that van Jaarsveld was the ranking company official on board required him to be more diplomatic.

The captain of the *Eagle* hated diplomacy. He much preferred maritime law, which made him king of the ship with unquestioned authority—and he *was* king when it came to the ship and the sailors. However, company officials—the owners of his floating kingdom— had certain privileges and immunities, which included the benefit of the doubt.

"Mademoiselle de Campion," the captain reasoned, "Monsieur van Jaarsveld might have been a little rough with you tonight. Men get that way sometimes. I'm not condoning it—that's just the way things are. But you have to admit that you were rough with him too."

"He got what he deserved," Margot replied curtly.

"Why don't you go back to the cabin?" the captain said pleadingly. "Maybe he'll apologize."

"I'm not spending another night in that cabin!" Margot folded her arms stubbornly. "I want my own quarters."

"There are no other quarters."

She bit her lip. "Before I agreed to come on board as Monsieur van Jaarsveld's chambermaid," she said, "he promised me separate quarters. He told me you were preparing a room for me—that it was being used as storage for sails and as soon as you moved them below . . ."

The captain scratched his head. This was the first time he'd heard any of this. "We stow all our sails in the hold," he said. "Maybe you misunderstood him. I don't know where Monsieur van Jaarsveld would have gotten such an idea."

Mademoiselle de Campion unsuccessfully fought back tears. "I know exactly where he got the idea," she said. "He fabricated it in that twisted mind of his."

Her tears caused the bulldog face to wince. The captain much preferred disciplining sailors. They didn't cry.

"Mademoiselle de Campion," he said, "you've shared Monsieur van Jaarsveld's bed for three nights now—I suggest you go back."

"I have not shared his bed!" she thundered. "He has not touched me! Except for tonight—when he tried to force himself. But I would never let him. I would never . . . let him . . ." Her voice was choked by tears.

The captain's head bounced helplessly from side to side. "Please don't cry, Mademoiselle de Campion."

Margot dried her tears. "I'm sorry to cause you trouble, Captain." She looked up at him. "I apologize—but I don't even know your last name."

"Danckaert," said the captain. "Captain Danckaert."

"Well, Captain Danckaert, I know it must be difficult for you to have one of the Lords XVII underfoot during this voyage."

"I beg your pardon? One of the Lords XVII?" the captain said.

"Monsieur van Jaarsveld."

The captain folded his arms. He rocked back on the edge of the desk and grinned. "Mademoiselle de Campion, exactly how did you become Monsieur van Jaarsveld's chambermaid?"

Without mentioning her ability to read or Monsieur Fabarez's charges of witchcraft, Margot narrated the events of her encounter with van Jaarsveld. And though she didn't tell him how she discovered it, she included van Jaarsveld's scheme to bed her.

Through most of the narration, the captain listened intently, quietly shaking his head.

"And he told you he was one of the Lords XVII?"

"He's not?"

"His father is. Monsieur Uys van Jaarsveld is merely a commissioner in his father's employ. And from what I've heard of him, he's gained that position by relationship, not merit."

Captain Danckaert mused for a moment. "It seems," he continued, "our Monsieur van Jaarsveld is a stranger not only to work but to truth as well. Which explains your presence on board." He sighed. "However, all this doesn't present me with any ready solutions."

"I'm not going back to his cabin," Margot insisted.

"Yes, you are," said the captain, pushing himself off the desk. "But you won't be staying. Come with me."

She followed the captain across the deck to van Jaarsveld's cabin. She stood several feet behind him as he rapped with authority on the door.

After a moment the face of Uys van Jaarsveld appeared.

"We've come for the lady's trunk," the captain said.

Van Jaarsveld looked past the captain and glared at Margot. "The lady"—he spoke the words with obvious distaste—"doesn't have a trunk."

"Come now, Monsieur van Jaarsveld. You had me delay the ship's departure twenty minutes until it was on board."

Van Jaarsveld's eyes snapped back to the captain. He addressed the officer as he would a slow-to-understand servant. "Everything in this cabin belongs to me. The dress she is wearing belongs to me. She owns nothing. Nothing!"

Standing behind the captain, Margot could see his neck turn bright red. His right hand pinched his trousers so hard they shook. "Monsieur van Jaarsveld," he said with great restraint, "surely you don't expect Mademoiselle de Campion to wear this same dress for the duration of the voyage, do you? Besides, what are you going to do with dresses? I'm sure they're all too small for you."

The captain's attempt at levity was lost on van Jaarsveld.

"If that is all, Captain, I must insist on bidding you good night."

Van Jaarsveld attempted to close the cabin door. The captain stopped him. At that moment Margot watched a transformation take place in the captain as the ill-at-ease diplomat gave way to the bulldog captain.

"Let me put it another way, Monsieur van Jaarsveld," the bull-dog growled. "Either you produce the trunk immediately, or I will consign you to a storeroom below—in chains if necessary—and Made-moiselle de Campion will enjoy your cabin for the remainder of the journey."

Van Jaarsveld straightened himself in superior fashion. "You forget who you're speaking to, Captain. I am a commissioner of the Dutch East India Company."

"No, Monsieur, you forget who you are speaking to. I am the captain of this ship. Let me remind you of the law of the sea. There is no justice or injustice aboard a ship. There are only two things: duty and mutiny. Carrying out the captain's orders is the duty of every person aboard a ship. Anything contrary to that is mutiny. So I ask you, Monsieur van Jaarsveld, are you intent on mutiny?"

Van Jaarsveld set his jaw. He stared at the bulldog face. "You wouldn't dare put me in chains."

"I will do whatever is necessary to maintain order aboard this ship."

"You will never sail for the Dutch East India Company again."

"Once you reach Amsterdam, you may do your best to have me relieved of duty. And I, in turn, will defend myself with a report that details how you lured an innocent young woman aboard by pretend-ing to be a member of the Lords XVII. Furthermore, that it was your intent to make a whore of her against her will. I'm sure the pious Lords XVII will be amused at the imaginativeness of your falsehoods and the extent of your lechery, you being their representative."

"I assure you, Captain—"

The bulldog went for the throat. "Which of us do you think the Lords XVII will favor? Me, for doing my duty as captain of this ship? Or you, for seeking only to satisfy your lust by seducing an innocent maiden?"

The trunk was on deck moments later. Van Jaarsveld dragged it out himself.

With two sailors trailing behind, carrying the trunk, the captain led Margot down into the hold.

"Where are we going?" she asked.

"To the only place I can think of to put you."

After stopping to light a lantern, he led her down two flights of steps into the belly of the ship. The sweet smell of the open sea was left behind as they entered a netherworld that was foul and stifling.

The first level beneath the deck was bad; the second level was intolerable. Margot choked and coughed as the sharp stench assaulted her throat.

"It's worse when the seas get rough," the captain said. "Stirs up the bilgewater. You get used to it after a while."

Margot doubted she would ever get used to such an oppressive odor. She followed the captain through a maze of compartments. If not for the lantern, it would have been pitch-black. The two sailors behind them were having a difficult time of it. The captain's and Margot's shadows blocked most of their light. They stumbled against hatchways and ran into beams, scraping their elbows and knuckles, no doubt, and mumbling curses.

The captain stopped at a door. It was late, and he rapped softly. Getting no response, he stepped inside, holding the lantern high. Another wave of odor tumbled out. The odor of sickness. This one made even the bulldog captain wince.

Following the captain through the doorway, Margot was surprised to see six young ladies in six hammocks, three on each side of a narrow room.

"The King's Nieces," the captain introduced her to the sleeping women. "You'll lodge with them for the remainder of the journey. As for your sleeping arrangements—" he swung the lantern around looking for space that wasn't there "—you'll just have to work something out with them."

He directed the trunk-bearing sailors to deposit their load in the middle of the floor between the hammocks. After lighting a candle for her, the captain bade Margot good night. Just before the door closed, he lifted the lantern high and took a long look at her. The light deepened the wrinkles on his face. He looked more like a bulldog than ever.

"Mademoiselle de Campion," he said, "it will take us four to five months to reach Cape Town. We're barely five days out of Amsterdam. You're not going to make trouble for me the entire journey, are you?"

As Margot fumbled to fashion some sort of a reply, the captain smiled at her and winked. Then he was gone.

No sooner had the door closed than one of the sleepers began moaning. Margot recognized the warning signal. She found a bucket and a cloth in a corner and managed to reach the girl just as she began vomiting. With each heave, the girl's face turned blood red, her neck muscles strained. She leaned so far over the edge of the hammock that

Margot feared she was going to fall out. After several heaves, the girl plopped back into the hammock, exhausted.

Margot looked in pity at the sick girl. She was fourteen, maybe fifteen, years old. "You poor, poor thing," Margot whispered soothingly as she mopped the girl's face.

The girl looked at her through half-opened eyes. When she failed to recognize Margot, she looked harder.

"Are—are you an angel?" she asked.

Margot smiled. "No, dear. I'm not an angel."

The girl wasn't convinced. "Have you come for me? Am I going to die?"

Margot wiped the girl's brow. "No, dear. You're not going to die."

Just then a second young woman began moaning. Margot hurried to her side and assisted her. Shortly after that, a third girl vomited.

For the better part of the night Margot went from one girl to the other, making each as comfortable as possible. Finally they all settled down. Between the sick odor in the enclosed cabin and her fatigue, she felt she would soon be joining them in their late night activity. She looked for a place to lie down. There was none. Her trunk took up most of the floor space.

Margot made herself as comfortable as possible by sitting on the floor and leaning against the trunk. The sleeping sounds of the women surrounded her.

O Lord, You have placed me in the belly of the whale this time, she prayed. *Am I to spend the next five months in here before this thing spits me out?* She reflected on her plight, then added, *And when it does spit me out, where will I be? What will life be like in this Nineveh? What do You want me to do in this Nineveh?* She sighed, thinking, *At least I've learned something about men through all this. I've learned that when you're running from a monster, before you jump into a rescuer's arms, make sure he's not a serpent.*

Pulling her legs against her chest, Margot made a pillow with her arms on her knees. Wearily she let her eyes fall shut. A series of unwanted images paraded through her half-conscious mind—Fabarez pointing an accusing finger at her; the gangwayman clutching her arm and leaning into her with his herring breath; van Jaarsveld clawing at her dress.

"Who are you, and what's this doing here?"

The unfriendly voice originated from behind her. Margot opened and reopened her eyes in an attempt to get them to function. The floor was stiff and so was she.

"Hey! Princess! I'm talking to you!"

Margot brushed back the lingering effects of sleep. She looked around. From every hammock, save one, a pair of inquiring eyes peered at her. The empty hammock's former occupant—a tall, thin young woman with a full head of long, curly, dark brown hair—stood behind her, one foot resting on the trunk.

"You on the floor. Are you dense or something? I asked you what you're doing here."

Struggling to her feet, Margot smoothed out a few of the wrinkles in her robin-egg blue dress. "The captain brought me here last night," she answered. Then, by way of belated introduction, she added, "My name is Margot. And you are—"

"There's no room for you here, Princess. You'll have to find some other place." The tall woman kicked the trunk. "And take this thing with you." Her voice and demeanor were loud and abrasive, a perfect match for the sneer on her face.

"According to the captain, there is no other place," Margot replied with an apologetic shrug. "And why do you keep calling me 'Princess'?"

"Look at you!" the woman scoffed. "Only rich people or royalty wear dresses like the one you have on!"

"I know who you are!" A brighter voice came from one of the hammocks. "You're the angel!"

Margot smiled. The first girl she had tended the night before was obviously feeling better. Her lids still drooped, but even so her eyes were incredibly round.

"I'm glad you're feeling better," Margot said. "But I'm not an angel—" she glanced back at the tall woman "—and I'm not wealthy or royalty."

"She comforted me last night too!" a second girl said.

"Me too. I remember now," said a third.

"I don't care what you did or what you're wearing," the dominant girl interrupted. "You can't stay here. We're too crowded as it is."

"That's Suzette," the round-eyed girl said. "She's always like that. My name's Katje."

"I'm glad to meet you, Katje," said Margot.

Katje took it upon herself to introduce the others as well. "And that's Anna and Aletta—they're the other two you helped last night.

Over there is Marie—she doesn't talk much. And finally, there's Clara."

Margot greeted each one personally.

"There, you've met everyone!" Suzette shouted. "Now get out!"

"Thank you for helping us last night," said Anna, ignoring Suzette's outburst. "That was kind of you."

Margot shrugged. "It seems I've spent a lot of time being a nurse to sick people lately." The thought of Sylvie resurrected sad feelings in her. She didn't bother to try to shoo them away. Feelings, even unpleasant ones, and memories were all she had left of the woman who raised her. "How long have you been sick?" Margot asked the girls.

Suzette answered for them. "Oh, we've had a regular carnival of sicknesses in here! They all started vomiting ten minutes after we set sail!"

"And they're still sick? That's odd," said Margot. "Monsieur van Jaarsveld was sick for only two days. After that, he was up and walking around the deck."

"If he were stuck down here in this rat hole like us, he'd still be sick!" Suzette cried.

"Surely you've not been down here the entire time, have you?" The very idea was abhorrent to Margot. They were so deep in the ship's hold that there was no way for them to tell if it was night or day without a timepiece. The atmosphere was stifling. And, of course, the smells were enough to make anyone sick.

"We're forbidden to leave the cabin." Suzette wrinkled up her face to look like a bulldog. She spoke with a gruff voice. "We'll disrupt the function of the ship!"

Margot readily identified the source. "Captain's orders."

Heads nodded all around her.

"Excuse me, ladies," Margot said, motioning to Suzette to step aside, "I need to talk to someone."

Suzette stepped aside.

Margot had to hold onto hammocks to step over the trunk and get past Suzette at the same time.

"Aren't you going to take this thing with you?" Suzette pointed at the trunk.

"I don't think you should go out there," Katje cried. "We're not supposed to leave the cabin."

"I won't be long," Margot replied. She stopped at the door to light another candle, using the flame of the taper in the wall holder.

"By the way," she said, "in that trunk you'll find dresses similar in style to the one I'm wearing. There are a variety of sizes. Help yourself to them. You're welcome to any of them that fit you, compliments of Monsieur Uys van Jaarsveld of the Dutch East India Company."

Even during the day, the hold was so dark that a candle was insufficient to light Margot's way. Her plan to go on deck and talk to the captain about the conditions in the women's quarters seemed simple enough when she conceived it. But now, after stumbling around in the dark for ten minutes, the plan didn't seem so simple after all. What was worse, she faced the frightening realization that she was lost deep in the bowels of the ship and had no idea where she was or how to get to where she was going.

To make matters worse still, she had started out with only a stub of a candle. It wouldn't be much longer before it burned out and she had absolutely no light at all. Margot began to wonder how many days she could wander about in the ship's belly before someone would come looking for her.

She began opening every door she passed. In doing so she discovered where the sails and rigging were stored. She found the shot locker and the powder room for the guns. She even found rooms stacked with water and beer casks. What she couldn't find was the passageway to the upper deck.

The candle burned precariously close to her hand. She could feel the heat of the flame. A sense of dread gripped her. She had made so many twists and turns that at this point she wasn't even sure she could make it back to the girls' cabin—*with* a candle, let alone without one.

Then Margot stumbled upon some steps. They led up. *Any way that leads up must be the right way,* she said to herself. She climbed the steps and pushed open the hatch at the top. The hatch had barely cracked open when she caught sight of a dozen or so sailors in various stages of undress.

"Oh!" she cried, letting the hatch fall closed.

The whoosh of the hatch extinguished the candle, leaving her in the dark. On the other side of the hatch, all manner of curses and clamoring could be heard.

"I swear it was a dame!" one voice cried.

An instant later the hatch flew open, and Margot was hauled up. She hastily explained her predicament and insisted that the sailors—all of them covered now—take her to the captain.

A company of seamen obliged—some in a sense of outrage that a woman, who was bad luck on a ship anyway, would be allowed to roam the vessel; others out of sheer merriment. Anything that broke up the daily routine was welcomed.

As her escorts led her to the upper deck, Margot tried to look at the positive side of her plight. At least she had found a way to get on deck. The negative side presented itself rather dramatically when she caught sight of the captain's expression upon their approach.

The bulldog did not look pleased to see her again so soon. Besides that, she was flanked by men who thought her either bad luck or a source of amusement. She clearly was not entering this discussion regarding the women's quarters on the best of terms.

So she decided to change the terms. She attacked. Pushing past her escorts, she marched up to the captain with a barrage of complaints before he, or anyone else, had time to utter a word.

"I would have expected something like this from an unscrupulous louse like Uys van Jaarsveld—but Captain, you surprise me! I would have thought this was beneath you. The conditions in which those six girls—those young, delicate ladies—are forced to live are intolerable! Do you realize that they have been sick ever since we left Amsterdam? Do you realize that, given the wretched hovel in which they are forced to dwell, you will be lucky if any of them survives this journey? It's shameless, Captain Danckaert. Shameless!"

The captain raised his hand to say something.

Margot wouldn't let him. Shaking her finger in scolding fashion, she continued. "If you had cattle in the hold, you wouldn't be treating them as poorly! You've shipped cattle to the colonies, haven't you, Captain? How would the colonists react if upon reaching Cape Town their cattle were skinny and diseased and near death? I'll tell you how'd they react! They'd be outraged! Furious! Well, Captain, you have six sickly, skinny women below. Women! Women, Captain; not cows, not casks of wine, not sacks of grain—women! Flesh and blood women!" Placing her hands on her hips, she concluded, "I want to know what you plan to do to remedy this abominable situation!"

The sailors stared at her as though she were demon possessed. Captain Danckaert looked as if he were about to bite her head off. Just when he was about to explode, Margot smiled at him and winked, just as he had done to her the night before.

It took all the wind out of his sails.

He turned to one of her escorts. "Where did this woman come from?" he shouted.

"She popped up the hatch in our quarters, Cap'n."

Eyebrows raised, the captain turned to Margot for an explanation.

"I got lost," she said apologetically.

The bulldog barked at the sailors. "Go back to your quarters. I'll handle this."

"But, Cap'n—"

The captain cut him off. "I'll discuss this with you later, Swenson! You have watch in two hours, don't you?"

"Yes, sir."

"Get some sleep!"

"Yes, sir."

To Margot, the captain barked, "You! Come with me."

The two of them sat opposite each other in his cabin just as they had the night before—he on the edge of his desk, she on the trunk.

"Now what's this all about?" the captain asked wearily. His bearing was much softer when he wasn't in the presence of his men.

"It's exactly what I told you on deck. Those girls are sick, and they're going to get worse unless something is done to improve their living conditions."

"They are in the place assigned to them by the Company," the captain explained.

"That's a cargo hold!" Margot cried.

"They *are* cargo!" the captain cried back.

Margot stared at him in disbelief.

"They're not paying passengers," he explained. "Those girls are orphans who have no future in Amsterdam. They're being shipped by the Company at Company expense to become wives for lonely farmers. As far as the Company is concerned, it's strictly a business proposition."

"But they're human beings! And I think I know you well enough to know that even though the Company may treat them like cargo, you are uncomfortable with the arrangement. Uncomfortable enough to look out for their welfare."

The bulldog looked at her with an amused expression. "You think you know me, do you?"

Deadly serious, Margot replied, "I know that you could have chosen to appease Monsieur van Jaarsveld by handing me over to him, but you didn't."

They stared at each other in friendly silence.

"What do you want me to do?" Captain Danckaert asked.

"Let the women come on deck to get some fresh air once a day."

"Out of the question!"

"Why?"

"They would completely disrupt the attention of my crew—they would be the kind of distraction that could result in injury or death! Sailing is dangerous enough without having the sailors mooning over some females on deck."

"Then let us come on deck at night. There's a minimal watch at night. I promise we won't do anything provocative that might cause a distraction."

The captain rubbed his chin. "It still doesn't sit well with me," he said.

"But you'll do it?"

"One hour a night. No more."

"Thank you, Captain Danckaert!"

The bulldog grinned wryly at Margot. "This is going to be a long five months, Mademoiselle de Campion—a long five months."

6

When Margot returned to the women's quarters—escorted by two sailors with specific instructions from the captain that no detours be taken—she found the women preening themselves and wearing the dresses from Uys van Jaarsveld's trunk. All of them except Suzette.

"Margot, they're lovely!" Katje cried, twirling around happily in a dainty yellow silk dress.

The whirling pixie brought a smile to Margot. *Much better,* she thought, remembering how miserable Katje looked the night before. Today her eyes were merry, though still not bright; her smile was accentuated by dimples. Margot imagined this was normal for Katje. Cheerful. Carefree. Though the three sick girls continued to exhibit signs of the lingering effects of their illness, the dresses provided them a moment of escape from their prisonlike confinement.

Four other girls joined Katje in a chorus of gratitude as a host of dresses swirled as best they could in such a cramped space.

Suzette leaned against the bulkhead, her arms folded, her face sour.

"Didn't any of the dresses fit you?" Margot asked.

"Don't know. Didn't try any of them on," Suzette replied testily.

"Why not?"

Katje answered for her. "She thinks we're making fools of ourselves."

With a scowl aimed at Katje, Suzette defended her reasoning. "I don't need no society dress to land me a husband. Thank you very much."

"The way I see it," Aletta chimed in, arranging the lace trim on her pink frock, "a dress like this one may well catch the eye of one of the wealthier men."

A ripple of giggles endorsed her analysis of the eye-catching power of the dresses.

Aletta added, "I don't know about the rest of you, but I'm tired of being hungry and poor. If this dress will make the difference between a dirt-scratching farmer and a prosperous wine plantation owner, it's worth it!"

"I don't care what my man does for a living," Katje cried, "as long as he's a man!"

The cabin bubbled with giggles.

Margot cringed. She thought of Fabarez and the gangwayman and van Jaarsveld. *If the man isn't the right man, having one can be worse than longing for one. Much worse.* However, she said nothing. She didn't want to spoil the girls' excitement over the dresses.

Suzette still stood off to one side and turned up her nose at the lot of them. "I've never once put on airs for a man, and I don't intend to start now. He can take me as I am or not at all."

"Just because you wear a nice dress doesn't mean you're putting on airs!" Clara insisted. It was the first time Margot had heard her speak. She was a plain girl with broad shoulders, dull red hair, and thick eyebrows. "For me, it's a practical matter," she said. "Margot can't wear this size. It's too big for her. Either I wear it or it sits in the trunk and is eaten by moths."

Suzette sneered. "As if a fancy dress will do you any good!"

Her barb hit its mark. Pain registered on Clara's face. In unison the other girls berated Suzette for her nasty comment.

Suzette shouted over them. "All I know is that I was raised an orphan! We didn't wear fancy clothes or go fancy places. I've never worn a silk dress in my life, and I don't aim to begin now."

"I hate it when you act so smug about being an orphan, Suzette," Marie replied. "We were all raised in the same orphanage! What makes you better than us?"

Suzette pushed off the bulkhead and took a threatening step toward Marie.

Margot moved quickly between them. "Suzette, I never wore a dress like this until two days ago," she said.

Her remark obviously came as a surprising revelation.

"We thought you were rich!" Katje exclaimed.

"Of course she's rich!" Suzette cried. "It's fashionable for rich people to tell everyone how poor they are!"

Margot laughed. "I'm not rich. In fact, I'm more like you than you think. I'm an orphan too."

"Sure you are!" Suzette laughed mockingly. "All orphans travel with a trunkload of expensive silk dresses!"

"You mean you're one of the King's Nieces too?" Katje cried.

"If you mean am I going to Cape Town to find a husband," Margot said, "then the answer is no."

Margot explained how she happened to be on board the *Eagle* and the events that led to her relocation below deck. She made it a point to mention Captain Danckaert's kindness toward her. Which led her to an announcement.

"The captain has arranged a little surprise for us tonight," she said.

"A surprise? What kind of surprise?" Katje cried, jumping up and down. In her excitement she looked like a little girl wearing her mother's dress.

Suzette looked at Katje with disgust.

Though pleased with Katje's enthusiasm, Margot couldn't help but wonder what the future held for this child, who was so young yet so obsessed with men and marriage. What would Katje be like ten years from now? Would the sparkle still be there? The innocence? Why couldn't Katje and the others be content to be young and un-attached?

Margot luxuriated under the dome of stars. With her face lifted heavenward, she found it difficult to decide which she enjoyed most —the panoply of spangling lights or the brush of the fresh breeze against her cheeks.

"Margot, this is a wonderful surprise! How did you ever manage it?" Katje squealed.

"Don't thank me—thank the captain," Margot replied, smiling at her young friend's joy.

Katje stood in the middle of the deck, arms fully extended at her sides, and spun in circles. Each in her own way, the girls basked in the night air. They scattered widely, enjoying the spaciousness as much as anything else. Their silk dresses—Suzette alone still wore wool—sparkled in the moonlight, adding splashes of bright color to an otherwise colorless deck. Giggles and squeals of delight bounced among the sails.

"Mademoiselle de Campion! May I have a word with you?" The captain's hard voice seemed out of place among all the feminine frol-icking.

There was a rush of silk as the King's Nieces converged on him, gushing with gratitude for allowing them this time on deck.

The bulldog brushed aside both the compliments and the girls, though his surly expression failed to dampen their exuberance.

Margot rescued the captain by reminding the girls that they had only one hour on deck. Before long, she and Captain Danckaert were alone.

"*My* surprise for them?" the captain roared as best he could with a hushed voice.

"I thought it would be nicer if the girls thought this was your idea. They love you for doing this for them."

"I don't want to be loved, Mademoiselle de Campion! I'm the captain! Nobody loves a captain! It just isn't right. Besides, I didn't agree to this!"

"One hour on deck each night!" Margot cried. "That's what you said!"

"But I didn't agree to a formal ball! Look at them! Listen to them! You promised they wouldn't be a distraction! When I came on deck a moment ago every one of my sailors—every single one of them —was ogling these women! They're supposed to be on watch—looking out for pirate ships, not wives!" He shook his head emphatically. "This isn't going to work! This just isn't going to work."

Margot had to concede that the sight of giddy, attractive women in bright silk dresses was a distraction to the seamen. But she wasn't ready to concede their hour on deck.

"Captain, the short time these girls have been on deck has done wonders for them. You're going to lose some of them if you keep them confined the entire voyage! I'll talk to them. We'll keep the noise level down. And I'll have them change clothes. Tomorrow night they'll be so colorless they'll blend into the deck. Give us at least one more night. Just one more night! If it doesn't work after one more night, then we'll stay below until we drop anchor at Cape Town."

The bulldog, Margot suspected, rarely conceded anything aboard his ship. He probably had given in more to her already than to any crew during his entire career.

He screwed up his face as if it were painful for him to say the words. "One more chance," he said.

The following night, the girls walked about the deck as though it were a cathedral. The captain appeared, glowered over them for several minutes, then disappeared. Nothing more was said. After that, the girls came on deck each night for one hour for the remainder of the journey.

For several days and nights Margot watched over the King's Nieces as though they were her flock and she their shepherd. She remembered the dream she had on the church steps her last night in Amsterdam—a dream of the poor children living in the shadow of the arched outer walls of the city. Vividly she recalled her feelings of helplessness as they begged her for food and money and she had nothing to give them.

Margot wasn't sure why she associated that dream with these girls, but she did know that—unlike the dream—when it came to helping the girls, she was not empty-handed. She had something to pass along to them. Not just dresses; dresses were trifles. She had compassion, and wisdom, and knowledge. The compassion she demonstrated on her first night with them.

And as she cared for them in their time of illness, she had learned something about herself. She learned that she didn't mind the mess, that bad odors didn't affect her as they did other people. She learned that as she cared for those who were sick, their well-being was foremost in her mind. It hurt her to see them in pain. And when those she was caring for showed signs of recovery, she felt a deep sense of satisfaction, more satisfaction than she had ever felt about anything else in her life.

But there was more she wanted to do for these girls than just care for them. She wanted to share with them a little of the wisdom Sylvie had given her. Thanks to her beloved Sylvie, she had a knowledge of the Bible that most women didn't have. And the more she thought of it, the more she craved to pass along to these girls some of that knowledge.

She had considered teaching them to read but dismissed that as too risky. Still, she could teach them God's ways. She could teach them wisdom that would be around to comfort them when she was not around; wisdom that would make them wise mothers; wisdom that would give them strength to survive the difficulties that most certainly lay ahead of them all.

"What is your favorite Bible story?" she asked them one afternoon.

"Bible story?" Suzette said with wrinkled nose.

"Certainly you have a favorite," Margot said.

The girls all stared at her as though they had never heard of the Bible.

"Surely you attended church while you were at the orphanage," Margot pursued.

They all looked at one another strangely, then shouted in unison, "Madam Hofmeyr!" They all talked at once about this Madam Hofmeyr.

"Who is Madam Hofmeyr?" Margot asked.

Katje explained. "Madam Hofmeyr was an old woman about four feet tall and four feet wide."

The girls all roared and nodded their heads at the description.

"Who marched us to church every Sunday in single file. She carried a switch and used it liberally on us. She would apply the switch if we so much as smiled on the Sabbath."

"One time she swatted Aletta for scratching her nose during a prayer," Anna said.

Aletta grinned a painful grin to confirm the story.

"Asking us about a favorite Bible story is like asking us to identify our favorite ache or pain." Suzette laughed. Leaning toward Clara, she said, "Which do you prefer? A slap on your cheek or a swat on your bottom?"

The girls laughed at the ridiculousness of the notion.

"And we had to sit perfectly still." Marie moaned. "Forever and ever and ever while the minister droned on and on and on!" To illustrate, she sat as rigid as a board with a pained expression on her face.

Laughter echoed off the cabin walls. Some of the girls grabbed their stomachs as they laughed, others fell over sideways, still others wiped away tears.

Margot smiled patiently. At first she smiled to mask her feelings of hurt and rejection. She had asked them a serious question, and they were amusing themselves at her expense. All she wanted to do was share with them something that was important to her, but they were making fun of it.

Then she realized that while she associated the Bible with her beloved Sylvie, they associated it with pain and boredom. She also realized that when Sylvie began teaching her the Bible, she already had a thirst for knowledge. These girls didn't have that thirst. She would just have to make them thirsty.

As she thought of thirst, an idea came to her.

"Have you ever heard of the Bible story of the woman who had five husbands?" she asked.

"Five husbands!" Katje cried with delighted shock.

Margot nodded. "And she was living with man number six."

The teacher had their attention.

"There's no such story in the Bible!" Suzette exclaimed.

"But there is!" Margot insisted. "Would you like me to tell it to you?"

Six eager faces, none of them more than a few feet from her, fell silent, waiting to hear the story of the woman who had five husbands. Margot narrated Jesus' encounter with the Samaritan woman at Jacob's well. How He asked her—a Samaritan woman, His enemy—for a drink; and how in return He promised the woman everlasting water. And how the woman in the story was further shocked to learn that Jesus knew all about her and her five husbands! Yet still He stayed to talk to her.

"Here was a woman who thought she would find happiness in her relationships with men," Margot concluded, looking directly at Katje. "After six such relationships, the woman was still unhappy. Jesus taught her that true happiness is not found in marriage; true happiness comes from God."

Margot gazed from face to face. They had new expressions. Expressions Margot had never seen on them. They were thoughtful! The girls were actually contemplating the things she had told them! She had given them spiritual food, and they were chewing on it!

"Margot, what's your favorite Bible story?" Aletta asked.

They wanted more! Margot could hardly contain her glee. Excitement bubbled deep inside her, rising to her throat and nearly spilling out her eyes in the form of tears. She smiled at the girls proudly in the same way Sylvie, her teacher, had smiled at her.

"Margot's favorite Bible story is probably about the Virgin Mary," Suzette said with a smirk. "Everyone I've ever met who walks around with their head in the clouds is fascinated with virginity! As if being a virgin is a good thing!"

So they weren't *all* eager to learn.

"Actually, my favorite story in the Bible is the story of Abigail," Margot said.

"Never heard of her," Suzette said with a note of dismissal.

She was shushed into silence by the other girls.

"Be quiet! I want to hear this," Aletta cried.

Margot began the story: "Abigail was a beautiful and wise woman who lived in the days when Saul was king of Israel.

"She had a husband, whose name was Nabal, which means 'fool.' Nabal was a wealthy man, but he was also ill-tempered, drunken, and evil in all his doings.

"These were perilous times for Israel. King Saul had fallen out of God's favor. And God had already appointed his successor—a shepherd boy named David. When Saul learned of this, he was furious, and he sought to kill David. So David had to flee to the hills for his life. Six hundred good men fled with him, and for years they roamed the countryside while King Saul's men pursued them.

"For a while, David and his men camped on Nabal's property. David sent messengers to Nabal with greetings, requesting that he share a portion of his abundance with David's starving men. David's request was not unusual. It was sheepshearing time, a festive occasion when there was plenty to eat. Nabal's shepherds told their master how David and his men had been good to them in the fields, protecting them from Nabal's enemies.

"But in response to David's request, Nabal said, 'Who is David? . . . There are many servants now a days that break away every man from his master! Shall I then take my bread, and my water, and my meat that I have killed for my shearers, and give it unto men, whom I know not?'

"When Nabal's words reached David, the shepherd-king cried out to his men to put on their swords, saying, 'This man has returned evil for my kindness!' And David and four hundred of his men marched toward Nabal's house."

Aletta's eyes were wide in anticipation of the story's outcome. Even Suzette was listening intently. Margot grinned inside.

She continued. "When one of Nabal's servants informed Abigail of David's kindness to the shepherds—and Nabal's rude response to David's request—she hurriedly ordered the servants to load up two hundred loaves of bread, and bottles of wine, and sheep already dressed, and several measures of parched corn, and clusters of raisins, and two hundred cakes of figs. Then she rode out to meet David before he reached Nabal's house.

"She fell at David's feet and said, 'May my lord pay no attention to that wicked man Nabal. He is just like his name—he is a fool, and folly goes with him.'

"David looked kindly on this brave woman. He said to her, 'Go home in peace. I have heard your words and granted your request.' He also told her that if she had not come to him, he would have killed every male in Nabal's household.

"When Abigail returned home, she found her wretched husband drunk, so she didn't tell him anything that day. The next morning she told Nabal all that she had done. He was so upset that his heart failed him and became as stone. Within days, God struck him dead. And that is how a wise and courageous woman saved her household from slaughter due to her husband's arrogance and stupidity."

Margot sat back and waited for their reaction to the story.

Suzette was the first to speak. "If Abigail was so wise, why did she marry a man who was named Fool in the first place?"

"Well . . . I suppose . . . you know . . . sometimes . . . marriages were arranged back then. Possibly her father arranged the marriage for Abigail."

Margot's lack of a ready response obviously pleased Suzette. "Her father must not have loved her then," Suzette concluded. "Who would arrange a marriage for his daughter with a fool if he loved her?"

Margot was content to let the blame for Abigail's marriage lie on a shortsighted father. "I do know," she said, "that even today many women marry foolishly. The wise woman who raised me, and taught me everything I know, married a man who was just like Nabal, only he wasn't rich. But he was certainly a fool. And I've come to the conclusion that sometimes wise women make foolish decisions when it comes to men. That is why I have decided that I will never marry."

"You're never going to marry? Ever?" Katje cried out in disbelief.

Margot was disappointed at the spirit in which Katje asked the question. She'd hoped that, of all the girls, Katje would be affected by this Bible story—not necessarily that she would put off marriage but that she wouldn't be so obsessed with the idea.

"I can only conclude that Abigail was better off after Nabal died," Margot replied.

For an hour or more a day, Margot led the girls in discussions and prayer based on Bible stories. She told them about courageous Deborah, the woman who led a nation when no man would; about gorgeous Queen Esther, who survived the vicious plot of an evil man; about Lydia, a wealthy businesswoman who financially supported the apostle Paul during his missionary efforts in Philippi.

After two months of stories, Margot had exhausted her supply and had told some more than once. She considered asking the captain if there was a Bible on board that she and the girls might use. Then, just as she was about to ask him, she realized that asking for a Bible presupposed that somebody would be able to read it. It went without saying that none of the girls could read. They were orphans. That left her. Asking for a Bible would be like announcing she could read. She decided not to ask him.

At first this limitation depressed her. Then she remembered that Christians had thrived for centuries without the aid of printed Bibles.

And if they could do it, so could the orphan girls in the *Eagle*'s smelly hold.

Another thought occurred to her that made the whole situation take on a new mood, a spiritually romantic atmosphere. They had no Bible, and they were forced to endure cramped quarters. Wasn't this just like the first-century Christians, who lived their faith in fear of discovery under the streets of Rome in the catacombs? The link of suffering to Christianity's past filled Margot with renewed vigor.

Even with the daily Bible and prayer time and the hour each night on deck, there was still sufficient time during the day for the girls to be bored. Their boredom usually manifested itself in one disagreeable form after another. After two months of close quarters, to her dismay Margot found herself getting caught up in the endless cycle of quarrels and sniping and bickering. Something had to be done.

Once more she approached the captain. She proposed that the women be given work to do.

"Out of the question!" Captain Danckaert's reply was lightning quick.

"But they'll tear each other apart without something to occupy their time!" Margot argued. "What would you do with idle sailors?"

"Put them to work."

"See?"

"No, I don't see. Those young ladies aren't sailors. And I have problems enough without having to worry about whether a bunch of women are sufficiently occupied."

"If they don't have something constructive to do, they'll kill each other!"

"Notify me if that happens."

Margot ignored his sarcasm. "We could clean something," she insisted. "We could scrub the floor."

"Swab the deck."

"All right, then. We could swab the deck."

"No. I was just correcting you. On a ship you don't scrub the floor, you swab a deck."

"Captain!"

"I'm sorry, Mademoiselle de Campion, but I can't have women swabbing my decks! Every sailor on board would be up here watching them! Besides, everything is already getting done in a timely and orderly fashion. Forgive me, but I can't think of a single thing your girls can do aboard a ship. You have to understand, men have been sailing for centuries without women, and somehow they've managed to survive. Everything that needs to be done, we do."

Margot rolled her eyes upward in exasperation. A square-corner tear in a sail above caught her eye. "What do you do about that?" she asked.

"About what?"

Margot pointed to the tear in the sail.

"We mend it."

"Women can sew," she said. "We've been doing it for centuries, and somehow we've managed to survive." As soon as she'd said it, Margot wished she hadn't thrown the captain's words back at him.

Captain Danckaert stared at her, then laughed. "You have a sharp tongue, Mademoiselle de Campion. But it's attached to a sharp mind. I like you."

High praise from a bulldog. It wasn't lost on Margot. It rendered her speechless. Then she began to wonder if the captain's compliment wasn't just another tactic to regain the advantage of the argument.

It wasn't. "All right," he conceded, "you can mend the sails. But there's a right way and wrong way to mend a sail. I'll have one of my men teach you the right way."

"Thank you, Captain," Margot said. She started to leave.

"One other thing."

She turned back.

"We're in constant need of line repairs. If your women can sew, they can also learn to repair rope lines. Both require nimble fingers. Do you think your ladies can handle that?"

Margot smiled. "Thank you, Captain."

The women discovered that the best part of repairing sails and lines was that they couldn't do it in their quarters, which were too small. They were taken up one flight of stairs to a hold that spanned the width of the ship. A large hatch opened up overhead, providing them with a window to the sky and, the biggest blessing of all, fresh air in abundance.

In two successive days a different sailor met them in the hold to instruct them in the sailor's way of repairing lines and mending sails. The first day, the assigned seaman became so flustered by the presence of seven females gathered around him that it took him three tries to mend a single line, though normally he could have done it atop a mast in gale winds while half asleep. The second sailor stabbed himself in the leg with a needle so badly he required medical attention.

Nevertheless, the girls caught on quickly. In a short time their work was proficient and timely. And at the end of their first week of duty, the captain made an unannounced visit to the hold to congratulate the ladies for a job well done.

Margot struggled to keep from drifting off. The girls had pulled crates into a circle and were sitting on them while they mended lines in the large hold. Coils of rope gathered about their feet and slithered between the crates like snakes. Overhead, their giant window to the sky boasted a cloudless stretch of blue. The combination of amiable chitchat and the warmth of the sun streaming through the hatch made Margot drowsy. Her fingers slowed, her eyelids drooped, her hands fell slowly to her lap as sleep covered her like a warm blanket.

"Van Doorn! Bring her around!"

The shout startled Margot awake. Then it sounded like a stampede across the deck overhead. The hatch slid shut with a bang. Latches clamped it in place.

As the girls' eyes adjusted to the dark, they stared at each other in wonder.

Katje spoke. "Margot, do you think they forgot that we're in—"

The ship leaned hard to starboard. The ladies tumbled off their crates.

"Man the guns!" The captain's voice was loud enough so that it could be heard through the closed hatch.

Soft, distant booms rumbled.

"Is that what I think it is?" Suzette said.

"What do you think it is?" Katje asked.

"It sounds like cannons firing," Suzette replied. "Someone could be firing at us!"

Overhead, the latches released. The hatch flew open. Sailors dropped in all around them.

"There!" One of them ordered the others to grab a sail the girls had patched the previous day. His jaw was clenched, his eyes were sharp with urgency. Turning to the women, he shouted, "Go back to your cabin! Now!" To the men: "Move! Move! Move!"

Like a mother hen, Margot reached wide her arms and gathered the girls, guiding them toward the steps that led down to their cabin. As she did, she yelled over the din at the sailor in charge. "What's happening?"

A line of seamen wrestled the sail toward the hatch.

"Move! Move!" he yelled.

"Tell me what's happening!" Margot shouted again.

The sailor shot her an annoyed look. Then he said, "We're under attack! Smythe! Grab that end! Pick it up! No—yes! Like that! Now move! Move!"

"Under attack by whom?" Margot cried.

"Lady, get back to your cabin!"

"By whom?" Margot insisted.

The sailor shoved her toward the steps. "Pirates!"

7

The ship leaned hard, throwing the girls against the bulkhead.

"What are we going to do?" Katje cried, grabbing onto a swinging hammock to steady herself.

"There's nothing we can do!" Suzette shouted at her. "If they board us, they'll rape us! And there's nothing we can do to stop them!"

The girls all began screaming and yelling at once. Katje wept.

"Quiet, girls! Quiet! Calm down!" Margot yelled over their shrieks. "The captain won't let that happen! Calm down!"

"How is he going to stop them?" Suzette cried.

"Raped? Will they really rape us?" Katje was nearly hysterical.

Marie fell into a corner, her eyes wild, her hands to her mouth. Anna knelt beside her, speaking to her in comforting tones.

"Won't be the first time for Marie," Suzette said callously.

"Shut up! Just shut up!" Anna screamed at her. Soothingly she said to Marie, "Don't listen to her. You'll be all right."

"Margot, what are we going to do?" Aletta cried. Her lower lip quivered. Tears were not far behind.

"I'll tell you what we're going to do," Margot said. "We're going to pray."

"A lot of good that will do!" Suzette cried. "Prayer can't stop pirates!" Her eyes were sharp with fear.

Margot knew that Suzette was just as scared as the rest of them, only instead of tears her fear produced hostility. Grabbing Suzette by the shoulders, Margot stared hard into her eyes. "Listen to me! 'God shall deliver thee in six troubles: yea, in seven there shall no evil touch thee.' That's God's promise to us, and we're going to take Him at His word!"

While the thunder of the *Eagle*'s cannons boomed salvo after salvo on the deck above, Margot gathered the girls for prayer. With Anna's help, she coaxed Marie from the corner. She had to pry Katje's hands from the hammock. Finally, with everyone on the floor, Margot began to pray. Though they were within inches of each other, she had to shout to be heard.

Suddenly there was a loud thunderclap overhead, followed by an enormous crack and creak of splintering wood. The ship shuddered violently. Smoke began pouring into the cabin, burning their eyes, choking them.

"Everyone out!" Margot yelled between coughs. She pushed on the cabin door. It was stuck. Leaning into it, she pushed harder. Still it wouldn't move. The smoke in the cabin grew thicker.

"Help me!" Margot cried to Suzette. The two women banged their shoulders against the door. It opened an inch, scraping hard against the deck. Smoke rushed to the crack, venting into the hold. Margot and Suzette choked and coughed and pushed. Clara pressed a broad shoulder between them. After several attempts, the three of them managed to push the door open enough to squeeze through.

Once everyone was out of the cabin, Margot gathered them all together. In this larger area, the smoke wasn't as bad. Still, the girls choked and coughed. They followed Margot single file down the walkway.

Margot felt her way from beam to beam in the dark. Though she was familiar with the way by now, it was slow going. Besides the lack of light, the *Eagle* took sudden course changes that threw them from side to side as the ship leaned hard one way, then another.

Boom!

A resonating explosion knocked the girls from their feet. Margot raised a forearm and turned her head to protect her face from the wood and splinters that showered down upon her. When she re-opened her eyes, she saw the most curious thing. A cannonball that had ripped a hole through the outer hull and upper deck completed its journey by rolling harmlessly against her foot. Smoke rose eerily from it. She pushed it away.

As the ship pitched on a downward swell, she could see the cannonball's point of origin in the distance—a ship shrouded in the smoke from its guns. Atop the vessel's mast fluttered the infamous Jolly Roger flag.

"Is anyone hurt?" Margot cried, scrambling to her feet.

There were a few splinters and bruises among them but nothing serious. As they were helped up, the girls gaped at the hole in the side of the ship. This evidence of the *Eagle*'s vulnerability seemed to paralyze them.

"Let's go! Come on, follow me!" Margot had to drag a couple of them away from the hole.

The scene on deck was chaos. Captain Danckaert stood beside the helmsman, alternating orders to him and to the men on the yard-arms. "Into the wind! Into the wind!" he shouted several times. "Don't let them get behind us!"

There were so many men in motion on the rigging and masts, and they looked so small against the huge sails, that they reminded Margot of an infestation of ants. The cloudless canopy of blue hung over them, the same canopy that had lulled her to sleep a short time earlier. It was oblivious to the frantic agitation aboard the ship, un-affected by the human drama that was being played out beneath it.

"Where are my cannons?" the captain screamed. To the first mate, "Van Doorn! Go below! Get those cannons firing!"

The distant booms sounded more sharply here on deck. They were followed by white puffs appearing on the side of the pirate ship. The air crackled overhead as cannonballs sailed past, narrowly missing the mainmast. One ball fell short of its target, sending a plume of saltwater skyward.

Uys van Jaarsveld, his ornamented sword drawn, danced about excitedly, thrusting at the pirate ship as if the threat of his sword would drive it away. His eyes were wide and glassy, his lower lip quivered. He looked as if he was about to cry.

Boom! Boom! Boom!

The deck quaked beneath Margot's feet. Huge clouds of white smoke billowed from the *Eagle*'s sides.

Moments later van Doorn reappeared. "We took a direct hit be-low, Captain! Heavy losses. Jacobus has four guns operational again."

"Grab anyone you can and help him! We need more guns!" the captain ordered. Just then, he spotted the women. Pointing to Mar-got, he yelled, "Get below! Get those girls below!"

"We can give aid to the wounded!" Margot cried.

"Get below! Now!" His face was lined with fury, but there was also a shade of concern among the lines.

Margot herded the girls to the steps that led below deck.

One level down, Margot heard moans and cries of pain. "Stay close!" she instructed the girls. She followed the sound of the cries. It led them to the gun deck.

Boom! Boom! Boom! Boom!

Four cannons thundered and spit fire and smoke. The sound reverberated off the timbers and caused Margot's ears to ring. Close to the doorway by which they entered was a gaping hole in the hull. Several feet beyond it, the ocean rushed madly by. Near the hole two cannons lay on their sides, looking like dead animals. Scattered around the deck were the wounded and dead.

First Mate van Doorn saw the girls. "Are you insane?" he cried. "Get out of here!"

"We can tend to the wounded!" Margot yelled.

"You could get killed!"

"We can get killed in our cabin! Already it's filled with smoke!"

The gunner grabbed van Doorn by the arm and shouted to him, pointing at one of the guns. The first mate's attention was pulled away from the women.

"Tear their shirts, trousers, whatever's at hand to use as bandages," Margot yelled to the girls. "If you don't think you can do this, just stand to the side."

Clara had a sick look on her face. She and Suzette stood against the bulkhead. The rest moved from sailor to sailor, binding up their wounds or, if they were dead, covering their heads.

Behind them, cannons spewed fiery destruction with thunderous, roaring booms. The deck was heavy with smoke and the gritty, acrid taste of gunpowder. The *Eagle* shuddered again as it took another broadside hit.

After the dead and wounded were attended to, Margot huddled everyone together and watched the guns being fired. Each was manned by a team that was coordinated by commands from Jacobus, the gunner in charge. Margot looked at the two cannons lying lifeless on their sides.

"Clara! Give me a hand!" Margot called to the broad-shouldered girl.

Clara had been squeamish at the sight of the wounded. She hesitated.

Margot went to one of the fallen guns. "Help me set this upright!"

Eager to help in a bloodless chore, Clara bounded over to the cannon. The two girls struggled to turn it upright, but it was too heavy. Suzette joined them, and they managed to get the large gun back on its wheels.

The sound of the cannon's being set upright drew van Doorn's attention. "What are you doing?" he bellowed. "Get away from that!"

Margot picked up the rammer, a long pole with a sponge at the end. "Show me how to load it!" she yelled.

104

"I'm not going to tell you again!" van Doorn screamed. "Back away from that cannon."

Margot stared at him. She didn't back away, nor did she put down the rammer. She pointed to a cup on the deck. "Katje! That's the measuring scoop. Fill it with powder!"

Katje looked questioningly at van Doorn.

Looking straight into her eyes, he ordered, "Stand against the bulkhead!"

The petite woman picked up the cup.

Van Doorn stormed over to Margot. His face was black and sweaty. "Leave this deck now!" he shouted, his nose just inches away from hers.

Margot refused to let herself be intimidated. "The captain said he needed more guns. We can give him one more."

"You'll blow us all up!" van Doorn screamed.

"Not if you teach us how to do it!" Margot screamed back.

Van Doorn grabbed the rammer. Margot refused to give it up. He tried to wrestle it from her. She held on. The next thing Margot knew, Clara was standing beside her. The broad-shouldered girl put her hand on the rammer too. So did Suzette and Aletta and Anna and Marie and Katje.

He stared at each one of them.

"All right!" he yelled.

The girls cheered.

"First, we have to anchor the gun down," he said. "Otherwise, when it recoils it will shoot clear through the bulkhead." Van Doorn knelt beside the gun carriage. He stretched a thick rope from the carriage to a hook screwed into the ship's frame.

Clara watched him and did the same thing on the opposite side.

Van Doorn assigned each of them a job, handing them the necessary equipment for their tasks. Pointing to the other guns, he stepped them through the procedure: load, prime, aim, fire, clean the cannon for the next shot. Clara and Suzette, being the strongest, were given the task of loading the shot and, at Margot's signal, pulling the line that moved the gun into firing position. Margot was placed in charge.

The other guns had fired twice before their gun was ready. With a nod from van Doorn, Margot gave the signal to fire. There was a moment's hesitation as Margot held the fire to the gun, then—*boom!* The gun recoiled with a vengeance.

Van Doorn's eyebrows shot up in an impressed manner.

Katje jumped up and down, clapping her hands.

"Not bad," said the first mate, "not bad."

"What do you mean?" Margot cried. "We missed. The shot sailed well in front of the pirate ship's bow!"

"But you got it off! That's a start," van Doorn said.

"It does us no good if we don't hit the ship!" Margot said angrily. "Load it up again, girls!"

Margot aimed the next two firings herself, then watched in frustration as each cannonball sailed in an erratic, harmless trajectory.

"Margot! Look!" Katje cried in tears. She pointed toward the pirate ship.

It had changed course and was heading directly toward them. They intended to board the *Eagle*.

"We've got to sink them before they get here!" Margot cried. "Let's give them a good one!"

Their fourth shot buried itself in the pirates' deck near the stern. Black smoke poured out of the hole. Several of the girls jumped up and down for joy. They even earned an approving nod from First Mate van Doorn. Their fifth shot hit the pirates' mainmast. Sails crumpled and crashed down upon the deck, taking the Jolly Roger with it.

The pirate ship turned into the wind and limped away.

The cheers on the *Eagle*'s gun deck were almost as loud as the guns themselves.

Exhausted, the girls sprawled on the gun deck, propping themselves against the bulkhead. Their faces and arms and clothes were black with powder.

A beaming Captain Danckaert strutted through the hatchway. "Fine shooting, men!" he cried. "Job well—" He pulled up short when he saw the women. "What's this?" he asked van Doorn.

"Meet your new gunners," van Doorn said with a grin. "It was their shot that hit the pirate ship's mainmast."

Hands on hips, the captain shook his head in disbelief. To Margot he said, "I thought I ordered you back to your quarters!"

Margot smiled at him. "Aren't you glad I don't take orders well?"

Four and a half months out of Amsterdam, a good number of the *Eagle*'s crew and passengers took sick. Scurvy. It was a dreaded illness, often deadly, but a common one on long voyages. So common was it that scurvy had prompted Dutch sailors to demand a refreshment station at the Cape of Good Hope, which lay approximately midway between the Netherlands and India. There they could eat fresh fruit and vegetables, rest, and bargain with the local Khoikhoi tribes for cattle. Those who were afflicted with scurvy would usually recover in a couple of days. Some would die.

Margot didn't take sick right away. Suzette was the first of the King's Nieces to feel tired and sore. Soon afterward, Katje developed similar symptoms; then Anna and Marie and Clara. From the reports Margot heard, forty-five sailors were in the same condition.

"Margot, I feel so weak," Suzette moaned as she lay in her hammock. She could barely keep her eyes open.

Margot caressed her hand. "Just rest," she said. "There's nothing you need to be doing anyway."

"I've never been sick before," Suzette said. "Never. Even at the orphanage. Thought it was a sign of weakness. Other girls got sick. Not me."

"You've been fortunate to be so healthy."

A weak smile. "Don't feel very fortunate now."

Once again Margot found herself playing the role of comforter at someone's bedside. *Lord, are you telling me something?* she asked silently. It hurt her to see Suzette so weak and helpless. Suzette had always been the strong one, even if her strength often exhibited itself in obstinacy.

"Remember when the girls were sick?" Suzette asked, "At the outset of the voyage—remember? The first night you were here."

"I remember."

"I despised them for being sick. For stinking up the cabin. Hated them. Hated you for treating them like babies. Thought they were weak. Didn't understand."

"Everybody gets sick sometime," Margot said.

"Not you."

Margot gently squeezed the girl's hand. She didn't tell Suzette, but she was worried that she wasn't going to escape this time. She tasted blood in her mouth. Her gums felt spongy, her teeth loose. Over the past couple of days her joints had grown stiff and sore, and she was beginning to bleed under the skin just like the others. But mostly she felt tired. So very, very tired. These were all symptoms of scurvy.

"I was wrong about you," Suzette said to Margot. "Forgive me?"

"There's nothing to forgive." Margot patted Suzette's hand. It was limp. "Suzette?"

No response.

"Suzette?" Margot caressed the girl's cheek. "Suzette?"

There was no life left in her.

"Oh, no!" Margot cried. Raising Suzette's hand, Margot kissed the back of it. She prayed, "Dear God, take her as a little lamb in Your arms."

"Margot? Are you all right?" It was Aletta. She was the only one of the girls who had shown no symptoms of scurvy.

"It's Suzette," Margot said. "She's—"

"Margot!"

Aletta ducked under Margot's arm to keep her from falling. "Come over here and lie down."

Through half-opened eyes Margot saw the forms of the other girls lying in their hammocks. Their eyes were closed. They were so still. So still—like Suzette? And now she was joining them. Tired. So very tired.

Aletta guided her to the only unoccupied hammock in the cabin.

Margot resisted. "Your hammock," she said.

"You need it more than me," Aletta insisted.

Still Margot resisted. She wasn't trying to be noble. Inconveniencing Aletta wasn't the real reason she resisted. The real reason was fear. Margot was afraid that, if she lay down, she would never get up again. Like Suzette—like poor, scared Suzette.

But there was no strength in Margot's fear. Her limbs were as weak as ever. And though her mind screamed warnings, she was helpless to combat Aletta's gentle but firm persistence. The beams of the cabin appeared overhead, rocking back and forth. Aletta's worried face moved in and out of Margot's field of vision.

"Dear Jesus, heal my dear Margot," Aletta prayed.

My dear Margot.

The same words Margot had used at Sylvie's bedside before she died—"my dear Sylvie"—were now being spoken over her. Over her deathbed? Margot rejected the idea. Yet try as she might, she could not stop the disease that was siphoning away her life.

My dear Margot.

What a sweet phrase it was. It meant that Aletta felt affection for her like that she had felt for Sylvie. The thought warmed her. It made her even more determined to live. If not for herself, for Aletta and the other girls.

108

A thought came to mind. A strong thought. She repeated it over and over: *I have fought off Monsieur Fabarez and his accusations of murder and witchcraft; I have fought off Monsieur van Jaarsveld and his lecherous advances and lies; and I have fought off pirates. Lord, I have not come this far to die from disease!*

Above her, the planks pounded with the sound of stampeding feet.

"What's that noise?" she moaned.

Aletta cocked her head and listened. "I don't know."

"Last time . . . ruckus like that . . . pirates." Margot tried to wave Aletta toward the door to investigate the commotion but found she couldn't raise her hand. Nor could she keep her eyes open any longer.

The next thing Margot knew someone was shaking her.

"Go see . . . the noise," Margot said.

"I did!" Aletta cried excitedly. "It's land! They've spotted land! We're one day out of Table Bay! One day! Margot, we've made it to Cape Town! We've made it!"

Margot made no response. She tried to smile but couldn't. It took too much effort.

"Now you must get well, Margot! You must!"

Aletta's words sounded like the droning of bees. To Margot, the world was fading away. She didn't care anymore. Let it go.

In the darkness she heard a voice. Not Aletta's. A different voice. Familiar. Soothing. Someone calling to her. Calling her name.

Sylvie! It was Sylvie's voice!

"Where are you?" Margot cried. "Sylvie! Call louder! I'm coming. I'm coming."

8

Three things I wish and nothing more;
Above all else to love my Lord and God
No overflow or riches—wealth
But to desire what the wisest prayed for:
An honorable life in this vale.

Like an echo the prayer resounded in the recesses of Margot's mind. It was a prayer she'd learned from Sylvie, one that godly woman had prayed daily. And it was Margot's first thought as she emerged from her dark delirium.

The rough timbers overhead were her first indication that she wasn't dead. Certainly her heavenly dwelling would not be made of aged beams jointed crudely together. Then there was the odor. Definitely not heavenly. Bilgewater. A disagreeable but recognizable smell. She was still aboard the *Eagle*.

She moaned, thinking a moan might bring someone. It didn't.

At least her mind was functioning, she thought, though she found it difficult to sustain the simplest of tasks, such as keeping her eyes open. Sitting up was out of the question. As she lay there immobile, she heard no sounds other than the occasional creak of the ship's timbers. Her mouth was dry, her tongue swollen, and her head ached terribly.

She moaned again. Still no one came.

"Aletta? Katje?" Her voice was breathy and barely audible. Her tongue stuck to the inside of her cheeks and lips as she formed the words. No one responded to her call.

Despite the anticipated pain, Margot decided she had to try to lift her head and look around. She took several deep breaths to prepare herself. On the third breath, she held it. Neck and stomach muscles strained. At first there was no movement, then slowly her head rose. It had the dead weight of a rock, yet she managed to lift it a few inches and turn it slightly toward the interior of the cabin. When she could hold it no longer, it plopped down heavily. Pain exploded behind her wincing eyes with a flash of light.

She had seen enough to know that she was alone. The other hammocks were empty.

Surely they're not dead, Lord. Not all of them!

The rapid click of wooden heels against planks started in the distance, then grew increasingly louder. Someone was coming. Since she did not know the fate of the other girls, an uneasy thought occurred to her. What if the approaching person was unfriendly? How would she defend herself? She was so weak, so vulnerable.

The footfalls stopped at the doorway. The door scraped the deck as it opened slowly. Margot struggled to lift her head again, to get at least some advance indication of the nature of her predicament. But try as she might, she couldn't do it. The harder she tried, the more frantic she became.

"Margot?"

The voice was soft. Feminine. Familiar.

The hopeful face of Aletta stepped into Margot's field of vision. Joyful tears glazed the young girl's eyes. "Margot! You're awake! Thank God! I thought I'd lost you."

Exhausted, yet relieved, Margot smiled weakly. Her eyes closed involuntarily.

There was a swish of water, then she felt the coolness of a moist cloth being placed on her forehead. It was accompanied by the distinct odor of aniseed. She moaned contentedly.

"Thank God! Thank God!" Aletta said repeatedly. Her voice was choked with tears. "Thank God you're awake!"

"The others?" Margot asked, opening her eyes again. "What about the others?"

"Oh, they're all fine!" Aletta blurted out enthusiastically and a little too loudly. "Except for Suzette, of course. She died. You remember that, don't you? You were standing beside her when you—"

"I remember." Margot matched the girl's suddenly solemn tone. "Where is everyone?"

Aletta giggled. Wrinkles in the corners of her eyes formed starbursts. "They're all off with their husbands!" She nodded enthusiastically. "Yes! Their husbands! Every one of us was snatched up the moment we stepped off the ship."

"You have a husband?"

Aletta beamed. "Oh, Margot! He's so handsome! And kind!

When I told him how much you mean to me, he agreed to let me come and care for you until you got better . . ."

Or died.

Aletta didn't say it, but it wasn't hard for Margot to complete the thought. "Klaas—that's my husband's name—" she blushed "—he said that once you were strong enough to move, perhaps we could take you to our house where I can care for you until you're well!"

"How long have I been asleep?" Margot asked.

"Four days, if you count today," Aletta replied. She moved to the edge of Margot's vision. "Don't go away. I'll be right back! Now that you're awake, I'll get you something that will make you feel better."

Don't go away? Margot would have chuckled had she the strength. *Where does Aletta think I'm going?*

When Aletta returned, she was carrying a pitcher and a cup. She poured a clouded liquid into the cup, then raised Margot's head and assisted her with a sip. The cool drink splashed against Margot's parched tongue. The next instant it seized her eyes and mouth from the inside and squeezed them together.

"It's tart," Aletta said. "I should have warned you."

Margot's head shook involuntarily. "I'll say it's tart!"

"Lemon water. It's pretty strong, but it's the best thing for you. Here, have some more."

The second sip produced the same involuntary response of Margot's facial features and another shake of the head.

"For some reason, I never did come down with the scurvy. Lucky, I guess. So I took care of the others, just like you took care of us that first night! After two days of drinking lemon water, everyone was up and about." Another giggle. "Well enough to be presented to the men!"

She let out a squeal. "Oh, Margot! You should have seen the men's faces when we came on deck wearing those silk dresses! I have never seen so many mouths hanging open in all my life! Within minutes, every girl was claimed. Every one! Even Clara! And there are about a dozen more men just waiting for you to get better!"

"No, thank you," Margot said. "I'm not interested."

"Maybe you should reconsider. There are some who—"

Margot cut her off. "What does your husband do for a living?"

Aletta beamed. "He owns a vineyard and a wine press in Stellenbosch!"

"Stellenbosch?"

"It's further inland. I haven't seen it yet, but the way Klaas describes it, it sounds too good to be true!"

"I'm happy for you, Aletta."

"Are you sure you won't reconsider? There are a lot of good—"

"I'm sure," Margot said. She closed the discussion by closing her eyes.

For the next two days Margot's world was the wooden box with six hammocks in the belly of the *Eagle*. The stronger she felt, the more oppressive was the box. For nearly five months it had been her home. And though it now seemed spacious, since she was no longer sharing it with six other people, she longed to see a color other than brown and to breathe air that did not have the tang of bilgewater to it.

Aletta was at her side during most of Margot's waking hours. At night, she disembarked and stayed in the colony with her husband. But she always arrived in the cabin shortly after Margot awoke each morning.

On the morning of the third day, Margot rose from the hammock and felt strong enough to venture topside. As she finished dressing, she heard approaching footsteps. They sounded too heavy and far apart to be Aletta's. The moment they stopped, there was a soft tapping on the door.

"Mademoiselle de Campion?"

With a smile, Margot opened the door to Captain Danckaert.

The bulldog face looked pleased to see her. "I'm glad to hear you're feeling better," he said softly, as if hard tones might hurt her.

"Thank you, Captain. I'm feeling much better. In fact, I was just waiting for Aletta. I thought I'd wander up on deck. That is, if you don't think it will be too distracting to the crew."

A lopsided grin indicated that the captain caught her reference. "Aletta will not be coming this morning," he said.

"Oh?"

"We just received a message. She wanted to come and say goodbye, but her husband decided they must leave for Stellenbosch at once."

Disappointment filled Margot's eyes. "I didn't get a chance to thank her for her kindness to me."

"The trip to Stellenbosch can be made in one day if you begin early and ride hard," said the captain. "And Klaas Starrenburg is a driven man. He isn't one to sit idle for very long."

The captain's portrayal of Starrenburg struck Margot as vastly different from the way Aletta described him. "What do you know about Aletta's husband?" she asked. "Will he treat Aletta well?"

"From my dealings with Klaas, he's a fair man. Hardworking. German temperament. Not overtly sentimental. He'll provide for Aletta and protect her. That's more than most men. Don't fret. You'll see her again, of that I'm sure. At a festival or the like."

Margot nodded, but her mind was not eased as she remembered the relationship between Sylvie and Monsieur Fabarez. She prayed a silent prayer that Aletta would be happy in her new life.

"Will I do?" the captain asked.

"Do? I don't understand."

The captain extended a crooked arm. "As company. You said you were going topside. May I escort you?"

Margot felt her cheeks flushing. It was a good feeling. Since her illness, every good feeling was appreciated. "How gallant of you, Captain!" she cooed. She took his arm. "I would be most honored."

Captain Danckaert led her through the now familiar, dark, wooden maze of beams and planks and storage holds that led up two flights of steps to the deck. As she remembered, the quality of air improved at each level.

From below she caught her first glimpse of sky through the deck hatch. It was only a patch of blue framed in wood; but after seemingly endless days of staring at nothing but rough brown timbers, it was the most exquisite patch of blue she'd ever seen. She paused just to stare at it.

The captain gave her a quizzical look. After a moment, they proceeded up the steps to the deck.

The patch of blue sky, as lovely as it was, had failed to prepare her for the panorama of colors that burst into sight the moment her head cleared the hatchway. At first, all the colors were glazed with the white light of the sun. Then, as her eyes adjusted from the darkness of the hold to the brightness of a clear day, the richness of the scene that surrounded her stole her breath away. Set against the sky's blue canvas was an imposing flat-topped mountain, its face a series of dramatically lit rocky crags. Then Margot watched in wonder while a soft white cloud, as if cued by God, appeared and draped itself across the top of the mountain, spilling over onto the cliffs below.

"Table Mountain," said the captain, equally captivated by the spectacle. "It seems it's trying to impress you," he added. "I've anchored here on many occasions, but this is only the second time I've seen the cloth of cloud spread neatly across the mountain like that."

There was a lesser peak situated to their right. The captain called it Signal Hill. The mast and flags atop the rounded hill readily explained its name. To a girl who had been raised in the lowlands, Signal Hill by itself would have been magnificent. But standing beside the glory of Table Mountain, the hill was nothing more than a slight curiosity.

Stretched along the base of Table Mountain was Cape Town colony. Whitewashed buildings with familiar curved Dutch gables lined broad dirt roadways. To the left was a massive fort made of gray stone. "The Castle," the captain called it. The red, white, and blue Dutch flag fluttered proudly over its ramparts.

Between the colony and the ship was a busy waterfront and some of the most curious people Margot had ever seen.

"Khoikhoi?" she asked, pointing to two short men at opposite ends of a pole, carrying a large, swaying bucket between them.

The hair on their heads was closely cropped and tightly curled. Their skin was leathery and dark brown. The man in front turned his head and yelled something to the man trailing behind. What came out of his mouth was a series of clicks and noises unlike anything Margot had ever heard before.

"You've heard of the Khoi?" The captain looked surprised.

"From sea stories that were read to me at home," Margot replied.

"Khoikhoi is the name they call themselves. We call them Hottentots."

"'Stammerers,'" Margot mused, upon recognizing the name. "It does sound like they're stammering."

Scattered among Dutch sailors and Hottentots were a host of other people of various nationalities—Frenchmen, Germans, brown Malaysians, black men from the interior tribes, and others Margot could not readily identify.

Suddenly the day's excitement caught up with her. She became light-headed and clung to the captain's arm to keep from swooning.

"I'll help you below," he said.

She gripped his arm. "Please let me stay—just a little while longer."

"It will still be here after you've rested," he said, leading her to the hatch.

After a long nap, she was on deck again, fascinated by the sights and sounds. As the sun set behind her and darkness crept over the colony, engulfing Table Mountain's steep ridge, she watched as torches and lanterns dotted the landscape—a secondary show of lights compared to the brilliant stars that spangled the heavens.

It was at that moment Margot realized she had fallen in love with South Africa on her first day. It was so unlike the crowded cobblestone streets and polluted canals of Amsterdam. This new land was spacious and green and fresh.

She folded her arms to ward off the stiff breeze that blew across the deck. She'd always imagined that distant lands would have a strange, exotic feel to them. But she felt no strange feelings as she stood before Cape Town. It was as though she was meant to be here. She belonged here. Though she had not yet set foot on the soil of the African continent, she knew this was home.

Margot de Campion leaned contentedly against the ship's railing. Recalling a verse from the Psalms, she whispered, "I called upon the Lord in distress: the Lord answered me, and set me in a large place."

Margot strolled arm in arm with Captain Danckaert. Two sailors followed dutifully behind, carrying her trunk. Neither Margot nor the captain were in a hurry. He seemed to take as much pride in showing her the bustling colony as she was anxious to see it.

They had just entered Greenmarket Square. A sampling of humanity crisscrossed the wide open area. Vegetable sellers. Sailors. A young Dutch boy carrying two buckets of water on a pole. Chained slaves, black and brown, escorted in single file. A pair of well-dressed, wealthy burghers standing belly to belly, sharing a laugh.

Margot turned to the captain. "How can I ever thank you for all you've done for me?"

The captain patted her hand. "You can repay me by promising me you won't give the governor a hard time."

They shared a smile.

"I'm serious," Margot said. "I wish I could do something for you. You've been so kind to me."

"Nonsense," he said. "If I've treated you differently from other people on the ship, it's because I respect you. And respect isn't given away—it's something you earn."

They left Greenmarket Square by way of a side street that was lined with shops of all kinds—cobblers, milliners, bakers, a tavern.

The end of the street opened up to an expansive parade field on the far side of which lay the gate to the gray stone Castle.

"I don't wish to argue," Margot said, picking up the conversation again, "but you haven't treated me like the other people on the ship. You have given me special treatment."

The bulldog face wrinkled. It was an instinctive response. The captain clearly wasn't accustomed to people's disagreeing with him.

"You went out of your way to secure a position for me here in the governor's house," Margot said. "You didn't have to do that. And I don't think you would have done that for just anybody."

"Some people deserve special treatment," he said flatly. However, there was a sparkle in his eyes as he said it.

Margot stopped, pulling the captain to a halt with her. Like shadows, the two sailors behind them stopped also. There was a soft thud as they set down the trunk on the dirt surface of the street.

Whispering so that the shadowy seamen couldn't hear, Margot said, "I understand your need to maintain a hard image. I just want you to know that you have made me feel special, and for that I will always be grateful."

From his pained expression it was clear the captain and sentiment were distant cousins at best. He glanced uneasily at the two sailors, then replied in a whisper, "I have never been married, nor will I ever be married. What woman in her right mind would ever want an ugly sea dog like me?"

The captain checked on the sailors. Though they showed no indication they were listening, he whispered even more softly, so softly Margot had to strain to hear him.

"And though I have no desire to marry, for some fool reason I've always wanted to have a daughter. Beats everything, doesn't it? Not a son—a daughter!"

Holding back her rising emotions, Margot smiled with warm understanding.

"And . . . well . . ." The captain looked down. "I've always imagined that if I had a daughter, she'd be just like you. So you see, that's why I act like I do with regards to you."

Tears glazed Margot's eyes. "Thank you, Captain," she said, squeezing his arm. "I feel proud that you think of me that way."

"Just don't go telling everyone what I just told you!" he ordered.

They walked in warm silence toward the Castle. Then, in a fatherly tone the captain said, "You will undoubtedly run into van

Jaarsveld from time to time during his stay in the colony. He will leave you alone. I've seen to that."

"Thank you," Margot said. "I'll not ask for the details."

"It's best that way," the captain replied.

Passing through the Castle's stone archway, they entered the Garden Court. From the inside Margot could see that the Castle was built in the shape of a five-pointed star with a bastion at each point. As the captain led her to the governor's residence, he explained that each bastion was named after a title of the Prince of Orange. Pointing to them one at a time, he called them by name—Buren, Leerdam, Oranje, Nassau, and Ketzenellenbogen.

In the center of the castle grounds was a well. The governor's residence was to the right. It was a long, white building with a balcony that featured a wrought-iron balustrade. The balcony was flanked by curved steps.

"You'll be in good hands here," said the captain. "And if I'm any judge of character, you will be the presiding governor by the time I make port here on the return voyage."

Margot grinned at his good-natured ribbing. The hardest part of getting on with her new life was going to be saying good-bye to him.

Their farewell came with surprising speed.

The captain announced himself at the door and stated his business. And the transaction that placed Margot in the governor's employ was handled with dispatch. In a matter of moments, the matron who oversaw the governor's cleaning staff—a tall, beefy woman with one long blonde braid coiled on the top of her head—appeared and whisked Margot away. The same sentiment would have been displayed had the captain delivered a sack of grain.

Margot's orientation lasted for as long as it took them to travel the length of the hallway. In crude fashion she was told to keep her mouth shut, her hands busy, and to mind her own business. If she was caught stealing, lying, or in someone's bed, she would be terminated. Likewise, if she became pregnant she would be terminated. All that was required from her was to fulfill her cleaning duties in an efficient and timely manner. For this she would receive room and board and a small wage.

"That is where you will sleep." The woman's extended arm was sturdy as a small tree trunk. She pointed to the first bed in a row of beds, five on each side of the room. There was barely enough space between the beds for a person to stand.

Two black servants appeared with Margot's trunk.

"Place it at the end of the bed," ordered the matron.

They did, then ran out of the room.

To Margot she said, "You have five minutes to unpack your things, then report to me at the front door where you came in. My name is *Mevrouw* Hilda."

The matron closed the door behind her.

The room in which Margot found herself was spartan. Beds. Small trunks at the foot of some of the beds, nothing as large as the one she had, which had once belonged to Uys van Jaarsveld. In fact, her trunk was so large it blocked half of the entrance to the aisle between the two rows of beds. The other girls would have to step around it to get to their beds. But there was no other place to put it. Nor was there any other place to put her clothes. So what did *Mevrouw* Hilda mean when she said to unpack?

Margot walked the length of the room and back, the sound of her heels on the polished wooden floor echoing against sterile, white-washed walls. For the remainder of the five minutes she sat in silence on the edge of her bed. Then she left to meet *Mevrouw* Hilda but not before first smoothing the wrinkles on her bed that she had made when she sat down.

For Margot there was something therapeutic about cleaning. Polishing wood and metal to a shine produced a glow of inner satisfaction. It gave her a sense of accomplishment. An aching back and sore muscles at the end of the day were a badge of pride for her. They were a testimony to her hard work. And Sylvie had taught her that the ability to work was one of the ways in which mankind reflected the image of God. For the Bible said that when God created the world, He worked for six days, then rested on the seventh. For Margot, on a much smaller scale, by cleaning she too was creating order out of chaos.

To be sure, she missed the mental stimulation and leadership role she had enjoyed among the girls aboard the *Eagle*. *Mevrouw* Hilda prevented any similar gathering among the cleaning girls by always keeping them in separate rooms during the day and working them late into the night. Even with the larger chores, those that required more than one person to complete, *Mevrouw* Hilda hampered social interaction by closely supervising the work. No conversing between the girls was needed or permitted. *Mevrouw* Hilda orchestrated each step. Hers was the only voice heard.

Isolation was the matron's way of maintaining order among the workers. This way there were no personalities in conflict, there was no chance of idle gossip and hurt feelings, and there was no chance of conspiracy against her. The matron went so far as to sleep in the same room with the girls to discourage any late night chatter.

Margot also learned that *Mevrouw* Hilda never complimented anyone for her work. On the other hand, if a task was not completed satisfactorily, she was at no loss for words. Several times a day Margot could hear the matron's shrill voice echoing down the hallway as she pointed out smudges and dust and cobwebs and spills. One would think by listening to her that dirt in any form was an inanimate demon waiting to spring to life if it was not immediately expunged.

Sometimes *Mevrouw* Hilda's harangues would last for nearly an hour. Except when she checked Margot's work. At those times the cleaning matron seemed almost disappointed that she could find so few things in Margot's rooms about which to scream.

Being an expert in exorcising filth, *Mevrouw* Hilda always managed to find at least one dirt demon in the rooms Margot cleaned. But Margot never let the woman's harangues bother her. She knew that if she cleaned as Sylvie taught her to clean, she could be proud of her work, even by *Mevrouw* Hilda's standards.

However, Margot got to wondering how *Mevrouw* Hilda would react if, despite her best efforts, she was unable to find a speck of dirt. It took several attempts, but one day Margot succeeded in cleaning a room until it was literally spotless.

When *Mevrouw* Hilda arrived to inspect, Margot watched with concealed glee as the overseer searched for preincarnate demons. When the matron's first tour of the room came up empty, she began another, this time doubling her efforts. After the second time around the room provided similar results, *Mevrouw* Hilda grew frantic. She became obsessed. For more than an hour she poked her head behind furniture, crawled on all fours, and stuck her fingers and nose into corners and crevices—wiping, sniffing, stretching, groaning. Finally she gave up.

Mevrouw Hilda stood before Margot, her shoulders slumped, her lower lip pouting. She looked like the disgruntled victim of a practical joke. Then she let out a *harrumph* and stalked out of the room.

From that day on, Margot always managed to leave at least one smudge for *Mevrouw* Hilda to find. It seemed the least she could do, since the discovery of dirt gave the matron a reason for living.

9

The governor and other company officials were careless about leaving revealing documents uncovered on their desks, just as van Jaarsveld had been careless about his journal in the *Eagle*'s cabin. For the most part there was no reason for them to be cautious. Common laborers were illiterate. In fact, the literacy rate was so low in the colony that most of the free burghers could shuffle freely through the papers on the governor's desk and be none the wiser for it.

Margot was the exception. And though she didn't snoop, the number of papers and letters left exposed to her view were enough to educate her on the general condition of the colony.

She saw a petition by French colonists to the governor protesting the suppression of the French language in the colony. According to the petition, the Huguenot colonists felt their very identity was tied to their language and that their opportunities to use French were growing increasingly rare since the majority of the colonists spoke Dutch. Furthermore, they believed that the decisions of the *Vereenigde Oostindische Compagnie*—the Dutch East India Company—were designed to force them to abandon their native language.

A letter lying next to the petition revealed that their fears were well grounded. From this Margot learned that not only was the Company unsympathetic to the French colonists' petition but that the governor was under orders to scatter the French colonists throughout the colony to keep them a minority. The Company fear was that, in a pinch, the Huguenots would side with a French squadron of ships should France ever decide she wanted Cape Town.

This kind of heavy-handedness was typical of the Dutch East India Company. From what Margot was able to learn, the Company kept strict control over prices and contracts and labor. From the Company's point of view, the colony existed only insofar as it served the needs of the mother country. Therefore the burghers were restricted to producing just enough corn, meat, vegetables, and wine to satisfy the limited demands of the Company at a price decided by the Company.

Naturally, this kind of relationship created disagreements between the Company and the free burghers who worked the land. It also invited corruption, as in the case of the former governor.

Margot learned that, seven years prior to her arrival, a major scandal rocked the governor's house. According to a complaint from the free burghers, Governor Willem van der Stel was an arrogant, ambitious, greedy, dishonest man who used the Company's materials, men, and time to build a personal country estate called Vergelegen. In addition to this abuse of Company resources, he used his power as governor to corner the colony's markets for himself and selected friends by issuing contracts to his favorites, including a valuable meat contract taken from the van der Kemps, a family whose name figured prominently in the records of the turmoil that followed.

Sixty-three free burghers signed a petition of complaint to the Lords XVII, which they smuggled to Holland aboard a ship.

When van der Stel learned of the petition, he took immediate action. First, he created a petition of his own which he induced 240 men to sign, using bribery, fraud, and force. In addition, he arrested many of the free burghers who had signed the original petition. Through imprisonment and torture he attempted to force them to recant. Many of them did. One notable holdout was Pieter van der Kemp, a prominent cattle merchant who owned a plantation named Klaarstroom—a large tract that was coveted by Governor van der Stel—at the base of the Hottentots-Holland mountain range.

In Amsterdam, after reviewing the free burghers' petition, the Lords XVII appointed a commission of inquiry. Based on its findings, Governor van der Stel was brought back to Holland and, after a long trial, was dismissed from service to the Company. Although his removal was a major victory for Cape Town colony's free burghers, it eased only slightly the tension between the burghers and the Company.

In addition to internal strife, there were also external threats. Margot learned that a short two years before she arrived, the settlement had been hit hard by a smallpox epidemic. According to the report she read, the tragedy began when a convoy carrying the disease limped into Table Bay. The fact that all those who had the disease aboard ship had recovered led to the disaster. Had they died, their clothes would have been burned. But since they recovered, their clothing was included in the laundry that was sent to the colony's slave lodge for washing.

Within days, slaves contracted the disease and were beginning to die like flies. Then the first whites began to display symptoms of the pox. Soon the death toll stood between two and five persons a day. Wooden coffins could not be made fast enough. And when pigeons began toppling from the roof of the governor's house and dying for no apparent reason, the people interpreted their deaths as an omen of catastrophe.

It was an accurate prediction. Before the disease had run its course, the epidemic killed off 25 percent of the colonists. The local Khoikhoi population was not as fortunate. With no resistance to the disease, scores of Hottentots died where they fell ill. Entire clans were wiped out.

According to a Dutch official, "the Hottentots died in the hundreds. They lay everywhere on the roads. Cursing at the Dutchmen, who they said had bewitched them."

Margot found other documents that further described the deteriorating relationship between natives and colonists. The San tribes, called Bushmen by the settlers, remained distant and threatening, occasionally raiding outlying farms. The Hottentots had traded with the Europeans for years. Although some clans took on an adversarial role, others worked for the colonists, especially with those families who raised cattle. The external threat of attack from either Bushmen or Hottentots was sufficient to warrant the organization of local bands of voluntary commandos who protected and policed the colony's fringe settlements.

Margot did not arrive at Cape Town with idealistic dreams of a land flowing with milk and honey—Sylvie's books had educated her well regarding the dangers of new settlements with strange geographies and climates, wild animals and unfriendly natives. But not until she read the unattended papers at the governor's residence did she realize to what degree her destiny was tied to that of the colony.

These papers were not a generalized narrative about a distant land. The people whose names appeared in these records walked the same streets she walked. The events and dates recorded here were a record of their lives. And from this point on, their history and her history were linked. Their risk was her risk; their danger, her danger. Together they would succeed, or together they would fail.

His voice made her shudder in the way a shiver rattled her spine whenever someone cracked his knuckles. It was van Jaarsveld.

A second pair of heels clicked in accompaniment to his on the hardwood hallway floor. Margot pulled back from the doorway of the room she was cleaning, hoping that van Jaarsveld and his friend would pass by. The lecherous commissioner was doing all the talking. His voice grew louder the closer they came.

"In here," she heard him say.

Margot rolled her eyes, expecting to see them at any moment. But no one came in. The next thing she heard was the sound of two chairs scraping the floor and a loud exhale and moan as van Jaarsveld settled into his chair. They had gone into the room opposite.

Her next thought was to slip out of the room. She didn't want to be anywhere near the man. In fact, she was willing to endure the wrath of *Mevrouw* Hilda for not finishing the room—something she had never done—rather than face him.

"When can I see Rachel?" he asked. "I have thought of no one else since I sailed for Amsterdam last year."

Margot froze. *The wretch!*

"Rachel is anxious to see you too," said the other voice. It was deep, smooth, confident.

"I'm disappointed you didn't bring her with you." Van Jaarsveld sounded hurt.

"This wasn't a social trip," came the reply. "You'll see her soon enough."

Good for you! Margot thought. Whoever he was, he wasn't intimidated.

"You will convey my love to her?"

"Of course."

There was a pause in the conversation. For a long time no sound came from the other room. *What are they doing?* Margot wondered. *Staring at each other?*

Then, "I like you, Jan," van Jaarsveld said. "Our families are going to get along famously. And this marriage is going to usher in a whole new age of cooperation between the Company and Cape Town colony. And like the marriage alliances of old, it will be based on the merging of two strong families—the van Jaarsvelds and the van der Kemps!"

I've heard that name before! Margot thought. *Yes—Rachel van der Kemp! In van Jaarsveld's journal. What was it he'd written about her? He called her an exotic African flower and, yes, he mentioned how he was unwise to propose marriage to her, that he'd learned to get what he wanted without resorting to such a drastic measure. That wretch! And that poor, poor girl!*

Margot listened as van Jaarsveld gushed on about the glorious future of the two families. Her hand clenched her cleaning cloth so tightly it shook. She knew what the true future held for Rachel van der Kemp if van Jaarsveld had his way.

I've got to stop him! But how?

She thought that if she could get a glimpse of the other fellow, van der Kemp, she could possibly catch him apart from van Jaarsveld later and warn him. From the clear sound of their voices, she determined they were close to the doorway. But would she be able to see them, and would she be able to see them without van Jaarsveld's seeing her? It was a risk she would have to take.

Standing against the wall next to the doorway, she leaned cautiously forward, poking her head slowly past the doorjamb. In the room across the hall, van Jaarsveld was sitting with his back to her. His meticulously groomed blond hair bounced side to side as he blathered on.

Opposite him in a matching chair was a well-tanned man in his early thirties. He seemed to be studying van Jaarsveld, weighing him in a balance. The man's features had hard edges; a triangular cleft cut deeply into his chin. He looked up. Sharp, pale blue eyes caught sight of Margot peering around the door. Full brown eyebrows furrowed at the sight as his and her gazes locked.

A faint cry escaped Margot's lips. She froze. What should she do? Draw back and hide? No, that would appear childish. Yet she couldn't remain where she was with her head poking out ridiculously from the side of the doorway.

Casually she inspected the doorjamb and pretended to notice a speck of dirt. She looked down her nose at the imaginary speck, used her fingernail to pick at something that wasn't there, then finished off the spot that didn't exist with a vigorous rubbing of the cloth. Moving into the doorway, she ran the cloth up one side, overhead, then down the other. She tried to act as though she were completely unaware of the men across the hall.

Van Jaarsveld's monotonous chattering indicated nothing was amiss. However, Margot couldn't keep herself from sneaking a peek at van der Kemp. Nonchalantly she let her gaze wander his direction.

He was staring at her! A raised, crooked finger held in front of his mouth failed to conceal an amused smirk.

Margot's face flushed. It was her turn to furrow a brow. In a huff, she turned her back on van der Kemp and retreated farther into the room out of his sight.

Van Jaarsveld droned on, oblivious to Margot de Campion and Jan van der Kemp's initial encounter.

"Monsieur van der Kemp! A word with you, please."

It was late afternoon. Margot was finishing her final room for the day, expecting *Mevrouw* Hilda to appear any moment, when she saw

Jan van der Kemp pass by the doorway. Not knowing whether he had heard her or not, she raced to catch him. She rounded the corner of the doorway the same moment he came in. She bounced off his chest and would have fallen had he not caught her by the arms.

She was taken aback by his size. He was much taller than she'd imagined him to be—nearly six feet. His grip was unyielding—it was as if she'd stumbled into a crevice between two rocks. Pale blue eyes looked down at her.

"Excuse me, Monsieur!" Margot cried.

"French." He said the word as though it left a disagreeable film on his tongue. "This is a Dutch colony. Speak Dutch. It's *mijnheer*, not monsieur.

The way he spoke to her—like an adult correcting a child—caused Margot's ire to rise. "Release me and I will speak Dutch, *Mijnheer* van der Kemp." Her tone mimicked his.

He didn't appreciate it. His already hard blue eyes narrowed to cutting sharpness.

Margot was determined not to allow herself to be intimidated into lowering her gaze, though in truth she found the strength of his presence unnerving. Stubbornly she held her ground.

He released her.

"What did you want?" he asked.

She didn't answer him immediately. First, she adjusted her sleeves and her dress though neither needed adjusting. She was stalling. She had carefully planned the words she was going to say, and now she couldn't remember them!

"*Mejuffrouw?* You did call out to me, didn't you?"

Margot smiled to herself. He'd called her Miss, not Mrs.

"Yes, *Mijnheer*," she replied. "I called you. It's about Rachel."

"My sister? What about my sister? How do you know her?" His reaction was intense. Guarded. Hostile.

"I–I don't know her," Margot stammered. The degree of his response startled her. "But I know *Mijnheer* van Jaarsveld. And . . . well . . ." She strained to remember how she'd phrased it earlier in her mind. "The marriage between your sister and *Mijnheer* van Jaarsveld . . ."

"Yes?"

"It shouldn't be. I mean, she shouldn't marry him." This was coming out all wrong.

Van der Kemp's blue eyes bored into her. "I don't see that it's any of your business," he said coldly. "Now if you'll excuse me."

Margot watched in dismay as he turned his back on her and proceeded down the hallway. "You're a sad excuse for a brother if you are willing to sacrifice your sister just to improve your relationship to the Company!"

The impact of her words hitting his back was noticeable. She doubted she could have made a greater impact on him had she hit him with her fist.

He whirled around. At first he didn't say anything. He took two, then three, steps toward her, his index finger extended in a threatening manner. He reined in his words as he would a team of spooked horses. "I'm warning you!" he seethed. "Keep your snooping nose out of my family's business!"

His anger was contagious; Margot responded in kind. "I wasn't snooping!" she yelled, genuinely offended by his accusation. "And I can't keep silent when a couple of self-serving men are more concerned with business than they are with human lives. All I can say is that you and *Monsieur* Uys van Jaarsveld deserve each other!"

"Margot! Hold your tongue!" A horrified *Mevrouw* Hilda appeared out of nowhere. She hustled her large frame between Margot and van der Kemp. Apologizing repeatedly to *Mijnheer* van der Kemp, she then poured a cascade of verbal abuses on Margot, demanding that she apologize.

"I'll not apologize for doing right!" she cried.

Hilda's oversized hand struck with a vengeance. The slap knocked Margot to the floor. Grabbing her by the hair, the matron pulled her down the hallway, all the while apologizing profusely to van der Kemp.

The broad-shouldered free burgher lifted a hand toward them and said something, but *Mevrouw* Hilda's curses drowned out his words.

Never before had Margot received a physical beating like the one *Mevrouw* Hilda gave her. The first night she was unable to sleep. The pain from her bruises caused her head to pound mercilessly. Besides, she couldn't get comfortable. Every position she tried aggravated one or more injuries.

But her physical pain was not the worst of it. Long after the bruises healed, *Mevrouw* Hilda continued to vent her rage on Margot. The stocky matron was not one to give a beating and then forget about it. She dragged Margot from room to room every hour of every day, never once letting her out of her sight.

All the dirtiest jobs defaulted automatically to Margot. She was forced to do them while *Mevrouw* Hilda hovered, shouting orders. No job she did was ever done fast enough. No job was done well enough to please the overbearing matron. The barrage of abuse took its toll. The fiery determination that once lit Margot's eyes was stamped out. All that remained was a blank stare and the resolve to do nothing and say nothing ever again. It wasn't worth it. It was better not to have an opinion, to mind one's own business, and not get involved in other people's lives.

One of *Mevrouw* Hilda's forms of retribution was to volunteer Margot for extra work. Following one full day of cleaning, she was enlisted to assist the governor's kitchen staff in a dinner reception for visiting Company official Uys van Jaarsveld. It was her task to serve the guests and then assist in the cleanup afterward.

If all went as scheduled, she would get three, maybe four, hours of sleep before having to rise for her next day's closely supervised cleaning tasks. But as rumor had it, if the reception carried on as long as it did last year when Uys van Jaarsveld was honored, she would barely finish in time to complete the one job before starting the other.

It mattered little to Margot. She no longer cared. There was something tragically wrong with a colony that honored men such as Uys van Jaarsveld, then blindly handed over to him an innocent girl for his pleasure all in the name of business.

10

The hardwood floor in the governor's dining room was so polished it doubled in appearance the number of people in the room. The guests' reflections served as color shadows of Cape Town's leading citizens, though the colors were mostly conservative black and white. Dutch men and women, Germans, French, all had broken away from the repetition of their daily-life activities for an evening of gaiety.

Long straight tables were decked out with spotless silver and blue-patterned china and arranged in a large U shape with the guests seated around the outside edge. Servants scurried around the outer perimeter carrying platters of freshly baked bread, sliced beef and mutton, fish, and dried fruits. The aroma of coffee was strong. A spinet and harp played in the background, though they could barely be heard over the din of noisy guests who were starved for social intercourse.

While serving, the servants painstakingly avoided the inside area between the tables. Standing there would be like standing center stage, and the servants knew better than to call attention to themselves and away from the governor and his guests.

Governor Chavonnes and Uys van Jaarsveld, the evening's guest of honor, sat prominently at the bottom of the U, facing the open end. This way all the guests could see them. To van Jaarsveld's left sat a radiant young woman—Margot assumed her to be Rachel van der Kemp—with dark, full hair that cascaded down to her shoulders. A pale complexion made her hair seem darker than it actually was. Her blue eyes had a natural sparkle to them. Her mouth was dainty, the corners turned up slightly. Her demeanor was innocent, carefree. She was an exotic African flower, just as van Jaarsveld had described her in his journal.

Seated next to her was an older man Margot presumed was her father. It was really more than assumption—a deduction. Jan van der Kemp sat next to him. The two men looked so much alike that, had there not been such an obvious disparity in their ages, one would have guessed them to be twins. To Jan's left was another van der Kemp, or so Margot deduced. He too bore a family resemblance, though more to Rachel than to the other van der Kemp men. His hair was dark like hers and long to the shoulders, as was the fashion. And whereas the other two wore shorter hair and were clean shaven, he wore a thin, stylish mustache.

These were Margot's observations gleaned from quick, covert glances for which she chided herself. Long before the guests arrived she determined to perform her duties and nothing more. Moreover, now that she knew where van Jaarsveld and the van der Kemps were seated, she would do her best to avoid that area. She determined not to look at anyone, not to speak to anyone. She would mind her own business and serve. Nothing more.

"*Mejuffrouw!* Oh, *Mejuffrouw!*" The voice that bounced off the rough white walls sounded irritatingly familiar. It belonged to Uys van Jaarsveld.

Margot pretended not to hear him. She concentrated on refilling a grinning Frenchman's goblet with wine. The bottle of wine she held was from the colony's own vineyards. Earlier in the evening the governor had proudly announced his wine choice, emphasizing its local origin.

"*Mejuffrouw!*"

The sound of van Jaarsveld's voice set her teeth on edge. A spike of dread jabbed her nerves. Intuitively she knew he was calling her. She ignored him, continuing to pour. But for how long? The wine was already close to the rim of the goblet. She raised the neck of the bottle to slow the flow.

"*Mejuffrouw!* You! Over there! Will someone over there please get me that servant's attention?"

A wrinkled hand reached out and gently tapped the back of her pouring hand. Margot looked up into the eyes of an older Frenchman with thinning gray hair. With an apologetic smile he pointed in the direction of van Jaarsveld.

Margot acknowledged the old man's silent message with a nod.

She could think of no way to avoid van Jaarsveld short of bolting from the room. Straightening, she proceeded along the outer edge of the tables toward the bellowing guest of honor. However, she kept her gaze lowered, refusing to look at him.

"No, no!" Van Jaarsveld's irritating voice boomed. "This way! Up the middle. You've taken too long to get here already!"

Margot looked up.

Van Jaarsveld was motioning for her to enter the area between the tables. The room fell silent. Now everyone was looking at her.

Reluctantly Margot retraced her steps and crossed the interior area in full view of all the guests.

As she approached van Jaarsveld, he held out his goblet to her. "It took you long enough!" he bawled.

Margot glanced up while she poured. The governor was scowling at her. She couldn't bring herself to look at any of the van der Kemps.

Once the goblet was filled, she turned to leave.

"Just a minute!" van Jaarsveld called after her. "Come back here, girl."

Biting her lower lip, Margot returned. She stood before him, her head lowered.

"Look at me, girl!" Van Jaarsveld boomed. He was determined to demonstrate his superior rank.

Margot knew it was unwise, but her stubbornness got the better of her. She refused to raise her head. "Would you like something else?" she asked politely.

A different voice sounded. Deeper. Authoritative. "Girl, what is your name?" It was the governor.

"Margot de Campion," Margot replied softly.

"Mijnheer van Jaarsveld is our guest," the governor said. "You will do what he says!"

Slowly Margot raised her head.

Van Jaarsveld's smug grin was infuriating.

"I couldn't help but notice," he said with an oily tone of superiority, "that of all the servants, you are the only white woman."

It was true. All the other servants were Malaysian or black.

"I take it you are Dutch?" he asked, playing with her.

Margot said nothing.

"Answer the man!" the governor shouted.

"French," Margot replied. "But I was raised in Amsterdam."

Van Jaarsveld's eyes lit up, truly surprised. "So tell me," he continued, "what is it that brought such a lovely Frenchwoman as yourself to this low level of servitude? Are you being punished for something?"

Reluctantly Margot nodded.

A rakish grin formed on van Jaarsveld's face. "It must have been something truly wicked to warrant something this demeaning. Care to tell us what you did?"

"I'd rather not."

"Tell him!" the governor demanded.

"I was disrespectful," Margot said softly. She wanted to look at Jan van der Kemp to see his reaction, since he was the one to whom she'd been disrespectful. But she fought the urge.

Uys van Jaarsveld nodded pensively. "I certainly hope you have learned your lesson well," he said in a superior tone. "One should never forget her place. That is all. You may go now."

It was all Margot could do to restrain herself from clobbering the smug van Jaarsveld over the head with the wine bottle in her hands. Instead, she lowered her head and moved to resume refilling the guests' goblets. But as she walked back across the open area she couldn't help but feel the gaze of Jan van der Kemp on her back.

As the evening progressed, van Jaarsveld turned his attention to Rachel. It sickened Margot to watch as the oily commissioner buzzed about her like a bee ready to pollinate a flower. The more wine he drank, the closer he leaned into her. To Rachel's credit, she matched his forward lean each time with a lean backward of equal degree. From the look on her face she was clearly uneasy with van Jaarsveld's public display of familiarity, if not downright disgusted.

Margot began to think of ways she might spill something on the commissioner. She didn't want to scald him; she just wanted to douse his flame. Then, catching herself mid-scheme, she remembered her self-imposed guidelines for the evening: *Don't look. Don't talk. It's none of your business. Stay out of it.*

But Margot didn't listen to herself. While removing a plate of fish bones and scraps, and wondering how they would look on van Jaarsveld's head, she happened to glance in the direction of the van der Kemps. Jan was staring at her. His eyes, normally a piercing blue, were soft and compassionate. Had he pieced it together? That her punishment was a result of their argument?

A sudden movement caught her eye. Van Jaarsveld made another lurch in Rachel's direction. The girl had just picked up her wine goblet and turned toward him. Rachel squealed as scarlet liquid splashed all over van Jaarsveld. Some of it hit her dress too. Van Jaarsveld jumped up, cursing and dabbing himself furiously with a napkin, concerned only with himself.

Rachel offered a string of apologies and hurried from the room. Jan tried to follow her; she waved him off.

The way van Jaarsveld was fussing and pouting, Margot had to turn away to keep from laughing out loud. It was perfect. And odd. In fact, the more Margot thought about it, the odder it became.

Then she realized the truth. The incident was no accident! Rachel had done it on purpose! Her hand had been resting on the goblet. Van Jaarsveld's swaying had grown predictable. The young girl had timed her move perfectly and did to van Jaarsveld exactly what Margot had wanted to do! Then there was the way she left—no tears, nor was her face red from embarrassment!

Margot set down the tray of fish bones to follow after Rachel under the pretense of rendering assistance.

She stopped. *It's none of your business. Do nothing! Say nothing!*

Margot followed after the girl anyway.

Margot whisked down a long, dark hallway, casting an occasional glance over her shoulder. She reached the room the ladies used for personal matters, with its full complement of mirrors and brushes and combs and basins of water and towels. She found it to be vacant.

Then she heard hurried steps echoing down an adjoining corridor. Suspecting there was a bit of deception going on, Margot kept out of sight to avoid detection. From behind a corner she listened as the rapid *click, click, click* of Rachel's shoes tapped against the wooden floor. There were only so many places the girl could go down this hallway, so Margot was content to wait. When Rachel's steps slowed, Margot listened for the sound of a door latch. Once she heard the click, she peeked around the corner just in time to see which door was swinging shut.

Margot carried her shoes so as not to announce her presence. Quickly but quietly she spanned the distance and stopped one door shy of the room Rachel had entered. Margot knew them to be connecting rooms. She worked the latch noiselessly and slipped inside.

She was in luck. The door between the adjoining rooms was closed. From the other side she could hear voices, more than whispers, loud enough to be heard clearly. Having crossed to the door, Margot eased the latch and pulled it open just a crack.

Rachel had lit no candles or lamps, but blue-gray moonlight streamed into the connecting room. One of the wide windows was open, and she was leaning on the sill, talking to someone outside.

Margot couldn't see the other person, but from Rachel's giddy voice and frequent giggling she had a pretty good idea what the deception and this mysterious rendezvous were all about.

Suddenly Rachel swung around and shot a glance behind her.

Margot jumped back. Had the girl spotted her? Her question was answered by the sound of more giggles and whispers. Margot leaned forward again until the girl and the window came back into sight.

She watched as a brown hand stretched forward and tenderly stroked Rachel's cheek. Closing her eyes in response to the sensation, Rachel reached up and caressed the hand that caressed her face. Her white skin, highlighted by blue moonlight, stood in stark contrast to the hand that touched her.

Then a face appeared. It was a young man. He had short, dark hair and dark eyes that were fixed, almost hypnotized, on Rachel. His full lips parted in a smile, revealing incredibly white teeth.

Rachel opened her eyes. She leaned forward. Their lips touched. Just barely at first. Then harder.

"Oh! I can't stay any longer," Rachel moaned. "I have to get back!"

"I know," whispered the boy. "But I don't want to let you go."

"And I don't want to go."

They kissed.

"Will we ever be together?" the boy asked.

"I wish I knew," she answered sadly. "I pray every day."

They kissed.

"I pray, too, that God will show us the way."

"There's got to be a way."

They kissed again.

"I must go, or someone will come looking for me."

"Good night, my love."

"Be careful, Matthew. Please, be careful."

Margot eased away from the door, stepped back into the hallway, and waited.

Moments later the door to the adjoining room opened. Rachel slipped out and eased the door shut. Not until she turned down the hallway did she see Margot.

"Oh!" A hand flew to her throat.

"Let me help you get that stain out of your dress," Margot said.

Margot rubbed at the wine stain as she and Rachel sat knee-to-knee in the ladies' room. Despite her fervent resolve not to get involved in other people's business, Margot found herself instantly fond of this girl and wanting to help her.

"That was brilliant—the way you orchestrated your exit from the banquet," Margot said as she rubbed the purple spot.

"Whatever do you mean?" Rachel cried innocently.

Margot stopped rubbing and looked at her.

"Was I that obvious?" Rachel asked. Her voice quivered; her fingers played with a bit of lace.

Margot reached over and patted the girl's nervous hands. She said, "Your secret is safe with me. But we have to talk about your dilemma." She turned her attention to the spot on the dress.

"My dilemma?"

"Mijnheer van Jaarsveld."

"Oh, *that* dilemma."

Margot stopped rubbing again. She looked up. "Did your brother say anything to you about me?"

"Which one?"

So there are two brothers, Margot thought. "Jan. Did he say anything to you about me or *Mijnheer* van Jaarsveld?"

Rachel shook her head innocently. "You spoke to Jan about me?"

"Indirectly. I was attempting to warn him about *Mijnheer* van Jaarsveld. I didn't start off well, and he thought I was trying to interfere in your business, and we got into a rather heated argument. Before I could say much, *Mevrouw* Hilda cut us off. That's why I'm here tonight."

Rachel's face lit up delightfully. "That's why you're serving? That awful scene with *Mijnheer* van Jaarsveld—oh, I'm so sorry for that. It was so rude of him. But—" Her hands flew to her mouth as she giggled. "All that was because of Jan? My brother Jan?" She became so excited she couldn't sit still.

Margot had to give up her effort to remove the stain. She couldn't help but laugh with Rachel, though she didn't know why she was laughing. "I'm glad I was able to amuse you."

"Please forgive me," Rachel cried. She reached out and took Margot's hand. "You have to understand my brother. He's so stern and serious all the time. The thought of him being reprimanded at the governor's residence by a woman is priceless! Simply priceless!"

When she finally quieted down, she wiped the tears from her eyes and added, "Please excuse me, but you have to know my brother to appreciate this. He's a good man, but he never has any fun. I don't think he knows how."

Margot took one last swipe at the stain and threw up her hands. "Be that as it may, this spot is not coming out, and you have to get back to the reception. You've been gone too long already. And I still haven't told you about *Mijnheer* van Jaarsveld."

"Can you tell me later?"

"I'll probably catch the back of *Mevrouw* Hilda's hand for leaving the dining room in the first place."

The instant the words left her lips, she wished she hadn't said them.

A look of horror crossed Rachel's face. "You will be punished for wanting to help me?" she cried.

"It wouldn't be the first time," Margot quipped. "Let's get you back to the reception."

Rachel didn't move. "It was Jan," she said. "You were beaten for trying to talk to Jan, weren't you?"

"It wasn't his fault."

Rachel took Margot's hands in hers. "I'm so sorry," she said. There were tears in her eyes.

Such a sensitive soul, Margot thought.

Instantly the tears turned to fury. "Jan should have defended you!" she fumed. "Believe me, I'll have words with him."

"He didn't know I'd be punished!" Margot cried. "He didn't know!"

The sound of someone clearing her throat came from the door. "I hope I'm not interrupting anything." A large woman in a plain woolen frock filled the doorway. "Rachel, are you all right? Everyone is asking after you."

"Thank you, *Mevrouw* Vermaas. I'm fine. This wonderful lady was kind enough to help me." Rachel's sparkling eyes flashed a message of gratitude to Margot. "Thank you, once again," she said. Then, bending down close to Margot's ear, she whispered, "I'll stop by in the morning. We can talk more then."

Margot nodded and watched *Mevrouw* Vermaas escort Rachel back to the dinner party.

As he had the year before, Uys van Jaarsveld milked the party until it was dry. At nine o'clock a gun fired from Signal Hill, the nightly signal for all good citizens to retire and for the burgher watch to parade the streets. But whenever guests tried to excuse themselves, van Jaarsveld insisted they stay longer. If that didn't work, he observed loudly that he always found it so much easier to grant favors to colonists he considered good friends and that there was nothing he liked more than an evening with good friends. His veiled threat caused many to stay longer than they had intended. But by one o'clock in the morning even those guests who were most easily intimidated had had their fill of wine and music and van Jaarsveld's tactics. The dining room was empty, and the cleanup began.

Three hours later Margot fell into her bed, tired to the bone.

Mevrouw Hilda lifted her head from the pillow and berated her for being so late and for coming into the room so loudly—Margot was too tired to be upset at the barbs thrown at her.

She got little more than an hour of sleep before the beefy matron was bouncing her bed, rousing her for another day's work.

Midafternoon the next day, the governor strolled down the hallway with Rachel van der Kemp hanging happily on his arm.

Margot was on her knees scrubbing the floor with a brush when the governor spoke to *Mevrouw* Hilda.

"This dear young lady—" the governor patted Rachel's hand "—would like a word with one of your workers, *Mevrouw* Hilda."

"Is anything wrong?" The matron looked worried.

"On the contrary," the governor replied. "It seems that one of your girls came to Rachel's aid last night during a very unfortunate mishap. *Mejuffrouw* van der Kemp merely wishes to convey her personal thanks."

"That's her! Over there!" Rachel broke free from the governor and stood over Margot. "Thank you so much!" she gushed. "I'm ever so grateful!"

Mevrouw Hilda's expression turned sour at Rachel's display of gratitude. Indeed, the governor's face was one of mixed emotions when he recognized Margot as the servant who had stood before him and van Jaarsveld the night before.

Rachel spun around. She addressed the governor. "Would it be too imposing if I were to request some time alone with *Mejuffrouw* de Campion? It would mean so much to me!"

If the governor had any reservations about Margot's influence on the girl, he pushed them aside in the face of Rachel's captivating smile. "It's not imposing at all," he said. "Is it, *Mevrouw* Hilda?" He didn't wait for an answer. Speaking to Rachel, he said, "But I'm afraid you'll have to excuse me, dear. I have a meeting in my office in ten minutes. Why don't you ladies take a stroll through the Company garden while you talk? My wife informed me just this morning that the Blushing Brides are in bloom!" The governor hurried out of the room.

Rachel extended a hand to Margot, and the two of them followed in his wake. Margot was certain Mevrouw Hilda glowered at their backs until they were out of sight.

Seated on a stone bench in the Company garden, Margot leaned her head back and let the sun bathe her face. She inhaled deeply. "I've been cooped up in that place for too long. I'd nearly forgotten how wonderful this land is."

Rachel sat next to her. She appeared to enjoy the female companionship even more than the peacefulness of the garden.

The two women were comfortable with each other—it was as though Margot had known Rachel for years. She had pondered this feeling of instant familiarity on the walk from the Castle to the garden. She figured that van Jaarsveld had something to do with it, based on the fact that people who endured a common disaster were often drawn together.

"How did you get promised to *Mijnheer* van Jaarsveld?" Margot asked.

"My father arranged it."

"To improve relationships with the Company?"

Rachel looked shocked. "No! Father would never do that to me. Where did you get such an idea?"

Margot shrugged. "From *Mijnheer* van Jaarsveld. Where else?"

Rachel shook her head. "That's not the way it is." She hesitated, picked at a fingernail, then said, "My father didn't tell me this directly—he doesn't discuss things with me like he does with Jan and Breyton—" her head popped up; her eyes were bright "—but he loves me. My father loves me very much, of that I have no doubt." Returning to her fingernail, she continued, "But according to my brother—"

"Jan?"

Rachel nodded. "Yes, Jan. He told me Father arranged the marriage with *Mijnheer* van Jaarsveld for two reasons. First, he thinks by marrying into a wealthy family, I will always be cared for. And second, he feels I'll be safer in Amsterdam—his grandchildren too, when they come."

"And your mother. How does she feel?"

"My mother's dead."

"Forgive me. I didn't know. I should have guessed that, since it was just you and your brothers at the dinner last night."

"Mother was killed in a raid. A Bushman's arrow. I think that's why Father wants to send me to Amsterdam. He thinks that by doing so he is protecting me from a similar fate. More than once I've heard him say that, as more and more settlers come to the colony, the raids by the Bushmen and Hottentots will increase."

"So instead he's going to deliver you into the clutches of *Mijnheer* van Jaarsveld?"

"What do you mean?"

"What do you know about Uys van Jaarsveld?"

Rachel shrugged. "That he's an important Company official. And that he says he loves me and wants to marry me."

Margot narrated her experience with van Jaarsveld, including his ploy about a girl waiting for him in Amsterdam and the lie about a separate cabin for Margot. She also told Rachel what she had read in van Jaarsveld's journal—his description of Rachel and his purported intentions for her. She mentioned the captain's threat should van Jaarsveld try to get even with Margot in Cape Town.

Thinking about it later, she was amazed at how easily the part about her ability to read had come out. She had always kept that a closely guarded secret, yet somehow she felt no threat in telling Rachel.

"You read all that yourself in his journal?" Rachel's face was flushed. "Once we got to Amsterdam—"

Margot finished her sentence. "He would have abandoned you."

Rachel turned pasty white.

Margot put an arm around the girl's shoulder.

"What am I going to do?" Rachel whimpered.

"Tell your father!" Margot insisted. "Tell him Uys van Jaarsveld is a lecherous wretch!"

Rachel appeared to envision her father's reaction. Her eyes darted to and fro. Then a transformation took place. She sat up straight. Her eyes donned a look of resolve. A hint of a smile punctuated the corners of her mouth with dimples. The change was dramatic, like the sun emerging from behind a dark cloud. And Margot had a pretty good idea what the girl was thinking.

"When are you going to tell your father about Matthew?" she asked.

Rachel's eyes popped wide. "How do you know? Of course! You saw us last night!"

Margot nodded. "Do you love him?"

A smile and glassy eyes were Rachel's answer. "And he loves

me," she added quickly. "But I can't tell Father about him. It's hopeless. He would never permit me to marry Matthew."

"Why not?"

"What do you mean, why not? You saw him, didn't you? Matthew is of mixed blood! His father is Dutch, but his mother was a Malaysian slave. My father would never agree to such a marriage!"

Margot felt foolish for not realizing this earlier. The Dutch Calvinists of Cape Town colony saw themselves as the covenant people of God. God's part of the covenant was to lead the people to a promised land, in this case South Africa. In return, the people promised to keep God's commandments, the same ones He gave to the people of Israel. Among these instructions was a warning against mixed marriages with 'the people of the land,' as in Deuteronomy 7:3–4: "Neither shalt thou make marriages with them; thy daughter thou shalt not give unto his son, nor his daughter shalt thou take unto thy son. For they will turn away thy son from following me, that they may serve other gods: so will the anger of the Lord be kindled against you, and destroy thee suddenly."

"At least," Rachel said softly, "when father learns of *Mijnheer* van Jaarsveld's true character, I won't be going to Amsterdam."

"We can be thankful for that."

"And who knows? I'll still be here. Matthew will be here. Maybe God will work a miracle, and we'll be able to get married. He's done greater miracles than this before!" Rachel beamed.

Margot did not share the girl's optimism. What was to keep Rachel's father from arranging a marriage to another Amsterdam man? Simply removing Uys van Jaarsveld from the picture didn't address her father's twin concerns.

However, Margot said nothing as the two of them strolled back to the Castle. The air was fresh, the sunshine warm, and Rachel was giddy. The combination of all these things gave Margot's spirits a needed boost.

But as the towering Castle walls loomed increasingly higher with their approach, so too loomed the oppressive presence of *Mevrouw* Hilda.

11

Two weeks had passed since Uys van Jaarsveld's marathon reception, and *Mevrouw* Hilda showed no signs of easing up on Margot. Day after day, from room to room, Margot was the woman's hands and arms and legs and knees. Each task was completed with the stern taskmaster looming over her, spewing an endless string of criticisms. Nothing she did was right. She was too slow. Too careless. Too lazy.

The overbearing *Mevrouw* Hilda delighted in quoting proverbs from the Bible to her girls while they worked. Unfortunately for them, the only proverbs she knew were regarding sloth. In the matron's hands each proverb became a club with which she bludgeoned the girl closest to her, in this case Margot.

"'As vinegar to the teeth, and as smoke to the eyes, so is the sluggard to them that send him,'" she shouted when Margot took a second to stretch her aching back. Another time, "'He also that is slothful in his work is brother to him that is a great waster.'" And, "'Slothfulness casteth into a deep sleep; and an idle soul shall suffer hunger.'"

There was no escaping the woman. Save for the times when *Mevrouw* Hilda left to check another girl's work, Margot was with the bombastic matron every waking hour. Her entire existence consisted of polishing floors and silver and furniture, scrubbing, dusting, wiping, and washing. The only time she saw outside the governor's residence was when she washed the windows.

After a full week of this routine, Margot had awakened one morning in a black mood. For days it dogged her every waking moment. No matter how hard she tried, she couldn't shake free. She found herself weeping for no immediate reason. There was no longer any rest in her sleep. Her only respite came in daydreams of running away.

At first Margot thought she was hearing things. She stood atop a ladder. Steadying herself against the wall with one hand, she reached with a rag as far as she could across the top of a picture frame, wiping away a year's worth of accumulated dust.

"Why are you stopping?" *Mevrouw* Hilda barked. "Reach farther. The middle is right here." A plump finger jabbed in the direction of the middle of the frame. "Farther! Here! Farther!" she shouted.

Margot drew back. She cocked an ear. "I thought I heard something," she said.

"You don't have time to hear anything!" *Mevrouw* Hilda bellowed. "The only sound you should be listening to is my voice! Get back to work! Finish this frame! We have to scrub the hallway next."

"It sounded like someone crying." Wrinkling her brow, Margot strained to hear past *Mevrouw* Hilda's discord.

Mevrouw Hilda stomped her feet repeatedly on the hardwood floor, making it impossible for Margot to hear anything. She took a swipe at Margot's ankles. That was as high as she could reach. "If you don't get back to work, you'll be the one crying!"

Someone appeared in the doorway.

"Rachel!" Margot yelled.

Margot descended the ladder, ignoring the protests of *Mevrouw* Hilda. By the time she reached the girl, Rachel was slumped against the doorjamb. Her hair was windblown, her eyes red, and her cheeks were stained with tear tracks.

"Rachel, what has happened?" With one hand Margot held Rachel up, with the other she brushed back stray strands of hair from the girl's face.

Mevrouw Hilda closed in on them, her hands on her hips, but said nothing. Rachel let loose a fresh burst of sobs. "Oh, Margot! Can . . . we . . . talk?"

"No!" *Mevrouw* Hilda cried. "Margot has work to do."

Turning red eyes to the matron, Rachel pleaded with her. "Please, *Mevrouw* Hilda. I must talk with Margot!"

The word *no* was on *Mevrouw* Hilda's lips. Surprisingly, she pulled it back. Margot never knew for sure, but she thought the matron might have remembered the way the governor had treated Rachel the last time Margot's presence was requested. Whatever the reason, *Mevrouw* Hilda granted Rachel's request.

"I have other girls to check on," she said. "Use this room."

"Thank you, *Mevrouw* Hilda," Rachel said weakly.

But the beefy matron was already out the door and clomping down the hallway. Margot helped Rachel to a couch. Producing a handkerchief, she wiped the girl's eyes and cheeks. "Rachel, what's this all about?"

The question itself prompted another storm of tears. But somehow, in the midst of all the wailing, Rachel managed to say, "Father insists I marry *Mijnheer* van Jaarsveld!"

Margot wasn't sure she'd heard correctly. "You told him about what *Mijnheer* van Jaarsveld tried to do to me?"

Rachel sobbed and nodded.

"And still he insists you marry him?"

"Yes!" Rachel's face was drenched with tears. "At first he wouldn't even listen to me, saying he refused to be party to chambermaid gossip. And when I finally managed to get him to listen, he claimed you were probably trying to get even with *Mijnheer* van Jaarsveld for dismissing you. He said he would be foolish to take the word of a chambermaid over that of a commissioner."

Margot put an arm around her and pulled her close. "I'm so sorry, dear," she murmured. "I'm so sorry." As much as Margot detested this development, she understood the reaction of Rachel's father. Not everyone knew Uys van Jaarsveld as she knew him. To most people he was a respected commissioner of the Company. And Margot was indeed a chambermaid. It wasn't surprising that *Mijnheer* van der Kemp would give him the benefit of the doubt.

"Somehow word of this got back to *Mijnheer* van Jaarsveld," Rachel said. She was gaining better control of herself now that the story was coming out. "Yesterday he rode out to Klaarstroom. He told my father he'd been informed that a malicious rumor was being spread about him, so he came at the earliest opportunity to refute it."

Rachel pulled away and looked at Margot in a most curious manner.

"What?" Margot asked.

"He was so sincere. So believable! I myself even began to think that maybe you were mistaken—that maybe you had exaggerated the incident."

Margot sat up straight. "Rachel, I assure you, with God as my witness—"

Rachel reached out and touched Margot's shoulder. "I know. I know. My father invited *Mijnheer* van Jaarsveld to stay for dinner. Afterward, just the two of us took a walk." Rachel's eyes brimmed once again with tears. "Oh, Margot—it was horrible! His hands were all over me! I couldn't get him to stop! He forced me onto the ground

—and if it wasn't for Old Knob walking by, I wouldn't have been able to stop him!"

"Old Knob?"

Rachel dabbed her eyes and nose. "A Hottentot who works for my family. His name is Knobkerrie, but everyone calls him Old Knob."

Margot nodded in understanding.

"What am I going to do?" Rachel cried.

Again Margot pulled her close. She stroked the younger woman's hair. "I don't know," she said softly. "If only Captain Danckaert were still here—" She sat up suddenly. "That's it! Captain Danckaert! He can confirm my story to your father when he gets back from India." Seeing Rachel's puzzled expression, Margot explained, "He's the captain of the *Eagle*."

"I still don't understand."

"That's the ship that's supposed to take you to Amsterdam. As soon as it anchors, I'll get Captain Danckaert to speak to your father and tell him."

"We're scheduled to sail for Amsterdam in three months aboard the *Pearl*. At least that's what *Mijnheer* van Jaarsveld told Father last night."

Before the Eagle *returns!* Margot thought. Van Jaarsveld had anticipated that Captain Danckaert could be trouble for him! The louse! He was cutting her off at every turn!

"There you are!"

A male voice resounded off the walls. Jan van der Kemp's shoulders filled the doorway. Margot had remembered the piercing blue eyes, but she'd forgotten how tall and muscular he was. The last time she'd seen him, he was seated behind a table of food. With just a few strides he covered the distance between them.

"I'm not going back!" Rachel cried. She snuggled closer against Margot's chest.

Margot responded by holding her tighter, daring the older brother to separate them.

The broad shoulders slumped. "Rachel! You have no choice—"

"Of course she has a choice!" Margot shouted angrily.

Jan ignored her. Speaking to Rachel, he said, "Father sent me to bring you home. I was supposed to ride out to the herd with Old Knob this morning, but when we discovered you were gone, Father told me to go after you instead."

"To round her up like a stray?" Margot cried.

The shoulders raised defensively. Jan's face reddened, his jaw clenched.

"Margot," Rachel said softly, "don't blame Jan, he's—"

"He's going to take you home so you can be handed over to a lecherous worm! That's what he's going to do!"

"Margot, you don't understand. Jan doesn't like *Mijnheer* van Jaarsveld either."

Margot stared in disbelief at the red-faced tower of manhood standing over her. To Rachel she said, "Then how can he stand by and do nothing while you are delivered to a man whose sole intent is to use you, then discard you?"

"Because that is Father's decision," Jan said. His voice was firm with conviction.

"But your father is wrong!" Margot cried.

Jan was unyielding. "Right or wrong, he is our father. Is that so hard to understand, *Mejuffrouw* de Campion? Or have they repealed the fifth commandment in Amsterdam—the one that says, 'Honor thy father and thy mother: that thy days may be long upon the land which the Lord thy God giveth thee.'"

The Bible reference caught Margot off guard. And the manner in which Jan spoke the words convinced her that the quotation was no mere argument. He believed the words—so much so that he would obey the commandment even though it went against his personal opinion. How was she to respond to this? She couldn't encourage Rachel to disobey her father, but neither was she willing to surrender the girl to van Jaarsveld.

"No, they haven't repealed the fifth commandment," she conceded softly. "But there has to be a way to prevent *Mijnheer* van Jaarsveld from having his way with Rachel."

"God will provide a way," Jan said. Again, the words were not spoken lightly; they were weighted with conviction. He reached out a hand to Rachel. "Come, let's go home."

Rachel looked from Margot to Jan. She lowered her eyes and began to rise.

"Wait!" Margot cried. "If your father knew *Mijnheer* van Jaarsveld's true character, would he still insist on the marriage?"

"Of course not!" Rachel said.

Jan squinted at Margot, unwilling to commit himself until he knew her intentions.

Margot continued. "So if *Mijnheer* van Jaarsveld's true character were to come to light for all to see—"

"Father would call off the wedding!" Rachel cried. Her sunlit hope was quickly overshadowed by clouds of doubt. "But how are we going to do that?"

How indeed? Van Jaarsveld was a master of appearances and charm. Then a thought popped into Margot's mind. His journal! Of course! But how to get it? They would have to steal it from his room. That didn't set right with her. Break a commandment to expose a wretch? Do wrong to expose wrong? No, Jan would never go for that, and neither could she.

Then it came to her. "'Therefore by their fruits ye shall know them,'" she said aloud.

There was a delay in Jan's reaction, but then he seemed to understand the direction Margot had taken. He smiled warmly.

Margot was pleased at his reaction, more so than she wanted to admit to herself.

"I'm not following you," Rachel said.

Margot explained. "We'll help *Mijnheer* van Jaarsveld reveal his true character by giving him exactly what he wants."

Rachel shook her head in confusion. But as Margot and Jan began to devise a specific plan, a light of approval flashed in Rachel's eyes.

To keep from being overheard, the three of them drew close together and spoke in whispers. To Margot's dismay, she discovered she was unprepared for the way Jan's closeness affected her. When he spoke, she found herself concentrating more on the way his lips formed the words than on what he was actually saying. She loved the way his eyes grew softer, resembling cool, pale blue ponds. His scent, like his complexion, was earthy; he was clearly a man who spent most of his life outdoors. While she was exploring the cleft in his chin, he suddenly turned to her.

"We'll need someone who knows the Castle grounds," he said. "That way we'll know if van Jaarsveld has taken the bait. Besides, I don't think we should leave anything to chance. Margot, can you get a servant or one of the other maids to help us?"

There was a prominent lapse between the question and Margot's answer. In truth, Margot was savoring the way he spoke her name.

Jan and Rachel looked at her expectantly.

Doing her best to gather her wits, Margot pretended to think. When a thought actually came to her, she first checked the doorway before speaking. It was clear. "No. Nobody I would trust. *Mevrouw* Hilda keeps us apart. I really don't know anyone that well."

146

"Matthew can do it!" Rachel cried, obviously happy to volunteer the boy.

Margot did her best to show no sign of recognizing the name. Not knowing whether Jan knew of Matthew's involvement with Rachel, she did not want to give anything away. But the look Jan gave his sister indicated some knowledge of the boy, and it wasn't favorable.

"But he's perfect! He's what we need!" Rachel insisted, tugging on her brother's arm.

Margot lost herself in the thought of what it must feel like to hold onto Jan's arm.

Reluctantly Jan agreed that Matthew could be part of the plan.

"We'll also need someone who can pen a message," Jan said. He added quickly, "A feminine hand."

"Margot can write!" Rachel cried.

It came out so quickly, Margot wasn't sure how to respond. Had it been wise to tell Rachel her secret?

"You can write, can't you?" Rachel asked. "I just assumed that since you can read, you can also write."

Hesitantly, Margot nodded. "Yes, I can write," she said warily.

Jan's blue eyes hardened. The friendliness was gone. His features were stone. "Then everything is set," he said coldly.

The brown-skinned Matthew Durbin did odd jobs for the governor's cook. Some days he worked. Some days he was turned away. He rarely got paid. Most often, he was able to take uneaten food home. On the night of van Jaarsveld's reception, the food that was left over was more than he could carry.

Jan and Rachel van der Kemp found him in the governor's kitchen. Matthew was eager to help Rachel and her brother with their plan, though he felt uneasy about the way Jan van der Kemp kept staring at him. He was told to be outside the commissioner's door shortly before 11:00 P.M. He was also told exactly what to say and do.

Their business concluded, the van der Kemps left. But Rachel cast one look back at him and flashed a loving smile, which set Matthew's heart on fire.

When *Mevrouw* Hilda returned and saw Jan sitting with Rachel and Margot, the matron had bowed slightly to him and left them alone. However, once Jan and Rachel left, Margot was once again at *Mevrouw* Hilda's mercy.

The domineering overseer kept her working late to make up for the time wasted talking to the van der Kemps. As it grew later and later, Margot was beginning to think their plan would die a stillborn death. It wouldn't have a chance to succeed if she was unable to pen the note and place it under van Jaarsveld's door.

Their plan was saved when one of the other maids came running to get *Mevrouw* Hilda. Apparently a worker had slipped on a wet floor and hit her head on a bucket, sustaining a gash on her forehead.

Before leaving to attend to the girl, *Mevrouw* Hilda ordered Margot to finish her work and retire for the night—which is exactly what Margot did after she pulled a sheet of paper from a desk drawer, penned the note to van Jaarsveld using the words the three of them had agreed upon, and slipped the message under the commissioner's door.

There was no way for her to know if he'd read it. She would just have to wait in the darkness. Of one thing she was sure. If he read the note, she would know about it in time. Everybody would know about it.

That night Margot lay on her bed, exhausted from the day's events. But a racing pulse kept any notion of slumber at a distance. From the opposite end of the room the sound of deep snoring told her that *Mevrouw* Hilda was asleep. She also heard an occasional moan or rustle of covers as the other girls slept. Margot turned her head and looked at the window shutters. They were outlined in white moonlight. A full moon, or close to it. Good. If all went as planned, a full moon would be helpful.

Margot tossed one direction, then another, entangling her foot in the covers. She tried to kick it free. It was caught. Reaching down, she freed the foot and pulled it loose. After rearranging the covers, she let out a sigh and wondered what time it was.

She wondered if van Jaarsveld had read the note. Or if he'd even been to his room since she'd slipped it under his door. She shook her head when she thought of how she almost didn't get it there in the first place.

Uys van Jaarsveld read the note in his hand:

Tonight. 11:00 P.M.

My room. A courtyard servant will guide you. I've not been able to stop thinking about you since the reception.

You don't know how long I've longed for this moment.

He'd found the folded note on the floor upon returning to his room. He read it again, this time with a wolfish grin. Absentmindedly he raised a hand and smoothed his long blond hair as he attempted to determine which of the many lovely ladies at his reception had penned the message.

"What time is it?" Rachel asked.

"Nearly eleven o'clock."

His arms folded, his forehead close to the windowpane, Jan was staring into the courtyard. The moonlight through the window softened his sharp features.

"Thank you for doing this for me," Rachel said softly.

A hint of a smile appeared on Jan's lips. "That's what families are for," he said, focusing his attention on the courtyard.

After securing lodgings for the evening for his sister and himself in the governor's residence, Jan had dispatched a messenger to Klaarstroom informing his father that he'd found Rachel and that they would be returning the next day.

"Do you think anything will happen?" she asked, looking across the courtyard. All was calm.

"If it does, it should be soon," Jan replied. He glanced at his sister, amazed that she had become such a lovely young woman in such a short period of time. He wished their mother were alive to see her. He was sure she'd be proud. Rachel caught him looking at her. "What?" she asked.

Jan turned his attention again to the courtyard. "Nothing," he said.

"Do you like Margot?" she asked.

His brow furrowed. He grunted something unintelligible.

"I like her," Rachel said. "I admire her for doing this for us. She doesn't have to, you know. She's not family."

Jan continued staring into the courtyard in silence.

"And the fact that she can read and write! It makes you wonder why a good Christian woman like her hasn't already been snatched up by some fine gentleman."

Rachel studied her brother's face. "I think she's attracted to you. I've seen the way she looks at you."

Jan sniffed. "I wonder what's keeping van Jaarsveld?" he said.

"What? Are you sure?"

Van Jaarsveld frowned as he stood in his doorway. He'd discov-

149

ered Matthew Durbin waiting outside his door shortly before eleven o'clock.

"Those were my instructions, *Mijnheer*," Matthew said.

Leaning close, van Jaarsveld whispered, "Who is your mistress? Come on, boy, you can tell me."

Matthew jumped, evidently with fright, his eyes wide and looking close to tears. "I'd be beat near to death if I were to tell you that!" he cried.

Van Jaarsveld studied the boy's reaction. It was a convincing performance, and he said, "Only my nightshirt?"

Matthew nodded. "That's what she said to me. Be sure to tell *Mijnheer* van Jaarsveld to wear only his nightshirt."

The commissioner ran his tongue over his lips. There was something perverse about parading around the governor's grounds clad only in a nightshirt on the way to a secret rendezvous. It appealed to him. Moments later he appeared again—dressed only in a nightshirt, bony white legs protruding from beneath.

"This way, *Mijnheer*," the boy said.

Matthew led the scantily clad commissioner the length of the back of the governor's mansion. Van Jaarsveld uttered several curses along the way as he stepped on an occasional sharp rock in his bare feet. Near the well, they rounded the corner of the building. The courtyard came into view.

"I'm not marching out into the middle of the courtyard in my nightshirt!" the commissioner whispered.

"It's just around the corner!" Matthew Durbin whispered back. "The second window. You'll be inside before anyone has a chance to spot you!"

Van Jaarsveld hesitated. Upon reflection, the added danger heightened his anticipated pleasure. He nodded. "Lead on!"

The shutters creaked as first one opened, then the other. Margot's head snapped in the direction of the sound. Her heart pounded in her chest as moonlight filled the windows. Van Jaarsveld had taken the bait. He was coming!

She watched as he pushed open the windows she had unlatched earlier. The figure in the moonlight paused and turned around.

Was he wise to them? She held her breath.

"It's dark in there," she heard him whisper. "Are you sure this is the right room?"

"Yes, *Mijnheer*," came the reply.

Margot recognized Matthew's voice from his encounter with Rachel.

The figure in the moonlight lifted a leg over the sill. Backlit by the moon, the familiar form of van Jaarsveld, with sloping shoulders and a slightly bulging midriff, filled the window. Behind him, Matthew darted away. His work was done.

Margot held her breath and waited as van Jaarsveld negotiated the step into the dark room. Once he was inside, it was her part of the plan to scream and wake everyone up.

"'Tis me, my dear," van Jaarsveld whispered into the darkness. His hand was groping like that of a blind man. "Speak, my dear, and I will come to you."

Margot took a deep breath.

But the commissioner stumbled before she could scream. Off balance, he teetered past a bed, his arms flailing, grabbing at anything. His hand found something and latched onto it. The exposed foot of *Mevrouw* Hilda, sticking out from under her covers.

The stout woman bolted upright. Her scream was deep and throaty. *"Aughhh!"*

The next instant bodies sprang up everywhere like souls in a graveyard on resurrection day. Everyone was screaming, including van Jaarsveld. Chaos reigned.

In the midst of the pandemonium, a large figure arose and took charge. *Mevrouw* Hilda. Somewhere she found a broom and was using it to exorcise the male demon from the room. The broom swooped high and swished down with mighty force, again and again.

Van Jaarsveld scrambled on the floor among the legs of the frightened girls like a cornered animal looking for a place to hide. Just as he got to his knees, another blow would knock him down. At last he managed to launch himself toward the window. For a moment he teetered half in, half out. With a wicked blow to his backside, *Mevrouw* Hilda helped him on his way. He crashed to the ground beneath the window of the maids' sleeping quarters.

At this point, the plan was to have Jan van der Kemp, aroused by the commotion, capture the lecherous van Jaarsveld outside the window. However, the plan took on a life of its own. And the person breathing life into the plan was *Mevrouw* Hilda.

Not satisfied that the intruder was outside, the matron went after him through the window. Leaning halfway out, she continued to pummel him with the broom, all the while screaming as though she were the one receiving the blows. When her target scooted beyond her reach, she continued after him by maneuvering her large self through the window.

Margot and the other girls took the easier route down the hallway and out the door into the courtyard.

The first thing Margot saw after clearing the door was a bewildered Jan van der Kemp stepping out of the way of the shrieking commissioner. Right behind van Jaarsveld was an equally loud *Mevrouw* Hilda, landing one blow after another on his head.

By now the whole courtyard was aroused. People came from every direction. Almost every window in the governor's residence held a candle and at least one inquisitive face pressed against the glass. A parade of people fell in line behind van Jaarsveld and *Mevrouw* Hilda, including the governor and his wife. Margot caught up with Jan and Rachel. The three of them exchanged shrugs and joined the parade.

They overtook the intruder and his pursuer at the fountain. Dancing round and round in the water, van Jaarsveld kept the center of the fountain between him and *Mevrouw* Hilda, who was also splashing about. It took Governor Chavonnes several minutes to restore order.

Then the story of Uys van Jaarsveld's late night foray came out.

Surrounded by a cloud of witnesses, *Mevrouw* Hilda described, with several threatening shakes of the broom in the commissioner's direction, how she was awakened by a crazed maniac intent on taking advantage of her.

All eyes turned to van Jaarsveld, who stood stoop-shouldered in knee-deep water in his nightshirt. After a couple of fumbling starts, he seemed to realize there was no defense for a man in his nightshirt climbing into a room full of young ladies. So he gave up and offered none.

The governor was incensed. He promised a full report to the Lords XVII and ordered the commissioner to return to Amsterdam on the first available ship.

However, the crowning blow came after the crowd began to disburse. Van Jaarsveld waited cautiously in the fountain until *Mevrouw* Hilda was a good distance away. Just as he was about to step out, a young redheaded woman approached him. Unsuccessfully trying to keep her voice low, she lambasted the drenched commissioner. As it turned out, he had canceled a rendezvous with her that evening for a more mysterious meeting with the unknown writer of the note that was slipped under his door. In her fury, the redhead gave him a final shove before walking away.

Van Jaarsveld lost his balance and splashed backward into the fountain.

The van der Kemps and Margot watched as he picked himself up. He saw them, started to say something, then thought better of it. Shaking his head, a dripping Uys van Jaarsveld walked across the open courtyard toward his room.

"I almost feel sorry for him," Rachel said.

Margot and Jan exchanged glances. Moonlight reflected in their eyes. They held their gaze much longer than a casual glance.

12

For reasons that were not explained to Margot, she was once again assigned work that was not under the direct supervision of *Mevrouw* Hilda. Possibly another girl had done something to warrant the matron's caustic attention; or possibly in the matron's judgment Margot had atoned for her indiscretion. Whatever the reason, Margot was relieved that she no longer had to work under the daily scrutiny of the proverb-quoting overseer.

Within minutes of being left alone, Margot realized how greatly she had been affected by *Mevrouw* Hilda's oppressive presence. Reveling in her regained freedom, she hummed; she quoted Bible verses—from books of the Bible other than Proverbs; she dwelt on memories of peaceful evenings with Sylvie; and she daydreamed of Jan van der Kemp, though she refused to think of that in terms of dreaming about him.

Margot preferred to characterize her daily thoughts of Jan in terms of concern for Rachel—how Rachel was fortunate to have a loving brother like Jan, now that her mother was dead; how Rachel was fortunate to know her brother was always nearby if she needed him; and how Rachel was fortunate to have a brother like Jan with such strong features and broad shoulders and blue eyes.

Being left alone also meant that Margot was again given opportunity to let her wandering gaze fall upon official papers that were left uncovered on the officials' desks. The documents for the most part defined and reinforced the myriad strict regulations the Dutch East India Company used to control the lives of the Cape Town colonists.

It became clear to Margot that all power in the colony resided in the governor, who, of course, was subject to the instructions of the Lords XVII in Amsterdam. A Council of Policy, composed of seven officials, assisted the governor in making local regulations. These regulations were numerous and affected nearly every aspect of business and life, down to the hours during which bakers could deliver bread.

Even private social concerns were regulated, such as whether or not a lady might wear a train or have silk and satin dresses; which ladies were allowed to use an umbrella or sunshade; how much money might be spent on a funeral or a bridal bed; how many servants people of different rank might employ; and whether a coachman might wear livery.

These heavy-handed rules reminded Margot of life aboard ship, where the captain's word was law—well, at least that's the way it was supposed to be aboard a ship unless the captain had a soft spot in his heart for someone, in which case that someone would be able to get him to do things he wouldn't normally do.

Margot smiled at the remembrance of Captain Danckaert. She missed his bulldog face and the way he had scowled at her and said, "You're not going to make trouble for me the entire journey, are you?"

Thoughts of life aboard the *Eagle* also brought to mind the King's Nieces. Margot wondered how each of the young ladies was faring. Since their arrival in the colony, she'd not heard from or seen any of them. Was Katje still happy now that she finally had a man? She thought of Marie and Anna and Clara and Aletta—Margot wished she could thank Aletta for staying with her when she was ill after all the others had gone.

Memories filled Margot's heart with a longing that weighed heavily on her. She walked over to a chair and fell into it. Her arms hung limp at her sides. She rested her head back against the wall.

It was ironic. Cooped up in the governor's residence the way she was, she might as well be on board a ship. Rarely was she allowed to wander outside. She had no contact with the rest of the colony. She never got to stand in the sun or gaze at the sky.

Who knew how many times God had draped Table Mountain with a cloud cloth since she'd been here? There was no way for her to know. She was cut off from the world. From the colony. From her friends aboard ship. From Rachel and Jan van der Kemp. It was as though she were adrift at sea in the governor's residence and *Mevrouw* Hilda was the captain and sole crew mate.

Margot closed her eyes. "Lord," she prayed, "if it be Your will, allow me to get outside occasionally, to interact with people." She didn't mention any names, but the image of Jan van der Kemp came to mind while she was praying.

The sound of heavy heels echoed up the hallway. It was either a good-sized man or *Mevrouw* Hilda coming to check her work. Margot jumped to her feet and rubbed furiously at the stinkwood chair upon which she'd been sitting.

The unsmiling man with a block chin held the door open for her. Margot walked in. The governor was standing tall behind his desk.

To her surprise, seated in a row of chairs on the far side of the room were Katje and Aletta. The two women were separated by two men. Both men sat with arms folded; their faces were stern, their eyes hard. It disturbed Margot that neither of the girls looked up when she entered.

The footfalls Margot had heard coming down the hallway in the governor's residence had belonged to the man holding open the door for her now. He had identified himself as *Mijnheer* Daniel Krog, an official of the Council of Policy. After verifying that he was indeed speaking to Margot de Campion, he instructed her to follow him to the governor's office.

Krog wouldn't tell her the nature of her appearance before the governor—only that her presence was requested immediately. When Margot voiced her concern that *Mevrouw* Hilda be informed of her whereabouts, Krog snapped something to the effect that the governor was more important than *Mevrouw* Hilda.

Now, without extending any pleasantries, the governor motioned Margot to stand before him. As she made her way to the spot he indicated with a rigid finger, she cast another glance at the girls.

Katje raised her head slightly. Red, sorrow-filled eyes met hers, then quickly lowered.

"Mejuffrouw de Campion?"

"Yes?"

"Seated over there is Danie Lelyveld and Klaas Starrenburg, both of Stellenbosch. I believe you already know their wives."

The men remained seated. They glared at Margot when she looked at them. Neither of the women looked up.

"Yes, I know Katje and Aletta. We sailed together aboard the *Eagle* from Amsterdam," Margot replied.

Hearing Margot say her name, Katje began to weep. Her husband leaned toward her and told her to shut up.

"And you shared quarters with these women?" the governor continued.

"Yes, we shared quarters."

"And during that time what did you talk about?"

Margot smiled. "It was a long trip, *Mijnheer* Governor. We talked of many things."

Council member Krog slapped Margot with an open palm. "For your insolence!"

The sound of the slap echoed across the hardwood floors. Katje jumped and whimpered.

Margot touched her cheek. It was warm from the blow. There was the taste of blood in her mouth.

"If the governor would be more specific," she said, "I will be glad to answer his question."

Another slap. Another echo. The first blow had stung and made her angry; the second brought tears to her eyes. Margot rubbed her cheek and worked her jaw.

The governor rapped his knuckles on the table impatiently. "Did you or did you not instruct these women to be disobedient and disrespectful to their husbands?"

Margot looked over at the men and Katje and Aletta. Their positions had not changed. The men glared. The women kept their heads down. Aletta's lips moved, but no sound came from them. Was she praying?

"No! I told them Bible stories!" Margot answered.

"Bible stories?"

"The story of Abigail and Nabal for one."

"That's it! That's the name!" Lelyveld was on his feet, pointing a plump, accusing finger at Margot. "Nabal! It means fool! Katje told me so. This woman taught my Katje that all men are fools!"

Katje raised her head. "That's not what I said!" she cried. "I said you were as hardheaded as Nabal."

The governor raised his hand as an indication for Lelyveld to calm down.

From behind her husband, Katje mouthed silent words to Margot. "I'm sorry!"

Starrenburg didn't want to let the matter rest. He jumped up. "That's not the only story this woman told those girls on the ship!" he shouted. "She taught them that when men are scared it's up to the women to step forward and take the lead!"

"The story of Deborah," Margot said quietly.

"And that when women have more money than men," Starrenburg continued, "the women are supposed to be sympathetic and help the men out by giving them some of it."

"Women with more money than men?" Lelyveld looked puzzled. Apparently he'd not heard that one from Katje.

Margot herself was having trouble matching his description with the appropriate Bible story.

For the first time, Aletta looked up. "Lydia and the apostle Paul," she said.

Margot noticed a bruise on the side of the young woman's face.

157

"Mijnheer Governor," Margot said, "there is nothing wrong with these stories. They're Bible stories!"

Her plea earned her another slap. "Speak only when spoken to!" Krog ordered.

Starrenburg shook his head. "They're not like any Bible stories I ever heard!"

Lelyveld jabbed a finger repeatedly at Margot. "The fact is, this woman has ruined our wives! My own wife called me a fool!"

This time the governor held up both hands. "I've heard enough!"

Lelyveld opened his mouth to say something else.

"Enough!" the governor roared.

The room fell silent. Lelyveld and Starrenburg remained standing.

The governor addressed Margot. "These may be Bible stories," he said, "but why these stories and not others, such as Paul's instruction 'Wives, submit yourselves unto your own husbands, as unto the Lord'? I fear you were meddling in things you did not understand, and in doing so you have done a grievous harm to these women and their husbands."

Margot bit her lower lip. She wanted to defend herself, but she knew that speaking out would only earn her another slap to the face. Even so, given an hour and a fair hearing, she doubted that she would be able to change the governor's mind.

To the men the governor said, "I will submit this woman for discipline to *Mevrouw* Hilda under whose supervision she now resides. You can be assured that she will have no further opportunities to corrupt other impressionable minds. As for your wives, the damage is done. Their correction and discipline is up to you. I don't know what else I can do."

The very thought of another beating by *Mevrouw* Hilda caused Margot's hands to shake. But even worse than the impending physical thrashing was seeing Katje and Aletta herded out of the room like stray cattle. Aletta walked past Margot and wouldn't look at her. Katje shot a quick glance at Margot, and it nearly broke Margot's heart. The small woman who had been so bright and happy, so much looking forward to marriage, looked at her with eyes brimming with fear.

Krog escorted Margot back to the room she'd been cleaning before she was summoned to the governor's office.

Margot tried to continue her work, knowing that it would go even worse for her if the work wasn't completed when *Mevrouw* Hilda returned.

But she couldn't stop thinking about Katje and Aletta. She had meant good for them, but it had turned to evil. Was she wrong in sharing her knowledge with the girls aboard the *Eagle?* Every time she thought of the look in Katje's eyes and Aletta's refusal even to look at her, it brought tears to her eyes.

Then there was the impending punishment at the hands of *Mevrouw* Hilda. She knew it would be worse than her previous beating. The thought caused her hands to tremble again. Nothing she did could get them to stop. Every sound in the hallway made her jump. *Mevrouw* Hilda? But when the matron didn't appear, she felt no sense of relief. Her coming was inevitable. The beating was inevitable. Margot looked in disbelief at her shaking hands. *Calm yourself!* She walked to a window and looked out, thinking the blue sky or a glimpse of the mountain would bring peace to her heart. But it didn't. In fact, what she saw struck her heart like lightning. Her knees felt weak. She grabbed the sill to steady herself.

She watched in horror as Monsieur Fabarez marched determinedly across the Castle grounds toward the governor's house.

"Come in, *Mejuffrouw* de Campion."

The disgruntled expression on the governor's face was not lost on Margot. It had been only a matter of minutes from the time the governor had dismissed her until the box-chinned Krog issued his second summons to Margot that day. This time she knew what to expect.

A wrinkled and soiled Monsieur Fabarez stood in front of the governor's desk. "That's the witch!" he cried, the moment she walked in the door. To Margot he said, "Think I wouldn't come after you, did you?"

The sound of his voice, the very sight of him, caused a shiver to travel the length of Margot's spine.

"Do you know this man?" the governor asked.

"Yes, *Mijnheer* Governor," Margot replied.

"Is what he says of you true?"

"What does he say of me?"

Krog raised his hand to strike her.

The governor shook his head.

Krog's hand hovered midair, then lowered to his side.

"Are you a witch? Did you kill his wife?"

All of this was too much for Margot. Seeing Katje and Aletta. Krog's slaps. The threat of *Mevrouw* Hilda. The sudden appearing of

Monsieur Fabarez. And now a reminder of Sylvie's death and the night she fled her home. Margot began to weep.

Through her tears, she said, "No, *Mijnheer* Governor. It is not true. I loved Sylvie Fabarez. She was a mother to me after my mother died."

"Are you a witch?"

"No, *Mijnheer* Governor. I am not a witch."

"She's lying!" Fabarez was hysterical. He moved threateningly toward Margot.

Krog stepped between them, and Fabarez backed off.

"An incantation!" he screamed. "She did it with an incantation! Put it in a nutshell and tied it around me missus's neck!"

"A Scripture passage," Margot explained. "Sylvie was sick with fever."

"There was also words I never seen afore!" Fabarez cried.

Margot hesitated. "Latin," she said.

The governor's eyebrows raised. "Latin? And who wrote the Latin phrase you tied around this woman's neck?"

Margot looked at Fabarez.

Dirty black eyes squinted at her with hatred.

Krog raised his hand to strike. "The governor asked you a question!"

"I did," Margot answered softly.

"You did?" the governor asked.

Holding her head high, Margot repeated in a clear voice, "I wrote the Latin phrase."

Skeptical, the governor shoved paper and pen across his desk toward her. "Show me," he said.

Margot picked up the pen, leaned over, and wrote in Latin: "God give you strength, my beloved." She held the paper up to the governor, who read it. "Those were the words that were in the nutshell."

The governor was clearly surprised that one of his maids could write in Latin. Holding out the paper to Fabarez, he said, "Are these the words that you saw on the nutshell paper?"

Grimy hands took the paper, leaving smudge marks in the margins. Fabarez strained to bring the words into focus. "Could be. Maybe not. One incantation looks like every other to me."

"It's not an incantation," the governor said. "She has written: 'God give you strength, my beloved.'"

"But she don't know how to read and write!" Fabarez shouted.

The governor looked to Margot for a response.

"Sylvie taught me," Margot said.

"Aha!" Fabarez wadded up the paper and threw it to the floor in triumph. "Now she's caught herself in one of her own lies! Me missus didn't know how to read or write!"

Again the governor looked to Margot for a response.

Everything was coming out now. Margot could think of no reason to hold back. "Sylvie's mother taught her, and she taught me. It was a secret kept in fear of how the menfolk would react if they knew their wives could read."

"Latin too?" the governor asked.

"And French. Sylvie's mother also knew Greek, but she died before passing it along to her daughter."

"Witchcraft plain and simple!" Fabarez screamed. "On the night me missus died, I went to get the burgomaster. When we returned, the witch had vanished! Disappeared—or flown away!"

"I escaped out the window."

"Why did you run?" the governor asked.

"I was afraid of what Monsieur Fabarez would do to me."

"Test her by water!" Fabarez cried. "That will prove I'm telling the truth!"

The governor addressed Margot. "Do you have anyone to speak on your behalf?"

Her first thought was of Jan van der Kemp, but she dismissed the thought quickly. He barely knew her; how could he testify to her character? "There is someone," she said, "though he's not readily available. Captain Danckaert of the *Eagle*. He can testify to my good character upon his return."

The governor looked down at his desk in a way that made Margot's heart stop. It was the way people looked whenever they were about to deliver unpleasant news. "The *Eagle*," he said solemnly, "went down off the coast a few days after it sailed. All hands were lost, including Captain Danckaert. I'm sorry to have to inform you of this."

This was all too much for Margot. First Katje and Aletta; then Monsieur Fabarez; and now Captain Danckaert. She felt faint.

The governor ordered a chair.

Krog managed to place one behind Margot just as she was falling.

"It's a witch's trick!" Fabarez screamed, jumping backward as though she were about to transform herself into a fire-breathing dragon.

161

"Be silent, man!" the governor ordered.

For Margot, the colors of the room were fading in and out. She found it difficult to hold her head up. Her stomach felt queasy.

The governor said to Fabarez, "Who can you get to speak on your behalf?"

"Me cap'n, of course," Fabarez said.

"Fetch him."

"What? Bring him here?"

"Yes! Bring him here!"

Fabarez screwed up his face. "I don't know . . . he's a busy sort of man . . ."

"Bring him here!"

Fabarez jumped, then scurried toward the door. While he was half in and half out, he turned back to say, "I'll tell him the governor wants to see him!"

"Just get him and bring him here!" the governor repeated.

Nearly an hour passed before Fabarez returned with a reluctant captain in tow.

In the interval, Margot did her best to compose herself. Keeping her head down, she would weep silently, wipe her tears, upbraid herself for not being strong, and then weep some more. Meanwhile, the governor and Krog shuffled papers on the governor's desk, discussed some things aloud, and whispered other things so that Margot could not hear.

Fabarez's captain was a hairy man. Thick black hair covered his head, his chin, and his arms.

The governor recognized him as soon as he walked in. "Captain Vorster." The governor greeted him with a nod of his head.

"Governor." The captain returned the nod.

The governor summarized the previous discussion for the captain. When he mentioned Margot's ability to write Latin, the captain looked at her suspiciously. When he described Fabarez's claim that Margot was a witch, the captain looked at Fabarez. The best Margot could determine, it was a look of frustration.

"She's a witch!" Fabarez cried, looking at his captain but pointing at Margot.

"Silence!" the governor screamed. Then, in a civil voice, he said to the captain, "I've asked you here, Vorster, to answer two questions."

"Which are?" The captain spoke in deep, clipped sentences. The voice of authority. Margot sensed none of the underlying warmth that she had experienced with Captain Danckaert.

"Question one, are you aware of any proceedings against this woman in Amsterdam?"

Vorster scratched his beard. It looked as if he were chasing a flea. "What was your name again, *Mejuffrouw?*"

"Margot de Campion," Margot said softly.

"De Campion . . ." Vorster repeated. He shook his head. "Not to my knowledge, Governor."

"I told you, she never came to trial!" Fabarez shouted. "She flew out the window, or vanished, or turned herself into a mouse, or something else witchlike."

The governor slapped his desk hard. "I told you to be silent!" he shouted. Captain Vorster shook his head and rolled his eyes.

"Question two," the governor said, still glaring at Fabarez, "can you testify to this man's good character?"

The captain's heavy eyebrows plunged together to make a bushy V. He pointed at Fabarez. "His character?"

The governor nodded.

A booming laugh bounced around the room. "He has no character!" the captain cried. "He's a bug! A nuisance!"

The captain's response took everyone by surprise, even Fabarez.

"Nobody on my ship wants him in their cabin. Nobody wants him on their watch. And I can't blame them. He's a braggart and a dullard. For nearly five months we've watched him spout lies like a whale spouts water. Twice I had to threaten his crewmates lest they throw him overboard at night. Quite frankly, Governor, I've had my fill of him, and so has my crew. No, I will not vouch for the man's character."

"I see," said the governor. "And in the little time I have known the man, I concur."

Fabarez rushed to the front of the governor's desk. Leaning forward, he shouted, "This woman is a witch! A witch! If you don't destroy her, this whole colony will be swallowed up by the sea within a year's time!"

"*Mijnheer* Fabarez, get your hands off my desk!" the governor ordered, leaping up.

Fabarez began to hop back and forth from one foot to the other, screaming, "A witch! God help us all! She's a witch!"

Krog called the guards. Within seconds, Fabarez was surrounded.

"Take him out of here. Out of the Castle. And don't ever let him back in."

The dirty, smelly, screaming Fabarez was carried out of the room. He could be heard all the way down the hallway and into the courtyard until finally his voice faded into nothingness.

The captain looked at Margot, then back at the governor. "The decision regarding this one is yours," he said, "but if Fabarez were to accuse any of my men, I would give them the benefit of the doubt just because it was Fabarez doing the accusing. Good day, *Mijnheer* Governor."

The captain exited the room.

With a sigh, the governor fell into his chair. Looking across the desk at Margot, he said, "Two times I have had to deal with you today. In one respect, I agree with the captain—I do not believe Fabarez's charges against you. But on the other hand, you have exhibited a pattern of disruptive behavior. I cannot continue to waste my time on matters such as these."

To Krog he said, "Take her to the slave compound and assign her work there."

With that, he picked up his pen, and Margot was dismissed.

13

A scarred, half-used candle flickered beside her, casting grotesque shadows against a textured, whitewashed wall. Margot lay on a pungent straw mattress and moaned. Her eyes stung from weeping. Her cheeks were damp. She trembled uncontrollably.

She wanted to close her eyes. To forget where she was. What had happened to her. To escape. But closing her eyes brought it all back. *Mevrouw* Hilda's face. Red with rage. Dripping with sweat. Arms as thick as tree trunks. Hands flying. When she closed her eyes, Margot felt the blows all over again. The pain. The fear.

After Margot's second appearance before the governor, she was kept at his residence just long enough for *Mevrouw* Hilda to beat her. Then she and her trunk were loaded into a wagon and carted to the slave compound, where she was dumped into the tiny room in which she now found herself.

The room was barely larger than the bed. Rough planks supported a soiled straw mattress. The bed sat upon a dirt floor that was moist and cold; its odor was musty with the strong scent of urine. Dirt stains crept upward from where walls and floor met. Iron chains and shackles provided the room with macabre ornamentation. There were brown splatters high on the walls. Blood?

Beyond the confines of the room Margot could hear an unending chorus of moans and cries. The sounds of misery frightened her even more. As did her shivers. And the lingering pain. Even wiping away a tear was painful. To do so she had to raise an injured arm and brush a bruised cheek.

What have I done to deserve this? It isn't fair. I'm not a bad person, am I? She winced as her tongue explored the inside of her mouth and found two cuts in her cheek made by her own teeth from blows to the face.

Why is this happening to me? Why has God abandoned me?

She didn't know which was greater, her pain or her anger. The two emotions vied for supremacy. She wanted to give in to them, to let them consume her. She wanted to give in to the hurt, to feel sorry for herself because nobody else did. She wanted to give in to her anger because of the injustice. They had no right to treat her this way. No right. She had done nothing wrong.

Yet in one afternoon she had lost everything—her position, her good name, Katje, Aletta, Captain Danckaert. Although Rachel and Jan van der Kemp were still nearby, she knew she'd lost them too. They had standing in the colony. They would never come to see her now. Not at the slave compound.

So who else was there? No one. What did she have? Nothing.

Fresh tears rose to the surface and spilled out the corners of her eyes. It was the thought that she was all alone that hurt most. That no one cared.

"I might as well sit in the ashes of my life and scrape myself with potsherds and curse God."

The sound of her own words quickened an impending revelation. Where had she heard them before? Sylvie. Of course, Sylvie. From the Bible. Sylvie had read them to her. The story of Job, the man who lost everything he had in one day. His livelihood. His family. His health.

Just like me.

Margot swung her legs over the edge of the bed, careful not to gouge herself with slivers from the wooden bed frame. She searched her memory to recall the night she'd heard the story of Job.

Sylvie had been sitting in a chair reading to her; the Bible was open on her lap. It was a cold night, for they were drinking hot tea and Sylvie's feet rested on a foot warmer smoldering with peat. She remembered Sylvie's contrasting Job's discomfort with their comfort, wondering aloud if she lost everything, like Job, would she be able to maintain her faith.

Margot could hear Sylvie's voice clearly: "Put yourself in his place! Everything suddenly taken away. Friends insisting you must have done something wrong to deserve your fate. A spouse telling you to curse God and die. I wonder, if that was me, would I remain faithful?"

Margot remembered how Sylvie returned to the open Bible on her lap and cried out excitedly, "Listen to this!" Then she read Job's words: "'What? shall we receive good at the hand of God, and shall we not receive evil? In all this did not Job sin with his lips.'"

"An amazing man, this Job," she had said. "In all this, Job did not sin with his lips! Unbelievable!"

She had read more: "'Though he slay me, yet will I trust in him: but I will maintain mine own ways before him.'" It was at this point, Margot remembered, that Sylvie closed the Bible and her eyes. Then, as though she and God were the only ones in the room, she prayed, "Lord, give me the faith of this man Job."

Margot brushed a tear from her bruised cheek. It hurt, but she no longer cared. In the middle of her small, musty room she knelt on the cold, damp earthen floor. She closed her eyes, but this time the image of *Mevrouw* Hilda did not appear. Nor did she tremble, for Sylvie's God was there to give her strength.

"Lord, forgive me for my lack of faith," she prayed. "Give me the faith of Job and of my Sylvie. In all this, may I not sin with my lips. Help me to say with Job, 'Though You slay me, yet will I trust You.'"

Margot stood at the entrance of the slave compound, a rectangular, walled structure with no roof. In the center was an open fire and a well. A lean-to in one corner covered a wooden bench, a small table, and one chair—the slave compound's office.

The open area beyond the single iron gate was a thick brown sea of mud. It was crowded with slaves who had been rounded up by the Company: Malaysians from the Dutch East Indies and blacks from Madagascar. Some were newly arrived slaves, waiting to be placed; others were runaways, who would first be punished, then returned to their owners. Along the whitewashed walls were rows of chains and manacles, all of them occupied.

Margot's presence at the slave compound was the result of a debate she had never heard. The debate was between the colonists and the Company regarding the colony's shortage of laborers. Which was better to use—free European labor or slaves?

The governor's brother, Captain de Chavonnes, was the most ardent advocate of free European labor. He pointed out all the disadvantages of using slaves: the fact that it was uneconomical, that it encouraged plantations rather than intensive cultivation, and that it induced habits of sloth and inefficiency among the owners.

However, de Chavonnes was a minority voice crying in the wilderness. The Company directors voted to import more slaves. That meant more workers were needed to control the slaves until they were disbursed to the owners.

"You *Mejuffrouw* de Campion?" The voice behind her had the quality of a piece of wood scraping against dry ground.

167

Margot turned in the direction of the grating sound. It belonged to a large-bellied man, whose enormous white paunch protruded between his shirt and trousers. Unkempt black hair thinned on top, while the sides were full and bushy. His face showed several days' growth of beard; and his mustache, which wiggled side to side under a bulbous nose when he talked, looked like a bristle brush.

"I am Margot de Campion."

The man sniffed, ran a finger under his nose, and scratched his belly, all the while looking her up and down, his gaze occasionally stopping long enough to make Margot feel uncomfortable.

"You doing anything later tonight?" he asked.

Margot crossed her arms. "To whom am I speaking?"

"Your boss," the man said with a grin that showed missing teeth. "Name's Hennig."

"Well, *Mijnheer* Hennig, if you'll show me what I'm supposed to do, I'll start my chores."

Hennig rubbed his nose again, cleared his throat, and spat. "Grab a bucket and water the slaves. Find out which ones is sick. Then come and tell me."

Margot nodded. She moved to enter the compound.

Hennig called after her.

"Hey!"

"Yes?"

"What about tonight?"

"I'm afraid that won't be possible," Margot replied.

"Know what you mean," Hennig said. "I got a crowded social calendar too."

Carrying a large bucket of water and a ladle, Margot passed among the slaves, giving them drinks. The reaction she received was varied. Most of them thanked her, some several times and with words she couldn't understand. But she knew they were grateful; their eyes conveyed their gratitude. Others were afraid. They shrank back when she approached. No amount of coaxing could get them to accept the ladle when she extended it to them. Still others glared angrily at her; murderous eyes peered over the edge of the ladle as they drank. The general health of the slaves was wretched. Caked in mud, nearly all of them had runny eyes and noses. At no time in the compound was there more than a five-second break in the sound of coughing. Many bore wounds that needed attention. From their capture? And many were rubbed raw by their chains. Most of the wounds were infected.

By the time Margot had circled the compound, the edge of her skirt was heavy with mud. It felt as though the ground were reaching up and trying to drag her down.

She found Hennig seated on the wooden chair behind his desk, his bulk falling over both sides. He was carrying on with three guards seated on the bench. When he saw her approaching, he pointed her out to the guards and raised his eyebrows suggestively.

"How many are dead?" he asked her.

"Dead?"

"Yeah. Not living."

The guards laughed.

"There are none dead that I saw," Margot said. "But there is a lot of sickness."

Hennig cursed and spat in the mud. "We got some kind of epidemic or something?"

"Nothing like that. General health concerns. And many of them are chafing on their ankles and wrists from the manacles."

"I thought you said we had sick ones!" Hennig boomed.

"That's what I'm telling—"

"How many will die afore mornin' if they're not treated?"

Margot hesitated. "None—at least I don't think so."

"Then we got no sick today! Why didn't you say so in the first place?" He pulled a muddy sheet of paper from a little drawer in the desk and laboriously made a large zero at the bottom of a column of numbers. He crammed the paper back into the drawer and slammed it shut.

"Now what am I supposed to do?" Margot asked.

Hennig looked at her as if she were crazy. Then a leering grin appeared. He winked at the soldiers. "I'm sure I can think of something," he said with a rakish chuckle.

"What *work* do you want me to perform?" Margot clarified.

"Nothing for you to do until midday, when we feed 'em," Hennig said. He waved casually at the compound. "You can tidy up or do whatever it is women do."

The guards laughed. That pleased him.

Ignoring them, Margot rummaged around the corner of the lean-to until she found some cloth. She tore the material into strips. Then she filled a bucket with water and worked from slave to slave, cleaning and bandaging wounds.

One little Malaysian girl had a nasty gash on her forehead. While the girl's mother held her, Margot cleaned the injury and wrapped it with bandages. As Margot gathered her things to move on to the next slave, the girl's mother took Margot's hands and, without saying a word, kissed them.

That night in the darkness of her room, Margot thought back over the day. As on board ship that first night in the girls' cabin, Margot was once again surprised at her ability to work with sickness and pain. Somehow blood and infection did not affect her as it did others. All she saw was a person in need. She had to render assistance. That's the way God made her. He made birds to fly and fish to swim. And He made Margot to render compassion and care whenever needed. Whatever the cost.

A girl, her hands bound at the wrists, was led into the compound behind a horse. What clothing she wore was nothing more than rags. Torn. Filthy. Covered by brown dust, as were her black arms and legs and face. Here and there were streaks of white and red. She looked as if she'd been dragged in the dirt.

"Runaway?" Hennig called out to the man on the horse.

The rider, a stout fellow with a horseshoe-shaped brown beard, nodded. Removing his hat, he wiped the sweat from his brow with a shirt sleeve. "Second time in as many months."

"Thought she looked familiar," Hennig sneered. "Bring her in."

Margot witnessed the girl's arrival while she was bandaging the infected foot of a middle-aged Malaysian man. She paused to see what would happen to the slave girl.

The horseman was a commando, a member of the burgher militia that supplemented the Company's regular forces. The need for the commandos had developed as the farmers expanded into the interior. These loosely organized bands of armed men were formed to protect the outlying regions from the frequent small-scale attacks of both the San and the Khoi. Over time, their policing activities had grown to include, among other things, the capture and return of runaway slaves.

From the youthfulness of the girl's face, Margot guessed the compound's newest arrival to be eighteen years of age. She was thin, yet well-developed, and had wide, attractive eyes.

The commando ordered the girl to stand against the compound wall. As he rode away, his duty fulfilled, she obligingly complied.

One of the guards handed Hennig a whip, multiple straps of leather woven together at the handle.

Margot rose slowly in disbelief. Everyone was moving like list-less players in a bad drama. The commando and his horse ambling offstage; the girl taking her place at the wall; Hennig holding the whip; the guards shuffling into position on each side of the runaway. The only hint of emotion in all of this was the thin smile beneath Hennig's bristle-brush mustache.

"How did you get away this time?" Hennig asked the girl.

Empty eyes stared at nothing. The girl made no reply.

"Where were you going?"

The girl mumbled something. It was unintelligible.

"You were locked in a shed. How did you get out?"

"Pushed a plank away. Crawled out."

"Did anyone help you?"

The girl made no response.

"I said, did anyone help you?"

"No, *Mijnheer*."

Hennig was silent for a moment, looking at her. Then he said, "That won't do. Turn around."

Dutifully, she faced the wall.

Hennig moved within arm's length of the girl.

"No!" Margot trudged through the mud toward him.

The compound overseer pointed the whip at her. "This is none of your business! Get back to work, woman!"

Margot stopped. But she didn't retreat.

Hennig turned his attention back to the girl. He struck her thirty or forty blows across the shoulders.

The strokes were well laid. At every stroke the girl winced, but she made no sound, not even a moan.

A knot of rage formed in Margot's stomach, hardening with each stroke.

"Turn around!" Hennig said to the girl, his breathing labored. "Now tell me the truth."

"A plank was loose. I pushed it away and crawled out."

The overseer shook his head. "You haven't had enough, have you? Hitch up your skirt."

Without hesitation, the girl gathered her clothing above her knees. Her expression remained unchanged. There was no shame. No embarrassment. She did it because she was told to do it.

Hennig continued to flog her, across her exposed legs and thighs, with as much strength as before.

This time, however, the girl writhed with every stroke, crying, "Oh, don't, *Mijnheer!* Please don't! That's enough! Stop! Oh, please stop!"

Margot could stand it no longer. She pushed past a startled Hennig and embraced the girl, shielding her from any more blows. The girl trembled in her arms, then tried to pull free. Margot held her close.

"I told you to stay out of this!" Hennig shouted.

"She's had enough!" Margot cried, without letting loose of the girl.

Hennig cursed. "I'm the one who decides when she's had enough!"

A hard, bitter voice came from within Margot's grasp. "Why are you doing this?" the girl cried. "You'll only makes it worse for me!"

"I'm warning you," Hennig bellowed. "Step aside!"

Margot held the girl tight.

One of the guards spoke up. "Do you want us to pull her off?"

"No," Hennig replied. "Any person in her right mind knows better than to step in front of a slave who is being whipped. Why, that person may accidentally get a taste of the lash herself!"

Margot tensed, but she didn't move.

"Let me go!" The girl squirmed. "I'm a runaway. I deserves to be whipped."

"Nobody deserves to be treated like this," Margot said.

"What a shame it would be," Hennig said in a loud voice, "if a beautiful woman were accidentally to step into a flying whip."

A guard stepped forward. *"Mijnheer* Hennig, don't do—"

"Stay out of this!" Hennig screamed.

The guard backed off.

"I'm raising my arm . . ." Hennig said.

"Don't do this!" the slave girl cried.

"Shh." Margot cradled the girl's head against her chest.

"I'm ready to strike . . ." Hennig said.

Margot braced herself.

"One more second and it will be too late . . ."

Margot closed her eyes.

For a moment, all was silent. Not a sound was heard in the entire compound. Not even a cough.

Whack!

Hot, searing leather fingers stroked Margot's back.

"Hennig! Don't!" the guard cried.

Whack!

172

Instinctively reacting to the pain, Margot pulled the girl even closer.

Whack!

Each successive stroke was harder than before. Margot squeezed her eyes shut so tight they hurt. Even so, tears managed to find their way out onto her cheeks.

Whack!

"Oh, Lord!" Margot whimpered.

Whack!

"That's enough!" the guard screamed.

After a moment had passed without a blow, Margot dared to look behind her.

The guard now held the whip. Hennig stood with his hands at his sides, his massive belly heaving from exertion, sweat dripping from his chin. A grin creased his face. "I never whipped a white woman before!" he said to the guard cheerfully. "I liked it!"

With an arm around the girl's shoulders, Margot began to lead her away.

"Where do you think you're going?" Hennig cried.

Margot kept walking. She didn't answer immediately, not until she could do so without her voice quivering. She would not give Hennig the satisfaction of knowing he had hurt her, even though the stripes on her back stung like fire every time her dress touched one of them. Biting back the pain, she managed to say, "I'm going to take care of this girl's wounds."

Hennig started to object, then he said, "Fix her up real good. Her master will want to beat her again when he comes for her in the morning."

As Margot led the girl to the well in the middle of the compound, the eyes of all the slaves followed her. They looked at her as they'd never looked at her before. It was a look of wonder mixed with thanks and admiration. Even those who had glared at her over the lip of the water ladle now looked at her kindly.

The whipping incident also drew the attention of Governor Chavonnes. That night he toured the compound, questioning Hennig, the guards, and Margot.

The governor conducted his investigation without ever actually stepping into the muddy compound. He performed his duty from atop his horse.

If there was any surprise or displeasure that Margot once again was in the center of controversy, the governor didn't show it. He addressed her coolly and dispassionately, first asking her to give her interpretation of the event.

"So, in your opinion, the punishment of this runaway was too severe?" he said, summarizing Margot's account.

"I prefer to think of her as a young lady," Margot said. "And yes, I believe her punishment was excessive."

The governor looked down in contemplation. After a moment of thought, he said, "If runaway slaves are not whipped, they will do the same thing the next day and the next. And all the other slaves would follow their example. Because you are new to the colony, you have no idea what it is like to work with slaves. They will never do any work if they are not afraid of being whipped. In the future, *Mejuffrouw* de Campion, you would do well to let those who are experienced in these matters do their jobs."

He didn't give Margot a chance to respond. Jerking the reins, he guided his horse out of the compound but not without first relieving Hennig of his duties as overseer for hitting a white woman with a whip.

The most surprising reaction to the incident came from the slave girl herself.

"You is a fool," she said as Margot again treated the girl's wounds.

Margot dabbed at one of the more vicious red stripes that extended across the girl's left leg and continued onto her right. "An interesting comment coming from someone who escaped some lashes from a whip," Margot said.

"I didn't escape nothing."

"How do you figure?"

"When my master learns what happen today, he'll beats me twice as hard."

Margot stopped and looked the girl in the eyes. She was striking in her natural beauty, yet there was a hardness about her. Her eyes were cold. Margot couldn't help but wonder how different this young woman's life would be if she were still in her native village, her innocence and youthfulness intact.

"What's your name?" Margot asked.

"Ndela."

"Well, Ndela, I just couldn't stand by and watch you get whipped. In the morning, I'll speak to your master when he comes to get you. I don't think he'll—"

Ndela shoved her dress down and pulled away. "Don't you do nothin' of the kind!" she screamed. "You jus' leaves me alone! Leaves me alone!"

Before Margot could do anything to stop her, Ndela ran and hid in a corner of the compound.

The next morning the compound gate swung open wide, and a half-dozen more runaway slaves were herded inside by two commandos on horseback. One of the commandos was Jan van der Kemp. He sat tall atop his horse. He didn't see Margot. His full attention was on the slaves.

They were a bruised and bloodied lot. Margot folded her arms in disgust when she saw their condition. Limping. Downcast. Beaten. Dirt and blood covering their legs and arms and bodies. She didn't want to believe that Jan van der Kemp could have anything to do with slaves, especially slaves in this condition. But there he was, prodding them like cattle.

The rage she felt inside began to build to such an extent that she knew exactly how a volcano felt just before it erupted.

Although Hennig was no longer overseer, the routine remained unchanged. The slaves were lined against the wall. Several guards appeared with whips.

"You're just going to sit there and let the guards whip those men?"

Jan looked down to see Margot standing beside his horse. His first expression was one of disapproval that someone was interfering with his business. Then, when he saw that it was Margot, he broke into a surprised smile; and then the smile faded when he realized where she was and when he saw her mood.

"You're just going to sit there and watch this?" she asked.

"They're runaways," he replied.

"They're human beings!"

"They're slaves who have done wrong and who deserve punishment."

"But they're slaves against their will! The fact that they ran away proves that!"

"But they are slaves nonetheless!" Jan's tone became heated. "And as slaves, they are under God's law to behave as slaves."

"God's law?" Margot cried.

"Yes, God's law." He looked hard at her. "Ephesians six: five, 'Servants, be obedient to them that are your masters according to the flesh, with fear and trembling, in singleness of your heart, as unto Christ.' Or how about this one? First Peter two: eighteen, 'Servants, be subject to your masters with all fear; not only to the good and gentle, but also to those who are harsh.' "

Margot was taken aback by Jan's ability to recall appropriate Scripture in support of his argument. Obviously he had given the matter some thought. But using Scripture as a justification to whip other human beings into submission didn't make him right.

The whippings proceeded. Margot tensed at the sound of each stroke. Her reaction brought fresh pain from the wounds across her back.

Jan sat emotionless on his horse. Neither looked at the other.

There were so many things Margot wanted to say to him. She wanted to ask him how Rachel was doing. She wanted to explain her presence in the slave compound. She wanted to let him know that she would be receptive should he ever want to visit her.

But she was too angry even to look at him. All she could do was glare at the atrocity taking place at the whipping wall. And the longer it went, the angrier she got. How could Jan van der Kemp believe that this was the right thing to do?

Following the whippings, Ndela was brought forward. Margot's heart nearly failed her as the thought came that Ndela might belong to the van der Kemps. To her relief, the slave girl was handed over to the other commando.

Hennig had prophesied correctly. Ndela's owner, an older man with a stern face and long white beard, ordered that she be whipped again, threatening that he would break her stubborn will if it was the last thing he ever did.

The girl was placed against the white wall.

Her owner began to dismount to administer the beating himself.

Margot started forward. It took every ounce of willpower she had, but she was not going to let the girl be whipped again.

Jan sat up straight the moment she came into his field of vision. "Cyrus," he said, holding out a hand toward the other commando, "we have a long ride back. It's going to be late as it is—even later if the girl is too hurt to travel. Save it for later."

The bearded commando fell back into his saddle and stared at the slave girl. From the look in his eyes, Margot could see that he wanted to beat her. He wanted to beat her to release his anger. Punishment was secondary.

Without waiting for an answer, Jan reined his horse toward the gate.

Cyrus sighed heavily. Pointing a finger at Ndela, he said, "We'll settle this when we get home. Meanwhile, I want no further trouble from you. Do you understand what I'm saying?"

"Yes, *Mijnheer*," Ndela mumbled. The way she looked at him was chilling.

Her owner almost got down from his horse and came after her. He probably would have done so had she not quickly lowered her gaze to the ground.

Standing in the mud, Margot watched as Jan rode out. She wanted to thank him for stopping Ndela's second beating. But for her to do so, he would have to turn around and look at her. He didn't.

14

BAM! BAM! BAM! BAM!

Margot was startled awake by a pounding on her door.

BAM! BAM! BAM! BAM! BAM!

Instantly her senses rallied. Her blood raced, and her mind did its best to keep up with it. She was alone with nothing to defend herself. What should she do? Should she answer the door?

BAM! BAM! BAM! BAM!

"Lord, protect me," she whispered. In a louder voice, "Who is it?"

"Margot?"

She recognized the voice. It was Jan van der Kemp.

"Jan? What's wrong?"

"Open the door!"

Margot put her hand on the latch. During the day she would have opened it immediately, but there was something about the dead of night that changed everything. People didn't come calling at this hour. Good news always waited until morning. Only dreadful things happened in the middle of the night.

"Margot? Please."

"Just a minute!" She lit a candle. Then she grabbed the blanket from the bed and threw it over her shoulders, drawing it tightly together in the front with a fist. She unlatched the door and opened it a crack. Even though she knew who to expect, what she saw caused her to catch her breath.

Behind Jan was a small army of armed horsemen with torches held high. The flickering lights coated everything with an orange glow set against black shadows. The lines on the men's faces were grim and forbidding. The reflected flames in the horses' eyes created the impression that they were possessed by demons.

With the torches behind him, Jan's face was dark. Troubled. Angry.

"What's wrong?" Margot repeated.

He peered past her into the room, giving no indication that he'd heard her. Putting his shoulder to the door, he pushed it open.

Margot stumbled backward, barely managing to keep her balance. "Jan van der Kemp!" she cried. "What are you doing?"

"Rachel," he said, his gaze darting around the room. "Is she here?"

"No, Rachel isn't—"

Not waiting for her to answer, Jan snatched the remaining cover from the bed and looked under it. Rachel would have had to have been as thin as a sheet of paper to be hiding there, but that didn't stop him from checking.

Since the bed, the trunk, and the two adults occupied every available space, it was impossible for Rachel to be in the room. And Margot was about to say something sarcastic to that effect. Then she got a good look at Jan's face. His brow was furrowed in anger, but his eyes betrayed a deeper emotion—worry.

"Rachel is missing," Margot said, sparing him from having to say it himself.

"I thought she might be here." He clenched and released his fists as he spoke. "I was hoping she would be here."

"How long has she been missing?"

It took a moment for her question to register with him. He was staring at the floor, concentrating on his thoughts. "What did you—"

"How long—"

"Oh." He nodded, the original question finally registering. "We're not sure. She went to her room early this evening, saying she was feeling uncomfortable. Old Knob—he's—"

"A Hottentot. Rachel told me about him."

Jan nodded again. "Old Knob discovered her window open just before sunset. It's not good to leave windows open at night—you never know for sure what's going to crawl in them. That's when we discovered her missing. I rounded up some of the commandos. We rode hard all night to get here." He looked one more time around the room —as if by his looking, Rachel would suddenly appear. He stepped toward the door. "Sorry to have bothered you."

Margot grabbed his arm. "There's something you're not telling me!" she said. "Why did you assume Rachel was with me? In fact, why assume she came to the colony at all?"

He looked at her, started to say something, then changed his mind and said, "It's family business. I have to go."

"No, you don't, Jan van der Kemp! You can't just barge into my room in the middle of the night, tell me Rachel's missing, then walk out on me!" She had him by the shirt sleeve now, but there was no doubt in her mind that if he decided to leave there was no way she could stop him.

Jan glanced toward the door. He edged his way back inside. When he spoke, it was in a low tone. He kept his eyes lowered. "Two nights ago she told Father about the Durbin boy."

"Matthew," Margot said.

"I've never seen Father so enraged."

"Because his mother is Malaysian."

Jan nodded. "Mixed blood—heathen blood."

"Did she tell your father she was in love with Matthew?"

He looked up at her with a surprised expression. "Rachel told you that?"

"Indirectly."

"Father leaped out of his chair." Jan shook his head slowly as he recalled the scene. "It was the first time I've seen him lose control. His voice quivered, his finger shook. He stood over Rachel and told her she was never to see the boy again. He said it would be easier for him to accept her death than to accept her marriage to someone of heathen blood."

"Poor girl," Margot said.

Her comment brought a disapproving glare from Jan. "Rachel is wrong in this."

Not wanting to engage him in an argument, Margot said, "The most important thing right now is to find her and make sure she's safe. So why did you think she would come here to me?"

"Rachel admires you for the way you handled van Jaarsveld, and you know about the Durbin boy."

Margot was surprised.

"Yes—she told me you saw them together the night of the reception. So I was hoping she would come to you for advice—or comfort. Otherwise . . ."

He seemed unable to complete the sentence, but Margot knew exactly what he was thinking. Otherwise, Rachel had run off with the Durbin boy.

"I'm coming with you," she said.

"No." He said the word emphatically. "I can't guarantee your safety."

"I didn't ask for your guarantee."

He shook his head and stepped toward the door.

She blocked his path. "What do you think Rachel's reaction is going to be when she sees a band of armed men coming after her? Maybe I can help ease her mind. Give me a minute to get dressed."

Margot shoved him out the door and tossed aside the blanket she was wrapped in. An uneasy thought struck her. What was keeping the commandos from riding off without her while she dressed? She listened for the sound of horses riding away as she hurriedly pulled on her clothes. Buttoning the last button, she threw open the door.

The commandos were still there.

A sea of disapproving eyes stared at her as Jan helped her up onto his horse. No sooner had she mounted than they were off. Margot grabbed frantically at Jan's midsection to keep from falling.

It took her a while to get into the rhythm, but then she found herself moving in stride with both horse and man. Being this close to Jan van der Kemp, her arms around him, brought about a giddy, girlish sensation. It confused her. Only silly, mindless girls who were looking for husbands felt this way.

At least Jan couldn't see the effect he was having on her.

Margot upbraided herself for her feelings. She reminded herself of Monsieur Fabarez. Demanding. Abusive. She reminded herself of *Mijnheer* van Jaarsveld. Selfish. Conniving. If she'd learned one thing about men it was that they used women to get what they wanted, then discarded them through neglect or abuse. It was best to avoid men altogether. Besides, she and the man sharing this horse were too different. She could never become romantically involved with a man as rigid as Jan van der Kemp.

Having renewed her resolve regarding men, Margot forced herself to think of Rachel and what she might do to help the girl. But as the red glow of morning light rimmed the eastern horizon, with her arms around Jan van der Kemp's waist, her cheek occasionally brushing against his back, she found her thoughts inevitably returning to him.

Cape Town colony's mixed race outcasts dwelled in a loosely knit district a respectable distance from the Castle. The area was cramped, primitive, and unsanitary, and the dwellings were a conglomeration of materials, more like the huts of the natives than the noble, white Dutch-gabled structures of the settlers.

Smuggling was the chief occupation of the district. Because of the Company's strict control over the buying and selling of goods, it was not uncommon for every family, regardless of social position, to circumvent the rules occasionally and deal directly with passing ships. For the district of outcasts, however, circumventing the rules was more than an occasional occurrence; it was a means of survival. Daily life consisted of clandestine encounters, deals with corrupt company officials, bartering, hoarding, and a home life in rooms that looked like small warehouses crowded with goods.

This was the environment in which Matthew Durbin, the eldest of five children, was raised. With his mother's black hair and dark skin, Matthew had to rely on his wit and charm to fend off the regular flurry of derogatory remarks that were cast at him like stones. It was the boy's exuberance in the face of adversity that initially caught Rachel van der Kemp's attention.

Rachel's favorite place in the Company Gardens was the pavilion. One summer afternoon, while sitting there in the shade, she watched as a boy approached two sailors, offering to sell them a speckled oriental vase. The larger of the sailors cursed and took a swing at the boy as he would an offending insect.

Given such a response, most lads would have taken the hint and moved on to a more amenable buyer. Not Matthew. The boy scurried in front of them and made a second appeal. Rachel was too far away to make out what he was saying, but she wasn't too far away to catch his infectious smile. As he held the vase in front of the sailors' eyes, his head bobbed happily side to side, and his mouth moved in a blur.

This second effort got the sailors to stop and look at the vase. Matthew displayed it by turning it around and around in his hands. The large sailor said something, and Matthew tilted the neck of the vase toward him, whereupon the sailor leaned forward to look inside. The sailor spit in the vase.

His companion thought this was hilarious, and the two men continued on down the street, playfully pushing and punching each other. Rachel watched as the young seller stood alone in the middle of the street, holding the vase. His smile was gone. He looked into the vase, then after the sailors, who were still enjoying their joke. It was what the boy did next that most impressed her.

He ran to a patch of wild beetle daisies by the side of the road. Grabbing several handfuls of flowers, he jammed them stem first into the vase and ran after the sailors, arranging the daisies as he ran.

Moments later the vase was once again in the sailors' faces, this time with a flower arrangement.

Rachel watched their reaction go from anger to interest as the smiling seller enacted a scene depicting how a woman might respond to the sailor who approached her with such a vase of flowers. The large sailor shook his head and started to walk away. His companion caught his shirt sleeve and said something that brought a grin to his friend's face. All the time, Matthew was grinning and holding the vase before their eyes.

The next thing Rachel knew, the large sailor was digging in his pocket for money. Matthew scowled at the first offer and put the vase under his arm. The second offer fared no better, and Matthew started to walk away. The large sailor looked angry until once again his companion said something. Then he reached for more money, and the transaction was made.

The sailors continued on their way, holding up the vase and nodding their heads.

Matthew walked in the opposite direction, grinning his infectious smile, doubly pleased. Not only had the sailor bought the vase and flowers but his own spittle as well.

Matthew spied Rachel looking at him before she could look away. He picked another handful of beetle daisies and extended them to her.

"Two *stuivers* for the lovely flowers, *Mejuffrouw?*"

Rachel didn't see the flowers. All she saw was a captivating smile and incredibly dark eyes. She looked down to hide the color in her cheeks.

"Only two *stuivers*. A small price to pay for a handful of God's creation."

Had she any money, Rachel would have given it to him. As it was, she engaged him on his terms.

"You would sell God's creation?" she asked.

"Oh, yes, *Mejuffrouw!* Look at the delicate craftsmanship of these flowers—unequaled by anything the finest artisan can manufacture. Such workmanship is surely worth ten pieces of gold, but for you, *Mejuffrouw,* two *stuivers.*"

Rachel smiled. "But *Mijnheer,*" she replied, "what is to keep me from walking across the road and picking my own daisies from the very patch in which these were grown?"

The boy's bright countenance faded, replaced by disappointment. "But *Mejuffrouw,* these flowers were harvested and transported across this treacherous stretch of road especially for you. Surely the worker is worth his labor."

He was better at this than she was.

"I'm afraid, *Mijnheer*," she said, "that I have no money. Even if I wanted to pay you for your labors, I could not."

The boy handed the flowers to her. "Then they are my gift to you," he said. "For in truth, because of your superior beauty, it is the flowers who should be paying you to sit among them."

From that day on, Rachel accompanied her brother whenever he came to the colony for business. She would sit in the gardens in the hope of seeing Matthew. Over the course of a year, their playful flirtation turned to the more serious talk of friendship, then of love.

It was that time of morning when it was no longer night but not yet day. A white mist hung between earth and heaven. Silently a young couple entered the slumbering district of outcasts, leading a horse.

The horse heard the sound first. He pricked up his ears, then moaned in complaint.

Now the couple heard it too. A low rumble.

Rachel tightened her grip on Matthew's arm. "You don't think—"

Matthew shushed her and listened. The rumbling grew louder.

"Oh, Matthew, it can't be them already, can it? It's too soon!"

Matthew responded with a single word. "Hurry!"

The thundering hooves of horses jolted the district awake as commandos flew up and down the streets, shouting, "Durbin! Durbin! Durbin!"

Men in nightshirts scurried from the houses, some with firearms, others with knives. The faces of frightened women and children peered from doorways and windows.

It disturbed Margot to be counted among the agitators that provoked such fear.

Jan pulled back on the reins. He spoke to a balding man with bare feet, holding a sword. "Where is the Durbin residence?" When the man answered him with nothing more than a scowl, he shouted, "We mean you and your family no harm. We're looking for the Durbins. Matthew has something that doesn't belong to him."

The man said nothing. He stood rock firm, gripping tight his sword.

Looking around, Jan caught the eye of another man. He had a long straight nose and a weak chin. There was no weapon visible.

"Tell me where the Durbins live," Jan yelled.

The man was shaking. Rapidly blinking eyes looked from Jan to Margot, then back to Jan.

Margot felt sorry for him and grew uneasier still.

"Now!"

The man with the long nose jumped. "Down there!" A quivering finger pointed down the street.

"The house with the thatched roof?" Jan asked.

Nervously, Long Nose nodded.

Without thanking him, Jan urged his horse forward. "Over here!" he yelled to several other commandos, who relayed his message to those on the outskirts.

Standing in front of the thatch-roofed house was a dark-haired Dutchman of medium height. A bulging nightshirt indicated a large belly. A full beard, flecked with gray, covered a firm jaw. The sleeves of his nightshirt fell past his hands. The barrel of a pistol protruded beyond the right sleeve.

"You Durbin?" Jan asked.

Eyes squinted at Jan beneath bushy eyebrows. "That I am," he said cautiously.

"You have a son named Matthew?"

A middle-aged Malaysian woman stood in the doorway. At the sound of Matthew's name, she covered her mouth with a hand.

"I have," said Durbin.

Jan adjusted himself in his saddle. The last of the commandos were arrayed a short distance away down both sides of the street. Beyond them, interspersed among the buildings, was a growing contingent of armed onlookers.

"I've reason to believe that my sister is with your son. I've come to take her home."

Durbin scowled. He looked back at the woman in the doorway. She shrugged and shook her head.

"You're mistaken," Durbin said.

Jan stared hard at him. "I'm not leaving without her."

Durbin's scowl deepened. He took two challenging steps forward. "Are you calling me a liar?" he cried.

"I'm saying I won't leave here without my sister. If I have to fight my way past you to get to her, I'll do it."

Durbin waved the pistol menacingly. "Come down off that horse and try it!"

Jan shifted his weight to dismount.

Margot clung tightly to his waist. "Maybe she's not in there!" she whispered.

He craned his neck to see her. His eyes were cold. "Let go of me!"

Then Matthew Durbin appeared in the road. Alone. He stood an equal distance from his father and Jan van der Kemp. *"Mijnheer* van der Kemp," he greeted Jan.

"Where's Rachel?" Jan thundered.

"She's safe," Matthew replied.

"You know where this man's sister is?" Durbin yelled.

"Yes."

"How do you know?"

"Rachel ran away from home last night to be with me," Matthew said to his father. "We're in love and want to get married."

"Never!" Jan shouted. The strength of his voice caused his horse to jump.

A sly grin grew on Durbin's face.

Margot imagined the man was remembering the reaction he got from family and friends when he announced his marriage to a Malaysian.

Durbin walked over to his son. He placed a hand on Matthew's shoulder and asked, "The young lady has consented to this?"

"Yes, Father."

"Why haven't you said anything about this before now?"

Matthew grinned sheepishly and shrugged.

Durbin stood next to his son. He draped an arm over the boy's shoulder, and together they faced Jan. "I have to stand with my son on this," he said.

"Then you will die with your son, unless I see my sister!" Jan shouted.

Durbin pointed his pistol at Jan. Suddenly firearms appeared from everywhere—the commandos aiming them at Durbin and the townspeople; the townspeople aiming at Jan and the commandos.

"Stop this!" Margot shouted. She slid from the horse before Jan could prevent her and ran toward Matthew.

Durbin moved his pistol toward her.

Matthew placed a hand on his father's outstretched arm. "It's all right, Father. I know her."

"Matthew," Margot said, "let me speak to Rachel."

The boy shook his head. "I'm sorry, *Mejuffrouw* de Campion."

"For just a few minutes," she pleaded.

"I can't risk bringing her out here," Matthew said. "Not with all these commandos around."

"I give you my word. They won't do anything."

Matthew smiled his infectious smile. "You I trust, *Mejuffrouw* de Campion. But I do not believe they would listen to you."

Margot swung toward Jan. "Move your men back," she said, "to the outskirts of the district."

"Not until I see Rachel," Jan said.

Margot walked over to his horse. Looking up, she said, "It's the only way they're going to let Rachel come out! Move your men to the outskirts."

Jan didn't move.

"What is it going to hurt?" Margot cried. "It will only delay the killing for a few minutes!"

Reluctantly, Jan motioned to the commandos. Following his lead, they moved to the far edge of the district, still within sight of the Durbin house but out of reach for any immediate threat.

Margot returned to Matthew. "Now can I see Rachel?"

Matthew thought a moment, then motioned toward the side of the road.

From the midst of the Durbins' neighbors a hooded figure stepped forward. The hood was removed, and Rachel greeted Margot with a hug.

"Alone, please?" Margot said to the two Durbin men.

Matthew looked at Rachel, who nodded in agreement.

A few moments later the women stood in the middle of the road, far enough away from everyone else to be able to speak softly without being overheard. Rachel looked tired and frightened.

Margot hugged the girl and released her; however, Rachel kept clinging to her for several seconds before letting go.

"Are you all right?" Margot asked.

"I think so." She glanced around her. "I'm scared."

Margot took Rachel's hands in hers. "Who wouldn't be?"

Rachel took a deep breath to compose herself. "How did you get dragged into this?"

"Your brother was hoping he'd find you with me."

"Maybe I should have come to you." Rachel's eyes filled with tears.

"Are you saying you don't want to stay with Matthew?"

"I love him!" Rachel insisted.

"But—"

Tears coursed down Rachel's cheeks.

Margot produced a handkerchief and handed it to her.

"But I love my family as well," Rachel said. "Why am I forced to choose one over the other?"

Margot didn't answer the question. The girl didn't need a reminder of her family's belief that they were God's covenant people. With that privilege came an equal responsibility to preserve the purity of that people—which meant she was forbidden to marry anyone other than a Dutch Calvinist, no matter how attractive or witty or charming he was.

"What do you want me to tell your brother?" Margot asked.

Rachel sniffed and dried her cheeks and eyes. "Tell him I love him. And tell him that I pray he will someday love someone as much as I love Matthew."

"Then you're staying?"

Rachel nodded.

"And you know what that means?"

Rachel looked at the people surrounding them. "We outcasts have to stick together."

Fighting back tears of her own, Margot opened her arms. The two women embraced. "God be with you," Margot whispered.

When she turned to leave, Rachel caught her by the arm. "One more thing—"

"Yes?"

"Look after Jan for me?"

Margot felt the color rise in her cheeks.

Rachel smiled warmly. "Don't be fooled by his crusty exterior. Inside he's a gentle, caring man."

The two women turned and walked in opposite directions—Rachel toward Matthew, and Margot toward the Dutch commandos and Jan van der Kemp.

15

Do you honestly think that by killing Matthew you will win Rachel's love?"

Margot and Jan were inches apart, but by the volume of their voices one would have thought they were communicating across a canyon. Jan was arguing that the commandos should ride back into the district and abduct his sister. "At least she would be where she belongs!" he insisted.

"She belongs with the man she loves!"

"She belongs with the family who loves her!"

"She's with Matthew. He loves her. Besides, if you really loved her, you'd let her go!"

"Out of the question! How can I leave her among these outcasts?"

"It's her choice."

"But it's a bad choice!"

"She's a grown woman," Margot said. "She knows the consequences for her choice. Don't make it harder on her than it already is."

Jan threw up his hands and paced. The rest of the commandos milled about in the distance, whispering among themselves.

"I just can't leave her here!" Jan cried. "What will I tell my father?"

"Tell him the truth! That Rachel loves him, but that she also loves the man who will be her husband. And that she is doing exactly what God planned for a man and a woman who love each other—to live together as husband and wife."

Jan rested his forearms wearily on the side of his horse, his head against the saddle. "But I'll never see her again," he whispered.

"That's not her choice. It's yours."

Jan shot her a cold look. Without another word, he mounted.

For a moment Margot thought he was going to ride off without her.

Then he offered his hand.

Margot grasped it, and he pulled her up.

Rejoining the commandos, he thanked them for their assistance and instructed them to return without him. He said he would take Margot to the slave compound, then catch up with them.

One by one the commandos rode by, offering him and his father and brother their condolences. The mood of the parting was as somber as that of a funeral.

It was a silent ride to the compound. Margot was struck by the difference between the man who had ridden out and the one who rode back. It was as if they were two different men. Riding out, Jan had sat tall and leaned forward, strong and determined. Coming back, he slumped from side to side, the rhythm of the horse dictating his movement.

Upon reaching her room, Margot invited him to stay awhile and rest before his journey home. She was hoping he'd want to talk.

He declined her invitation. She watched as he dejectedly turned his horse toward the flatlands and home.

Then, for no discernible reason, he stopped. Was something wrong? Was he feeling ill? Slowly he dismounted. The reins fell from his hands. He just stood there, his back to her, staring at the distant peaks.

Quietly Margot walked up behind him. Should she say something? Or did he want to be alone? Was he even aware that she was directly behind him?

"Care for some company?" she asked softly.

He didn't turn around. Nor did he acknowledge her question.

She waited a moment, then started to leave.

"Please stay," he said with a dry, raspy voice.

Margot stopped and came back to face him, folding her hands in front of her. She could tell this was difficult for him by his downcast eyes; he wanted to say something, but the words weren't coming.

Jan reached down and plucked a leaf from a fynbos bush. He worked the leaf absentmindedly with his fingers, plucking pieces from it and flicking them with his thumb and forefinger. "Walk with me?" he asked.

Margot moved to his side. She matched his slow, aimless pace.

"I promised Mother I'd take care of Rachel," Jan said, flicking another piece of leaf. His voice was heavy. "I made the promise to her the day she died."

"How did your mother die?"

190

Jan threw his head back. He grimaced and inhaled deeply.

Margot had touched an invisible wound. At first she felt a pang of regret for asking the question. Then she thought of how sometimes while treating the slaves she had to hurt their wounds in order to heal them. She decided to wait and see what he would do.

His words came out haltingly. "The San tribes had been raiding our cattle. Father requested soldiers to drive them back into the wilderness, but the governor said we were situated too far from the settlement. He couldn't spare the men. There was no commando organization in those days, so Father enlisted the help of a few neighbors. One night we lay in wait for the San. Sure enough, they came. Father fired a warning shot. They ignored it. A skirmish broke out. Some of the San were killed. They got none of our cattle that night, and we thought that was the end of it."

Jan stretched his back—a delaying tactic. Margot sensed that the emotional part of the narration was nearing. He started to speak several times before any words came out.

"One afternoon Mother was riding with us. She loved horses and always managed to find some reason to get out of the house and go riding. It wasn't that we didn't want her along. She was great fun to be with. The excuses were for herself. She felt she needed some kind of justification for neglecting her chores to do something pleasurable."

The memory of his mother and her excuses obviously hit him hard. He pressed his lips together to fight back the rising emotion.

"There was no warning," he said. "A San hunting party attacked us. We managed to frighten them away with our firearms, but not before one of their arrows struck Mother on the side of her neck." His chin quivered as he fought back tears. "The arrowheads are quite small actually, made of ostrich bone and not much larger than the tip of your finger. It didn't even penetrate! It was just a scratch."

Margot furrowed her brow. "How can a scratch—"

"Poison," he said, his voice choking. They walked several steps before he could continue. "Mother insisted she was fine. She said it felt like nothing more than a tiny sting. And when nothing seemed to happen to her, we thanked God for His protection and started for home. Along the way, her neck began to itch—she did her best to keep from scratching it. Still, the itching grew worse. By the time we reached the house, she was feeling dizzy, and her speech was slurred. Her legs failed her on the front steps. We helped her to her room and onto the bed. It wasn't long before she was fighting for each breath."

He was losing the battle to control his emotions. Tears escaped, falling on weathered cheeks.

Margot couldn't remember having seen a man's tears before. It had a powerful, contagious effect on her.

"She died shortly thereafter."

"I'm sorry, Jan," Margot whispered.

They walked in silence for a time.

Then he cleared his throat as a signal he was ready to continue. "When it became clear to Mother that she was dying, she called each of us to her bedside and spoke to us separately. That's when she asked me to watch over Rachel, who was twelve at the time. I was twenty-five. Mother was afraid Rachel—being the only girl—would be neglected.

"You have to understand my father. He would never intentionally neglect Rachel. It's just that he's single-minded. All of his energies are focused on the farm. It has to be that way if we are to survive out where we are. Mother knew that. But she also knew that she would no longer be there for Rachel. That's why she asked me to look after her. Rachel became my responsibility. My mother's dying request. And I failed her."

"It's not as though Rachel has died," Margot said.

"She's as good as dead!" Jan shouted. "Don't you understand that?"

"No, I don't understand that!" Margot yelled back. She would treat the wound, as painful as that might be.

The color rose in Jan's face. "Rachel's an outcast now! We can have nothing to do with her!"

"What if Matthew embraces Christ?" Margot offered. "Would he still be an outcast?"

"From what Rachel has told me, Matthew is a Christian."

"And you would still reject him?"

"Yes."

"Why?"

"Because of his heathen blood!"

"But what of forgiveness? Doesn't the Bible teach that Christ broke down the barrier of blood so that there is no difference between Jews and Gentiles? Can't He do the same between Dutch and Malaysian?"

"You are new to the colony. You don't understand," Jan said. "It's different here."

"How is it different?"

192

Jan spoke slowly. Each word was delivered with force. "We're a covenant people. It is our covenant that defines us. It ties us to the land. If we break the covenant, how can we expect God to bless us? Our very survival is at stake! Rachel has broken that covenant. Her own actions have judged and condemned her."

"That's rather harsh, don't you think?"

"Harsh? She's fortunate we don't stone her."

"But she's your sister!"

Agony twisted his face. The dam burst. Tears flowed unhindered. "Don't you think I know that?" he cried. "Don't you think I know that?"

For a month Margot went over the conversation in her head. She heard from neither Jan nor Rachel, nor was she given any opportunity to initiate contact with them. With no news, she finally gave up thinking about it. What good would it do to go over it again? There was nothing she could do. She stood on the outside looking in.

Besides, she had her own news to worry about. Marc Fabarez had been killed in a tavern fight. He was knifed by one of his own shipmates.

Margot wasn't notified of his death. There was no reason she would have expected to be notified. Other than the governor and a few members of his staff, no one knew there was a connection between her and Fabarez. She came upon the news of his death by chance.

She overheard a group of guards reveling over the fight as if it were a sports event. According to the man who was relating the incident, a smooth-faced boy who looked and sounded too young to be a guard, Fabarez had been loud and obnoxious all night. When Fabarez was not looking, one of his shipmates placed a dead mouse in his mug of ale as a practical joke.

The young guard described how they watched with amusement as the first attempt to deposit the mouse failed when Fabarez whirled suddenly around. The mouse flopped onto the table and was covered quickly with a hat. Fabarez suspected nothing. On the second attempt, the mouse made it into the mug, but the tail stuck out over the rim. Several anxious flicks of the hand later, the mouse was completely inside Fabarez's mug. He still suspected nothing.

The entire tavern waited for him to take a drink. For the longest time he bragged and boasted and swung his mug without ever lifting it to his mouth. Finally, the shipmate who placed the mouse offered a toast to the ship. With everyone peering over the rim of his mug,

Fabarez took a large swig of ale and wound up with the mouse's tail in his mouth. The entire tavern erupted with laughter.

It didn't take long for Fabarez to identify the prankster. A scuffle broke out and quickly escalated into a knife fight. The young guard telling the story grew animated as he described how Fabarez took a knife to the belly, then staggered backward into a huge cauldron of soup simmering in the fireplace. Boiling soup cascaded onto his face and chest and hands and arms up to his elbows. No one knew for certain whether he died from the knife wound or the burns.

The impact Fabarez's death had on Margot surprised her. The absence of grief didn't surprise her—she'd always suspected that someday Monsieur Fabarez would get his due. It was the flood of associated memories that overwhelmed her. His death opened up the possibility of returning to Amsterdam.

She thought of the house in which Sylvie raised her. Margot knew every inch of it, had scrubbed every inch of it. She remembered Sylvie's pots and pans and the medieval cupboard, the secret repository for Sylvie's books. Did the house still belong to Fabarez? And Sylvie's things, were they still there? The neighbors would know. Surely they could speak to the burgomaster on her behalf. Margot thought of what it would be like to go back there. To sit at night at the table and read. To live again in the home she knew so well. Only this time it would be *her* home. She could possibly take in a boarder. An orphan. And pass along to her the knowledge she herself received from Sylvie.

The pull to return was strong. She looked around her. Slaves chained to the walls. Guards sitting under the lean-to, swapping crude jokes and stories. She was ankle deep in mud. Her hands were dry and gritty. The edges of her mud-encrusted dress weighed heavier on her than ever before. Her room was a filthy holding cell for slaves. What did she have here that could possibly compare to her life in Amsterdam?

Margot lifted her eyes. Table Mountain stood on the horizon. She remembered the first time she saw it, standing on the *Eagle*'s deck with Captain Danckaert. She remembered how at that time it had seemed so majestic. Somehow, as she stood in the mud of the Company's slave compound, it no longer had the same allure. The images of home were too strong.

Sloshing across the compound floor, she continued her duties.

But her mind was on Amsterdam and how she might secure passage aboard a returning ship at the earliest possible date.

Later that night Margot returned to her room, her muscles weary and her back aching as usual from trudging and bending and kneeling. It was twilight. The sun had gone down, but the sky still reflected its glory in deep hues of orange. When her door came into sight, she saw a horse and the figure of a man waiting for her.

"Lovely evening," Jan said.

"Yes, it is."

"Nothing like it anywhere else in the world."

"Oh? You've traveled the world?"

A lopsided grin creased his face. "Don't have to. I just know that you can never find another sunset in the world like the sunsets we have here."

Margot folded her arms. She too was grinning. "And how do you know that?"

"Because this is home."

She tried to show no reaction. His comment was nothing more than coincidence. He couldn't possibly have known that she was thinking of leaving, of trading in her new home for her old one.

"What brings you to town?" she asked.

"You."

"Me?"

He folded his arms as well and grinned at her reaction. Apparently her face had registered every bit of the shock she felt.

Margot refolded her arms, tighter. She was almost afraid to ask the question, but she asked it anyway. "And what do you want from me?"

"Do I have to have a reason? Can't I just ride in to see you?" His blue eyes twinkled with humor. His smile was inviting.

Margot's breathing became shallow. Her heart thumped madly. Somehow she managed to say, "I guess that would be . . . I mean . . . is acceptable. At least, it's fine with me. I have no objections."

His smile increased. He closed the distance between them. "Actually," he said, "it's a matter of business."

"Business?" It was amazing how one word could send her toppling down the other side of her emotional mountain.

Jan explained. "Father, Breyton, and I were talking, and since we no longer have a woman around . . . well . . . since Rachel . . ."

"I understand," Margot said.

"We've decided we need a housekeeper. Naturally, I thought of you."

"Naturally."

"I mean, since that's what you were doing when I first met you."

She said nothing.

"So how about it?" he asked.

"How about what?"

"Would you be interested in becoming our housekeeper? I'm sure I could get the governor to release you to us."

Margot stared at him. He was all business.

For the rest of her life Margot was never able to comprehend, let alone explain, what happened next. She felt her lips move. The voice was her own. And the words she heard were words of acceptance. Without thought. Without any consideration of her plans to return to Amsterdam. They just came out.

"Great!" Jan said. "When can you be ready to leave?"

"When will you talk to the governor?"

"Already have. We can leave as soon as you get your things together."

16

The colony lay behind them, the flatlands stretched in front of them. The sun crested over the distant eastern peaks, throwing shafts of light at their eyes. Already they'd been traveling an hour. During that time Jan had spoken seven words in toto, and those he spoke soon after they mounted the horses: "It's going to be a long ride."

Margot followed behind him two horse lengths. Never once did he check to see if she was still with him. *This is a mistake,* she thought. *A big mistake. How could I have been so foolish?*

She surveyed her surroundings and wondered why anyone would want to live out here. Nondescript scrub brush littered the landscape. The land was parched, and the only sign of life was the occasional slithering of a reptile.

Regarding signs of life, the man on the horse in front of her was exhibiting very few of them. He just plodded along. Margot considered falling off her horse to see if he'd notice—or possibly stopping to see how far he'd go before looking back. But she thought better of it. If the last hour was any indication, he'd go for miles before missing her.

Margot filled her time by turning her thoughts to ways she could back out of her agreement. Jan hadn't mentioned the length of her employment. She wondered how long she would have to stay to be polite. Was a month too short? A week?

She sighed heavily and looked for a response from Jan. There was none. How could she possibly spend an entire week with this man and his family? The slaves in the compound were more courteous and certainly more talkative! The two of them had been riding only an hour, and already it seemed like a week. A week would seem like a year. A month would be an eternity!

Margot glared at his dusty back. He was so unpredictable! Usually he was distant and unresponsive—which suited her just fine. The less involvement she had with men the better. Then, at other times, he did things that made her want to throw her arms around him—like the time he plotted with her and Rachel to reveal van Jaarsveld's true character; and more recently, like the walk they took together the day Rachel ran away.

He was open, warm, vulnerable—and stubborn. Mostly stubborn. Just when she thought he was different from the Fabarezes and van Jaarsvelds of the world, he said or did something that was totally male. And then they'd argue.

Margot sighed again. Maybe it was best they rode in silence.

She wondered if Jan's father and brother were like him. Of course they were! Look what they did to Rachel! *This is a mistake. A big mistake!* Margot said to herself over and over again. How could she possibly have agreed to work for the very men who had disowned Rachel? She must have been out of her mind to acquiesce to this arrangement.

By the time they stopped for a midday meal, Margot had planned how and when to inform Jan that she would not be able to work for his family. They sat a comfortable distance from each other at the base of a large bush. With the sun high overhead, there was little shade.

Jan handed her some bread and cheese and, not waiting for her, took a bite of bread and chewed with purpose. He never looked directly at her, choosing instead to stare at the desolate landscape through squinting eyes.

"How much farther?" Margot asked.

"We're halfway there." He took another bite, never taking his eyes off the flatlands.

Five minutes of silent chewing passed before Margot spoke up again. "Living out here," she said, "I imagine it's quite a treat when you get to go into the colony."

"How so?"

"The change of scenery. Everything is so brown and flat out here. And the colony is so beautiful with the blue expanse of ocean on one side and Table Mountain rising on the other. I fell in love with the scenery the first time I saw it from the deck of the ship."

"No comparison," Jan said matter-of-factly, without interrupting his chewing.

There's an understatement, she thought.

"It's much more beautiful out here," he said.

Margot had known that she and Jan saw things differently, but she never knew how differently until this moment. How could he prefer this flatland wilderness to the scenery at the Cape? The man had absolutely no taste at all.

As if he heard her thoughts, he explained, "I don't mean this." He waved a piece of white cheese at the flatlands before taking another bite. "This is nothing. Wait until you see Klaarstroom."

"That's right." Margot remembered. "'Clear stream.' The name of your family's estate." She looked at the parched landscape again and wondered if the name was derived by wishful thinking. "Describe it to me," she said.

"Klaarstroom?" A sparkle appeared in his eyes.

Margot found herself fighting off a pang of jealousy. It was the kind of sparkle she'd fancied he would someday have when he thought of her. *In the days before I realized how different we are,* she reminded herself.

Jan shook his head and stuffed the last of the cheese into his mouth. "I'd rather you see it for yourself," he said, his mouth full.

Margot was content to wait and judge Klaarstroom's beauty for herself, but anything that might get Jan talking was worth an extra effort. "Please tell me," she said as she stood and brushed off her dress. "You can tell me while we're riding. It will help pass the time."

Surprisingly, he didn't object. This time when they mounted, he waited until she was beside him before starting off, though he didn't begin talking right away.

Margot had to prompt him with upraised eyebrows as if to say, "Well?"

A boyish grin appeared. "At night you can hear leopards," he said. "Or sometimes, earlier in the evening, you can hear baboons shouting at one another. If you like antelope, we have a dozen or more different kinds, whole herds of them blazing across the valley. And the mountains—" his gaze rolled heavenward in search of the right words "—the mountains are indescribable! You'll just have to see them yourself. Some of the trails along the cliffs are so narrow and steep they'll make you dizzy. The heights are covered with towering pines that point straight to God. And the rivers are great! They're cold and fast-flowing and bursting with trout and bass. And birds! Birds of every description. And if you're really lucky—I've seen them twice in my lifetime—you can spot a hippopotamus in the river!"

For two hours Jan described in detail his experiences growing up in the valleys and mountains of interior South Africa.

Several times Margot had to remind herself to close her mouth, so dumbfounded was she at his level of excitement. This was a side of Jan van der Kemp she had never seen before. And though, given the barrenness of the land surrounding them, she was sure he was exaggerating, still he managed to create in her a sense of wonder at what actually lay ahead. She found herself casting an occasional glance at the approaching mountains.

With each look they loomed larger. Soon the foliage of the flatlands grew more dense, and a river came into view.

"For me, crossing this river is like crossing a boundary line into a different world," Jan said. "I always look forward to crossing it because it reminds me I'm not far from home."

Apprehension rose inside Margot like storm waters behind a dike. She took a deep breath to force them back. Why did the thought of being near Jan's house affect her this way? *Because this is a mistake, that's why!* she told herself. She tried to concentrate on the scenery. She still hadn't seen anything that compared with Jan's descriptions.

"They're called the Hottentots-Holland Mountains," Jan said of the peaks ahead. "When the early settlers from Holland first traveled this far inland, it was inhabited by Hottentot tribes. One of the settlers described his homeland to the chief. In reply, a Hottentot chief said, 'This is our Holland, the Hottentots' Holland.' It's been called that ever since."

They crossed the river.

Margot knew better, but for some reason she expected more. The grass wasn't greener on this side. The sky wasn't bluer. It made her remember a time when she was growing up. A friend of Sylvie's moved to a larger house and couldn't stop talking about it. For weeks all they heard from the woman was descriptions of the new house. How magnificent the kitchen was, the staircase, the upstairs bedroom. When Sylvie and Margot finally visited her, Margot was sorely disappointed. It wasn't nearly as grand as the woman had described it. On the way home, she mentioned her disappointment to Sylvie, who patted her warmly on the hand. "She described the house the way it looks to her," Sylvie said.

The same thing is happening now, Margot concluded. *Jan is describing his home the way he sees it.* It didn't matter whether she thought it was grand, as long as he did.

Jan pulled to a stop, so she did too. "Let's follow the river upstream," he said.

"Is this the way to your house?" Margot asked.

"Mmm . . . no," he said playfully. "But I want to show you something."

Amused, Margot said, "You're the leader."

They turned their horses upriver and began a slow climb. Bushes gave way to thick pines around which they began to weave. Within minutes the temperature grew decidedly cooler.

Suddenly a pinecone fell from above, hitting Jan on top of the head. He yelped in surprise and rubbed the spot.

Margot started giggling. "I'm beginning to like this place!" she said.

Her levity was short-lived as a pinecone whizzed past her own head.

"Hey!" she cried as she ducked.

Jan looked into the trees. He pointed upward. A monkey—a mother with a gray coat and black face—and her two offspring sat on a branch high overhead. Looking down on them, the mother picked another pinecone and dropped it. The two younger monkeys leaned over to watch it fall. It almost hit Jan.

"How adorable!" Margot cried.

"You wouldn't think they were adorable if you were the one they hit on the head!" Jan turned his face to the monkeys and howled at them. Startled, the mother leaped from tree to tree with one baby on her back, the other one trailing close behind.

"You scared them!"

"Of course I did! I didn't want another lump on my head." He explored the bump with his fingers. "It's bleeding!" He extended his fingers to show her.

She saw a spot of red on one finger. "Don't be such a child!" she said. "You act like you're going to die."

Jan dismounted. Kneeling beside the river, he wet a handkerchief and applied it to his head with a wince.

Margot took the opportunity to stretch her legs. She hadn't realized how stiff she was until she arched her back.

Wandering to the river's edge, she stared at the water, allowing it to entrance her with its rushing motion and gurgling sound. In some places she could see all the way to the bottom; multicolored, smoothly polished stones were stacked as neatly as tiles. In other places the riverbed was obscured as the water tumbled madly against exposed rocks. The resulting collision created white foam and a rising mist that looked as if the river were giving up its ghost. After a day on the arid flatlands, the moist air and the rushing of water combined to create a wonderfully invigorating feeling.

"Will you look at my head?" Jan asked. He leaned toward her, parting his hair to reveal the spot where the cone had hit.

Margot glanced at it. "It's just a scratch!"

"Feels like more than that," he said. He straightened up and smoothed his hair back in place. "Ready to continue on? We need to hurry—otherwise it will be dark before we reach Klaarstroom."

Climbing ever higher, they cleared the trees. As they did, Margot uttered a small cry.

Jan looked back at her, seemingly pleased at her reaction.

Pressing a hand to her chest, she exclaimed, "Oh, Jan! It takes my breath away! You didn't do this place justice."

A bed of flowers spanned the width of an enormous open meadow like an intricate oriental carpet. Purple ericas mingled with scarlet wild irises and bright orange flame flowers. Patches of white-and-blue wood orchids swirled among them.

"Now I know where Jacob got his idea for Joseph's multicolored coat," she said.

In the background a series of staggered cliffs stood over the delicate carpet like silent sentinels. Mysterious alabaster clouds crept on cat's paws between their dark, chiseled faces.

"So what do you think of my home now?" Jan asked.

Margot shook her head in disbelief. "I'm speechless."

"Just a little farther and I'll show you why I brought you up here."

"There's more?"

Crossing the meadow was like gliding on a floral sea. Even Margot's horse seemed to sense the beauty of the place. The plodding rhythm that carried her across the flatlands was gone. The horse moved smoothly, effortlessly through the colors.

Jan led her between two cliffs spaced widely apart. Margot thought they looked like two massive rock forearms pointing toward heaven. She picked up the sound of the river again. And as they traveled deeper into the ravine, the gentle roar of falling water grew ever louder.

Dismounting, Jan stepped forward proudly, his hands on his hips. He didn't say anything. He let the scene speak for him.

From a cliff high above, the river threw itself over a rocky precipice. For an instant the water hesitated as though surprised it had run out of riverbed, then it plunged with ever-increasing speed toward the rocks below, where it crashed and—like caterpillar to butterfly—was magically transformed into a luminous mist that danced around a rainbow. A clear pond gathered the fallen drops and shepherded them into a gorge, where the river continued its journey through the meadow and beyond.

Margot stood on a cool green flooring of moss that stretched to the base of the cliffs, where it made several futile attempts to climb them. The late afternoon sunlight sliced into the ravine at a dramatic angle, splashing the valley with bright colors wherever it touched.

"This is my most favorite spot in the world," Jan said.

Margot performed a slow pirouette as she gazed in wonder at God's handiwork. No European cathedral had ever been built that could rival this ravine in its ability to draw a person's attention toward God.

"Jan, thank you," she said. Her words sounded flat and mundane, given the magnificence of the falls, but she could think of no others. "Thank you for bringing me here."

"I wanted to share it with you," he replied.

He moved to her side, close enough that she could feel the warmth of his arm next to hers. A moment before, Margot would have thought nothing could easily distract her from the beauty of the ravine. She would have been wrong. Surrounded by natural splendor, she was now aware of only one thing—how near Jan van der Kemp was standing.

He lowered his head and spoke in a voice barely audible over the roar of the falls. "Ever since this morning I've been trying to find the words to thank you for helping me with Rachel. First with van Jaarsveld, then . . . then on the day she ran away. I was glad when you insisted on riding with me to get her. If Rachel would listen to anyone, she would listen to you. I don't know if you're aware how much she admires you."

"The feeling is mutual," Margot said. "Rachel and I are a lot alike."

Jan stepped in front of Margot so that they were face to face. The pale blue eyes that had the ability to cut right through a person were as tranquil as the pool of water behind him. "Rachel isn't the only van der Kemp who is fond of you," he said.

"Oh?" Margot felt a rush of blood in her cheeks. She tried to be bold, to hold his gaze. But she couldn't. She lowered her eyes.

His hand lifted slowly. The warmth of his palm pressed against her face. She closed her eyes, and the sensation heightened. Slowly his thumb caressed her cheek with a single stroke.

"I think you know how I feel about you," he whispered.

Lifting her head, she opened her eyes, hoping to communicate to him that if he attempted to kiss her she wouldn't resist. But when her eyes opened, he was gone! That same instant his hand had left her face. All she saw was the back of his head.

"It gets dark around here quickly," he called happily over his shoulder. "I want you to see the house before the sun sets."

Margot scrambled to collect her wits. It was as though her emotions had spilled out on the ground and were rolling every which way. She didn't know which one to grab first—anger, joy, frustration, love.

Somehow she managed to climb onto her horse and follow after Jan, who was already on his way out of the ravine.

As they approached the van der Kemp estate, the sun was snuggling close to the western horizon.

There was a discernible change in Jan's demeanor the closer they got to Klaarstroom. Gone was the warmth and the friendliness. His back straightened, his eyes hardened in intensity, his mouth formed a thin, straight line.

"Almost there," he said.

Margot nodded tensely. Her apprehension was rising again, and Jan's tenseness wasn't helping. She would soon be meeting his father and brother. *This is a mistake.*

Riding side by side, they traveled a road lined with maturing oaks. "All these trees were planted by order of the Company," Jan explained. "One of our former governors had a fondness for oak trees. Part of our agreement for the right to use this land was that we would plant oak trees. As a young boy, I helped dig the holes." They reached a lane that jutted off to the right. "Here we are."

His words rolled up into a ball and sat heavily in Margot's stomach. Following Jan, she urged her horse down the wide lane that led through a grove of fruit trees. A large, white Dutch-gabled house came into view at the end of the lane.

"It's lovely!" she exclaimed.

Hers was not an empty compliment. She was genuinely impressed that such a structure existed this far into the interior. The van der Kemp house was a wide, spacious structure with the traditional whitewashed exterior made from seashells. The front of the house boasted a large central facade that rose to a rounded peak. What looked like the end of two large scrolls adorned the edges halfway up the sides, with two smaller ones closer to the peak. A mullioned window for the upstairs room sat in the center of the facade.

A raised porch spanned the width of the house. Matching windows were on either side of the door. Four square, ivy-covered pillars supported the roof. One could not approach the porch directly from the front. Two sets of steps sat at right angles to the veranda, leading to a central adjoining landing.

"Do you like it?" Jan asked.

"It is beautiful."

"I can't take credit for it," he replied. "My father and brother built it. Though the two of them nearly killed each other before it was finished."

The ball in Margot's stomach tightened.

"Let's go in. I'll introduce you."

As Margot took one more look at the house, the sun touched the horizon behind her. Suddenly the rays caught the windows just right. Reflecting the sun's glory, the windows shone as if they were made of gold.

17

The van der Kemps' house was of typical design for houses on the Cape. When Jan escorted Margot through the front door, she found herself in a home that was spacious, light, and airy—a mansion, compared to the small, dark rooms in which she was raised in Amsterdam.

The shape of the house was a large T, the front forming the wide top. The dining room and kitchen were to the left. To the right the entryway opened up into a sizable sitting room. The rest of the house stretched back along the stem. There was a stairwell where the top and stem met. She supposed it led to the single upstairs room whose mullioned window was situated in the center of the house's grand facade.

Bright yellow wood ceilings were accentuated by rich, red stinkwood beams. The darker wood was used again for the flooring, which made the ceilings stand out even more. The rooms were furnished with handsome, handmade stinkwood furniture carved with simple inlaid patterns.

Margot ran her fingers along the polished arm of a chair sitting beside the door. "What beautiful craftsmanship!" she exclaimed. "These are much finer than the chairs at the governor's residence. I wasn't aware there was a craftsman in the colony who could do work like this."

"There isn't," Jan replied. "The man who made that chair lives here. My brother, Breyton. In fact, he made all the furniture in this house."

Margot's gaze traveled from piece to piece. "They're all lovely!"

"Breyton is good at what he does," Jan said. "Just don't tell him I told you that."

While she admired the furniture, Margot also made a quick evaluation of the condition of the rooms. She wanted to know how much work and what kind lay ahead of her. To her pleasant surprise—considering that three men were the primary occupants of the house—the rooms were not in bad shape. They needed work, to be sure, but nothing more than a good cleaning. Within days she could have the floors and furniture shining as brightly as anything in the governor's residence.

Jan walked her to the stairs. "Your room is up there."

Margot peered up the staircase.

"It was Rachel's room," he added. His voice wavered momentarily when he said her name.

"And my trunk?"

"As I mentioned before we left the colony, I arranged for its delivery. Cyrus Steenkamp, our closest neighbor, will bring it with him when he returns with supplies. Should be here in two days."

Jan hadn't expected her to have such a large trunk in her possession when he went to get her. Otherwise, he said, he would have taken a wagon. Margot wondered how he would react if he knew that the trunk was once the property of Commissioner Uys van Jaarsveld.

The front door swung open. Margot recognized Pieter van der Kemp and Breyton from van Jaarsveld's reception. Sharp anxiety pricked her insides. She recognized them from the reception; would they remember her? Van Jaarsveld had done a good job of humiliating her that night in front of everyone.

"Where have you been?" Pieter thundered. "It took you long enough to get here. Come by way of Batavia?" There was no sign of humor on his face.

Jan ignored his father's exaggeration. And he didn't respond directly to the question, saying instead, "Father, Breyton, this is Margot de Campion—our new housekeeper."

Pieter stepped forward and took her hand. Seasoned eyes met hers. They were polite, not friendly.

Margot was once again struck by the similarities between Jan and his father. The man holding her hand looked exactly like Jan, only an older version. Then her heart sank as she saw a glimmer of recognition light up in his eyes.

Using the tone of voice a judge might use when passing sentence, he said, "You're the girl at the reception!" He dropped her hand.

Margot felt her face growing hot.

"That's where I've seen that face before!" Breyton chimed in from behind his father. Jan's younger brother wore an amused but charming smile. "You'll have to admit, though, Father," he said, "van Jaarsveld was quite unfair to her."

"Retribution," Jan added. "Van Jaarsveld attempted to deceive Margot on the ship coming down here. She thwarted his intentions."

Both boys spoke van Jaarsveld's name as if it were something they would scrape off their shoes.

Pieter still seemed not totally convinced that Margot didn't in some way deserve her treatment at the reception. But he said slowly, "Well, we know all about *Mijnheer* van Jaarsveld, don't we?"

"I'm Breyton," the younger brother said, stepping between his father and Margot.

He was thinner than the other two men, and his hands were more delicate, lacking their calluses. His hair and eyes were dark, and while he bore the family resemblance, she noted again that he more closely resembled Rachel than his father and brother. But the most distinguishing quality of his appearance was his neatly trimmed, stylish mustache.

"I've been admiring your craftsmanship," Margot said, indicating the furniture.

Breyton appeared pleased by her compliment. "Thank you, my dear lady," he said. There was a gracefulness and polish about his personality that was lacking in both his father and Jan.

"So this is the girl who's caught your eye," Pieter said gruffly to Jan. "Well, she's pretty—and mighty skinny. Can she cook and clean?"

Jan turned red.

"I am a good housekeeper," she assured him, doing her best to hide her embarrassment.

"Don't listen to him," Breyton said. "It's just that Jan is thirty-one years old and you're the first girl in whom he's ever shown any interest."

Margot blushed.

"I brought her here to be a housekeeper, nothing else!" Jan insisted.

"Do you believe in God?" Pieter asked her, folding his arms.

"Yes," Margot replied, pleased but astonished at the sudden change of subject.

"The Bible?"

"Father, this isn't an inquisition!" Breyton objected.

Pieter turned on him with a fury that was greater than the moment warranted. The intensity of his reaction gave evidence of a history of conflict between father and son.

But it was Breyton's reaction that most frightened Margot. The younger man's demeanor changed completely. If she hadn't witnessed the change herself, she would have thought he'd donned a mask. His eyes blazed; his face grew dark, even evil. Margot wondered how anyone capable of such a demonic presence could produce such heavenly handcrafted furniture.

"I'll not have a heathen living under my roof!" Pieter bellowed.

"I don't mind answering the question," Margot said, hoping to diffuse the conflict. "Yes, I believe in the Bible."

"Your parents both Christian? Both Dutch?"

Breyton threw his head back and laughed. "This is ridiculous!"

Margot jumped in quickly. "My parents were killed when I was small. They were French Huguenots."

To his father, Breyton yelled, "What about Old Knob? He's a heathen, and he lives under your roof."

"He lives in his own hut!" Pieter roared.

"Which is situated right next to our house—on our property," Breyton shouted back. "In my mind, that's the same as living under this roof."

"Of course it is, in your mind!" Pieter cried. "But then there are a lot of warped and perverted ideas floating around in your mind."

"Father—" Jan interceded by touching his father's arm. He spoke in soothing tones. "It's been a long ride for Margot. If you're finished, I'll take her to her room."

"Do that!" Pieter yelled, still angry. He never took his eyes off Breyton. Breyton snorted, shook his head, and stalked out, slamming the front door.

Pieter glared after him.

Jan motioned for Margot to go upstairs, which she willingly did.

The room at the top of the stairs was the finest room Margot had ever stayed in. It had the same yellow wood ceiling and stinkwood beams and floor as the rest of the house. The bed rested on an exquisite four-poster frame; bed frame and matching chair and chest with mirror all were made of the same rich, red wood.

The view from the mullioned window looked out over the orchard in front of the house. From her high vantage point Margot could see that the boundaries of the orchard gave it an octagon shape with two lanes crossing in the middle like a large plus sign.

Yet despite the elegance of her accommodations, Margot could not get comfortable. For one thing, the room smelled like Rachel. It was an eerie reminder of the girl's absence and fate. And then there was Margot's mixed reception by the van der Kemps. What kind of feud had she stepped into? And what had Jan said to his father and brother, if anything, that would prompt their remarks about his being interested in her? Visions of van Jaarsveld came to mind. Had she once again been lured into a situation for some perverted purpose?

Like a haunting refrain, the words from the flatlands kept coming to her: *This is a mistake. This is a mistake!*

Margot spent her first night at Klaarstroom sitting in the stinkwood chair, unable to quiet her mind. She didn't get up from the chair until after the morning sun had cast a long shadow in the shape of the house's facade over the octagonal orchard.

Margot was relieved to discover that her first day would be spent alone.

She came downstairs and encountered in the kitchen a black slave who identified himself as Ding. He was a happy man with large white teeth. When she first appeared, he was sitting on a counter. The moment he saw her, he hopped off and told Margot that the *Mijnheers* van der Kemp would be gone all day—Pieter and Jan rode out to inspect the herd, and Breyton was . . . away. Once he delivered the message, Ding announced that he would be going back out to the fields. White teeth flashed as he proudly informed her that he was the foreman of the field slaves.

"Wait!" Margot cried. "Will the *Mijnheers* van der Kemp be home for dinner?"

"Oh, no, *Mejuffrouw*. They be out late."

"Then is there someone around here who can show me where things are?" she asked.

"Things?"

"Cleaning supplies, brooms, those kinds of things."

Ding nodded. "You'll find things in the closets." He turned to go.

"Wait!" Margot cried again. "Will there be any others in the house?"

"Others?"

"Servants, relatives I don't know about . . ."

Ding gave her a puzzled look. "You is all there is," he said.

Margot pictured the long hallway and wondered how many rooms there were that she hadn't seen yet. "Well, if that's the way it is—I suppose I can handle it."

Ding cocked his head. "You afraid of work, *Mejuffrouw*?"

"What? Oh—no, not at all," she stammered. "Thank you—" she couldn't remember his name "—Dong."

"Ding," he corrected her.

"Sorry. Ding."

"I be going then." He turned to the door.

"All right, and thank you again."

"You repeat yourself," Ding said, hanging half in and half out the door. He showed his teeth, a lot of them. "You be fine, *Mejuf-frouw*. But in a new land it is always good to remember a saying my mother told me: 'The housefly does not play a sticky drum.'" The grin grew even wider, then he was gone.

By the end of her first day, Margot was exhausted. Having spent the first part of the day exploring the rooms, she spent the second half cleaning, sweeping, and polishing. Other than an occasional servant walking in and out and eyeing her curiously, she had no contact with anyone. Nor did she eat anything, preferring to work. Once she started, she didn't want to stop. It felt good to clean again, to take pride in a room that was spotless and shiny. It reminded her of Sylvie and Holland.

The hour was late when she climbed the stairs to her room and fell onto the bed. Within minutes she was asleep. She didn't hear the men when they rode in.

The next morning when Margot rose, the van der Kemps were gone again. This time no one was left behind to give her a message, so she made herself breakfast and began cleaning.

Shortly after noon, Jan rode in and came into the house just long enough to tell her that they would want dinner that evening. When she asked what he wanted her to cook, he shrugged, told her to fix whatever she could find, and rode out again.

"How about some soap and water? I've managed to find that," she said to the closed door.

After poking around the larder, Margot prepared a meal of mutton and cabbage and carrots. She also found some bread and cheese. The dinner was ready long before the men returned.

Margot nearly killed herself with anxiety while she waited. She had no idea when to expect them; she didn't know what they liked and disliked, or how they liked their food prepared; and the later it became, the harder it was to keep the food warm without ruining it. Her heart jumped every time she thought she heard horses approaching. She wanted them to get home before the meal was ruined, yet she personally dreaded their arrival.

It was late when Pieter and Jan finally rode in. Breyton wasn't with them.

Pieter barged through the door first, his hands, face, and clothes covered with dust. Without greeting Margot, he asked her if she'd seen Breyton. When she said she hadn't, he mumbled something unintelligible and stomped toward the back of the house.

Jan followed in his wake, dirtier than his father, if that was possible. He barely made eye contact with Margot, then followed his father down the hallway.

Margot returned to the kitchen and waited for them to return, fussing over the meal nervously.

Nearly half an hour passed before the two men appeared again. When they did, they were washed and wore fresh clothes. They sat at the table, and Margot dished up the food.

Just then the front door swung open, and Breyton strolled in. There was an absence of dirt on him. He walked straight to the table and sat down.

Pieter glared at him.

Breyton deliberately avoided looking at his father.

Margot busied herself by placing the serving dishes on the table. While she made several trips back and forth to the kitchen, the three men sat in silence. They didn't look at her, nor did they look at each other. When the last dish was placed on the table, she turned to go back to the kitchen.

"There's a setting missing," Pieter said.

"I'm sorry," Margot said, "I wasn't aware you were expecting anyone else. I'll bring one out right away."

She returned moments later with another place setting.

Pieter indicated that it was to be set next to him and across from Jan.

Margot placed the china plate and utensils, then turned again toward the kitchen.

"Where are you going?" Pieter asked her.

"I'll be in the kitchen should you need anything," she replied.

"Have you already eaten?"

Margot indicated she had not.

"You'll eat with us," said Pieter. He motioned to the setting beside him.

Margot looked at Jan and Breyton, who were both watching her.

"I really don't think that would be appropriate," Margot said.

"Why not?"

"Well, I'm just the housekeeper," she replied.

"Nonsense! Sit down," Pieter said.

Self-consciously smoothing her dress, Margot pulled out the chair and took her place next to Pieter van der Kemp.

No sooner was she settled than the van der Kemp patriarch bowed his head and offered thanks to God for the food.

Then for the longest time the only sound at the table was the clanking of silver utensils against china plates.

Margot kept her eyes focused on her plate.

"What ship brought you down here?"

Margot looked up. Pieter was addressing her. She swallowed hastily to answer. Too hastily. The bite didn't go down right. She covered her mouth and coughed and swallowed again. This time it went down.

"Excuse me," she said. "The *Eagle*. I sailed down on the *Eagle*."

Pieter's whole face lit up. "Hans Danckaert's ship! A good man. Did business with him for years. Did you know his ship went down off the coast?"

"That's what I heard," Margot said sadly.

Pieter stared at nothing reflectively for a moment, then he began to chuckle. "Strangest thing—" he chuckled some more "—last time I saw Danckaert, he told me an unbelievable story." He stopped to chuckle again. "Seems one time his ship was under attack by pirates. And in the middle of the battle a dozen or so of the King's Nieces he was transporting came on deck!" He laughed. "In the middle of battle! So Danckaert is forced to stop fighting long enough to deal with these women!"

Jan and Breyton followed the story with huge grins on their faces.

"So he orders them to go below. And they refuse!" Pieter was howling at this point. "Finally he gets them to go below deck. But instead of going to their quarters, they go to the gun deck! The ship's being bombarded by deadly accurate pirate guns, and here these women are standing in the middle of the gun deck! The first mate orders them back to their quarters. And they refuse again!"

"Why did they refuse?" Jan asked.

"They wanted to help fight the pirates!" Pieter roared.

By now Jan and Breyton were laughing too.

Pieter put down his utensils. He waved his hand at Jan to indicate there was more. "That's not the best part! One of the guns was unmanned. The crew had been killed by a direct hit. So these women talk the first mate into teaching them how to load and fire the gun!"

"No!" Jan cried.

Pieter's head was bobbing up and down. "Can you imagine that? They're being pulverized by pirate guns, and the first mate is trying to make sailors out of these women! But even that's not the best part. It was the women who drove the pirate ships away! Drove them all away!"

"The women?" Jan cried.

"The women!" Pieter said. "Scared off two or three pirate ships!"

"There was only one ship," Margot said quietly.

Pieter scowled, clearly not pleased with her assertion that his facts were in error. He wasn't laughing anymore. "I'm sure Danckaert said it was more than one," he said firmly.

"Then Captain Danckaert was exaggerating," Margot replied. "There was only one pirate ship. We hit its mainmast."

"You?" Pieter said.

The eyes of all three men were on Margot. She placed her hands demurely in her lap. "I was one of the women on the gun deck," she said, trying her best not to look as pleased as she felt at the open-mouthed stares she was getting from the van der Kemp men.

Pieter looked at her admiringly. "And the rest of the story—is it true?"

"It happened pretty much as you described it," she replied.

"Then if you were one of the King's Nieces—"

Margot shook her head. "No. I was aboard the ship but not as a King's Niece." Briefly she described the events that landed her on board the *Eagle*. She began with Fabarez's accusation of witchcraft, including the nutshell and her ability to read, and ended with his recent appearance in the colony and his death. She told her tale with boldness. Part of her was hoping that the conservative patriarch would take offense at something in her story and would conclude she was not a fit housekeeper for them. She reasoned that, if he released her, she wouldn't have to quit. When she finished her story, she watched closely Pieter's response.

The elder van der Kemp turned to Jan and said, "This girl is strong and intelligent like your mother. She is going to do well out here. She's a survivor." Turning back to Margot, he said with respect, "You say you can read?"

Margot hesitated out of reflex, then nodded.

"That's more than I can say for these two," Pieter commented, disdainfully regarding his sons. "Since they were boys, both of them have exhibited an intense dislike for any kind of mental activity. They avoid it at all costs, even though I tell them over and over that it takes more than a strong back and strong will to make it in this world."

Jan was clearly uneasy with his father's words.

A faraway gaze indicated that Breyton's attention had drifted. He was no longer paying attention to the conversation.

Pieter sat up straight in his chair. "My father was a baker in Utrecht, where I was born," he said. "There were ten children altogether. I was the oldest and learned to put in a hard day's work when I was still young." He extended massive arms. "That's where these forearms came from—from kneading dough. Every day I worked next to my father. And every day he taught me that in order to make it in this world you need two things: you need to work hard, and you need to be smart.

"He used to say to me, 'What good does it do to work hard if you don't know what you're worth? And what good does it do to be smart if you don't work?' So every night, after working all day in the bakery, I was forced to study my letters and numbers. More than once I remember my father slapping me on the back of the head and yelling, 'Think, Pieter! Think!'"

Pieter van der Kemp paused and looked at both his boys. "Sometimes I think I should have slapped my boys on the backs of their heads more often. Maybe then they'd know how to read."

Jan listened with his head lowered. He didn't look up.

Breyton plainly didn't hear a word of his father's story.

"What attracted you to Cape Town colony?" Margot asked.

"Nothing. I never intended to come here."

He smiled at her puzzled response. "Have you ever heard of the *zielverkoopers?*"

"The sellers of souls?" Margot shook her head.

"Recruiters for the Dutch East India Company," Pieter explained. "As I said, I was the oldest son in my family. So my father expected me to become a baker, just like him and his father and his grandfather. But I hated everything about the baking business. Loathed it. And though my father never knew it, his insistence on my learning to read was largely responsible for my discontent. A friend loaned me a book of sea stories. And after reading that book, more than anything else I wanted to become an adventurer. So one day while I was making deliveries, I happened to meet this *zielverkooper,* who was trolling the streets looking for boys just like me."

Margot leaned forward, intrigued. The mention of sea stories stirred memories of her evenings with Sylvie when the two of them would travel together to distant lands in the safety of their sitting room.

Pieter continued. "Every Thursday for weeks I would rush through my deliveries so that I could meet the *zielverkooper* at a local tavern without my father knowing about it. The *zielverkooper* would buy me a drink and tell me one tale after another about how young men signed on with the Company and sailed to Batavia. Within months of their arrival, every single one of them was wealthier than he ever could have been in Utrecht. And though the wealth appealed to me, it was the adventure of sailing to distant lands that intrigued me even more." Pieter paused in his narration long enough to take a drink. He chuckled. "I could have used one of my father's slaps on the back of the head right about then! As you might guess, I never made it to the East Indies. The ship dumped all of us who were foolish enough to sign promissory notes to work for the Company onto the shores of Table Bay. It seems the Company needed workers to build the Castle, and this was their way of securing common laborers. My life has been tied to the Company ever since."

"What made you stay?" Margot asked. "Surely at some point you could have gone on to Batavia or back to the Netherlands."

"Two things." Pieter smiled. "The land—and a good woman. The way I see it, God used my foolishness for His purpose and my good." A hand waved in the direction of the front of the house. "Where else could I live in a more beautiful and spacious place? And it was here that I met and married Antijie, the only true love of my life. Out of God's goodness, He made it possible for me to become a free burgher. I can't begin to tell you the excitement I felt the day Antijie and I staked out this farm. The center is in the middle of that orchard in front of the house."

"Where the two lanes cross," Jan interjected.

"Following the Company's guidelines, we started at that point and rode our horses at a walking pace for one half hour in each of the main compass directions. Everything within the circle of those connected points became our estate. Everything you see around us—the house, the slave quarters, the orchard, the farm, everything—Antijie and I built or planted."

"This isn't exactly our land," Jan explained. "We pay the Company to use it."

"They may own the land," Pieter thundered, "but this house is mine!"

His outburst caught Breyton's attention. The younger brother's face soured from a look of indifference to one of loathing.

Nodding in concession to his father, Jan said to Margot, "It's a sore point. The Company keeps changing its policies. Last year they decided that not only do we have to pay for the use of the land but we also have to give a tithe of the crops and herds on the land."

"Thieves!" Pieter barked. "With our own sweat and blood we work this land and make it something we can be proud of. Meanwhile, rich Company directors in Holland sit on their bench and decide they want more money. So do they work for it? No, they pick our pockets!"

The room fell silent.

"It's not an easy life out here," Pieter said more quietly, reflectively. "But we've done well. We buy sugar, spices, coffee, our clothes from the colony. Other than that we keep to ourselves and take care of our own. Our slaves are treated kindly as long as they obey. We are a godly people, and I believe God will bless us according to our faithfulness."

A chair scraped at the end of the table. Breyton stood.

"Where do you think you're going?" Pieter asked.

"For a walk."

"No, you're not. We need to get an early start tomorrow."

"I'm not going with you," Breyton said.

"Yes, you are!"

Breyton shook his head. "You know I'm no good to you out there. You're the one in love with those cows, not me."

"It's about time you began pulling your weight around here!"

Pieter's words quickened a transformation in Breyton, the same one Margot had witnessed the night she arrived. His normally charming features twisted into a dark, evil persona of hatred. "I pull my weight!" he thundered. "Who do you think built this house?"

"You wouldn't have known where to start if I didn't show you! Besides, that was years ago. What are you doing now?"

"I want to add more rooms on the second story, but you won't let me!"

"A waste of time and money!"

"In your opinion."

"Yes, that's my opinion! And if you had a brain, it would be your opinion too!"

Breyton turned to leave.

"Get back here!" Pieter roared.

Breyton ignored his father and went outside.

After the dinner table was cleared and the dishes were washed, Margot retired for the night. She dressed for bed and brushed her hair

217

as she thought over the day's events. As it turned out, her fears about the dinner had been unfounded. All three men liked it. Not that they told her so. But when she cleared the table, there was not a scrap of food left on any of the plates.

Then there was the way she was treated. Invited to the table. Accepted. No, more than accepted. Pieter was clearly impressed with her, and she with him. The patriarch's outspoken affection for the land and the van der Kemp estate raised her appreciation for it as well. As for his attention, she was flattered, but it made her feel trapped. He had made it even harder for her to leave.

Then there was Jan. He was so different when he was around his father. From the first time she met Jan, she had always seen him as a walking stone statue of Dutch manhood. It wasn't that he was without emotion. She had witnessed his emotions, but they too seemed fitting emotions for someone who was a monument to men. For example, when he was in anguish over Rachel, the tears on his cheeks were stone tears. And standing at the base of the waterfall, the statue wore a stone grin. All of that changed when Pieter was in the room. Next to his father, Jan was a little boy. The stone man became flesh and blood.

Just then Margot heard something outside. Her brush paused mid-stroke. It was the distant cry of a large cat. Breathless, she waited and listened. There it was again. *At night you can hear leopards,* Jan had said. Her reaction surprised her. She felt her blood rush, not from fear but from exhilaration. It was as though the leopard were the land's ambassador. Welcoming her.

She moved to the window. Her hairbrush went to work again as she stared into the night. She doubted the leopard would be bold enough to approach the house, so she didn't expect to see it. But for some reason, it thrilled her to think that somewhere in the darkness the leopard might be looking at her.

A movement caught her eye. In the orchard. Not a leopard but a man—a man leading a horse. The dark figures crept slowly in the shadows. They stopped. The man mounted. Turning onto the lane that led away from the house, the man and the horse moved into the light from Margot's window.

The rider kicked the horse's sides and rode quickly away but not without first looking back. The light caught him squarely in the face. Breyton.

For an instant he locked eyes with Margot. Then he was gone.

18

With speed Breyton put distance between him and Klaarstroom under cover of darkness. It disturbed him that Margot had seen him ride away. Would she say anything?

He answered his question with another question: What purpose would she have in saying anything? He could think of none. He was none of her concern. Besides, it didn't matter. He was away. On the return trip he could create a plausible story or two to cover his departure, just in case. For now, he had more pleasant things to think about.

Breyton van der Kemp knew that what he was doing was wrong, but he didn't care. That was something he'd resolved months earlier. For him, it was no longer a matter of the mind; it was a matter of the heart.

Not everyone could understand that; his father, for example. If Pieter van der Kemp knew what his son was doing, the old man would turn red and die of apoplexy. Breyton chuckled at the thought. It would serve the old man right for loving his covenant with God and the land more than he loved his son.

Breyton knew he could never change his father's mind. Hence the secrecy, the late night rendezvous. He knew that if he was caught he would lose everything—the van der Kemp house, a lifetime of crafted furniture, his family, his free-burgher status. He would be like his sister, Rachel, only worse—a pariah, a leper. His father and brother would disown him. He would never again be able to work, or trade, or buy, or sell in the colony. But Breyton didn't care. She was worth all that and more.

The dark outline of Cyrus Steenkamp's farm gradually took shape in the distant night. Not a light was on. Breyton dismounted a good distance from the buildings. Having tied his horse to a tree limb, he covered the remainder of the way on foot.

There was a chill in the air, which, combined with a sense of forbidden excitement, caused him to shiver involuntarily. His insides churned like a windmill, only instead of milling wheat into flour, it took the risk of capture and turned it into heightened anticipation.

At the barn's rough timber door, Breyton rapped twice softly and waited.

"Go away! This is *Mijnheer* Steenkamp's barn!"

Breyton smiled. He recognized the voice—but more important, he recognized the correct answer to his knock. It indicated that she was there and she was alone. Taking one last look around outside, Breyton pulled open the door. It creaked in complaint for being pressed into service at such a late hour. With no moon visible, the landscape behind him was dark, but it was darker still inside the barn. Eagerly he stepped over the threshold and into the darkness.

"Where are you?" he whispered.

"In the loft."

His hands probing, Breyton felt his way forward, shuffling through dirt and straw. "I can't see anything!" he whispered.

"Your eyes will adjust. Keeps coming."

Forms of posts and stalls slowly began to appear. He made his way past them, his heart racing at the thought of this clandestine tryst. Still shuffling, he caught sight of the wooden ladder that led to the loft. He climbed to the top and searched for her but saw nothing, conscious that each stage of his approach had grown increasingly darker.

From the blackest corner came a feminine voice. "Over here. Hurry."

Breyton's heart beat faster at the note of urgency in her voice. He crawled toward her over the hay.

"Should I lights the lantern?"

He stopped. "You have a lantern?"

"Yessuh."

"If you have a lantern, why did you make me come all this way in the dark?"

"To see how bad you wants me," she cooed.

A playful smile spread across Breyton's lips. "You vixen!"

The lantern was lit. Sitting coyly in the corner of the loft, with wide, innocent-looking eyes, was Ndela, the sixteen-year-old black slave of Cyrus Steenkamp.

She opened her arms, and he rushed into them.

At that moment, for Breyton everything else in the world ceased to exist. All thoughts of what others might think and how they might react to seeing him embracing a black slave dissipated in the warmth of her arms. The only thing that mattered was that the two of them were together.

Breyton was smitten with Ndela the day she arrived at the Steenkamp farm. No matter how hard he fought his urges to be near her, he found himself a helpless captive of her beauty. When opportunities to ride to the Steenkamps did not present themselves frequently enough, he created them.

All he wanted was to look at her, or so he told himself. As an artist, he was fascinated by the grace with which she carried herself, the fluid motions of her arms, the slenderness of her fingers. And as his stares grew lengthier, bolder, she took notice of him.

At first, Ndela dutifully lowered her eyes in keeping with her position. Then one day, to his surprise and delight, she brashly met his gaze with a boldness of her own and held it. One second? Two seconds? Breyton had no idea. For him, time ceased. All he saw were dark, saucy eyes, and he was lost.

Breyton began to notice that Ndela would go out of her way to offer him refreshment, to see that his horse was taken the moment he arrived, and to express admiration for the beauty of his work whenever he delivered a piece of furniture to her master. Moments between them blossomed into romance. An exchange of words or laughter. A brushing touch. A lingering touch. Hurried, private moments together. A kiss. Then Breyton was sneaking over to the Steenkamp farm late at night. He would do anything, say anything, go anywhere just for the chance to lose himself in Ndela's arms.

"Puts out the light," Ndela said. "The smoke's hurtin' my eyes."

Breyton raised up and blew out the flame. Then he resumed his position, cuddling close to her, his head in her lap.

Ndela stroked his hair. "I's gonna run away."

"You promised me you wouldn't do that again!"

"I gots to. Your father is never gonna buys me."

It was true. When the decision was made that the van der Kemp household needed a housekeeper, Breyton urged his father to buy Ndela. Pieter rejected the suggestion outright. He said he wanted nothing to do with a slave who had already run away twice. His father laughed derisively when Breyton suggested that maybe she ran away because of ill treatment at the hands of Cyrus Steenkamp. Before Breyton could mount a third attempt to secure the housekeeping position for Ndela, it was decided that Jan would ride to Cape Town and offer the position to one Margot de Campion. And though Breyton had seen Ndela since the position had been filled, he hadn't found the words to tell her yet.

"I'll find a way to raise the money to buy you," he said. "I'll make more furniture and sell it. I know several people in the colony I can approach."

"That will takes too long! I's gots to run away now."

"You'll just be caught and whipped again!"

"Not if I has a horse."

"Where are you going to get a horse?"

She snuggled close to his ear and whispered, "You can gets two horses, and we can runs away together."

He wanted to do it. The thought of the two of them together, free to live as they pleased, had been his fantasy for nearly a year. But each time he considered it, a sliver of reality worked its way under his skin. Where would they go? How would they live? Their only option was to flee into the desert. But then how would they survive? He was a craftsman, not a farmer or a cattleman.

"We's could be together always," Ndela cooed.

Breyton closed his eyes. She pulled his head against her, cradling it as though it were her baby. The heat of her body penetrated her clothing and warmed his cheek. The last of Breyton's remaining resistance melted.

"It will take me a couple of days to get everything together," he said.

Ndela rocked happily, holding his head tighter still. In the darkness, Breyton couldn't see the glint of cold triumph in her eyes.

The next instant the barn doors burst open, kicking up a cloud of dust and straw. Three lanterns held high rushed in through the swirling dust, followed by musket-toting Cyrus Steenkamp.

Ndela screamed and dropped Breyton's head, her legs churning, pushing herself into the darkest reaches of the corner. Breyton scrambled to his knees, positioning himself between her and the light.

"Move and I fire!" Steenkamp aimed the musket at the loft.

Breyton froze. Behind him he could hear Ndela weeping, her legs still writhing though she was as far back in the corner as she could get.

One by one the lanterns, held by three black slaves, came up the ladder. Without exception the slaves' jaws were set, and their eyes bulged an angry white. The lanterns bathed the loft in light. The only darkness remaining was Breyton's shadow, which stretched toward the corner and covered Ndela.

Laboriously, gray-bearded Cyrus Steenkamp made his way into the loft, carrying the musket. With his feet planted firmly on the loft floor, he rose to full height, his weapon at the ready. Squinting eyes recognized Breyton, then peered around him at Ndela. His mouth curled in disgust as he slowly shook his head.

Margot told Pieter and Jan she had seen Breyton ride out the night before, only when she learned that the youngest van der Kemp was missing. Breakfast was eaten in silence. Pieter chewed angrily, and Jan stared at his plate during the entire meal. When Pieter's chair scraped backward, Jan took one last hurried bite and then followed his father.

From the window Margot watched them ride out. Their silence served to remind her that she stood at the edge of the family. She was allowed to watch, but she was not a part.

Since there was nothing else she could do, Margot set to work cleaning off the breakfast table.

Once the dishes were washed, she carried a pail of dirty water out to the orchard to dispose of it at the base of a tree. From the side of the house came a curious clicking noise, accompanied by what sounded like small animal yelps. With empty bucket in hand, she went to investigate.

On the western side of the house she saw a hut, made of poles planted in the ground in a circle with their tops drawn inward and tied together to form a dome. Thin strips of wood were woven between the poles for siding. Woven reed mats were secured over this framework, and over the mats—spaced at times unevenly—were animal skins.

Sitting in the dirt at the hut's entrance, the door flap tossed back, was a half-naked, brown-skinned man who was covered with wrinkles and sagging flesh. He was clucking like a hen while his hands played with pieces of cow dung. The dung had twigs protruding from it in a way that resembled the legs of animals. Catching sight of Margot's shadow, he jumped slightly. He scooted the dung behind him like a child hiding his toys.

"I'm sorry to have startled you," Margot said.

The little brown man cocked his head and studied her, and she him.

Margot had never been this close to a Hottentot before, so she was unprepared for the odor. It was so overwhelming she had to fight to keep from swooning. The man looked as if he had rolled in dirt and dung, as if he had never bathed in his life. But he alone was not the cause of the stench. Atop his head he wore a covering resembling a skull cap, which was made of cow dung mingled with a stinking grease. Draped around his neck were the entrails of an animal. Margot was not expert enough to know what kind of animal, but from the contents, which were clearly visible in several places, it had been a grass-eating beast.

She was reminded of a comment she once read. An early settler had described Hottentots as "beasts in the skins of men rather than men in the skins of beasts." If the man sitting in front of her was any indication of the general population of Hottentots, Margot concluded that the description was an understatement.

The little brown man stood up. He was under five feet tall. Scratching his short, curly black hair much as a dog would scratch a flea, he said, "Are you Jan's woman?"

What has Jan been telling everyone about me? Margot was incensed. "No, I am not Jan's woman!"

"Good. Too skinny to be a cattle farmer's wife."

Although Margot could understand him, his speech was poor Dutch intermingled with the clicks of his native tongue.

"My name is Margot. I'm the housekeeper."

"Then you are Jan's woman!"

Margot flushed with anger. "No, I am *not* Jan's woman!"

The little brown man shrugged. "You confuse me." Entering his hut, he motioned to her. "Come, come." The hide flap lowered, and he disappeared.

Margot stared at the flap. She did not want to go into the Hottentot's hut. Would she offend him if she refused?

A dung-covered head with black peppercorn hair popped out of the opening. "Come! Come!"

Bending low, Margot entered.

The odor was worse inside. Stifling. Hanging on the sides of the hut were water bags made from the stomachs of cattle. Also hanging on the walls was a variety of foodstuffs stored in nets—strips of dried meat, roots, herbs, and other odds and ends.

"Sit! Sit!" The little man motioned to the floor. He squatted on his heels.

Margot examined the floor before sitting. It was stamped hard and seemed to have been treated with some kind of dark stain. Her hand touched the surface as she lowered herself to her knees. She felt wax. Probably beeswax to give a shiny appearance.

"Knobkerrie. That's me." The brown man patted himself on the chest.

"I've heard of you. From Rachel."

The man grinned and nodded. "Old Knob. Knobkerrie. That's me."

"I'm pleased to meet you."

"Nice?" Old Knob motioned to the interior of his hut.

Margot followed the sweep of his arm. "Nice. Yes, your hut is nice." She couldn't help but be amused at what Sylvie would say of the hut—the woman who scrubbed the front porch step until she nearly wore it away.

"Marry, you and Jan?"

"I don't know what *Mijnheer* van der Kemp has told you, but he and I are not getting married. I am the van der Kemps' housekeeper. Nothing more."

"Good people. Jan. Pieter. Not all settlers good. Van der Kemps good to the land, good to Old Knob." His words were not merely gratuitous. The brown man's eyes glistened with genuine feeling.

Margot did not want to appear unfriendly, but neither did she want to stay inside the Hottentot's hut any longer than necessary. To be polite, she inquired about his family.

Sadness swept across his face. "Dead. All dead. My whole village. Dead. Great sickness from ships. Many Khoikhoi die."

"I'm sorry," Margot said. "Truly, I am." She realized now that she was sitting in the presence of one of the native survivors of the smallpox plague of 1713.

"When my village died, Pieter let me build my hut here. In place of honor. Fitting for a king with no village."

"Place of honor?"

"Western side of settlement. First to catch the rising sun."

Margot glanced around the hut's interior before asking, "Would you like to move into a room inside the house? I could ask *Mijnheer* van der Kemp for you."

Old Knob shook his head emphatically. "He asked. I refused. Not good the way they live. Not healthy."

Margot suppressed a laugh. Here was a man, filthy dirty, with dung on his head, wearing animal entrails for a necklace, and declaring that the van der Kemps' house was unhealthy. Preparing to rise, she said, "Thank you, *Mijnheer* Knobkerrie, for your hospi—"

"Sit! Sit!" Old Knob urged. "Listen to story of my ancestor, Xhore."

The way Old Knob insisted she stay reminded Margot of some of the elderly ladies in Amsterdam. Lonely, eager for company, they always hated to see visitors go. Apparently loneliness transcended cultures.

"Xhore was my father's father," Old Knob said with a wistful look in his eyes. "When the ships sailed for England, they took Xhore with them. He did not want to go. He was aboard ship to look. Sailors sailed. Xhore told them over and over, 'Xhore go home—Saldania go!'"

"Saldania?"

"This place Saldania."

Margot nodded in understanding. Saldania. The Khoi name for South Africa.

"Xhore dressed like Englishman. Long sleeves. Shoes with buckles. Hat with feather. Met king named James of England. The king had many questions for Xhore. Laughed at Xhore's stories of Saldania. But Xhore not happy away from home. Kept saying, 'Xhore go home—Saldania go!' Feared he was because people stare at him. He the only Khoikhoi in England."

"I can see why that would be frightening."

"I remember day when Xhore return. He looked like small Englishman. We thought him rich. Much brass. Brass necklace. Brass rings. Brass buckles. He say brass not valuable in England. James the king looking for gold in Saldania. He want Xhore to help him find gold, not brass. When Xhore leave English ship at Table Bay, he promised to return in three days. But when he talk with his village, they tell him not to go back. He didn't. From that day we ask for more from Englishmen. Cattle worth more than brass—Xhore learned that. Englishmen not like lesson Xhore learned." Old Knob shook his head mournfully. "Lesson Xhore learned brought hate between English and Khoikhoi."

Margot sat silently as the old man retreated for a moment into his memories. She was willing to wait while he selected the ones he wished to share.

Suddenly the brown man jumped up. "Stay!" he said. "Not go away."

He rushed to the far side of the hut where he rummaged through a pile of miscellaneous clothing items and skins. Finding what he was looking for, he turned around proudly, holding a copper breastplate against his chest and a javelin in his hand.

"From England. Xhore wore when he return home. Xhore gave to me. His best grandson. Xhore love Knobkerrie very much. He say Knobkerrie be great king some day."

Margot smiled at Old Knob's unabashed pride in the articles. "Those are fine items. Family heirlooms. Thank you for sharing them with me." She began to rise again.

"Sit! Sit!" Old Knob cried, hopping from one foot to the other. "Story not finished. Xhore find greater treasure than brass in England. Greater than James the king's gold."

Margot took her seat. "What did he find?"

"Heard Xhore myself. It was like this. Captain of ship came to trade with Khoi. He talk to Xhore about England and God of England. Captain asked Xhore who was God of Khoi. Xhore say, 'England God—great God. Saldania—no God.'" Old Knob said the last three words with great sadness. Then, much brighter, he added, "Then Xhore say, 'But England God, my God!'"

Margot smiled at the thought as well as at the enthusiasm with which Old Knob pronounced his grandfather's faith.

"Now. Today. I say, Xhore's God my God. England God, my God too!" Old Knob beamed.

Never before had Margot heard such a simple yet heartfelt statement of faith.

"That is why Old Knob stay with Pieter and Jan. Same God."

The light in the old Hottentot's eyes confirmed that what he was saying was true. And from that moment, whenever Margot saw the little brown man, his personal hygiene would no longer seem as offensive. For inside the crusty old shell beat the heart of a true believer.

"Van der Kemp!"

The voice came from outside the hut.

"Van der Kemp!"

It was an ugly sounding cry, not the cry of someone bringing good news nor of someone coming for a social visit.

Margot ran from Old Knob's hut with the Hottentot close behind.

Cyrus Steenkamp sat on his horse yelling at the house. A musket was tucked under one arm, and his free hand held the reins of a second horse. Breyton, his hands bound and his head bowed, sat atop the horse under Steenkamp's control.

"Van der Kemp!"

"They're not here."

Steenkamp whirled in Margot's direction. Eyes squinted as he stared at her. He recognized her, she saw, but was having trouble

227

placing where he'd seen her. Then he nodded, his long gray beard swinging back and forth like a pendulum. "The slave compound," he said. "You're the one who took the lashes for Ndela."

Breyton's head snapped up. From his reaction it was clear this was the first he'd heard of that incident.

"What are you doing here?" Steenkamp asked.

"I'm the van der Kemps' housekeeper."

"That was your trunk I hauled up here?"

"Yes."

"Had I known it was yours I would have left it in Cape Town."

"I'm sorry you feel that way."

"I feel that way about anyone who undermines God-given authority!" Steenkamp bellowed. Looking at Breyton, he added, "Or who makes a fool of himself because he has no more sense than a rutting animal."

Something caught Steenkamp's eye. He looked up, past Margot. Behind her came the sound of approaching horses. She turned as Pieter and Jan rode up.

Anger flashed across Pieter's face as he looked at Breyton and the ropes that bound him.

"What's going on here?" Pieter demanded.

The gray-bearded neighbor looked with disgust at him. "There was a time when I respected you, van der Kemp," he said. "But no more."

Jan dismounted. He stood beside Margot but couldn't take his eyes off the ropes that bound his brother. "What is this all about?" he whispered.

"They just arrived," Margot replied.

Pieter remained on his horse, keeping at eye level with his neighbor. With reins still in hand, he leaned forward. "Why have you bound my son?" He managed to restrain his tone, but the redness of his neck indicated it was not without great effort.

Steenkamp tossed the reins of Breyton's horse in Pieter's direction. They fell limp to the ground. "I caught this one in my loft last night with one of my slaves."

Pieter looked at his younger son.

His eyes lowered, Breyton refused to look at his father.

"By all that's holy, van der Kemp, what have you been teaching your children? One of your offspring runs off with a Malaysian, another beds my slave, and now you invite this woman of questionable character into your house." He glanced at Old Knob as though to say something about him too, then apparently thought better of it. "Van der Kemp, have you no fear of God?"

The reins shook involuntarily in Pieter's hands. It took him a moment before he was in control enough to speak. "We have been neighbors too long to warrant that kind of talk, Cyrus. I'll forget you said those things. And you can be sure my son will get what's coming to him."

"See that he does. And keep him off my slave!" Looking at Margot, he added, "And keep her away from my farm. She's trouble." With a hard jerk of the reins, Steenkamp rode off.

Pieter van der Kemp watched him leave. He sat back and exhaled loudly. However, that did not appear to diminish the level of his anxiety. His face and hands were crimson, all except for the white creases in his hands from gripping the reins.

Old Knob returned to his hut without saying a word.

Margot decided to follow his example and go into the house. With her back to the van der Kemp men she heard Pieter's voice.

"I'll talk to you later, Jan. I want to know what it is you haven't told me about that woman. As for *you*, come with me."

Margot busied herself in the kitchen for a time. When she went upstairs to get a handkerchief, a slapping sound caught her attention. She walked to the window. Breyton and Pieter were beside the barn. The younger van der Kemp was leaning against a post. Behind him his father, leather whip in hand, applied one stroke after another to his son's bare back. With each stroke Breyton's head snapped back in pain.

Pieter was a portrait of vengeance. Face red with rage. Teeth clenched. Right arm strong and held high. The whip hesitating at its apex, then lashing down in judgment.

The hand holding the handkerchief flew to Margot's mouth. She bit down on it. It was too much for her to watch. As she turned, she happened to see Jan standing behind a tree, watching his brother's whipping. He turned away, wiping tears from his cheeks with both hands.

19

Margot tried not to think about the whipping. In the kitchen she chopped carrots and greens. But the sound of the knife against the cutting board reminded her of the lash striking Breyton's back. From the larder she pulled out meat for stew. Holding it in her hands, she saw the exposed red flesh of Breyton's back.

She kept telling herself she'd seen men whipped before. It was a daily occurrence in the slave compound. Why did Breyton's whipping disturb her so? Family. That's what it was. What was happening out by the barn wasn't some overseer beating a disobedient slave. It was a father beating his son. A father laying an angry lash on his own flesh and blood.

With an anguished cry, Margot ran out the back door. She closed her eyes and breathed deeply. *Try not to think about it,* she told herself. *Force it from your mind. Think of the sunshine on your face. The clean scent of the air. The—* A cry came from the direction of the barn. It was Breyton. Though she couldn't see what was taking place, she could still hear it.

Margot covered her ears. "Please, Lord, make him stop! Make him stop!" Pressing her hands against the sides of her head, she tried her best to shut out the sounds.

Something tugged at her apron.

Startled, she opened her eyes. As she did, she was greeted with a foul but familiar odor.

Old Knob was looking up at her. *"Mejuffrouw* Housekeeper in pain?"

"As soon as that stops, I will be fine." She motioned toward the barn just as another wail pierced the air.

Old Knob looked in the direction of the beating even though the house blocked any view of the barn. *"Mijnheer* Pieter do right thing."

"How can you say that?" Margot cried.

"Breyton must learn. He plant seeds of his destruction. *Mijnheer* Pieter try to destroy them before they take root."

"I can't believe that whipping a son like that is the best way to correct him!"

Old Knob stared at her a moment, then walked toward an elm tree. "Come!" He motioned to Margot to follow him. "Come. Come."

At the base of the tree Old Knob sat. The old Hottentot, who would have looked out of place in the van der Kemp house sitting in its finely polished stinkwood chairs, looked totally natural at the foot of the tree. The man and his environment were a perfect match.

"Tell you old story. Story my father's father told me."

Margot sat beside the old man on his upwind side.

With great relish, Old Knob launched into his tale.

Spring it was in Saldania. Plum trees in bloom. High in one plum tree lived mother dove and her two fat babies. One day while she sing to her babies, a jackal heard her.

Jackal calls up to dove, "How many babies do you have?"

Mother dove said, "Two. Two."

"Throw one down," said jackal. "Then you only have one to feed."

"No! No!" cried mother dove. "Both babies are dear to me."

Jackal leaped high toward her. "Ow! Ow!" he cried. "Throw down one baby, or I will climb tree and eat them both!"

Mother dove so frightened by jackal, she forgot jackals could not climb trees. So to save one of her babies, she threw other one down.

Dilak! Jackal swallowed the baby dove whole!

(Margot jumped when Old Knob simulated the jackal's gulping sound, much to the delight of the aged storyteller.)

"My poor baby!" cried mother dove.

Jackal ran around tree to see if anyone was looking. "Grrr!" he growled. "Throw down other baby, or I will climb up and eat it and you and nest of sticks too!"

Mother dove was so frightened she threw down other baby to him.

Dilak! Jackal swallowed other baby dove whole!

(Margot didn't jump this time. Old Knob looked disappointed.)

Then, smacking his lips, jackal went away.

Mother dove looked into empty nest. "Woo, woo, woo! What have I done? How can I live without my babies?"

A blue crane heard dove's cry. "Why are you so sad?" asked crane.

Mother dove told crane what happened.

231

"Your babies were safe!" cried crane. "Who told you that jackals can climb trees?"

"Jackal started to do it! He made it halfway up trunk. And I didn't think he would stop there."

"Jackal tricked you," said crane. "Well, now it is our turn to trick him. Jackal made you believe he could climb tree. I'll make him believe he can learn to fly." And with that crane flew away, looking for jackal.

The crane found jackal running fast. His fur was wet with sweat.

"Slow down!" cried crane. "You will run yourself to death!"

"A storm is coming," said jackal. "I must get home before it breaks."

"Too bad you have to run on ground," said crane. "To us who fly, long distances are nothing. Why don't you meet me here when storm is over, and I will teach you to fly?"

Jackal liked that idea, so he promised to return. As soon as storm passed, he came back. Crane was waiting for him. "Now teach me to fly," said jackal.

Crane told jackal if he wanted to fly he would have to rub gum all over himself. So jackal rubbed gum from mimosa tree all over himself. "It makes my hair stick together!" jackal said. "I do not like way it feels."

Blue crane said nothing. She plucked feathers from herself and stuck them to jackal's gummy coat.

Jackal was delighted. "I am a bird!" jackal cried. He ran on his hind legs and flapped his front paws. But he could not get off ground. "You made me a bird that can't fly!" he complained.

"I will have to teach you to fly like I teach my children," crane said. "Get on my back. I will fly you into air. When we are high enough, you must jump off and fly."

Jackal looked up at the sky.

"You are not afraid, are you?" crane asked.

"No, no," said jackal. "I was just measuring height of sky."

So jackal climbed onto crane's back. Crane flapped her wings faster and faster. Finally she rose into air. When they were high in sky, crane told jackal to jump off. When he hesitated, she pulled herself out from underneath jackal. And jackal fell all the way to earth. He hit ground hard, and when he did, the two baby doves popped right out of his mouth!

Crane flew down and gathered up baby doves and carried them back to their nest.

Mother dove was happy to have her babies back. She thanked blue crane again and again.

Jackal was not dead. He dragged himself to river and began to clean sticky mess from his body. All the other animals laughed at jackal, who had feathers stuck all over him.

Blue crane flew overhead. She said, "It is a true saying: 'Whoever sows evil will see it come forth in his own garden!'"

Old Knob rocked back and forth, enjoying the wisdom of his story. He concluded, "*Mijnheer* Breyton must learn the lesson of jackal, or he will soon have evil growing in his own garden. Do you like Xhore's story?"

"It's a wise story," Margot said. "However, I still don't think—"

"Margot?" The voice was Jan's. He was standing nearby. "May I speak with you?"

Old Knob and Margot stood.

"Thank you, Knobkerrie," she said.

The old Hottentot shook his head. "Thanks not wanted or needed. In Saldania we help each other survive. It is law of wilderness. No thank yous. Why thank someone merely for behaving well?" Then he disappeared around the corner of the house.

"Margot," Jan said, "you treated a lot of wounds in the slave compound . . ."

Margot nodded. She'd seen enough wounds for a lifetime.

"Will you . . . that is, would you be willing . . ." Jan struggled to find the right words.

Margot placed an assuring hand on his arm. "I'll need clean water and plenty of clean cloths," she said.

Breyton sat on a stool in the barn. For half an hour Margot tended the stripes on his back. Neither of them spoke. Rarely had she seen a whipping worse than his. With each application of the cloth he flinched and closed his eyes to fight back the pain. Several times he reached up and wiped away tears. But never once did he make a sound. And when his eyes were open, they focused on the floor with an icy stare. The shadow of hatred that she had seen cross his face on occasion when he and his father quarreled was now fixed and hardened with resolve.

"We'll have to do this once every day for a while," Margot said, "to keep the wounds from festering."

Breyton didn't acknowledge her.

"I met Ndela when I was at the slave compound. She had run away," Margot said. "I treated her wounds too."

She paused, waiting for some kind of response. She was hoping Breyton would talk to her. The thing she most remembered about Ndela was the young girl's cold eyes and her odd disdain for Margot's intervention on her behalf. It puzzled her what Breyton saw in the girl. They were from different worlds, different backgrounds. One slave, one free. One who did menial labor and the other who crafted immaculate furniture . . .

Breyton's back rose and fell with each breath. It was the only sign he gave that he was alive.

"You're going to hurt for some time. Sleeping will be most difficult." Margot dabbed the last of the stripes. "It would be best if you not wear a shirt for a while."

Breyton stood. He grabbed his shirt. He winced as he arched his back to get his arms into the sleeves.

"Here, let me help you then," Margot offered.

Breyton pulled away from her. Gritting his teeth and clenching his eyes tightly, he slid one arm, then the other, into the sleeves. Several times he had to stop. He breathed heavily for several seconds before resuming. Finally he managed to get the shirt on by himself. He walked toward the door. Red stains began appearing where the shirt touched his back.

Without turning around, he said, "Something happened in the slave compound that I'm not aware of. Otherwise Steenkamp would not have treated you as he did. For whatever it is you did for Ndela, thank you."

"Why thank someone merely for behaving well?" Margot replied. "Out here we have to look after each other."

Carrying the bundle of bloodied rags, she made her way toward the house.

As Margot reached the front steps, a figure caught the corner of her eye. Standing where the roads crossed in the front orchard was—*Rachel!* It took a moment for Margot to recognize her. The girl's hair was plain, her dress simple; she was unlike the primped and pampered Rachel that Margot was used to seeing. Matthew stood behind Rachel at a good distance.

"Helloa, Margot."

"Rachel!"

Realizing what she was carrying, Margot cast aside the rags and rushed to meet her.

The younger girl waited for her in the center of the crossroads but received Margot's embrace eagerly when it came. While holding her tightly, Margot looked over Rachel's shoulder at Matthew.

He flashed an infectious smile and waved.

Stepping back, Margot asked, "Are you married?"

Rachel blushed and nodded.

"Congratulations!" Margot gave her another hug.

"And I'm pregnant," Rachel whispered.

Margot pulled away. "You're sure?"

Rachel's eyes twinkled excitedly. She nodded again.

"That's wonderful!" The third hug was harder than the previous two. "I'm so happy for you!" Margot exclaimed.

"Helloa, Breyton," Rachel called over Margot's shoulder.

Releasing Rachel, Margot stepped to one side. Breyton stood near the steps of the house, his back arched. Margot knew it was to prevent his shirt from touching raw flesh. There was no smile. He said nothing. He just stood there.

Pieter and Jan emerged from the house.

"Helloa, Father. Helloa, Jan," Rachel said softly.

Pieter walked to the edge of the steps. Jan remained behind him. Like Breyton, their faces were emotionless. They stared but said nothing. The men looked like three cattle farmers posing for an oil painting.

"I had to see you," Rachel said hesitantly. Her voice was barely audible. She couldn't look at her father when she spoke; she stared at her hands as they squeezed each other reassuringly. "I have news," she said.

There was a pause as Rachel glanced up briefly, evidently hoping to catch some sign of encouragement from her family.

There was none. Three stony male faces stared back at her.

Rachel continued anyway. "Matthew and I are married," she said, glancing back at her husband.

Matthew's eyes were fixed on the van der Kemp men. There was no infectious smile for them like the kind he had flashed at Margot. Instead, he met their icy glare with one of his own.

Rachel lowered her head. She began to weep. "I shouldn't have come," she whispered so that only Margot could hear.

"You're doing the right thing," Margot replied. "Tell your father about the baby."

"I can't!" Rachel was weeping openly now.

"Get off my land!"

Pieter's thundering words hit Rachel with a force sufficient to halt the flow of her tears. Her face froze into a look of disbelief. It took her several moments to recover. When she did, to Margot's dismay a glaze of loathing covered the girl's young, innocent eyes.

Margot had seen the look before. It was chillingly cold. It was the same look she had seen in Breyton's eyes.

Rachel spun around and started to leave.

"Wait! Rachel, don't!" Margot ran after her and blocked her retreat.

"Let her go!" Pieter yelled.

Rachel tried to step around Margot, but she blocked the girl's path again. Yelling to Pieter, Margot said, "Rachel and Matthew came all this way just to tell you something! The least you can do is listen to them!"

"They can talk to the wind for all I care."

Margot whispered, "Tell him, Rachel! Tell him! He's your father!"

The glaze of hatred had crystallized in Rachel's eyes, transforming her entire appearance. If Margot had not already known it was Rachel who was standing in front of her, she wouldn't have recognized her as the same woman.

"If you don't tell your father, I will!" Margot threatened.

The look Margot got in response made her want to cry. Rachel's features grew harder. Her eyes no longer harbored hate; they generated it. The tender, carefree Rachel that Margot had known was being eaten up from the inside. In its place was a frightened, defensive animal. Margot knew that unless she did something soon, she was to lose Rachel.

Yelling over Rachel's shoulder, Margot cried, "Your daughter is expecting!"

The three men showed no reaction.

"She is going to have your grandchild!"

There was no immediate response. But the message had been delivered. The only thing the messenger could do now was wait for Pieter van der Kemp to decide what he was going to do with it.

In a low, bitter tone Pieter growled, "I have no grandchild, because I have no daughter."

Rachel flinched.

A rising tide of anger rose inside Margot with a fury she'd never known before. With it came trembling and tears. Her words weren't spoken—they catapulted from her mouth. "What kind of father are you? What kind of Christian man would say something like that to his daughter?"

Jan took a step forward, his hand outstretched, "Margot, don't—"

Pieter cut him off. "Nobody in this household is to have anything to do with that woman and her husband. Nobody! Ever! That includes you, *Mejuffrouw* de Campion! Either step away from her now, or get your things and your self off my property!"

"Or what? You'll whip me too?" The words flew out of her mouth before she could stop them.

Pieter balled his fists.

"Margot, don't." It was Rachel. For the moment she was back, the Rachel Margot knew and loved. "Please, don't. You can't help me. But you can help Jan. He loves you, and you can save him. Nobody else can. Only you. Walk away from me. Please, walk away."

"Rachel, I can't live in a house like this."

"You must. You can change them. Jan will listen to you."

Margot shook her head.

"Please."

Margot stared at the men. Stern. Unyielding. Even Breyton, who wore fresh stripes on his back. And Jan. Was there really a spark of humanity behind that stony exterior? With tears, Margot embraced Rachel. "God be with you," she whispered. Then she stepped to the side to let Rachel pass.

Silently Rachel walked away from her family. After several steps, she took one glance back. The glaze in her eyes had returned. When she looked at her father there was no warmth, no longing; only bitterness, and hurt, and hate.

As soon as Matthew and Rachel were gone, the three van der Kemp men went inside the house. Not another word was spoken.

For the longest time Margot stood alone on the road while reason and emotions fought a bloody war inside her. She staggered to the point where the roads crossed, the place where Rachel stood during her attempt at reconciliation. It was there at the crossroads that Margot's emotions overwhelmed her. She collapsed onto the dirt and wept. Unable to think, unable to pray, all she could do was hurt.

20

For weeks following Rachel's visit, the van der Kemp household was like a tomb that had been sealed for two hundred years. Her visit was never mentioned. It was as if it had never occurred and Rachel never existed. Jan and Breyton shuffled around the house barely uttering a dozen words between them. Dinners were the worst. Four people shared a table in solitude. If any words were spoken, Pieter spoke them.

And the words he spoke were sharp-edged and cutting. He worried aloud about what their neighbors were saying. If Steenkamp, their closest neighbor and friend for years, questioned the morality of their family, what must their other neighbors be saying about them? And who could blame them, when none of his children exhibited the values that had made them a covenant people?

He harped on Jan's inability to read, complaining that when business needed to be transacted in Cape Town, he was forced to accompany Jan into town as he would a little boy.

He accused Breyton of being a freeloader and lacking manhood, because he avoided the work as a cattle farmer and had to resort to chasing after slaves instead of courting acceptable women.

There were no rebuttals to his harangues. No objections. Jan and Breyton sat sullenly at the table and took the abuse. Night after night.

Margot began to thank God daily for the daylight hours when the men were away, because those hours afforded her a measure of peace. While they were out with the cattle or working the farm, she cleaned and scrubbed and polished until her arms ached, her anger dissipated, and her soul felt renewed. Cleaning was the best thing for her. It gave her anger and frustration an outlet. The tumultuous feelings that stewed inside her somehow worked their way into her arms and out her fingers until the floors of the van der Kemp household shone like mirrors and the dishes so reflected the candles that the room was twice as bright.

During these days of silence, Margot found companionship and common ground among some of the other workers, notably Old Knob and Ding, the black foreman. Both agreed that never had they seen the van der Kemp house in such a black mood.

Referring to Pieter's concern about his neighbors, Ding said, "As my mother used to say, 'The staring frogs do not prevent cattle from drinking.' In other words, don't worry about other people's opinions."

When he wasn't out with the cattle himself, Old Knob would stop by the kitchen door and beg for some of Margot's pancakes. The Hottentot proclaimed the flour disks to be the perfect food. Those he didn't consume on the spot, he stuffed inside his clothing to eat later. Between Ding's optimistic sayings and Old Knob's reassuring presence, Margot managed to maintain a level of hope that the stormy mood among the van der Kemp men wouldn't last forever.

Then there was the land itself. It became as much a companion to her as Ding and Old Knob. Once a day, usually at sunset, she took a walk. In the quiet of twilight, she found comfort and a sense of stability in the solid presence of the mountains. She would perch on the edge of a rock and be as still as she could, her eyes scanning the land for signs of life.

This time of day reminded her of the evenings when she and Sylvie would sit on the bench in front of the house in Amsterdam and pass the time with their neighbors. Here, her neighbors were an occasional antelope, aardvark, or porcupine. She shared the sky with flocks of geese or the blackhead ibis, and sometimes a blue crane swooped across the sky and reminded her of Old Knob's story. One evening she sat enraptured by the effortless soaring of an eagle against the darkening sky. The longer she watched, the more it seemed the bird had the power to pull her spirit heavenward, away from the oppressive mood of the van der Kemp household.

However, as alluring as the South African land was to Margot, for some reason it also provided grist for a recurring nightmare.

She seemed to be taking her evening walk. The air was cool. The night's first stars were peeking through the blue veil of sky like little children hiding behind a curtain. In the distance, a herd of antelope skimmed the horizon, sleek and graceful.

Then, for no discernible reason, the antelope changed course and headed straight for her. The pounding of their hooves set the earth to rumbling. Naturally, as they approached they grew larger. Unnaturally, they grew larger because they were changing. They became more muscular. Their faces grew wide. Enlarged nostrils flared angrily. Eyes bulged white and wild. They weren't antelope anymore. They were horses. Horses with riders. Men. Strong men, their arms raised in fury just like Pieter's arm when he whipped Breyton.

Frightened, Margot ran for cover. But there was no house to run to. Only bushes. Bushes with woefully inadequate coverings of leaves.

Then, from out of nowhere, her mother appeared. Not Sylvie, but her birth mother. With arms waving, Mother attempted to divert the horses and riders from Margot's path. Then Father appeared. Together they waved and yelled. To no avail. They placed themselves in the path of the oncoming stampede. Nothing they did altered the horses' course.

Now flashing swords were brandished over the riders' heads. They were for Margot. No one swung a sword at her parents. They did not need to. The first horses to reach her mother and father opened wide their mouths and swallowed them whole. The horses didn't have to slow to do it. And they kept coming, ever faster. The swords flashed high against the sky like lightning. Ready to strike. Eager to taste her blood. Margot dove into the bushes and covered her head. She was helpless. Defenseless. She could only watch as horses and riders and swords came closer and closer.

High overhead, an eagle stopped his circular pattern to watch the spectacle. Huddled behind a rock an aardvark wept; a porcupine turned his face away at the sight. The sun stood still. The wind refused to blow. All nature held its breath, shocked that man could be so filled with hate that he would willingly, gleefully spill the life force of God's creation in the dust.

The leaves on the branches could not hide her. The ground trembled. The horses were so near now that Margot could hear their snorting, a breathy chant. She bit her fingers to keep herself from crying out. She bit them until she tasted blood. She closed her eyes. Her only hope lay in the dubious reasoning that if she couldn't see them, they couldn't hurt her.

She waited and waited. Nothing happened. Had it worked? Had they gone away? Slowly she separated her fingers. Just a crack. Just enough to see. A horse screamed, the rider's eyes spit fire, his silver blade hovered high, then ripped through the air with a mighty swish.

Margot screamed. Her attempt to raise her hands to intercept the blade was hindered by her bedcovers. Feet kicked and struggled in an attempt to escape.

Then she awoke, surrounded by dark forms—a cabinet, a window, a nightstand. There were no horses, no riders, no silver blades, only silver moonlight streaming through the window. But familiar surroundings and logical observations did little to calm Margot's racing heart, or stop the perspiration from flowing, or return her breath that had fled like a bird from a cage. Gradually, as her awakening senses rallied, she began to feel pain in her fingers. They bore teeth marks. Her own.

Margot didn't know what exactly prompted the nightmares. She'd had them when she was little, in those early days with Marc and Sylvie Fabarez in Amsterdam. But that was years and years ago.

Fully awake now, Margot rose and walked to the window. The orchard was bathed in moonlight. The mountains looked flat black against the horizon. There was no sound. No movement. The world was asleep. All but Margot.

Still, something was not right. The calmness of the night seemed only a cover for some raging horror that lurked beneath the earth's surface. The world could not hold it back forever. It would some day burst forth. That's what her nightmares were telling her. Warning her about. Death would come from the wilderness. And she couldn't stop it.

He led the horses through the darkness until they were out of sight of the house. Before mounting, he mentally checked his provisions. Clothing. Food for a week; he wished it could be more, but that was all he could manage to obtain. A musket and ammunition. He would have to make shelter out of whatever materials he could find in the wilderness. That did not concern him. He was good with his hands.

Having inspected his supplies, he mounted without hesitation. He was riding away from nothing. The crisscrossed wounds on his back reminded him of that. There was nothing for him at Klaarstroom any longer. Nothing he wanted, at least. Tonight he was riding away from ridicule, insults, and abuse. With the dawn of a new day he would start a new life with the woman he loved. Breyton had never felt more alive in his life.

The Steenkamp farm appeared out of the darkness. As before, he approached the barn on foot, having tied up the horses a good distance away. He checked the area for movement. All was still.

With his cheek against the barn door Breyton whispered, "Ndela?"

He waited for a response. When one was not forthcoming, his heart began to sink inside him. Had someone intercepted his message? Or had Ndela decided it was too dangerous to meet him? If she

241

wasn't here, how would he find her without waking up the entire slave population? A sense of dread took root inside him. Were all his efforts tonight in vain?

He whispered again. "Ndela?"

All was silent.

Then the barn door opened a crack. Moonlight poured through the opening, illuminating her wide eyes.

"You got my message!"

"I was afraids to believe it!"

"Believe it! I have two horses waiting for us."

"You really has two horses?"

Breyton twisted about to look behind him, and stripes of pain crossed his back. "Hurry! Before someone comes," he said.

The barn door creaked open just enough for Ndela's slim frame to slip through. She was carrying a bundle of clothing.

"Do you have everything? We can't come back."

"I's go naked just for the chance to get away from here!"

His head darting from side to side, Breyton scanned the terrain. With his arm around the slender shoulders of Cyrus Steenkamp's youthful slave, he led her to the horses. He felt a shiver shake her body.

"Frightened?"

Ndela looked up at him, her face highlighted with the moon's blue light. Bright eyes and a quick smile answered him. "Not scared," she said. "Excited! I's finally gonna be free!"

"You do know how to ride a horse, don't you?"

"Just tries and keeps up with me!"

Within moments two figures rode off together into the darkness. They headed toward the hills, beyond the boundaries of the colony's outlying settlements.

"Have you seen Breyton this morning?" Jan stood in the kitchen doorway.

Margot was mixing a large batch of pancakes, half for the van der Kemps and half for Old Knob.

"I haven't seen him."

Jan shook his head. "He's not in his room. I'm afraid he took off again."

"To see Ndela?"

"Possibly. I don't know."

Behind Jan, the front door slammed violently. Heavy boots clumped across the wooden floor. Pieter appeared.

"Two horses are gone," he said.

"Two?"

Pieter's mouth formed a thin line. He confirmed Jan's question with a nod.

"Do you think he went after her?"

Before Pieter could answer, a bellowing came from the front of the house.

"Van der Kemp!"

Jan looked at his father. "Steenkamp," he said.

"Van der Kemp!"

Pieter went out onto the porch. Jan was right behind him. Margot trailed after.

The van der Kemps' gray-bearded neighbor sat on his horse, a musket draped across his lap. "Where's that boy of yours?" Steenkamp thundered. "My slave Ndela is missing."

"Breyton's not here," Pieter said.

Eyes squinted at him. "Where is he?"

Pieter crossed his arms. "I don't know. But two of our horses are missing."

Steenkamp lifted his face heavenward in disgust. As he did, his long beard jutted out parallel to the ground. "This wouldn't have happened if you'd controlled your boy, van der Kemp!"

A thick finger jabbed the air in Steenkamp's direction. "Don't you lecture me on raising my boys!" Pieter threatened. "Breyton's wearing stripes that will take a good month to heal! Besides, we don't know that he had anything to do with your slave's disappearance. She's run off before without his help!"

"What else could it be?" Steenkamp boomed. "Two of your horses are gone. So is Breyton. He can't ride both horses—the other one must be for somebody else. My gut tells me it's Ndela."

Jan spoke up. "There's only one way to know for sure. Cyrus, you ride up the road and alert the other commandos. Tell them to bring three days' worth of provisions and meet us here. And tell them to hurry. If Breyton and Ndela are together, they've already got several hours lead on us."

Cyrus Steenkamp nodded, obviously pleased with Jan's initiative. He rode out.

Jan turned to Margot. "I'll need three days' worth of food," he said.

She nodded and turned toward the kitchen.

Behind her, she overheard Pieter's words to his commando son. "You find him and bring him back here. If he has indeed helped that slave escape, heaven help him. He won't be able to sleep on his back for a year!"

Breyton and Ndela emerged from the mountain pass. Before them stretched a seemingly endless plateau of wilderness. This was the home of the San tribes and the Khoi tribes and the Boers, nomadic raiders who lived off the meager offerings of the wilderness, supplementing their stock of supplies with stolen sheep and cattle from the ranches in the valleys below. As of this particular morning, the wilderness population had increased by two.

Having ridden hard throughout the night, the weary travelers rested themselves, taking refuge in a dry riverbed. Breyton relaxed with his arms behind his head in the shade of two large fynbos bushes. Through half-closed eyes he watched as Ndela arranged and rearranged the foodstuffs and clothing and miscellaneous tools and utensils packed on the horses.

Then kneeling by the small campfire, she poked it to flame with quick jabs.

"Quit worrying," Breyton told her. "We've got a good lead. Besides, the horses need rest, and so do we."

She shot a glance at him. "I knows that!" There was an edge in her voice. She jabbed the stick into the fire twice more, sending a flurry of embers heavenward.

"Come here." Breyton reached out an arm to her.

"I's not in the mood for that."

"For what? All I want you to do is relax for a few minutes. You'll feel better."

Without looking at him, she said, "I feels just fine rights here."

With a groan, Breyton stood and walked up behind her. He placed pale hands on her dark shoulders.

She tensed.

"Come lie down."

"I don't wants to lie down."

"Ndela, you'll feel better—"

She whacked his shin with the stick. "I tells you, I feels just fine rights here!"

Breyton jumped back and grabbed his shin. "That hurt!" he cried.

Ndela softened. Hostility fled her eyes. "Looks, I's real sorry," she said. "I's jus' nervous. Jus' gives me time. I's gets over it. Now you goes over there and gets some sleep. When you wakes up, I's probably be jus' fine."

It was obvious that something was bothering her, and that disturbed Breyton. But he didn't know what else to do at the moment. He wanted to take her in his arms and assure her that everything would be all right. At the moment, however, she wouldn't let him get close to her. So he chose a patient course of action. The reality of her freedom and their new life together was no doubt overwhelming. He'd just have to give her some time.

In keeping with her wishes, Breyton made himself comfortable in the shade of the fynbos bushes. He figured he would sleep for a short time and regain his strength before continuing on, even though he still had no clear idea where they were going.

He closed his eyes and invited slumber to cover his thoughts like a blanket. But try as he might, his thoughts would not settle down. Restlessly he hovered in limbo between unconscious sleep and waking thought. Images of Klaarstroom appeared and disappeared—the grand edifice, the stinkwood floor that he had laid plank by plank, the inlaid patterns his hands carved in the furniture.

These were surreptitiously supplanted by images of the Steenkamp farm and Ndela—private moments, stolen glances. Losing himself first in her eyes, then in her arms. He remembered the horrified look on old Cyrus Steenkamp's face when he caught them in the loft— and wondered what his face looked like this morning when he discovered Ndela was missing.

A rustling pulled him back toward consciousness but not enough for him to open his eyes. Ndela moving about the fire.

A smile formed happily on his face as his thoughts drifted to the woman he loved and their new life together. He had given up everything for her. But she was worth it. There wasn't anything he wouldn't do to make those eyes dance and sing. And her smile, so playful— inviting. Gone for the moment. But it would return. She was frightened. Who wouldn't be? He was scared too. Give her time. By nightfall he would see that look in her eyes again that so captivated him. What a wonderful thought. Tonight, just the two of them—snuggling by the fire and dreaming of what their life would be—

A click startled him. It was one of those distinctive sounds that cuts through the fog of slumber and instantly charges a person's senses. A lightning bolt could produce no greater effect. It was the click of a musket trigger.

His eyes flew open.

Ndela stood over him, the musket in her hand. Its deadly end was pointed at his head. That sight alone was enough to start his heart racing, but the thing that whipped it into full gallop was her eyes. They were icy cold and emotionless.

"Ndela, be careful with that gun! It's dangerous to point it like that."

"I knows whats I's doing." Her voice was as cold as her eyes.

Slowly Breyton pushed himself into a sitting position. "I don't understand. Just what is it you think you're doing?"

"Course you don'ts understand. You is a fool."

"Ndela, you're just afraid, and that's understandable—"

"I's not afraid! I knows exactly whats I's doin'. I's escapin'."

"We've already done that! You're free, Ndela! Free!"

"Not quites yet," she said evenly. "But soon. I's be free when you is dead and I rides away from here alone."

Breyton shook his head. "No—no, you're just frightened. I will never treat you like Steenkamp. I love you. You know that. And you love me. I've seen it in your eyes."

"I's never loved you. Never! I's surprised you couldn't tell how disgusted I was every times you touched me. I jus' lets you touch me so's you would help me escape."

"No, you love me."

"I's would do anything to gets free. Anything! Even lets some rich settler boy paws me! But now I gots what I needs. A musket and a horse." She smiled a wicked grin. "Two horses."

Breyton shook his head. He refused to believe this.

"It makes no matter whether you believes me or not. In a few minutes you's will be dead, and I's will be free." With a coolness that was completely devoid of feeling, she pointed the musket barrel at his stomach.

"Ndela, don't do this!"

Blam!

A hot fist slammed into Breyton's stomach, doubling him over. His hands flew instinctively to the wound. They provided no comfort—they only confirmed what his mind still refused to believe. What he didn't want to believe.

But rational thought would no longer allow him to suspend belief. Like a lawyer, it pieced together evidence into a compelling argument. Pain. Intense pain. That was the first piece of evidence. Red fingers. Blood. His strength waning. His head swimming. Darkness pressing against the edges of his mind, trying to force its way in. Yet still there was a part of him that wanted to believe she didn't mean to do it. That it was an accident.

That was when rational thought presented its strongest item of evidence. Ndela's confession. She stood tall over him, smoke from the musket swirling upward around her head. Her eyes. Cold. Vindictive. A smile. No, a laugh. Boastful. Triumphant.

"Every times you touches me," she sneered, "I closes my eyes and thoughts of this moment. But you knows what? Now that I shots you—now that I sees you lying there on the ground and dying—I does it all over. Just for the chance to shoots you again."

Rolled up like a ball, the side of his head in the dirt, Breyton watched Ndela pack the last of the provisions onto the horses. She was happy. Carefree. And as she rode away, leaving him to die, she hummed a merry tune.

21

Breyton prayed he would die. He wanted the pain to stop. He didn't want to feel anymore. He didn't want to think. He wanted to slip into unfeeling darkness, to disappear forever. All his life he'd been taught to believe in life after death. He prayed there was none. For if there was, there would be questions, an accounting, judgment, and condemnation. He wanted none of that. All he wanted was to be left alone. Forever.

Pain squeezed an involuntary moan from him. He rolled his head. Sweat from his brow rolled down his temple and into his ear.

He cursed God for not killing him. Why didn't God just let him close his eyes and return to the dust of the earth as though he'd never been born? What kind of a God would leave him to roll in the dirt in pain, neither dead nor alive?

The longer he lay there, the more he died emotionally until all emotions were gone save one. Anger. It burned in his belly next to his wound. Festering. Intensifying until it was all-encompassing. It was his anger that kept him physically alive, that nursed him in the wilderness. And by the time the sun touched the western horizon, Breyton felt comfortable with his new companion. When all others deserted him, he knew he could count on his anger. It would never forsake him. Whenever he needed strength, his anger would be there to give it to him.

Voices echoed against the walls of the riverbed. Male voices, talking casually.

Grimacing in pain, Breyton managed to scoot himself behind the fynbos bushes that had earlier given him shade. He gulped back the moans that attempted to escape his throat during the effort. Once in place, it wasn't difficult for him to lie still. The effort had drained him of strength. He could barely keep his eyes open. His only hope was that he would not be detected, because he was in no condition to defend himself.

The thought amused him. Why would a person who wanted to die think of defending himself when the instrument of death was so readily at hand? With one moan or a rustle of the bush he could invite a poison San arrow or possibly a Khoi spear to do for him what God refused to do.

The voices grew louder. They were accompanied by the soft thud of horses' hooves on the dry riverbed. San didn't use horses. Neither did the Khoi. Boers did. Even better. Boers carried guns. His death would be quicker.

Breyton peered through the branches and waited for the instruments of his death to appear. Reaching out, he gripped a large branch. He would wait until they were close to him. Then he would scream and shake the bush, hoping to startle them into sending a friendly musket ball his direction.

Horses' heads came into view. Then the hands and arms of the riders. When their faces appeared, Breyton's hand fell noiselessly from the branch. His eyes narrowed, focusing his hate on the faces of men he could see but who had not spotted him.

Cyrus Steenkamp and Jan rode side by side up the dry river bottom.

"There. A campfire." Jan pointed to the pile of ashes beneath the bushes behind which his brother was hiding.

The two men rode to the site and dismounted. While Jan bent down and checked the ashes for warmth, the older man placed his hands in the small of his back and stretched.

"Ashes are cold," Jan said.

Steenkamp shook his head. "I'm selling her this time for sure. Never had one like her before. I treat them well. They live better than they do out with their tribes. You'd think they'd be grateful."

Jan stood and stretched as well. "We won't catch up with them tonight. Do you want to bed down here or continue on?"

Steenkamp didn't answer immediately. He stretched once more, this time vocalizing it. Then, with hands on hips, he surveyed their surroundings, looking upriver, at the sky, at the riverbank. Squinting eyes stared at the pair of fynbos bushes situated along the bank.

Breyton held his breath, as if by doing so he would be harder to spot.

The old man with the gray beard just stood there, frozen for the longest time. "Let's head upriver," he said at last, turning in that direction. "Maybe we'll run into some of the other commandos. No offense, but I'll feel safer out here if we set up camp with more than just the two of us."

Jan apparently took no offense. He mounted.

Steenkamp had to take several extra bounces to get his leg high enough to clear his horse's back, and then only with a loud grunt. "She's gonna pay for this," he said. "I'm too old to go chasing after slaves. What do you think your father will do with Breyton?"

"It frightens me to think about it. Father is ready to kill him. You didn't see the whipping he gave Breyton the last time. I thought he was going to kill him then."

Steenkamp harrumphed. "A lot of good it did."

"Breyton's not a bad sort. He and Father have always seen things differently—placed values on different things. But Breyton was always good with his hands, and he loved creating things. I just can't imagine him living out here."

"Then why did he do it?" Steenkamp cried.

Jan shook his head. "Something came over him. Since we were kids, he and I have always been different, but it never bothered us. We understood each other. Until recently. He's changed. I don't understand him any longer. If I didn't know better, I'd think he was bewitched or possessed."

"Ndela. She has a way of getting people to do whatever she wants them to do."

"Possibly. But Breyton is old enough to think for himself. And he's made some stupid choices recently."

The two commandos turned their horses upstream.

"There's a part of me that doesn't want to catch up with my brother," Jan said. "Maybe he'll find peace out here. He certainly didn't have any at home."

Steenkamp and Jan rode out of earshot.

Breyton flopped over onto his back. Crisscrossed wounds complained, forcing him to his side, which aggravated his stomach wound. It felt as if he had taken a boot to the abdomen. A white fog covered his eyes as he began to pass out.

His last conscious thought was his brother's words *Maybe he'll find peace out here.* He chuckled bitterly. Not peace. Anger. Consuming, driving anger. That's what he'd found. And for the first time since being shot, Breyton knew he would live. His anger would keep him alive. More than that. His anger gave him a reason to live.

For two days Breyton tossed back and forth between consciousness and unconsciousness, baking during the day and shivering at night. Then, on the third day, a clan of Boers found him.

Four days after they set out to find Breyton and Ndela, the commandos returned home empty-handed. The van der Kemp household of five, once a model of the Dutch colonial dream, now consisted of two cheerless men and their housekeeper.

Margot's first return visit to Cape Town colony since arriving at Klaarstroom came a week after Breyton's disappearance. Jan appeared in the kitchen and announced that he and his father had business to attend to in the colony and that she would be accompanying them. He gave no reason for her presence on the trip, only that she would be going.

Pieter rode ahead of the wagon that carried his son and Margot. It was a quiet ride, as though the men had packed up the tomblike atmosphere that had so pervaded the household and brought it with them.

For Margot it was just as well. It felt good to get out of the house. The sky stretched in cloudless blue from horizon to horizon. Even the desolate flatlands were a welcome sight. The air was fresh. And except for the few times she placed her hands near her face, there was nary a scent of polish or soap or any other cleaning product.

She felt the ocean's presence long before she saw it. Having spent most of her life near the sea, until now she never realized how much she missed it. The first thing that she noticed was a change in temperature. A moist coolness kissed her cheeks and hands. It was so distinct, like stepping from an enclosed sunlit room onto a breezy shaded porch. A full rush of ocean air greeted them as they traveled the pass that connected the colony with the flatlands.

At the summit, the full expanse of the ocean opened up to her. The ships anchored in the bay. The busyness of the wharf with men and women and carriages intermingling below while a variety of sea-birds circled and darted overhead. Like an inset jewel, the colony buildings sparkled proudly against the bay. Then, as the wagon descended into town, the familiar sight of Table Mountain appeared. Of all the mountains she'd seen since her arrival, this one was still her favorite.

The absence of conversation gave her the freedom to reminisce as they made their way to the Castle. Not all the memories were pleasant, but they were all a part of her. They rode past the slave compound and the little room she had called home for a time. Though they didn't pass the Company Gardens, she was able to catch a glimpse of them as they turned toward the Castle. And while the men rode solemnly across the parade plain, Margot recalled with fondness her first walk across it with Captain Danckaert. How she missed him.

In the Castle courtyard they passed the fountain. Margot bit her lower lip to conceal a smirk as she remembered van Jaarsveld's dancing around in the water trying to escape *Mevrouw* Hilda's late night wrath. She glanced at Jan beside her to see if he shared her recollection. His face was as it had been the entire trip. Emotionless. Withdrawn.

The wagon stopped. Pieter dismounted and was making his way to the door that led to the governor's residence. Jan climbed out of the wagon but had given no indication to her what she was to do.

"Should I come in or wait here?"

"Yes."

Without looking her in the eye, he helped her down. Why wouldn't he look at her? Margot began piecing things together. What reason did she have for accompanying them to the colony? None that she was aware of. And if there was a reason, why did Jan not tell her—unless he didn't want her to know or couldn't bring himself to tell her. Then there was the trip itself. She had concluded that the silence was caused by continuing grief over Rachel and Breyton. But what if there was another reason?

Margot followed Pieter and Jan up the steps to the governor's residence. As they walked through the doors, the familiarity of the surroundings generated a devastating thought that explained everything. They were bringing her back. They were going to leave her here. Hand her back over to *Mevrouw* Hilda.

And at that instant *Mevrouw* Hilda appeared, emerging into the hallway with a young girl in tow. The matron was shaking her thick index finger at the girl, berating her for inadequate work. The girl, young and frightened, was close to tears. The steady flow of abusing words halted abruptly the moment *Mevrouw* Hilda caught sight of Margot. There was a flash of surprise in the matron's eyes, which was quickly replaced with a well-practiced expression of haughty contempt.

Pieter and Jan passed by the matron without so much as a glance. Margot followed them but not without an increasing feeling of dread that she would soon be at the mercy of this domineering woman once again.

The governor greeted Pieter and Jan van der Kemp with professional warmth. *Mijnheer* Daniel Krog, the heavy-handed Council of Policy official, stood dutifully to one side. The faces of both the governor and the block-chinned official showed surprise when Margot trailed in behind the van der Kemps. Without offering any introductions,

Pieter instructed Margot to sit in a chair against the wall while he and Jan conducted business.

The four men discussed matters related to cattle farmers. Papers were produced by the governor and handed to Pieter, who read them carefully while the governor pointed out several paragraphs with his finger. Looking over his father's shoulder, Jan focused on the documents as though he were reading them too. The subject at hand was a matter of increased control and regulations over cattle farmers; stipulations handed down to the governor from the Lords XVII. Pieter seemed none too pleased with them.

However, Margot caught little of the content or significance of the matter. Her mind was preoccupied with the business that she was sure would come next—the matter of her disposal.

She refused to become emotional about it. It was for the best. She had known, going out to Klaarstroom, that her stay would be a brief one. In fact, that was her preference. They were doing her a favor. She could get on with her plan to return to Amsterdam.

Asking for a few moments alone with his son, Pieter pulled Jan aside. In hushed but fiery whispers, Pieter jabbed at a couple of paragraphs on the paper. Jan, in turn, leaned forward and pretended to read them, nodding his head at everything his father was saying. Once, while his father was railing, he looked up and caught Margot's eye. A guilty look crossed his face, then quickly disappeared as he furrowed his brow and concentrated again on the documents.

His glance confirmed Margot's suspicions. When Jan and Pieter van der Kemp left the governor's residence that day, they would do so without her.

The matter of the regulations concluded with neither side pleased with the other. Talk turned to other mutual concerns. There were indications that the wilderness Boers were growing increasingly restless. The governor told Jan to pass the word along to the other commandos. In his opinion, the Boers were looking for an excuse to raid the outlying cattle farms. And if hostilities escalated, troops could be sent.

Pieter asked for an update on general colony matters, and discussion ranged from ship arrivals and departures to mutual friends to the weather. Nothing of consequence. The men were oblivious to Margot's presence, except for Jan, who sent expressionless glances her direction a couple of times.

There was a knock at the door. Krog answered it for the governor. It was *Mevrouw* Hilda. The matronly overseer frowned disapprovingly at Margot as she made her way to the governor's desk.

Despite Margot's self-assurances that this was what she wanted, a lump of pain lodged in her chest as she thought of what life would be like returning to the dormitory and the confines of the governor's residence and the iron authority of *Mevrouw* Hilda.

The governor excused himself. *Mevrouw* Hilda whispered something in his ear, to which he responded with an angry look and emphatic gestures. His voice was kept low so that no one other than *Mevrouw* Hilda could hear what he was saying. The matron nodded, then left the room, but not without casting one more angry glance at Margot.

"You must excuse the interruption, gentlemen," the governor said. "We have just welcomed some visiting dignitaries from Utrecht —commissioners, actually—and, as usual, preparations are inadequate to their tastes." Then, as an afterthought, he added, "Would you care to join us tonight? We could set two extra places and put you up for the night."

"That would be grand!" Pieter said. "As long as we could excuse ourselves early. We must return to Klaarstroom tomorrow."

"Understood," the governor said. "Krog, see that the arrangements are made."

Jan spoke up. "Sir, if I might add—"

"Yes?"

"We would need three places at dinner. And an extra room. *Mejuffrouw* Margot de Campion would be joining us."

It was as though Margot had suddenly appeared out of nowhere. One moment she was of no more importance than a piece of furniture; the next moment she had every man in the room staring at her.

With an amused grin the governor said, "Any guest of yours is welcome here."

As they left, both the governor and Krog kissed the back of Margot's hand.

Margot floated down the steps leading from the governor's residence into the courtyard. Jan assisted her into the wagon, something he hadn't done when they first started out. As before, Pieter led the way while Jan and Margot followed behind in the wagon.

Passing through the outer gates, Margot said, "Thank you, Jan. That was kind of you."

"Not at all."

"But I can't attend a reception."

He seemed genuinely disappointed, a reaction that pleased her.

"Why not?" he asked.

"For one thing, I have nothing to wear. I didn't bring anything that is suitable for a dinner with the governor and his guests."

"The governor's staff is prepared to accommodate you. You should know that."

"But that's not the only reason."

"What's the other reason?"

"Jan, I'm your *housekeeper!*"

"So?"

"Men don't take their housekeepers to dinner at the governor's residence!"

"Maybe other men don't. I do."

Margot shook her head. "I can't do it."

Exasperated, Jan cried, "Why not?"

"I used to work there! I served people in that room. If I were to go there tonight and someone needed his mug refilled, I'd probably jump up and fill it for him!"

"If that's your only concern, then it's settled. You're going."

Margot looked at him incredulously.

With a boyish grin, Jan said, "I'll hold you down if you show any inclination to jump up and serve someone."

Margot laughed at the thought.

"So accept my invitation to go as my guest."

Her head was swimming. A few moments earlier she was convinced she was being abandoned; now, she was being invited to the governor's reception as the guest of Jan van der Kemp.

Her cheeks flushed as she said, "I accept."

22

I just have too many emotions.

That was the conclusion Margot came to as she lazed comfortably on a bench in the Company Garden's pavilion. She sat alone. With eyes closed, she allowed the sun to caress her face with its warmth. It was this peaceful feeling and the memory of sharing the Gardens with Rachel that she would always associate with this place. Allowing her mind to wander freely, Margot thought of the range of feelings she'd had since entering Cape Town earlier in the day.

Her introspection was occasioned by the fact that Pieter and Jan were at the docks, renewing friendships, transacting business, picking up supplies, and bartering directly for a variety of goods with the captains of the ships currently anchored in Table Bay. Observing how Margot was shunted aside during the meeting with the governor, Jan had asked if she wanted to visit anyone or shop while he and his father took care of business. Margot asked him to deposit her at the Company Gardens.

Which brought up the recurring question, Why had she been brought along in the first place? She chuckled to herself. Her overreaction to that question earlier had caused her a good deal of needless suffering. She had jumped to conclusions, and now that it was over she felt foolish. Yet the question remained unanswered. Why *had* she been brought along?

Deciding she would just have to be patient and let the answer reveal itself, Margot let herself relax. It was a luxury. Days without scrubbing, polishing, and cooking did not come along often, and she was determined to make the most of it. She inhaled the fragrance of the flowers and stretched leisurely. Opening her eyes, she blinked until they adjusted to the light. The green of the grass and the rainbow of flowers set against Table Mountain came into view, and Margot moaned contentedly.

"Take your time," Margot whispered to her absent traveling partners. "I could do this all day."

A deep gruff voice spoiled the peaceful mood. "Get away from me! I don't want it!"

A black-haired young man holding a speckled vase danced in front of a sailor. "But, sir, this Chinese vase has great value, not only monetarily but in its ability to attract women!" The young man swooped over, picked some flowers, and placed them in the vase. Holding vase and flowers in the man's face, the seller said, "What woman could possibly resist such a gift?"

"Back off!" yelled the sailor. "I don't have a woman, and I don't want one!"

The black-haired seller started to make another attempt when his eyes caught sight of Margot sitting in the pavilion. Flashing a white smile, he left his customer.

"Buy a vase, m'lady?"

Margot smiled warmly at Rachel's husband. "Matthew," she said, "does that vase really come from China?"

The young man shrugged. "Does it matter? Sailors don't buy them for their value—they buy them as gifts for their girls. If the vase pleases the sailor's young lady, it is worth every *stuiver* he spends on it, is it not?"

Margot laughed. "Which are you, Matthew—a romantic or a swindler?"

Matthew flashed his best smile. "I've been accused of both."

"It's good to see you. How's Rachel?"

"Sick in the morning and tired much of the time, but I'm told that's to be expected."

Margot nodded. "How is she doing emotionally?"

Matthew's smile vanished so suddenly it was dramatic. He looked around the Gardens. "Are you alone?"

"Pieter and Jan are at the wharf. I'm alone for the moment."

Matthew checked about him again, as though the two might appear at the mention of their names. When he didn't see them, he said, "Rachel has not been the same since that day we were at Klaarstroom."

Margot's face drew up with concern. "I was afraid of that. Just as she was leaving, I saw a mixture of pain and anger in her eyes that frightened me."

Matthew sat on the pavilion steps; Margot invited him to join her on the bench; he declined, saying it wouldn't be appropriate for them to share a bench in public. Margot said she understood and thanked him for being considerate of her.

"Rachel has changed," Matthew said sadly. "There are moments when I still see in her the woman I fell in love with, but those moments are few. I've tried everything I can think of to make her feel better, but nothing seems to make a difference."

"Matthew, I'm so sorry. I wish there was something I could do to help."

"I wish so too." His face brightened. "Can you come talk to her? She thinks so highly of you. Maybe you can make her feel better."

"I would love to see her, but I can't leave here. I don't know when Pieter and Jan are going to return. And I don't know what they'd do if I wasn't here when they came back."

Matthew shook his head sadly. "I had to ask," he said. "It's just that I feel helpless, not being able to cheer her up. Having a baby is supposed to be a happy time for families. She's treating it like it was a funeral."

"Matthew . . ."

"Yes?"

"What do you do when you offer a vase to someone and they say they don't want to buy it?"

"I offer it again."

"And if they refuse again?"

Matthew shrugged as if the answer to Margot's question was obvious. "I switch tactics and offer it again. Sometimes I add flowers. Sometimes I appeal to their good taste. There are a lot of ways to convince people they need to buy my vases. All it takes is to find the right reason that will get them to buy."

"Good. Now think with me. Say I want to communicate with Rachel, but I can't go over to her house to talk to her. Use that creative mind of yours. What other way could I communicate with her?"

Matthew rolled his eyes heavenward as he thought. "You could tell me what you wanted to say, and I could tell Rachel."

"That might do for today, but I was thinking of some kind of system in which we could communicate with some regularity."

"You're right—our meeting today was by chance. We can't always count on that." He thought some more. "It would help if you knew someone who could write . . ."

"I can write."

Matthew looked at her skeptically.

"I can read and write," Margot assured him. "But Rachel can't. Can you?"

"No, but my father can! He could read your letters to her and write down her responses to you."

"But how do we get the letters back and forth?" Margot asked.

Matthew's brow wrinkled as he thought. "Postal stones!" he cried.

"Postal stones? What are they?"

Jumping up, Matthew hurried over to a square rock near the pavilion. "This is a postal stone. This one is set here as just a sort of memorial. But in the early days of the colony—before the Castle or any other buildings were built—ships used to leave each other messages here at the Cape by placing documents and letters under stones like this. The etching on the top of the stone indicated who the letter was for."

Margot picked up his line of thought. "So then, whenever I'm in town I can slip a letter to Rachel under that postal stone . . ."

"And I can check the stone periodically for letters from you—and place Rachel's responses under it for you."

"How is it that you know about postal stones?" Margot asked.

"My father was a sailor. He told me about the old days." Matthew grabbed up his vase and started to run away.

"Where are you going?"

He turned around just long enough to answer. "To get you paper, pen, and ink so that you can write Rachel a letter."

A half hour later, with Matthew watching, Margot penned her first letter to Rachel.

The young man stared in fascination as she scratched letters onto the paper as though she were performing some magical feat.

She rested the pen. "Would you like me to read it to you?"

Matthew nodded.

Margot lifted the letter and read aloud:

Dear Rachel,

There is not a day that goes by that I do not think of you. I feel your presence in every room at Klaarstroom. But no more so than in your bedroom. I will always think of it as your bedroom, which you are kind enough to share with me. And every day when I think of you, I pray that God will bless you with good health and happiness.

My dear Rachel, my heart goes out to you when I think of how you were treated during your last visit to Klaarstroom. But what disturbed me even more was seeing how it affected you. I pray to God that you and your father and brothers will one day be reconciled. But until that day comes, do not let their shortsightedness rob you of the joy and love that was once so much a part of you. Don't give in to your anger. Don't let hate rob you of the blessing God has given you. Blessings? Oh, yes! You have a husband who loves you. And the fruit of your love is now growing in your womb. Be happy. Teach your child to be strong in love and forgiveness.

Pray for your brother Breyton. He has run away into the wilderness with a black slave girl. We do not know his condition or whereabouts. And pray for your father and Jan. They don't want to admit it even to themselves, but they love you.

Keep me informed of the progress of your pregnancy. I will leave you a letter every time I come to Cape Town and hope to hear from you.

Thank God for Matthew. He adores you.

Margot lowered the page. "Then it's signed with my name. Is there anything else you would like me to add?"

"Well . . ." Matthew hesitated.

"What?"

"You could tell her that you love her. You do, don't you?"

Tears filled Margot's eyes. "In the short time we've been together, I've grown to love her an inordinate amount."

"That means a lot?"

Margot laughed. "Yes, that means I love her a lot."

Having inked her pen one last time, Margot added above her name:

With much love. Your friend,

As soon as the ink was dry, Matthew took the letter, folded it, and prepared to place it under the postal stone.

"What are you doing?" Margot asked. "Why don't you just deliver it to her yourself?"

Matthew shook his head. "I'll bring her here tomorrow. Rachel loves surprises. This way she can find the letter herself. It will mean more to her that way."

"You're a thoughtful man, Matthew Durbin."

Once the letter was placed, Matthew looked around again for any sign of the van der Kemps. "Thank you," he said. "You are a special woman with a special gift."

"I can't take credit for it," Margot said. "My mother taught me to read and write."

Matthew looked at her quizzically. "I wasn't talking about that."

"Oh?"

"You have a special way of helping people—of making them feel good about themselves."

Margot blushed. "There's nothing special about what I do."

"Oh, but there is!" Matthew exclaimed. "Rachel is the one who pointed it out to me. Since then, I've seen it myself. You're always helping someone, bringing out the best in them. That's what Rachel loves most about you."

"That's very kind of her, but—"

"You really don't see it, do you?" Matthew leaned back in surprise.

"Matthew, you're embarrassing me."

"I'm serious," Matthew said. "You make a difference when you're around. I'm surprised you don't realize that."

"I–I don't know what to say. But thank you, Matthew. That's very sweet."

After they had exchanged good-byes and best wishes, Matthew left her.

Alone again, Margot thought about what he had said. She had never thought of herself as a person who made an impact on people's lives. But she liked the fact that Rachel saw that quality in her. Was it really true? Or was Rachel merely being kind? If it was true, why hadn't she realized it before?

As Pieter and Jan rode up to the Company Garden pavilion, Margot asked God to confirm this gift if she really did have it. And if she did, she prayed that she could make a difference in life among the family van der Kemp.

The whole experience of the governor's reception was like a fantastic dream.

When they arrived back at the residence, Margot was shown to her room. She knew every part of it because she'd cleaned it at least fifty times. Then three female members of the governor's staff brought an assortment of dresses and shoes and jewelry for her to select from to wear that evening. She chose a conservative but stylish green silk gown and a modest diamond necklace.

Jan appeared shortly before dinner to escort her to the dining area. He too had been outfitted by the governor's staff and was barely recognizable, wearing a silk shirt with ruffles, and gloves, and stockings stretched over his muscular legs. His manner and conversation were restrained but cordial, an improvement over the silent moodiness that characterized their journey across the flatlands.

But it was the reception itself that Margot most enjoyed. Although the guests were outwardly happy and festive, it was her interaction with the maids and servers she most enjoyed because many of them recognized her. Whenever they served her, she thanked them and complimented them on their efficiency, or their pleasantness, or whatever else came to mind. To say that they appeared shocked at her kindness would be an understatement. She would ask them their names, and the very question would bring fear to their eyes. But when they learned that she merely wanted to thank them by name, the entire staff began competing, it seemed, to serve her first.

But the thing that made it all worthwhile for Margot was that other guests noticed the attention she was getting. They began to thank the servers too and soon were enjoying the same attention. After a time, the entire atmosphere of the reception turned from cordial formality to genuine laughter and goodwill. And it all started with simple courtesy to those who were serving.

That night, alone in her room, Margot lay wide awake. She thought about what Matthew had said of her. A gift he called it. The ability to make a difference. She had made a difference aboard the *Eagle*, hadn't she? And with Rachel. Then tonight—such a simple thing to do, but it changed the complexion of the whole evening. And this was just a dinner reception. Could she make a difference in things that really counted for something?

23

The next morning Pieter rode out early, leaving the slower wagon behind.

"Father always goes on ahead on the return trip," Jan explained as he navigated the wagon through the bustling early morning streets of Cape Town. "He can never stay away from Klaarstroom for long. That's why Rachel would always come along to keep me company going back. Well, that was one of the reasons. She loved going to the colony. Even as a child."

It was good to hear Jan talk about his sister. He never would have said that if his father were nearby. "Is that why you brought me?" Margot asked. "To keep you company?"

"Partly." He reined the horses to a stop and jumped out. "Be right back."

He disappeared through the door of a shop that had no sign.

"Partly?" Margot said to herself.

Moments later Jan reappeared with a large sack of grain over his shoulder. He tossed it into the back of the wagon and returned for another. Margot saw no workers. She witnessed no transaction. And he moved with a briskness that went beyond eagerness to start their journey back.

He jumped onto the seat beside her and urged the horses forward. A quick glance at Margot prompted him to furrow his brow. "What?" he asked.

"I didn't say anything."

"You didn't have to say anything. What's that look on your face?"

Margot turned away. "No look. It's just my normal face."

Jan shook his head in disagreement. He glanced over his shoulder at the bags. "We purchased them yesterday," he said.

"I wasn't accusing you of stealing them!" Margot cried.

"I didn't say you were!"

"You implied it."

"Well, you implied I was doing something wrong."

"I did not!"

"You most certainly did—with that look!"

Innocent eyes stared at him. "There was no look!"

Jan grunted and turned his attention to driving the horses. "We bypassed the Company, all right?" he said. "With Company regulations the way they are, it's the only way we can survive. Everybody does it."

"That doesn't make it right."

"What else can we do? We would be out of business if we observed every regulation set down by the Company. If you want to know what isn't right, I'll tell you—the way the Company strangles us isn't right!"

"That still doesn't make what you are doing right, does it? How can you be so strict about what is right and wrong in some areas of life and then do something illegal like this?"

Anger reddened his neck. "I think we'd better find something else to talk about."

They rode in silence for a moment.

With a soft voice, Margot said, "I'll be baking bread with smuggled grain."

Jan's jaw clenched tightly, but he didn't say anything in response.

Neither spoke for a time. Margot watched as the Company Garden slid by them on her side of the wagon. She saw the pavilion and remembered the moments of leisure she had spent there. She saw the postal stone and thought of Matthew and Rachel.

Should she tell Jan about Rachel? He'd already mentioned her once this morning. No. She decided to keep her communication with Rachel a secret. She couldn't risk Jan's disapproval of the letters. For a moment, a pang of guilt struck her. Was *she* doing something wrong by communicating with Rachel? Or by being secretive about it? Brushing aside the feeling, she decided she wasn't doing anything wrong. It was the van der Kemp family that was shunning Rachel, not her. As for the secrecy, it was done to protect Rachel, not to hurt or deceive anyone. Margot decided that if her actions ever became known, she would in no way feel ashamed of them.

The wagon carried its two silent riders up the pass to the flatlands. Margot turned to take one last look at Table Mountain, the colony, and the ocean. She didn't know when she'd see them again.

"Thank you for taking me as your guest last night," she said.

This brought a smile to his face. "Thank you for attending. I know it wasn't easy for you."

Wagon wheels crunched across dirt and rock and in and out of ruts, jostling the two riders from side to side and occasionally into one another.

"How do you do it?" Jan asked.

"Do what?"

"Last night. At the reception. How do you do it?"

A combined smile and puzzled look formed on Margot's face. "I still don't know what you're talking about."

Jan turned and studied her. "You really don't."

Margot shook her head.

"Remarkable."

"What are you talking about?" Margot cried.

Jan drew a deep breath and settled back into his seat. "Not long ago you stood in that same room at a similar reception as a servant. Last night you socialized with some of the same people you waited on the previous time. And you bore them no ill will. I watched you. You weren't pretending. It was genuine."

"Why should I bear them ill will?"

"Because of the way they treated you when you were a servant! They were rude. Demanding. And when van Jaarsveld did his best to humiliate you, they were eager to have great fun at your expense! Had it been me, I would have had nothing to do with them!"

"Is that the reason you invited me to be your guest? So that I could have a chance to get back at them?"

"That was part of the reason."

Again, part! When would she know the whole reason she had been brought on this trip? But at the moment that was secondary. "I'm sorry I disappointed you, then," she said.

"Disappointed me? Not at all! You were great!"

Margot was still puzzled.

"You shamed them!" He laughed victoriously. "Don't you see? It caught them completely off guard. They had done their best to humiliate you, and you got even with them by showering them with kindness. It was great! They felt so foolish—so ashamed!"

"Is that why you think I acted like I did? To shame them?"

She saw that he read her expression. All signs of levity drained from his face.

"If that's what you think, Jan van der Kemp, then you don't know me at all." She fought back tears, but the hurt was too deep to do it alone. With the assistance of her rising anger, she managed to keep her cheeks dry. But not without a stiff battle.

"Now what did I say?" Jan asked lamely. "I was complimenting you!"

Margot crossed her arms and turned away from him. The wagon rolled into the flatlands with the mood in the wagon as desolate as the landscape.

Between the edge of the colony, which marked one flatlands boundary, and the river that marked the other, neither Margot nor Jan spoke. The entire journey across the flatlands, she wrestled with her feelings as hurt and disappointment gave way to smoldering anger.

Try as she might to convince herself that, deep inside, Jan was different from the other men she'd known, she concluded now that she'd been mistaken—had been looking for something inside him that wasn't there. He was no different from Fabarez. Van Jaarsveld. Katje's and Aletta's husbands. Hennig. The van der Kemp men—unfeeling brutes, all of them. Selfish. Demanding. To think that she was realizing this about Jan only now made her so furious she wanted to hit something or cry or both.

She'd found only one exception to the rule. Captain Danckaert. Now there was a man with a good heart. And it didn't make him weak either. She remembered his bulldog face. *You're not going to make trouble for me the entire journey, are you?* Margot discreetly raised a handkerchief to dry her nose. She wished she could see him again. Talk to him. He was the only decent man she'd ever known.

The wagon splashed through the river. And without so much as a word or a glance, Jan turned upstream.

"What are you doing?" Margot asked.

Jan didn't reply.

"We don't have time for this," she said. "Take me straight to the house."

He didn't move.

"You are so stubborn! Well, I don't know what you think is going to happen, but let me assure you that I am going to sit on this wagon seat until we are in front of the house! And there is nothing you can do or say that will change my mind."

He showed no sign of having heard a single word she said.

Head down, eyes narrowed, jaw set, Margot determined she would not allow Jan van der Kemp to use the beauty of the land as a weapon to get her to lower her defenses and forget her anger.

Emerging from the pines, the wagon glided effortlessly across the floral sea. Purple, scarlet, orange, blue, and white petals swirled in intricate design. Towering, mist-enshrouded stone sentinels kept watch over them. For some reason Margot had thought the scene would not have the enchantment it had when she first saw it. There *was* a degree of difference in its power over her between her first and second visit—this second time she was affected by its beauty even more.

Anger, frustration, disappointment—all were undesirable foreigners in this kingdom, banished forever from this world of enchantment.

Passing between the two lofty outstretched arms of granite, they entered the natural cathedral with its impressive rock cliffs, roaring waterfall, and glistening pond. The wagon stopped, and Jan stepped out onto the mossy green carpet, his eyes tracing the waterfall to the top.

He did not ask Margot to join him.

"This is why you brought me along on the journey," Margot said.

Jan turned toward her. With the waterfall and cliffs and pond behind him, he no longer looked like the unfeeling ogre she had made him out to be. His eyes were soft, his features calm. "The last time we were here, I saw a look on your face that I had never seen before or since."

"A look?"

Jan stared at the ground, searching for words. "Heavenly—angelic."

"Angelic?" Margot chuckled.

Jan frowned. "You're laughing at me."

"Jan, no. I'm sorry. It's just that no one has ever referred to me as angelic before." From the look in his eyes, she was sorrier still. He was serious.

Speaking to the ground, he said, "The expression on your face that day was a look of innocence. Of wonder. The kind of look I imagine we'll all have on our faces the first time we see God."

"I have a look that looks like that?"

His head down, Jan nodded.

Margot climbed out of the wagon. The coolness of the moss penetrated her shoes, refreshing her feet. Jan was right about the ravine. It was like being in the presence of God. All her anger and resolve from the flatlands dissipated in His presence. Her indignation seemed petty and childish in the midst of such grandeur.

She stood beside him, facing the waterfall; he kept his back to it.

"I'm sorry for making you angry," he said.

Now it was her turn to be silent. She didn't want to forgive him too quickly. It wasn't enough for him to be sorry that he had made her angry. He needed to know that he'd misjudged her intentions. That's what had hurt her.

"Every time I'm around you, I think of an Old Testament Bible story," he said.

"Which one?"

He shook his head.

"Please tell me."

"It's not a well-known story," he said. "You might not know it."

Margot waited. She wasn't going to drag it out of him. If he wanted to tell her, he would tell her.

Jan cleared his throat and rubbed his nose. "It's the story of Nabal and Abigail."

Margot's head snapped his direction. Had he been talking to the husband of one of her girls? She searched his face for some kind of indication that he was jesting.

There was none. His eyes were introspective. Serious. "If you're not familiar with the story, it's about a man and his wife. The man is a fool, but his wife is not only beautiful, she's intelligent. Only he's too much of a fool to notice it."

"I'm familiar with the story."

He glanced at her self-consciously, then looked away. With a shrug of his shoulders, he said, "Then you can understand why I'd think of that story. Of course, we're not married or anything like that, but on the one hand you're beautiful and intelligent—and so much so that it makes me feel like a fool."

Margot wasn't sure what to say.

"I've been thinking all the way across the flatlands," he said. "And I realize now that you're not the kind of person who sets out to get revenge against someone. I was wrong to think you were. You're not that way at all."

"Thank you," Margot said softly.

"Like I said, a fool."

The waterfall played a short interlude. Jan turned and faced the same direction as Margot.

"So why did you do it?" he asked.

Margot crinkled her nose. "Do what?"

"Why were you kind to the people who hurt you?"

"I'm not responsible for their actions," Margot said. "But I am responsible for mine. Just because they are rude and selfish doesn't mean I have to be rude and selfish."

Jan worked that thought as though it were a bite of beef that didn't want to go down. "But the Bible says, 'An eye for an eye.'"

"The Bible also says, 'Ye have heard that it hath been said, An eye for an eye, and a tooth for a tooth: but I say unto you, That ye resist not evil: but whosoever shall smite thee on thy right cheek, turn to him the other also.'"

"That's not possible," Jan said.

"Then answer me this: Why would God give us a command that He knew would be impossible for us to do?"

"But if someone does wrong—"

"It's up to God to judge him—not up to us to take revenge," Margot cried. "In your world everything is black and white, good or bad. Everyone is an enemy or a friend. If people can't live up to your expectations, you cut them off." Margot knew she was saying too much, but these words had been building inside her for too long. They just had to come out. "In your world love is dispensed only if a person lives up to your standards. One slip, one error in judgment, one mistake, and that love is withdrawn. What a miserable existence it must be to know that on any day one wrong decision can ruin your life."

Jan appeared stunned. Then, in a voice that was barely audible, he said, "It's worse than you think. In my world, not only can you lose favor by making the wrong choice, but you can also lose it by not making enough right choices—by not being good enough."

Margot had seen Jan in a devious mood when they plotted van Jaarsveld's unveiling; she had seen him weeping in anguish over the loss of his sister; and she had seen him looking like a little boy at the dinner table next to his father. But she had never seen him like this. Fearful. Broken.

"Nothing I do pleases him," he said. His voice was not bitter; it was the voice of one resigned to inevitable fact.

Margot's instinct was to reach over and touch him. She countered the impulse by folding her hands in front of her.

"I'm not an adult in his eyes. Maybe I never will be." But then he chuckled. "I used to think that if I'd learned how to read, things would be different."

"I saw you in the governor's office."

Jan closed his eyes. "Pathetic, wasn't it? He does that every time. He's ashamed of me because I can't read. Maybe he has a right to be."

"Jan, the measure of a man is not based on a single skill."

"Try telling my father that. Besides, it's easy for you to say that. You can read. Did you see the way my father's eyes lit up that night at the dinner table when he learned you could read? He was impressed."

Margot searched for words to comfort him. None were forthcoming.

"Do you want to know the hardest part?" he asked. "I'm his last hope, and I think that frightens him."

"Frightens him or you?"

Jan smiled. "Both of us. What if I'm not good enough? I could lose everything we've built over the years."

"And what if you did?"

Jan looked at her as though he couldn't believe she'd said that.

"Really, what if you did lose everything? There is nothing you can lose that can't be rebuilt. The most important thing in life is relationships—first with God, then with other people. Everything else is dross."

"You are remarkable," Jan said softly. "You see things so clearly. All my life has been spent on things—raising cattle, working the land, building an estate . . ."

"Take away those things, and what do you have left?"

"God."

Margot nodded. "And your loved ones."

Jan walked toward her until they were standing face to face. He reached down and took her by the hands.

Margot flinched. "What are you doing?"

He just looked at her.

She tried to pull her hands away.

He held them tight.

"What are you doing?" she asked again.

"Margot, I think you know how I feel about you."

Her hands struggled like rabbits in a trap. "Jan—let go of my hands."

With a frown he released them. "What's the matter? I've made my intentions clear, haven't I?"

"To whom?"

"To you."

Margot shook her head. "Maybe you've made your intentions clear to everyone else in the world, but they've not been so clear to me."

"What do you mean?"

Margot's hands flew to her hips. "Just what have you been telling everyone about us?"

"What do you mean?"

"Your father, your brother, Old Knob—"

Jan matched Margot's hands-on-hips stance.

"Old Knob?"

"Yes! Do you know what he said the first time I met him? He said, 'Are you Jan's woman?' Now where would he get an idea like that if you didn't tell him?"

"I never told Old Knob anything that would give him that impression!"

"Well, he had to get it from somewhere!"

Jan threw up his hands and walked in a small circle. "I don't know what to say . . ."

Hands still on hips, Margot was content to wait until he thought of something. She watched as he went in circles, his facial expression changing from flustered to defeated.

He walked toward the wagon. "We'd better get going," he said. "Whether or not I've made my feelings clear to you, it's quite clear how you feel about me."

Margot walked to her side of the wagon. "Jan—"

He held up a hand to stop her. "It's all right. I understand," he said. "Nabal and Abigail."

It was late by the time they reached Klaarstroom. Ding and a couple of field servants rushed out to unload the wagon. Margot followed Jan up the front steps to the porch.

"Look at the moon," she said.

A large white disk was just beginning to emerge from behind the Hottentots-Holland mountain range. Jan stopped a moment to look.

"Thank you for taking me to Cape Town," she said. "And to the waterfall."

"You're welcome." He turned toward the front door.

"Jan?"

"Hm?"

Margot glanced first one direction, then another.

Jan followed her glances with a puzzled expression.

271

She leaned close to his ear. "If you want, I'll teach you to read."

Jan pulled away to look at her.

"You think I can't do it?" Margot asked.

"I'm a grown man! I can't learn now."

"Why not?"

"You either learn it as a child or not at all."

Margot folded her arms. "Who told you that?"

"No one told me that. It's just the way of things."

"Maybe you're right. I apologize for bringing it up. I was under the impression that learning to read was important to you."

"Knowing how to read is important to me; learning to read is for children."

Margot cocked her head in quizzical fashion.

"That didn't make sense, did it?" Jan said sheepishly.

Margot shook her head.

"You really think I can learn to read?"

"Yes, I do."

"How long will it take?"

"That depends on two things: How hard are you willing to work at it? And when do you want to start?"

"Can we start tomorrow?"

24

The offer to teach Jan how to read did not come easily to Margot. For one thing, it altered the lifelong illusion that she would one day sit down and introduce her own daughter to the world of words the same way Sylvie had introduced her. Margot never imagined that the face beside her would belong to a full-grown man.

The other thing that had caused her to hesitate was the fact that although reading had been a wonderful boon to her over the years, it had also caused a good number of problems. It was difficult to forget how the nutshell Scripture she'd placed around Sylvie's neck had changed her life; or the trouble her Bible stories had created for Katje and Aletta. She'd learned that not everyone embraced knowledge as she did. And she had no way of predicting the way it might affect Jan van der Kemp's life.

"When will your father be home?" Margot asked.

Jan shrugged. "He usually stays out until after it gets dark. But there is no way of knowing for sure. We'll just have to listen for him."

It was Jan's decision to keep his reading lessons a secret. He reasoned that if his father knew about the lessons, he'd want to have a part in them. It was his father's early attempts to teach his boys to read that had put them off reading for good. Margot accepted his decision but realized that Jan's wanting to keep his learning to read a secret would make it easier for him to quit if it got hard for him. She would just have to make sure that didn't happen.

"You brought the Bible?" Margot asked.

Jan placed a Bible on the dining room table.

Margot thumbed through it. It was written in Dutch. Beside it she placed a pen, an ink well, and paper.

"You sit there." She pointed to a chair.

"What if I don't want to sit in that chair?"

Margot gave him a frustrated look. "Are you going to—"

He was grinning from ear to ear.

Margot laughed with him. "Already I can see who the trouble-makers are going to be in this class."

As they sat side by side, Margot folded her hands on top of the Bible. "First, we pray," she said.

"For a miracle?"

"Jan van der Kemp, get serious. This is the way Sylvie taught me, and this is the way I'm going to teach you. Sylvie always said, 'The effort will succeed if God blesses it.' So bow your head."

Jan closed his eyes and bowed his head.

So did Margot. The room was silent. Several seconds passed.

Jan opened his eyes. "What are you waiting for?"

"With Sylvie it was different. I've never prayed with a man before. You pray."

"No, you're the teacher. You pray."

Margot shook her head. "I can't. God will give you the words. You pray."

They bowed their heads.

Jan prayed. "Almighty Father in heaven. All my life I've been like Nabal in the Old Testament. I don't want to be like that anymore. Please make me wise by letting me learn to read. Amen."

"That was nice," Margot said. She opened the Bible to the first book and the first verse. "Now, see this?" She pointed to the first letter. "This is a letter. Words are made up of letters."

Jan fell back into his chair. "I know that!" he cried.

"Jan van der Kemp, you're never going to learn to read if you keep interrupting me!"

"So teach me something I don't know already!"

Margot lifted her head to indicate a quote. "'Always begin at the beginning.'"

"Sylvie?" Jan asked.

"Sylvie. Now may I continue?"

Jan leaned forward and focused on the word directly above Margot's finger.

"These spaces separate the words. And a sentence is made up of a string of words that is concluded with some form of punctuation—in this case a period. Any questions?"

"This may be easier than I thought."

"Don't count on it. Now, do you know your letters?"

"Most of them."

"What letter is this?" Margot pointed to the first letter of the first verse.

"That's an *I*."

"A capital *I*," Margot corrected him. "All letters have an uppercase and a lowercase. This is an uppercase *I*. All sentences begin with a capital, or uppercase, letter." She pulled the paper toward her and loaded the pen with ink. She printed an uppercase *I*. "There. I did the first one for you. Now you print a row of uppercase *I*'s." She pushed the paper in front of him.

He took the pen, holding it awkwardly.

"Here . . ." Margot reached across and positioned the pen correctly in his hand.

As she did, he looked at her. Their faces were inches apart.

"Try concentrating on making uppercase *I*'s," she said.

With determined effort on Jan's part, a row of *I*'s appeared at the top of the page. The row started straight, then sloped downward near the end.

"We'll work on your penmanship as we go along. Now, what is the next letter?"

"*N*." Then, before Margot could correct him, "Lowercase *n*."

"That's correct. Here is how you make a lowercase *n*." She made the first one for him.

He pretended to forget how to hold the pen.

Margot chuckled. "I'm not falling for that one, *Mijnheer* van der Kemp."

He corrected the position of the pen and made a row of lowercase *n*'s.

"Good. These two letters form the first word in the sentence—*I* and *n*. Together they form the word *In*." She had him write a row of *In*'s on the paper. In this fashion Margot led Jan word by word through the first half of the first sentence of the first verse of the Bible. Most of their time was spent on the word *beginning*.

Jan completed another line.

"Now read it to me," Margot said.

He picked up the paper, squinted his eyes, and read, "In . . . the . . . beg . . . beg . . ."

"Beginning. Start again."

Jan sighed. "In the . . . begin . . . ning . . . God."

"In the beginning God," Margot repeated. "That's good, Jan. You're off to a good start."

Letting the paper fall to the table, Jan let out a huge sigh. "This is more tiring than herding cattle."

Just then the front door opened.

"Jan? You in here?" Pieter's voice boomed through the house.

Margot and Jan scrambled to clear the table. Jan slipped the Bible onto the seat of a chair that was pushed under it. The papers he slipped under himself and sat on them.

Jumping up, Margot grabbed the ink and pen and hid them behind her back just as Pieter came into view.

"Oh, there you are—" He stopped mid-sentence and looked from Jan to Margot, then back to Jan. With a sheepish grin, he said, "Um . . . I didn't know . . . I guess the two of you want to be alone. I'll just be out . . . Jan, when you're done . . . or free . . . I'd like to speak to you. I'll just be . . . just be outside." He cleared his throat and excused himself and left.

No sooner had the front door closed than Jan burst out laughing. "He thought we were—"

His laughter died when he saw the expression on Margot's face.

Pieter never mentioned what he saw or didn't see or thought he saw when he burst in on Jan and Margot during Jan's first reading lesson. But whatever he saw, he appeared to like. Almost overnight the mood around the van der Kemp household began to improve. Gone was the brooding over Breyton. Good-natured laughter, once thought to be extinct in the house, made a strong reappearance. Meals were no longer marathons of misery but were once again congenial occasions.

Several months after Jan's first reading lesson, the three of them were enjoying morning breakfast when Ding bounded through the front door.

"*Mijnheer* van der Kemp—it's horrible—" The young black man, normally cheerful and happy, was doubled over, out of breath, and shaking with fright.

Pieter and Jan were by his side in an instant. "What is it, Ding?"

"It's horrible, that's what it is!" Ding cried, trying to catch his breath. "Raiders!"

"Here?" Pieter shouted.

"No, not here—at the Steenkamps—last night."

"Jan, fetch the muskets."

Ding waved him back. "They gone now, but, oh—the mess—the mess!"

"How do you know this?" Pieter cried.

"Fanie told me—one of *Mijnheer* Steenkamp's slaves. She escaped. Came here."

"Were the raiders Boers?" Pieter asked.

Ding nodded.

Margot remained behind as Pieter and Jan rode over to the

276

Steenkamp farm, so she didn't see the results of the raid herself. But she saw its effect on the two van der Kemp men. The entire Steenkamp family had been murdered. Their house and all adjoining buildings were burned. The crops were destroyed and the cattle and sheep herded into the hills. For weeks afterward, whenever an unexpected noise sounded in front of the house, Jan and his father would jump to a window. They wouldn't relax until the sound had been identified as harmless.

"Old Knob knows you're learning to read," Margot said.

"You told him?"

"Of course not."

"Then how does he know?"

Margot laughed. "He listens at the window."

"Why, that sneaky Hottentot!"

"I told him it's a secret. He promised not to tell anyone."

Jan sat back in the wagon seat with the Bible on his lap. He had been reading for ten months and was making good progress. He had reached chapter twenty-four of Genesis.

Margot held the reins as they traversed the flatlands on their way to Cape Town. Every other month the two of them traveled to the colony to pick up supplies. Jan didn't like leaving Klaarstroom with the increase in Boer raids, but the idea of Margot's journeying to Cape Town alone was unacceptable. It was her idea to make the most of the time by having him read as they traveled.

"Continue reading," she said.

Jan lifted the Bible. It took him a moment to adjust to the bouncing motion of the text. "And Isaac went out to—" He held the book toward Margot.

She glanced over to where his finger was pointing. "Meditate," she said.

"Meditate in the field at the eventide: and he lifted up his eyes, and saw, and, behold, the camels were coming. And Rebekah lifted up her eyes, and when she saw Isaac, she lighted off the camel. For she had said unto the servant, What man is this that walketh in the field to meet us? And the servant had said, It is my master: therefore she took a veil, and covered herself. And the servant told Isaac all things that he had done. And Isaac brought her into his mother Sarah's tent, and took Rebekah, and she became his wife; and he loved her: and Isaac was comforted after his mother's death."

Jan dropped the book into his lap.

"That's one of my favorite Bible stories," Margot said. "I didn't

277

used to like it. I guess it's one of those stories that has to grow on you. Are you going to read some more?"

Jan shook his head. "My eyes are tired. I think I'll rest them awhile." He closed his eyes and let his head fall back.

"You're doing well!" Margot said. "You're mispronouncing a few words, but overall you're doing well."

Jan's head bounced up. "I'm not mispronouncing words!"

"Sure you are!" She gave him a couple of examples.

"No, *you're* mispronouncing them."

"How do you figure?"

"Everybody around here pronounces them like I do."

"Just because everyone does something wrong doesn't make it right."

"Sure it does!"

Margot laughed and shook her head. "If you were to go to Amsterdam, you would hear the words pronounced correctly."

"But we're not in Amsterdam. We're in Cape Town, Africa. And the people who live here pronounce the words differently."

"Well, we may be living on a different continent, but we're still Dutch."

"No, we're not."

Margot looked over at him. "You're not Dutch?"

"No. I don't consider myself to be Dutch. I was born and raised here on the African continent. I am an Afrikaner."

It was the first time Margot had heard anyone describe himself in that way. But from that time on, she began to notice that the people of Cape Town colony took pride in the ways they were distinctly different from their Dutch forefathers. And the longer she lived in Africa, the more she thought of herself as an Afrikaner too.

Margot sat in the pavilion at the Company Garden. She held a piece of paper in her hand as Jan approached.

"What's that?" Jan asked.

She held the paper out to him. "Read it yourself," she said.

He looked at her to see if she was joking.

"Go ahead. I'll help you if you need it."

Sitting next to her, Jan took the paper and studied it. "It's about Rachel!" he cried, almost dropping the paper.

"Read it," Margot said.

"I don't think I should."

"It's a letter written by Matthew's father as told to him by Rachel. She and I have been corresponding for months." Margot explained how she and Matthew had revived the old postal stone system to exchange letters. "So go ahead, read it. In fact, read it out loud."

"Margot, you shouldn't be doing this. If Father—"

"Read it!" she cried.

Jan reluctantly lifted the letter. He read:

Dear Margot,

It is with joy that I say these words. I am a mother. Little Deborah—such a big name for such a little baby—was born to us one month ago today. The entire Durbin clan is so pleased to have such a beautiful little girl added to their family. You should see how Matthew looks when he is holding his daughter. You would think his chest is going to burst.

Since we don't know what day you will come, Matthew has agreed to check the stone every day to see if you have received this or not. Margot, may I make a request of you? Would you permit me to show you my baby? I think you will love her as much as I do. I know it is asking too much for you to come to our house. But if you consent to my request, Matthew has agreed to come and get me and the baby. We will meet you at the pavilion.

However, if you don't think this is a good idea, I understand.

Love,
Rachel

Jan lowered the letter.

Before he could say anything, Margot said, "Matthew has already been here. They're on their way."

It was difficult for Jan to stay, but he did.

Within minutes, Matthew and Rachel Durbin approached the pavilion. Rachel was carrying little Deborah. When she saw her brother standing next to Margot, she stopped and clutched the baby close to her. Matthew placed a protective arm around his wife. A scowl creased his forehead.

"It's all right," Margot said. "He read your letter and agreed to stay."

Rachel didn't move. She wore a betrayed look on her face.

So Margot took the initiative. She descended the steps of the pavilion and went to Rachel. "Can I see your baby?"

Motherly pride won out over distrust. Peeling back layers of blankets, Rachel showed the newborn to Margot.

"She's adorable!"

Mother and father beamed.

"May I hold her?"

Rachel looked to Matthew, who nodded. The exchange was made with care. Margot felt the warmth of the infant as she held the baby tight. She rocked Deborah for a moment, then without a word she turned and crossed to the pavilion.

"Margot—" Rachel said.

Calling over her shoulder, Margot said, "I'll take good care of your baby."

She ascended the pavilion steps.

Jan backed away.

"There's no need to fear her," Margot said. "She doesn't have teeth yet."

He stopped and let Margot get closer.

"Deborah, I'd like you to meet your *Oom*—your uncle. Jan, this is your niece. Her name is Deborah."

Jan leaned forward for a quick look, then moved back and forced a smile.

"Oh, this just won't do," Margot said. "Here." She gave the baby to Jan so quickly that he had the infant in his arms before he knew what had happened. Margot stepped away.

"Margot," Jan said, "please, take the baby back." He inched toward her cautiously.

"No," she said, "I think the two of you need to get acquainted." She went down the steps and back to Matthew and Rachel.

Matthew said, "Margot, I really don't think Jan is enjoying—"

"Of course he's enjoying it," she said. "He just doesn't know it yet." Margot glanced over at Rachel.

She wore the biggest smile Margot had ever seen on her.

"If you don't look a sight, Jan!" Rachel laughed. "Never did I imagine that you would ever hold a baby! I don't know who is more scared—you or Deborah!"

Indeed, Deborah had started to wail, which only seemed to add to Jan's anguish.

"Will someone please help me?" he said. "Please?"

"Would you like to rescue your brother from his dilemma?" Margot asked.

Rachel went up the pavilion stairs and took her baby from Jan's arms. Margot and Matthew followed close behind.

The four of them sat and talked for nearly an hour before Jan and Margot began their return trip to Klaarstroom.

25

The thing that nearly knocked Margot off her feet was Jan's parting word to his sister and Matthew. He asked for one more look at Deborah.

Rachel drew near the wagon and leaned forward, lovingly obliging.

Reaching out a thick rugged finger, Jan tenderly stroked the baby's velvet cheek. Then he said to her, "You'll come see me, won't you? And bring your mother and father with you."

Rachel drew back, holding her baby close.

Jan was not put off by her reaction. "I'll speak to Father. But whether he wants you there or not, I do. You will be welcome at Klaarstroom. You will always be welcome." With that, he drove away.

Margot stole glances at Jan all the way across the flatlands. Had he changed that much in the last few months, or was she just getting to know the real Jan van der Kemp? The secret hours they had spent together as he learned to read had revealed a side of him she had never seen before.

He had a passion to learn—and not just reading. They talked a lot about life situations, usually centered on Bible stories such as Nabal and Abigail. And though he expressed a certain comfort in his own brand of legalism, he also felt deeply its limitations and sorrows.

He described it to Margot this way: "You were right when you accused me of painting everything either black or white. Life is so much easier when you have only two brushes and two shades. But all that changed for me at the governor's reception when I saw the effect you had on the people who had once sought to hurt you. When I tried to paint that black and white, you took offense. I didn't know why. But I learned today. When I saw Rachel's smile again—and heard her laugh. And when you shoved little Deborah into my arms. The feelings I felt for her—Rachel's baby! My niece. Suddenly I could see the colors. And I don't know if I can ever go back to black and white again."

When Margot heard those words, she wanted to throw her arms around his neck. She didn't, of course.

I don't think I could ever grow tired of this place, Margot thought. She sat on a blanket, following the length of the waterfall from bottom to top and back again.

"Here it is . . ." Jan was stretched the length of the blanket, lying on one side. He propped himself up with an arm while the other hand flipped pages in the Bible. He read: "And they heard the voice of the Lord God walking in the garden in the cool of the day." Genesis chapter three, verse eight.

"That's nice," Margot murmured.

"I like it. It reminds me of this place. Whenever I come here, I can hear the voice of God walking about."

Margot looked at him and smiled.

"The only bad part about it is that it didn't last. Not even for one verse."

"What do you mean?"

Jan read again. "And Adam and his wife hid themselves from the presence of the Lord God amongst the trees of the garden."

"That's right," she said. "Chapter three—the temptation that brought sin into the world."

"Why is it that good things can never last?"

"Is that your subtle way of telling me it's time for us to go?"

Jan laughed. He closed the Bible, set it aside, and scooted closer to Margot.

Her first thought was to scoot away and maintain the distance between them. She didn't move, but she remained keenly aware that he was close.

"I was thinking of other things. There have been so many changes in my family, all of them bad—my mother's death, Rachel, Breyton, the way these things have affected father—"

"Hiring a housekeeper," Margot added.

"You're about the only pleasant thing that has happened—except, of course, the birth of little Deborah." He reached over and stroked Margot's shoulder.

She flinched. Then, to cover her reaction, she straightened her dress and stood. "Don't be silly," she said. Without looking at him, she walked a few feet from the blanket, arched her back in a stretch, and stared at the waterfall.

Only she wasn't thinking about the waterfall. She was thinking about the warmth of his hand when it touched her shoulder. When she felt her heart quickening and realized her breathing was shallow, she chided herself for feeling the way she did.

"What are you afraid of?" The voice startled her. It was close to her ear. She hadn't heard him come up behind her.

Margot folded her arms. "Afraid of? What makes you think I'm afraid of something?"

"You won't let anyone get close to you."

"I don't know what you're talking about." She wanted to step away from him, but that would only prove his point, so she couldn't.

"I've watched you long enough to know this to be true. Whenever someone gets close to you, you back away."

"You've been watching me?"

"It won't work."

"What won't work?"

"Changing the subject. Why won't you let anyone get close to you? Has someone hurt you that badly?"

Emotions began welling up inside Margot. She hastily erected control dikes to keep them from spilling over. "It's time we should be heading back," she said, turning toward the wagon.

Strong, warm hands grabbed her shoulders from behind, holding her in place.

"Don't run away from me," Jan said. "I have to know."

Margot pulled against his grip, testing it to see if it would give. It didn't. She closed her eyes and sighed heavily. "Have to know what?"

"Is it all men who scare you? Or just me?"

"Men don't scare me," she said flatly.

"Then it's me."

"Jan van der Kemp, you don't scare me."

"They why are you trembling?"

She was. Much to her dismay.

"You know what I think?" he asked.

Margot slumped her shoulders, hoping that, if she indicated she was resigning herself to this discussion, he would turn her loose.

He didn't.

"What do you think?"

"I think you're doing exactly the same thing I've been doing, only you do it with men."

"What?"

"Black and white. Every man you've ever known you've painted as either black or white. And my guess is that most of them have been painted black."

"That's ridiculous." She fended off the words quickly before they had a chance to work their way into her mind.

"No man will ever be good enough for you, because every man has faults. You paint him black. Unacceptable. There is no room in your world for the possibility of an imperfect man loving you."

"That's not true," Margot whispered.

"No?"

Gently Jan swung her around until she was facing him, his hands still holding her in place by the shoulders.

Margot glanced up. The way he was questioning her, she expected to see a superior look in his eyes, tinted with control—or possibly mischief, should he be enjoying himself. Instead she saw a deepness; and in those deep recesses of his eyes there was pain. She looked down again.

"Look at me!" he whispered.

Slowly, cautiously, she raised her head.

"It's not true? Then, *Mejuffrouw* Margot de Campion, what are you going to do with me?"

"What do you mean?"

"Standing before you is a man with faults. One who loves you."

Margot closed her eyes. "Please don't say that!" she whispered.

"Am I that repulsive to you?"

Tears came to her eyes. She shook her head.

"Then why don't you want me to say it? That's how I feel."

"Because it scares me." Margot sniffed and wiped away tears.

"I scare you?"

She didn't respond.

"Nabal and Abigail," he said sadly.

"Will you stop saying that!" Margot cried.

"It's true. Nabal didn't deserve Abigail. And I don't deserve someone like you."

He released her arms.

The portions of Margot's shoulders that had been covered by his hands were touched once again by the misty air. It chilled her. She shivered.

"Let's get you into the sun," he said.

Margot didn't move. "I'm not too cold," she said. She raised her head to look at him. There was no restraining force to keep her this close. Yet she stayed. "I told you I was scared. But not of you. I'm scared of me. I have feelings for you I've never had for another man. They scare me."

"What can I do to help you?"

She could contain the rising tide no longer. The dam inside her burst. "Hold me," she whispered.

In an instant she felt herself crushed against his chest; his arms encircling her, holding her tight; his cheek pressed against the top of her head. She lost herself in the warmth and scent of his embrace. Hers was a tiny universe. Dark. Warm. Secure. And she knew she could live there forever.

26

Do you want to know when I was first attracted to you?"

Margot looked up at the man who asked the question. She was seated in the wagon close to Jan, her arm in his, her head against his shoulder. His features were outlined with moonlight. A panorama of stars provided a backdrop behind him.

"It was in the hallway at the governor's palace."

"No!"

Jan nodded. "You called me a sad excuse for a brother because you thought I was making Rachel marry van Jaarsveld."

Margot laughed and buried her forehead against his arm. "If I recall," she countered, "you berated me for calling you Monsieur."

"French! That's right! I'd forgotten that."

"So what was it that attracted you to me?"

Jan smiled lovingly at her. "Your compassion and forthrightness. You were trying to protect Rachel, and you didn't even know her."

Margot bolted upright. "You yelled at me! You said it was none of my business!" Her tone was playful.

"It wasn't! But then van Jaarsveld's intentions and character became clear, and I learned you were no idle busybody. I realized how difficult it was for you to do what you did. How compassionate. That's when I fell in love with you."

"You had me fooled," Margot replied. "You hid your feelings well."

Jan shrugged. "It's one of the things I do best."

Margot giggled. The sound of her giggle surprised her. It was light and airy, like Katje's giggle when she talked excitedly about men. Margot had never heard a sound like that come out of her mouth. It unsettled her. The idea that she might be turning into a giddy little girl over a man unnerved her. Look how things turned out for Katje.

"Do you want to know the first time I knew I was in love with you?"

"My, we *are* full of confessions tonight, aren't we?"

Jan shrugged again. He was in a playful mood. "No use keeping it bottled up now, is there?" Then at the remembrance, his face sobered. "It was the day after we picked up Ndela in the slave compound. That's when I learned what Hennig did to you." The memory was sufficient to cause him to grit his teeth and clench his fists.

Margot felt his arm harden until it shook. Instinctively, ever so slightly, she moved back.

"Cyrus Steenkamp physically had to restrain me from riding back to the compound and tearing Hennig limb from limb. Had I gone back, I would have killed him—I know I would have killed him."

"Jan!"

He nodded at her reaction. "It scared me too. I never felt that strongly about anyone. It made me realize how much you mean to me."

The next few moments passed in silence. Margot's thoughts swirled in confusion. She was uncomfortable with the serious turn in their discussion. The idea that a man could feel the way Jan felt about her warmed her, yet at the same time frightened her so much that she wanted to jump from the wagon and run. She longed to embrace the warmth, but her fear of his strength held her back. What would happen when the warmth cooled and only the strength was left? Isn't that what happened to Sylvie and Monsieur Fabarez?

"What are you thinking?" Jan asked.

His words jarred her loose from the conflicting feelings that had entwined about her. With a light but forced tone she said, "So then you did tell everyone at Klaarstroom how you felt about me!"

He laughed. "No! Honest! I never said anything to anyone! I'm as baffled as you as to how they guessed."

The wagon reached the end of the lane that bisected the orchard and led to the house. Jan started the wagon up the lane, and the whitewashed Dutch gables came into view.

I have too many emotions! Margot moaned to herself. She wanted to run. But how could she? The tiny universe that existed in the circle of Jan's arms pulled at her with invisible force. She reached over and touched his shoulder.

"There you are!" Pieter's voice boomed from the porch. He rushed down the steps and toward the wagon. "Where have you been? You should have been home hours ago!"

Margot's hand retreated to her lap. Something was wrong. There was a worried look on Pieter's face that was more than just concern over the tardiness of their return.

Apparently Jan didn't see it. "We stopped at the waterfall for rest," he said.

Pieter didn't hear him. He reached the side of the wagon. Placing a strong hand on his son's arm, he said, "Two more farms have been hit by the Boers. Both of them were burned to the ground. The families killed."

"Lord have mercy on them," Margot cried, lifting a hand to her mouth.

Jan closed his eyes and grimaced.

"Slabbert and Nortje were here when I arrived. They're worried one of us might be hit next. We worked up a plan whereby we will keep check on each other. Also we drafted a letter to the governor requesting troops. But God alone knows whether they'll arrive before the Boers decide to strike again."

"We'll just have to leave it in His hands," Margot said.

The two men nodded in agreement.

"There's more," Pieter said. "It doesn't look like the Boers are doing this alone. The San may have joined them."

His hands folded and resting between his knees, his head down, Jan sat alone in the sitting room. It was his favorite chair. Breyton had made it especially for him. When Margot emerged from the stairway, making last-minute adjustments to her hair, she saw his downcast posture and knew immediately what was wrong.

"Where's your father?" she asked.

Without looking up, Jan said, "He rode out early this morning."

"I'm sorry."

"Me too."

Margot walked over and put a comforting hand on his back. "I've been praying that he would change his mind."

"God won't force a change on my father he is not willing to accept."

"Do you think Matthew and Rachel will be disappointed?"

Jan chuckled wryly. "I'm sure it would have been a greater shock to them had they found him here. And least he didn't forbid them to step on his property."

"Thanks to you," Margot said.

For two weeks a running battle had taken place following Jan's announcement that he had invited Rachel to visit Klaarstroom and bring her new baby. It was a two-man battle. There were times when Margot resisted the urge to have a say in the matter. She did so by reminding herself that she was only the housekeeper.

As it turned out, her voice was not needed. Jan stood toe to toe with his father. He argued strenuously and passionately on the side of compassion and forgiveness. In the end, Pieter relented insofar as admitting that Jan had a right to offer the invitation, no matter how ill-conceived—but that he had no right to expect Pieter to be party to his sin and error.

"They're here." Margot moved to the window and confirmed the arrival of their guests.

Jan swung open the door for her, and the two of them stepped onto the porch. In the middle of the orchard where the lanes crossed, Matthew and Rachel stood side by side. It was the identical spot Rachel had occupied when her father threw her off his property nearly a year earlier. Little Deborah was bundled deep in Rachel's arms.

For a moment, time was frozen. Even at a distance Margot could see the fear and uncertainty in Rachel's face.

Tossing aside her role as housekeeper, Margot swept down the steps, "Matthew, Rachel—thank you for coming. Let me see that little one again."

Jan followed her at a slower, more casual pace. When he reached the four of them he greeted Matthew warmly and thanked him for coming. Turning to his sister, he said, "Welcome home, Rachel."

Margot whisked the baby out of Rachel's arms so that she would not get in the way of the hug between brother and sister that followed.

They visited for more than an hour, sitting comfortably in an informal circle in the sitting room. The sun streamed through the windows, creating a lazy afternoon atmosphere in the room. Little Deborah lay asleep in Margot's arms. When the infant turned fussy and Rachel began to fashion a bed for her with blankets on the floor, Margot insisted on holding her while she slept. It delighted Margot the way Jan would sneak peeks at her holding the baby.

They spent the time sharing news—Matthew and Rachel describing their life as new parents and Jan telling them about the status of the farm, the events that led to Breyton's departure, and Pieter's health, which had always been vigorous but had shown significant decline in the last year.

Both couples avoided the topic of Pieter's absence. Neither Matthew nor Rachel asked; Jan and Margot offered no explanation or excuses.

Nor did Jan or Margot say anything about developments in their relationship, but by the way Rachel glanced from one of them to the other, it became evident she had her suspicions.

Then the front door flew open with a crash. Startled, little Deborah began to cry. Ding stumbled through the open door. *"Mijnheer van der Kemp, come quickly! The Boers. They're attacking!"*

27

Pieter and Old Knob huddled behind an outcropping of rocks. Pieter was armed with a musket. Together with the field hands they had successfully fought off the Boers' initial attack. Pieter had sent three men in as many directions for assistance from the nearby farms, knowing that it would be hours before help could arrive. He told them also to inquire about the governor's promised troops.

"It's been two weeks, and we've heard nothing," he complained to his Hottentot partner. "Isn't that just like the Company? Quick with the outstretched hand when they want something from us, lagging when we need something from them."

"Jan come. He'll help us," Old Knob said.

"Let's hope he gets here soon."

The Boers had swept out of the hills earlier that morning. From their dress, weaponry, and various skin colors, it was obvious they were a conglomerate group that had banded together to survive outside the bounds of normal society. Nomads, Boers wandered the high plains wilderness, occasionally raiding outlying settlements for their meat. This particular band was more ruthless than the others and more vindictive. Not until recently were the Boers known to destroy property and kill settlers. There were theories as to why the sudden change, but they were just theories. No one could come up with an adequate explanation for the wanton killing.

Old Knob crawled a short distance away to his things. Lying low, he uncovered a metal breastplate and retrieved a javelin from between two rocks.

"What are you doing?" Pieter asked him.

"I came to do battle," Old Knob replied. He set about strapping on the breastplate—which was not easy, considering his horizontal position.

"That's the one Xhore gave you."

Old Knob nodded. "From England. Like in the Bible, breastplate of rightfulness."

Pieter grinned. "Breastplate of righteousness."

291

"That too."

The sound of horses came from behind them. Whirling around, Pieter saw his son approaching. At a safe distance, Jan abandoned the horse and ran the remainder of the way, crouching low. A hail of musket balls greeted his arrival. A couple of them whizzed past his head, sending him crashing to the ground. He scrambled to safety behind the rocks.

"You all right?" he asked his father.

"Five field hands are dead. We've managed to keep them pinned up in those ravines." He pointed across an open expanse to the craggy cliffs of the mountainside. "The way it stands right now, it's like we have a wolf by the ears—as long as we got hold of him, he can't bite us, but then neither can we let go. What about Margot and—" he started to say Rachel's name but found he couldn't "—the others?"

"I left Ding with them. Matthew is there too, but he's only fired a musket once in his life. I gave him a quick lesson."

Pieter winced and turned his eyes back to the crags. "Guess we'll just have to keep them from reaching the house."

"Obiqua! Obiqua!" Old Knob yelled. "Robbers and murderers!"

After the first shots, the cattle had settled to Old Knob's right. Now, from beyond them, six San approached the beasts in their half-crouched hunting position. Each held a small bow in front of him, an arrow in place, fingers pinching the string. For hundreds of years the nomadic San had stolen the pastoral Khoi's cattle. Centuries of animosity lay behind Old Knob's use of words.

Old Knob stood up, jumped excitedly from foot to foot, and beat the air with his fists. *"Obiqua! Obiqua!"*

Pieter shouted, "Knob! Stay—"

Musket balls sprayed the rocks all around the Hottentot. Old Knob fell to the ground.

"Knob!"

The small black man rolled over and over.

Keeping low, Pieter and Jan rushed to him on their hands and knees.

Old Knob came faceup and stopped. His eyes flickered open. "Knobkerrie almost see God's face that time."

After he was sure Old Knob wasn't hit, Pieter scolded him for being careless.

The Hottentot tapped his chest. "Breastplate of rightfulness protect me."

Their attention was drawn again to the encroaching San warriors. Pieter and Jan agreed that if all they suffered was the loss of a few cattle, they could indeed count themselves fortunate.

But Old Knob insisted that if the San were allowed to take the cattle, they would soon come back for more.

Before either van der Kemp could stop him, Old Knob was scrambling toward the herd. There was nothing Pieter and Jan could do but watch and attempt to cover him from a distance. Reaching the animals, he began working his way between their legs. Soon they lost sight of him among the mass of cattle legs.

"If we can't see him, neither can they," Jan hoped aloud.

"The San show no indication of seeing him," Pieter added, equally hopeful. They watched as the warriors began separating some animals from the rest of the herd.

Suddenly Old Knob popped up from among the cattle, calling the San names and shaking his javelin. The San were so startled that they broke and ran, but not before they released a volley of arrows at Old Knob. When the Hottentot saw the arrows coming, his face showed surprise and shock. But then, when the arrows hit his breastplate and fell harmlessly to the ground, he shouted and danced and shook his javelin all the more vigorously. Beating his chest with his hand, he cried, "Breastplate of rightfulness save Old Knobkerrie!" He turned toward Pieter and Jan and shouted, "*Obiqua* defeated by Xhore's breastplate of rightfulness!"

While the San warriors retreated to the hills, Old Knob danced and sang among the cattle. Having made his way back to Pieter and Jan the same way he came—by crawling among the cattle's legs—he emerged triumphantly to the laughter and cheers of his two friends.

Knobkerrie beat on the breastplate. "San arrows just bounce off. Xhore would be happy for Knobkerrie. He told me one day I would be a great king."

While he spoke, Old Knob scratched his shoulder. Several minutes later he was still scratching.

Pieter called him over to look at it.

While Pieter examined Old Knob's shoulder, the Hottentot bent his head and looked too. "Oooo, not great," Knobkerrie said.

Pieter looked at him, then at Jan. "There's no arrowhead, but there's a cut in the skin."

"Lord, no," Jan said.

Knobkerrie smiled. "Not worry," he said to Pieter. "Your God, my God. Knobkerrie see God's face today. Maybe see Xhore. Tell him breastplate of rightfulness miss one arrow."

Within minutes, Old Knob was growing dizzy.

"Look! They're coming again!"

The six San warriors had recovered from their fright and were stalking the cattle again.

"Obiqua!" Old Knob jumped up.

Both Pieter and Jan attempted to grab him, but he slipped away, running toward the herd this time. His line was not direct—it was more like a series of half circles in which every third step he fell to the ground.

"Obiqua! Obiqua!"

Reaching the edge of the herd, he managed to pull himself onto the back of a bull. Riding cattle was nothing knew to Old Knob; he did it all the time. Only this time he struggled to maintain his balance.

With a yell he turned the beast toward the San warriors, who stared at him in disbelief. The old Hottentot with his dung cap and brass breastplate charged the bull through the herd, which parted like the waters when Moses led the people of Israel across the Red Sea.

The San let loose another volley of arrows. Some hit the breastplate and fell harmlessly to the ground. Old Knob screamed with delight in praise of his breastplate of rightfulness. If others found fleshy targets, these didn't bother him either.

"San arrows no longer hurt me!" Old Knob cried. "Can die only once! No longer afraid!"

The bull charged the San. Old Knob bounced side to side. Twice he nearly fell off. Somehow he managed to hold on.

"Ahhhheeeeeee!" he cried happily.

The San dropped their weapons and fled before him. They scattered in six different directions.

"Ahhhheeeeeee!"

He was heading straight toward the mountains and the Boers.

"Ahhhheeeeeee!"

BLAM! BLAM! BLAM!

The Boers opened fire. The bull carrying Old Knob stumbled and fell. The old Hottentot sailed over the animal's head, hit the ground hard, and rolled awkwardly. Then all was still. Neither the bull nor the man moved.

"What do you see, old friend?" Pieter mourned. "When you look into the face of God, what do you see?"

28

Van der Kemp!"

Pieter and Jan looked at each other. The voice that called to them came from the craggy cliffs.

"Pieter van der Kemp!"

"What do you think they want?" Jan asked.

Pieter shrugged. "We're going to find out." Turning toward the rocks, he shouted, "This is Pieter van der Kemp!"

The two men waited for an answer. When one didn't come, Jan said, "Either they don't believe you, or you scared them off."

Then, "Indicate your location!"

Jan looked at his father and shook his head.

"We have to resolve this one way or the other," Pieter said. He took his handkerchief, tied it to the end of his musket, and waved it over his head.

All around them the field hands, hiding behind anything large enough to protect them, watched in silence.

Pieter lowered the flag and waited for further contact.

"Step out from behind the rocks. Come to the center of the field. Do not bring a weapon."

With a look of disbelief, Jan said, "What kind of fools do they think we are?"

Pieter handed him his musket.

"Father, don't go out there!"

"Son, this isn't the first risk I have taken to save Klaarstroom."

"Let's hope it's not the last," Jan replied.

With his hands held out to his sides, Pieter stood and faced the mountains. When the Boers didn't shoot him, he figured they had something else in mind, so he stepped over the outcropping of rocks and walked toward the center of the field, ever mindful of the lifeless body of Old Knob to his right. When he reached midfield, he took his stand and waited.

For several moments nothing happened. Pieter stood alone as the wind whipped through the rocky crevices, at times making a mournful cry. From his improved vantage point he could see faces peering around rocks and trees. The enemy. And he exposed like this.

The figure of a Boer stepped from a ravine and began making his way toward him. The man wore a large, bulky coat—to conceal a weapon? His hair was dark and full, as was his growth of beard. From a distance his face was nothing more than two eyes and a nose poking out from behind a hairy bush. The man stopped several yards away. For what seemed a full minute he did not say anything.

"You haven't changed much, Father."

Pieter peered past all the hair. *"Breyton?"*

The man didn't respond.

Pieter leaned forward, searching for some recognizable feature. "Breyton?"

"Are you trying to pretend you don't recognize me?"

The voice belonged to Breyton.

"You've changed so much."

"I figured you would like the new me," Breyton said. "You always complained that I was too soft, too lazy—that I was less than a man because I didn't handle cattle well. Surprise. Now I do."

"You're the one behind all this? And the Steenkamp farm? All the destruction—the killing—the families—the children?"

Breyton didn't answer. He didn't need to. The devil danced in his eyes. Not only was he responsible, he took pleasure in it.

The realization of the truth was more than Pieter could take. He staggered to one side, catching himself just before he fell. "You—are—not—my—son!"

"I was never your son! Never your son! Never!" Breyton ranted at the sky. His eyes looked like those of a cornered, wounded animal that was still trying to protect itself even though it knew it was going to die. There was no anguish in his scream, no grief—only anger, a thirsty anger that needed violence and destruction and pain to quench it.

Pieter backed away. He spoke as he would if he were describing a nightmare, not wanting to believe what was so evident. "Just like a rabid wolf. You have to be destroyed. For everyone's safety, you have to be destroyed."

Breyton produced a large knife from beneath his coat. "This wolf has teeth!"

Pieter stepped back.

Breyton moved toward him. "All the other farms? They were just to get your attention. I killed all those people just to get your attention. And I did, didn't I?" He laughed like a sick hyena. "Don't you see the irony in that? All my life I've been trying to get your attention." He thrust his face forward, clenched his teeth, and added, "And—I—finally—found—a—way!"

Pieter took another step back.

"I just wanted you to know that before I kill you. Because I want you to feel responsible for their deaths. I want you to agonize over their deaths before you join them!"

"Breyton." Pieter stopped as he said the name. He pulled himself upright. He took a step toward his son.

The boy cocked his head and screwed up his face. His father's initiative took him by surprise.

"Breyton," Pieter said again, "I can understand why you hate me and that you want to kill me. Fine. I'm willing to die at your hand."

With a sneering smile and a guttural groan Breyton gripped the knife for use.

"I'll let you kill me," his father said. "But then it's over. You will have had your revenge. Go back to the wilderness and never return."

The sheer wickedness of Breyton's laugh covered Pieter's skin with chill bumps.

"You don't understand, old man. I don't want just to kill you. I want you to suffer, to writhe in agony on this field, to wish for death yet know it's still standing a long way off, to watch everything you've worked for burn to the ground, to watch as your favorite son is disemboweled before your eyes and you are too close to dying yourself to help him. Maybe then you will know the kind of suffering I endured year after year after year as the son who never could do anything good enough for you."

"You are mad!"

"Quite!" Breyton came after his father with slow, tantalizing steps.

Pieter stepped back. His heel struck something, and he stumbled, falling backward, hitting ground, knocking the breath from his lungs.

"Ho, ho, ho, ho!" Breyton cried. "You're making this too easy for me, old man!" He raised the serrated blade to strike.

BLAM!

Breyton spun around. The knife flew from his hand. He clutched his shoulder. Scrambling to his feet, Pieter sucked as hard as he could for air and stumbled back toward the rock cover.

BLAM! BLAM!

Musket balls whizzed past him, some ricocheting off the boulders. He tumbled down next to Jan, who was staring out at the field, his musket at the ready, his eyes wide with terror.

In the field, Breyton had recovered his knife and was angrily attacking the ground, plunging the blade into the earth over and over as he cursed and growled.

"Kill him!" Pieter cried. "Kill him while we have the chance!"

Jan looked helplessly at his father. "I can't kill my own brother!"

"He would kill you!" Pieter shouted. "Kill him!"

"I can't do it!"

Pieter grabbed the musket from him and threw it on top of the rocks into firing position.

It was too late. Breyton was running toward the ravine. He was quickly out of range.

Pieter flung the musket to the ground. He sat down, his head resting against the rocks, his chest heaving.

"Lord, forgive me!" His face was twisted with anguish. "Forgive me. Please, forgive me!" He squeezed his eyes shut as hard as he could, trying to forget the mad look in Breyton's eyes. But he couldn't. Breyton's rabid glare and sneer and hyena laugh taunted him in the darkness of his own mind.

Something touched his arm. He jumped.

It was Jan. "Father?"

Pieter reached over and patted his son's hand. "The boy's mad. He'll not be satisfied until he has killed all of us and burned Klaarstroom to the ground."

It was as though his words themselves sparked a flame to life. In the distance, in the direction of the house, a column of thick smoke arose.

"See that, old man?" Breyton stood at the edge of the ravine. "That's your house! Your precious house."

"Margot!" Jan bolted upright.

"My, what fine-looking smoke! I knew all those chairs and tables I made would make a good fire someday!"

"Father, I must go back. Margot needs me."

"You always treated me like I was the dumb one! But who's dumb now? While you focus on one threat, another one sneaks behind your back and burns your house down. Not a bad plan for an imbecilic son, is it, old man?"

"Go," Pieter said. "Somehow we'll hold things down here."

Jan looked toward the house, at his father, then back toward the house.

"Go!" Pieter said again, this time emphatically.

29

Jan gathered up his musket and, keeping low, ran toward the horses. He signaled a handful of workers to take a wagon and follow him. Then he jumped onto his horse and urged it into a gallop, all the while staring ahead at the column of smoke. He chastised himself for not leaving more men at the house to protect the women. If anything happened to them because of his shortsightedness, he knew he'd never forgive himself.

"Lord, cover Margot and Rachel and Deborah with Your arms," he prayed. "Please, Lord, cover them with Your arms."

Margot saw them from the window. Boers. Ragged. Dirty. All of them armed. They were in the orchard, moving from tree to tree, coming toward the house.

"Matthew! They're coming in the front!"

The half-Malaysian boy emerged from the hallway, musket in hand. "How many?"

"I counted five. Maybe six."

"Four are approaching from the back," he said.

Rachel whimpered. She was sitting in a chair, rocking Deborah feverishly. The baby fussed, perhaps sensing her mother's anxiety. "Matthew—" she cried.

"Where does this go?" Matthew pointed at the stairs.

"My room," Margot and Rachel said in unison.

"Does it have a doorway that leads outside?"

"No," Margot said.

Rachel was on her feet now. Crying. "Matthew, don't let them kill my baby!"

Matthew looked helplessly toward the back of the house, then at the front door. "How can I hold them all off? We only have the one musket!" He looked frantically at his wife and child. His feet shifted nervously but with no direction. Beads of sweat cascaded down his cheeks.

"Matthew!" Margot said. "Think. Someone wants to get in. How do we convince them to leave?"

Matthew sucked in his lower lip as he thought. His feet continued to shuffle nervously. "We can't force them . . . they're stronger. Convince them to leave . . . convince them . . ."

Margot and Rachel exchanged worried glances.

"You make them *want* to leave!" he said. "Make them think it's in their best interest to leave!"

Margot checked the window. The Boers were almost to the house. "Hurry, Matthew! How do we make them want to leave?"

His feet danced as he tried to hurry his thoughts. "Make them want to leave . . . what would make the Boers want to leave . . ."

Rachel shouted, "Use their character against them! Like we did with van Jaarsveld. Turn their character against them!"

"Good!" Margot cried. "What is their true character?"

The first of the Boers were venturing out from the cover of trees.

"They attack to get something," Matthew said.

"They want something," Rachel echoed.

"They want something. Take away what they want!" Matthew shouted. His eyes lit up. His eyes crystallized with the look of a man who had a plan. "Everyone upstairs!"

"But there's no way to get out if we go up there!" Rachel cried.

Margot grabbed her by the shoulders and led her to the stairway. "Trust his instincts! Do what he says!"

As Rachel carried the baby up the stairs, Matthew grabbed Margot by the arm. "We need things that will burn and make a lot of smoke. A lot of smoke!"

Margot nodded. She ran into the kitchen. She grabbed oil, candles, bags of herbs and spices, anything she thought might produce a lot of smoke.

Matthew was waiting for her at the bottom of the staircase, his musket trained on the front door. Margot heard what he heard—footsteps on the porch.

"Up the stairs! Quick!" he cried.

Margot felt his hand on her back, pushing her upward just as the front door crashed open. The sound of their pounding footsteps bounced loudly against the stairwell.

Rachel jumped when the two banged through the bedroom doorway and slammed the door shut behind them. The baby started crying. Rachel shushed her and held her close.

Matthew's eyes darted around the room.

"What are you looking for?" Margot cried.

"There!" He pointed to the trunk in the corner. The one that had once belonged to van Jaarsveld. To Margot, whose hands were still full of the things she'd collected, he said, "Listen at the doorway. Tell me what you hear." As he passed by Rachel, he thrust the musket at her. "Hold this."

It was an odd sight to see Rachel sitting on the edge of the bed with a baby in one arm and a musket in the other.

"I hear noises downstairs," Margot said. "Can't make out what they're saying."

Matthew threw open the trunk lid. Grabbing handfuls of clothing, he emptied it in two seconds, then scooted it toward the door. "Place everything in here," he said. "Give me that oil lamp too!" He pointed to the lamp on the bedside stand.

Margot retrieved it.

"Bring the stand too!" Matthew said.

It was a small night stand; like most of the furniture, it had been made by Breyton.

Shouting could be heard downstairs and the sound of furniture being thrown against the walls.

"All right, listen," Matthew said to the girls. He threw a heavy quilt into a far corner and began to drag the mattress to the window. "We need to convince them to leave, right? Who wants to stay in a house that's on fire? Here's what I want you to do . . ."

He put the remaining combustibles in the trunk while he described their roles to them. Then, with the lit lamp in his hand, he waited to hear footsteps on the stairs. He didn't have to wait long. He pointed to Margot.

She screamed. "What are you doing? No! You're crazy! Don't! Don't!"

Matthew threw the lamp into the trunk and jumped back. He pointed to Rachel.

"I'm sorry, little one," she whispered. Then she pinched the baby hard. Little Deborah's squeal split the air. It was followed by her mother's scream. "Put it out! Put it out! Please, I don't want to burn!"

Margot joined her. So did Matthew. The fire in the trunk grew in intensity. The room was filling with smoke. They started to choke and cough, but they kept screaming.

"Get us out! Get us out!" Margot cried.

Matthew pounded on the door with his foot. To do so he had to kick through the fire. He winced as the flames licked his leg. On the fourth kick the door flew open. When the air from the stairwell rushed in, the flames shot up even higher. Smoke billowed down the stairway. Matthew screamed and fell backward, his pants leg on fire.

Margot threw a blanket over his leg and smothered the flame. From downstairs she could hear men yelling, "Fire! The house is on fire!"

Rachel looked out the window. "It's working!" she cried. "They're running out!"

The fire in his clothing extinguished, Matthew ordered, "Under the quilt! Hurry!"

Coughing, Rachel ducked beneath the bedcover and sat on the floor. Margot followed her.

"Is the second fire necessary?" she asked Matthew.

"We've got to convince them, or they'll be right back in here."

He set the mattress on fire, fanning the flame with his hand. Then wrapping his fist in a blanket, he punched at the windowpanes, knocking out several of them.

"Aaaahhhhhhhh!" Matthew cried and waved his arms frantically. "Help us! Help us! My wife! My baby!" The smoke cut him off. He coughed and choked.

"Hurry, get under here!" Margot held up the edge of the quilt. He slid under it and joined her and his family.

Beneath the covering the baby screamed while the three adults coughed and gagged. Matthew frequently lifted the corner of the quilt to check the fires to make sure they didn't burn beyond where he wanted them to burn.

"How long do we have to stay under here?" Rachel yelled.

"Just a little while longer," Matthew answered. "If they're not convinced soon, they never will be." He checked the fires again.

The blaze in the trunk burned as planned, but the mattress fire began to creep along the floor.

"Stay here!" Matthew said. He flipped back the quilt and jumped out.

Grabbing a corner of the cover, Margot held it against her mouth and coughed repeatedly and uncontrollably. Through burning, watery eyes she watched as Matthew beat down the mattress fire. Then he checked to see what the Boers were doing, and his shoulders slumped. Margot knew it wasn't good news.

"They're just standing there watching!" he cried in disbelief. "Why are they still standing around? Don't they have other people to kill today?"

Rachel was coughing so hard she could barely get her breath. Margot felt as though she would turn herself inside out with each cough. Matthew stood beside the window, his arm against the wall and his forehead against his arm.

"The moment we go down, they'll be waiting for us. Why didn't I—"

All of a sudden he straightened up. He stared in disbelief out the window.

"What is happening? Why are they—" His face broke out in that huge toothy grin that Margot always associated with him. "It's Jan! It's Jan!"

While Margot helped Rachel to her feet, Matthew kicked aside the burning trunk so that they could get by. Then, as they began to work their way down the stairs, leaning heavily against the walls with each cough, he beat out the fire in the trunk with a blanket.

After helping Rachel into a porch chair, Margot collapsed into one herself. The air had never smelled or tasted as sweet. She wanted to drink it in with huge gulps—but each time she breathed, it set her to coughing. She had to content herself with little sips of air.

Jan bounded onto the porch just as Matthew emerged from the house. He yelled to the servants to get buckets to put out the house fire. He grabbed Margot. "Are you hurt? Are you burned?" Anguished eyes looked her over for burns.

"Not hurt," she said, then coughed into his shoulder. She tried to tell him the house wasn't on fire, but she couldn't get the words out.

Jan pulled her head against his chest, his lips rested on the top of her head. "I was afraid I'd lost you. I never would have forgiven myself. Never." His arms fell over her shoulders, and she found herself once again in her safe little universe. He held her tightly against him until she stopped coughing.

One of the servants stepped from the house. "The fire was in a box," he said, clearly puzzled. "A lot of smoke. And other than a mattress, nothing else burned."

Jan shared his puzzled look.

Margot pulled away from Jan just far enough to see his face. "Matthew saved us by making the Boers think the house was on fire."

Cradling his wife and child in his arms, Matthew said, "It wasn't a good plan. It nearly didn't work."

"It was a clever plan!" Margot insisted. "And it worked as long as it needed to."

"It was the smoke that brought me back here," Jan said.

Rachel looked up at her husband proudly. "It did better than you think it did," she said.

Jan looked around. "This isn't over yet. Already we've lost several men." With downcast eyes he added, "Including Old Knob."

"No," Margot said softly.

"It gets worse," Jan said. "Breyton is the one who is leading these raids."

"Breyton?" Rachel cried in disbelief. "I don't believe it!"

"Neither do I!" Margot said.

Jan's eyes filled with fear. "He's changed."

30

Maybe I can say something that will make a difference!"

Jan folded his arms and shook his head. "Margot, if you saw Breyton, you'd realize nothing you say will have any effect."

"At least let me try!"

"No."

"Let me see him for myself!"

"No!"

Margot crossed her arms. "Why are you being so stubborn about this?"

"Stubborn?" Jan threw his hands high in the air. "It's not a matter of stubbornness. I won't take you out there with me because I love you and don't want to lose you!"

"You can't protect me from everything!" she cried.

"Maybe not, but I can protect you from my brother!"

For the moment it was an impasse. Margot sat in a chair on the front porch; Jan stood over her. They were alone. Matthew and Rachel had taken the baby inside the house, hoping to quiet her long enough so that she would fall asleep.

Margot slapped the arms of the chair and stood, even though he gave her little room to do so. He didn't move. She stood anyway. They were inches from each other. "I'm going out there," she insisted.

"You're staying right here."

She pushed him away with both hands. Though she pushed hard, he barely moved. "Jan van der Kemp, get out of my way."

"I can't let you go out there," he said.

Margot felt her anger rising. "Let's get one thing straight," she said. "You do not own me. We are not married. And there is no reason why I have to listen to you."

"Other than the fact that you work for us."

"Then I quit!" She walked past him.

"Margot—" His tone was soft. Conciliatory. He touched her arm; she pulled away. "All of my life I have waited for someone like you. Most of those years I didn't even know I was waiting. Now, in such a short time, you have created a desire in me and filled it all at the same time. I admit I'm being selfish. I don't want to live with an emptiness that only you can fill."

Margot stopped at the edge of the porch, looking out over the orchard. Her back was to him; her voice matched his in tone. "Jan, I feel exactly the same way. You have awakened feelings in me that I had told myself for years did not exist. And as hard as it is for me to admit it to myself, I like them." She closed her eyes. Tears came. She whispered, "I don't want to lose you either."

She felt his large hands cover her shoulders, his lips and nose touch the back of her head. Pushing him back, she swung around. "But I am not a Chinese vase for you to set on some mantel and admire! Like it or not, I love this land as much as you. And if there is any hope for a relationship between us, we're going to have to save this land together!"

She was talking to a stone face. Hard, unyielding features stared at her. Then, to her amazement, the stone melted and became human. A solitary tear rolled down a cheek of flesh. He pulled her against him with a warm ferocity and said, "I only have the one horse. You'll have to ride with me."

For the rest of her life Margot would remember the expression on Pieter's face when he saw them running low toward the outcropping of rocks that had been the van der Kemp defense since the initial attack.

"What are you doing bringing a woman here?" he yelled.

Margot didn't wait for Jan to reply. "I came to talk to Breyton," she said.

They fell to the ground behind the boulders. Jan was between his father and Margot. He turned to her. "I didn't say you could talk to him. You said you wanted to see for yourself!"

Pieter poked his son in the kidneys to get his attention. Jan turned his head toward his father.

"This is no place for a woman!" Pieter said. "What were you thinking?"

"She insisted on—"

Margot punched Jan's shoulder. He turned back toward her.

"I thought we agreed that we were in this together!"

"We are!" Jan cried. "But I never agreed to let you go out there—"

Pieter jabbed his son again. "Son, look at me when I'm talking to you!"

Jan turned toward his father.

While the two men argued over the wisdom, or lack of it, in bringing Margot to the fighting, she surveyed the field in front of them. In the distance she caught an occasional glimpse of a head poking from behind a tree or rock. At times an arm appeared as it was raised and then lowered.

She looked at the back of Jan's head. It bobbed emphatically. He and his father were both talking. Neither one was listening.

Margot stood up and walked into the field toward the Boers.

Frantic voices shouted behind her, first Pieter. "What is she doing! Grab her!"

Then Jan. "Margot! Come back here! Stay down!"

A swish of his hand brushed her dress but came up empty.

Margot glanced back but kept walking.

Jan started over the rocks after her.

BLAM! BLAM!

She stopped. The bullets hit the rocks, spraying him with chips. He fell backward. The musket fire was meant to keep him back, not her, Margot concluded. Ignoring Pieter's and Jan's pleas, she walked to the middle of the field and waited.

The faces scattered about the craggy ravine were clearer now. Dirty. Hungry-looking. Hard, uncaring eyes stared at her. Something to her right caught her attention. A dead bull. Just beyond it, a body. Small. Broken. Brown skin. A brass breastplate caught a ray from the sun and threw it back.

Margot closed her eyes. Her heart ached. Old Knob. She remembered him seated at the entrance to his hut, playing with dung-and-stick animal toys. She remembered his story of the jackal and the mother dove. It seemed the old Hottentot's fears about Breyton had come true. The seeds of destruction had been planted, and now they were bearing fruit.

Coming from the ravine, a bearded figure wearing an oversized coat strode toward her. As he got closer, Margot noticed a rip in the right shoulder. It was stained with blood.

Jan had said she wouldn't recognize Breyton. At the time she took it as an exaggeration. Now she wasn't so sure. The man who approached her looked nothing like the Breyton she knew. Was it he? She looked harder. Hair covered so much of the face, it was hard to pick out distinguishing features.

Just when she decided that the man coming toward her was not a van der Kemp, he said, "Margot. What a curious surprise."

It was Breyton's voice. And now that he was closer, she could see that the man had Breyton's eyes.

"Why are you doing this, Breyton?"

A grin appeared. It wasn't a human grin; it was more like one a person would expect to see on a jackal. "Straight to business." He shook his head in mocking sadness. "Jan seems to be a bad influence on you. I would have expected our conversation to begin with a few pleasantries."

Margot conceded. "All right, how is Ndela?"

The jackal's smile disappeared. Breyton's lips quivered. Like lightning bolts, his eyes flashed rage. And for the first time Margot was truly afraid that she would not leave the field alive.

"She's dead. I tracked her down and killed her."

Margot's fingers rose to her mouth in shock at the coolness with which he admitted the killing.

His eyes widened. "A lovers' spat." He chuckled at his morbid humor. "I was merely repaying her for what she did to me." Breyton pulled back his coat and raised his shirt.

Margot winced at the sight. His stomach was caved in on one side. The flesh that was there was pocked and black and red.

Lowering the shirt, Breyton shook a finger at her. "Never fall asleep when the person you love has a musket!" He laughed hard. The jackal was back.

"Breyton—"

He held up a hand to stop her. "I don't want to hear it. Besides, it wouldn't do any good."

"Then why did you come out here to talk to me?"

"To convince you."

"Convince me? Of what?"

"That I'm going to kill all of you and burn this farm to the ground. I told the old man I was going to do it, and I don't think he believed me. But they'll believe you if you tell them."

"I don't believe you'll do it," Margot said.

The jackal laughed. "Before today is over you'll believe it!"

"Rachel is here. At the house. She has a baby named Deborah. I don't believe you want to hurt either one of them."

"Rachel has a baby?" His angry eyes softened.

"Little Deborah. She's your niece."

"How old is she?"

Margot smiled. "Just a couple of months old."

Breyton smiled too, but there was no warmth in his smile. "Then she'll die in innocence, never knowing how truly evil this world can be!"

"You would kill an infant? Your own niece?" Margot cried.

Breyton's eye widened wickedly. He nodded his head. "Anything that belongs to that old man I will destroy. Anything! Anything!" His jaw jerked erratically to one side as he yelled, yet his eye remained fixed on Margot. The man was an animal. There was no goodness left in him.

"Do you plan to murder me too?" Margot couldn't believe how controlled her voice sounded. It did not reveal the growing terror she felt inside.

The jackal grin appeared in response. "You belong to him now. You have to die."

Margot took a deep breath. "Then get it over with. Kill me."

The jackal stared at her in a way that reminded Margot of Old Knob's story. It was the way she had imagined the jackal looked when he told the mother dove to throw down her babies so that he could eat them.

Breyton shook his head. "Not yet. Soon. But not yet. I'm going to let you live for a while longer."

"For what purpose?"

"Purpose? Purpose?" He threw his hands out to his sides and lifted his head toward the sky and screamed at someone—God? a demon? the sky itself? "Why must everything have a purpose?" Then to Margot he said, "Purpose? Do you really need a purpose to die? Why can't people die just because someone kills them?"

The man was raving. Margot took a step backward.

As instantly as he had flown into a rage, he was back again. Calm. Quiet. "I'll give you a purpose," he said. "That is, if you indeed need a purpose."

Margot didn't respond.

He continued anyway, speaking like a kind father instructing his daughter regarding a particular matter of etiquette.

"You see, my dear lady, I will not kill you this moment because it suits my purpose. By not killing you now, I demonstrate great patience and goodness. After all, we are kindred spirits, are we not, you and I? Each of us at one time or another has succumbed to the wild but wicked charms of a wide-eyed Ndela. You, on the one hand, took lashes for that poor, unfortunate soul; while I, on the other hand, provided her a means of escape. Both of us were deceived. Kindred spirits and all that. Don't you think?"

Margot took another step backward. The charming Breyton was more frightening than the raving madman. With lightning speed, he lashed out and grabbed her by the wrist. His grip was like iron.

Behind her, Margot could hear Jan calling her name.

"But we are different in this—" the charming Breyton clenched his teeth "—only one of us fell to the dubious charms of Pieter van der Kemp. Only one of us is still allied on his side. Only one of us realizes the true evil of the man who quotes from the Bible yet hates his own son. And that one must die with all the others. It's a matter of principle, my dear. As much as I'd like to make an exception in your case, I'm afraid it would set a bad precedent. I'm just going to have to kill you!"

He released her arm with the same suddenness with which he'd seized it.

Until that moment Margot hadn't realized how strongly she had been pulling away. She stumbled backward at the sudden release, yet managed to catch her balance before she fell.

Using his large coat for a cape, Breyton turned around with a flourish and walked back toward the crags. Then suddenly, he twirled around again. A rigid finger pointed at Margot. "You tell that old man that he is going to die today! But not before he sees everything he loves destroyed! You tell him that!"

Breyton left Margot standing alone in the middle of the field.

31

The moment Margot was behind the rocks, Jan had her in his arms. She had walked calmly back across the field, but now that it was over she found herself shaking uncontrollably and struggling to hold back an onslaught of tears.

"Everything I said, everything I did—nothing! I thought I could make a difference—reach the old Breyton—appeal to his humanity. But nothing I said or did mattered to him. Nothing! He wants to kill us. And unless we can find a way to stop him, he's going to succeed."

She composed herself long enough to fill them in on the parts they had not heard. No sooner had she finished than a cry went up along the van der Kemp lines.

"They're coming! They're coming!"

Hordes of Boers poured out of the ravines onto the field, screaming and waving their weapons.

"They must have been waiting for reinforcements!" Pieter yelled.

They kept coming, countless numbers of them.

Jan grabbed his musket and took aim.

BLAM!

A stocky Boer grabbed his leg and rolled in the dirt.

Pieter placed a hand on Jan's shoulder. "There are too many of them!" he shouted.

Jan looked again and acknowledged that his father was right.

"Fall back to the house. We can defend ourselves better there! Go!"

Jan reached out his hand for Margot. To his father he said, "You're coming too, aren't you?"

Pieter nodded. "I'll pass the word along. Then I'm right behind you!"

Running low, Margot and Jan retraced their steps to the horse. Musket balls whistled by them. Jan mounted, then pulled Margot up.

She took an anxious look for his father.

Pieter ran to one side of the rocks, cupped his hand and shouted, then ran to the other side and did the same thing. Men began emerg-

311

ing from behind boulders and trees and the foliage in the field. All ran in the direction of the house. Ding appeared on one side, driving a wagon. Field hands all around him ran beside it and then jumped onto the bed.

The horse turned suddenly as Jan urged it toward the house. The animal picked up speed, and soon the distance between them and the running Boers increased. The wind rushed past them, and Margot's heart beat so loudly in her ears that she could barely hear anything else. What she did hear caused her heart to leap with fear.

It was Ding's voice.

"Mijnheer van der Kemp! *Mijnheer* van der Kemp!"

She turned to see Pieter struggling to his feet. His fallen horse thrashed about beside him but seemed unable to get up. A cloud of dust encircled Pieter. He checked himself and his horse for injuries. Behind him came a wall of Boers. "Jan!" Margot shouted. "Go back! Your father!"

Jan looked behind them. The instant he saw his father's predicament, he slowed the horse and turned it around.

Ding saw Pieter too. He steered the wagon toward him. The wagon was closer and reached him first. The van der Kemp patriarch jumped onto the bed. No sooner was he aboard than Ding laid into the horses with the whip. They charged forward as everyone in the wagon reached for something to hold onto to keep from falling off.

From the back of the wagon Pieter saw Jan and waved his son forward.

Jan pulled the horse over hard and spurred him toward the house, but not without checking behind them every few minutes to assure himself that his father was still there. However, because of their difference in speed, the wagon eventually fell out of sight.

Matthew was standing on the porch with musket in hand when they arrived.

"They're coming!" Jan yelled to him and the servants within earshot. Without exception, they all looked to Jan for orders.

Margot jumped from the horse and joined Matthew on the porch.

"Where's Rachel?" Jan cried, dismounting.

"Lying down with the baby in your room."

"Get them upstairs. Matthew, you stay upstairs and guard them."

Matthew nodded and disappeared into the house.

To the hands standing around, Jan yelled, "Find defensible positions in the house and barn and slave quarters."

They all scrambled in different directions.

"Where do you want me?" Margot asked.

"Upstairs with Rachel and the baby."

Margot glared at him. "I thought we'd settled this."

Jan shook his head. "Someone has to defend the upstairs." He handed her his musket. "Do you know how to fire one of these?"

"I think so."

He took her answer as a yes. "Matthew has a musket too. One of you guard the window, the other the door. If anyone comes toward either of them, shoot. Don't talk—shoot!"

Margot took the musket. "What will you use?"

"I'll find another musket."

"And where will you be?"

"Probably downstairs. Now hurry!"

Margot nodded. She started for the front door, then ran back to Jan and threw herself into his arms, kissing him with all her might. "I love you! God be with you," she whispered.

"And with you."

Matthew was helping Rachel and the baby up the stairs when Margot got there. "Seems like we've done this before," Matthew said as he guided his wife through the smoke-blackened stairway.

"Let's just hope we don't have to start another fire," Margot replied.

The charred remains of van Jaarsveld's trunk was the first thing she saw when she entered the room. The charred mattress and broken window were next. This room had been the nicest she'd ever lived in. It was difficult to see it like this. She imagined it was even more difficult for Rachel.

Matthew dragged the burned mattress to one side while Rachel positioned herself in a corner with the quilt.

As he checked the window, Margot went over to mother and baby. "How's little Deborah?"

Rachel looked at her baby with sad eyes. "She's still coughing from the smoke—" she coughed herself and laughed "—and so am I. But other than that she seems to be doing well."

Margot bent down and pulled back the edge of the baby's blanket to get a better look at her. Little Deborah's tan cheeks had a pinkish tint to them. Her mouth moved in a sucking fashion for a moment, then was still. Her eyes were closed peacefully; she was oblivious to the strife all around her.

"Lord, have mercy!" Matthew said from the window. "I can see them coming. Hundreds of them!"

Rachel's eyes showed alarm.

"God will see us through this," Margot said, touching Rachel's cheek with the back of her hand in motherly fashion.

"I know He will. I believe in miracles."

Margot smiled and nodded.

"Who wouldn't?" Matthew said from the window. "The very fact that we're here is enough to convince anyone of miracles."

The girls managed to laugh. Jan's invitation and the Durbins' arrival at Klaarstroom seemed a lifetime ago.

There was a pounding of feet on the stairs. Matthew and Margot swung their muskets toward the door.

"Don't shoot! It's me!" Jan appeared, waving a leather bag similar to one he had strapped over his shoulder. In his other hand he carried a musket. "Extra ammunition," he said. "Let's hope you don't need it."

Matthew thanked him and slung the bag across his shoulder.

Jan walked over to his sister and kneeled beside her. "Looks like I didn't pick a very good day for you to come home."

Her face warmed with a half smile. "We were just talking about that. You sure do know how to organize a grand reception, Jan."

"I feel I must complain about the guest list," Matthew added, looking out the window again. "I think next time you ought to pare it down a bit."

Before joining Matthew by the window, Jan said to Rachel, "May I kiss her?"

Tears came to Rachel's eyes as she peeled back the blanket. Jan leaned over and gave little Deborah a kiss on the cheek. While his head was down, Rachel looked up at Margot as if to say, I can't believe this is my brother!

At the window, Jan checked on the progress of the Boers. They looked like an approaching storm, he reported, with Ding's wagon right in front of them. "Father and Ding are in the wagon. From the looks of it, they're in no immediate danger."

Suddenly shots rang out, hitting the front of the house. From the orchard. Boers?

"Where did they come from?" Jan cried. He looked again in the direction of the approaching wagon. "They're riding into a crossfire! I've got to warn them away."

He bolted for the door, then swung back around.

"Remember. If anyone comes up these stairs, shoot them! And stay clear of that window!"

The door slammed shut, and he was gone.

Margot looked at Rachel and Matthew, and they at her. An image came to mind from one of the tales in Sylvie's sea-story book. It was as though the three of them were stranded on an island, and Jan was swimming for help through shark-infested waters. Margot couldn't but wonder if she'd ever see him alive again.

32

Jan stood helplessly beside a front window watching the wagon carrying Ding and his father approach the house. He checked the orchard. It was packed with Boers. Where had they come from? Back to the wagon. The only face looking forward was Ding's—all the others were looking at the horde chasing them.

Somehow Jan had to warn Ding off before the wagon reached the front of the house. But how? He couldn't step outside to signal them. He'd checked with those guarding the back of the house. Anyone stepping outside either back or front would be a prime target. The cost of signaling the wagon would be a human life, and even then there was no guarantee that the signal would be received.

A deep breath affirmed what in his heart he already knew to be true. If it cost him his life to save the wagonload and his father, he would do it. But then again, he didn't want to throw his life away frivolously if there was another way.

Then he had an idea. He broke out a windowpane.

The wagon continued coming. It was beginning to slow now.

Jan poked the deadly end of his musket out the broken window at the wagon. What better way to warn someone off than with a warning shot? He took aim. Where to shoot? Over their heads? They would hear the sound, but, with the noise of the wagon, would they be able to determine the direction from which the shot came in time? He decided to fire at the ground. An explosion of dirt coupled with the sound of musket fire would give them a double warning. He picked a spot and waited for the wagon to get a little closer.

Ding's face was clearly visible now. Sweating. Scared. Pieter was on the seat beside him but was facing backward.

Jan pulled on the trigger just as his father turned forward. Something had caught Pieter's eye. Now he saw the Boers in the orchard! He yelled at Ding.

The startled driver stared wildly into the trees, then pulled the reins hard to the left and away from them.

Jan let up on the trigger. Too late.

BLAM!

A small explosion of dirt flared in front of the horses. They reared and bolted sharply left. The wagon skidded, its wheels kicking up a spray of dirt. Suddenly the skid halted abruptly as the wheels caught hold. The wagon rolled sideways.

"No!" Jan cried.

He watched in horror as bodies flew every which way. The horses stumbled and fell, one crashing on top of the other. Dust clouds plumed, engulfing the scene of splintered wood and strewn bodies.

The wagon emerged from the cloud, its momentum causing it to skid to within several hundred feet of the house. The horses jostled to get to their feet. Their ties to the wagon broken into splinters, they ran off. Some of the men, likewise, staggered to their feet and ran. A volley of shot and smoke issued from the orchard. Those who were mobile enough to run for it were massacred by musket fire. One by one they arched their backs and fell.

Jan pounded his fist against the wall. "Noooo!"

Upstairs Margot peered over Matthew's shoulder. They watched in horror as the wagon tumbled out of control. It was a hideous action, the kind they didn't want to see but couldn't help but watch.

Matthew described the scene to Rachel who was still sitting in the corner holding Deborah.

"My father! Do you see my father?"

"Too much dust. I can't see anything right now."

A series of loud blasts echoed as muskets spit smoke and death from the trees. Margot hid her eyes against Matthew's back.

"What's happening?" Rachel wailed.

Still hiding behind Matthew, Margot said, "The Boers are shooting at them."

"Father!" Rachel shifted the baby to one arm so that she could push herself out of the corner with the other.

Margot shook her head at Rachel. "No, honey, stay there!"

"My father's down there!" Rachel said, ignoring Margot's instructions.

"I see him!" Matthew cried. "He's alive!" He looked at Rachel. "The wagon is on its side. He and Ding are behind it on this side. He's safe for now!"

Rachel abandoned her effort to get up. Her head fell back into the corner. She was weeping softly; her eyes were closed.

Peering over Matthew's shoulder again, Margot pointed toward the wagon. "Pieter's favoring his leg. And Ding is holding his arm." To Rachel she said, "But they're both sitting up. The wagon is protecting them from the Boers' muskets. They look scraped and bruised, but other than that they seem to be all right."

Rachel looked at her and nodded, appreciating the news.

"I don't see any weapons," Matthew said.

Margot looked. "I don't see any either. But the Boers don't know that they don't have weapons."

"At least not yet," Matthew said.

"At least not yet," Margot echoed.

From his vantage point at the sitting room window Jan breathed easier when, as the cloud of dust rose, he saw his father and Ding sheltered in the hollow of the wagon bed.

"But they don't have any weapons," he whispered to himself.

He glanced at the approaching band. He recognized Breyton's gait, and now his beard and oversized coat. They would be here in a matter of minutes.

Jan had to find a way to get a musket and ammunition to his father and Ding before they arrived. If he could make it to the corner of the porch, he could toss a weapon and an ammunition pouch to them.

He went to the front door. His plan was simple. Throw open the door. Run from pillar to pillar to the end of the porch and toss his musket and pouch to his father.

Jan placed his hand on the latch. Took a deep breath and pulled. *BLAM! BLAM! BLAM! BLAM! BLAM! BLAM!*

Musket balls peppered the front of the house like hard rain. Glass from the windows sprayed all over the furniture and floors. Jan jumped back. The door beside him gaped open like a portal to the afterlife, inviting him to step through. Only, if he did, it would be the last thing he ever did in this life.

Margot grabbed Matthew's shoulder.

"What was that?" she cried at the sound of a musket storm.

"I think Jan's thinking what we're thinking, and he tried to get help to the wagon."

It took only an instant for Margot to understand the possible consequences. "Jan?" she cried softly at the realization. Then frantically, "Jan! Jan!" She ran to the bedroom door and threw it open. *"Jan!"*

"Stay up there! Don't come down!"

318

The sound of his voice meant he was alive. She fell against the doorjamb in relief. "Are you hit?" she cried.

"No! But the door is wide open. So don't come down!"

"You're sure you're all right?"

"Yes! I'm all right."

Margot placed her head against the doorjamb. "Thank You, Lord. Thank You."

Matthew called to her from the window. "I have an idea!" He left the window. "How do you stop people from shooting at you?"

Margot looked at Rachel. Neither was following his line of thought.

"How do you stop people from shooting you?" he asked again, this time showing teeth.

The way he smiled, Margot could tell he liked his idea better the more he thought about it.

He answered his own question: "By making them think you're already dead!" He grinned in triumph.

Rachel didn't share his smile. "I don't think I like this plan."

"It sounds intriguing. What's your plan?" Margot asked.

Matthew described it.

At each step of the scheme, Rachel shook her head harder. "No, no," she said.

"What do you think, Margot?" Matthew asked.

"It's risky. Very risky."

"But will it work?"

"It could."

"No! I won't let you do it!" Rachel cried from her corner.

Staying clear of the window, Matthew crossed over to her. Kneeling beside her, he caressed her cheek.

"No!" she insisted, beginning to cry.

"Rachel, I can do it. But more important, I have to do it."

"No, you don't have to do it!"

"Yes, I do. Those men out there want to kill us. Your father and Jan and all the others are endangering their lives to stop them. I've got to do my part. I can't sit up here and do nothing!"

Rachel turned her head. She refused to look at him.

"And if by some miracle we do get out of this alive," he said, "how will I ever convince your father and brother that I am worthy to be a member of this family if they know I could have done something to help but didn't?"

"They would never need to know!" Rachel said.

"But I would know!" Matthew shouted. "Look at me!"

Rachel refused to turn toward him.

Laying aside the musket, Matthew placed gentle hands on her face and turned her toward him. "Either we are part of this family, or we are not. Their approval of us is secondary. If we're truly a part of this family, we have to act like it."

Tears rolled down Rachel's cheeks in a steady stream.

"So you tell me, are we part of this family or not?"

Through watery eyes Rachel looked lovingly at her husband. "We're a part of this family," she whispered. "Be careful."

"I love you," he said. He kissed his wife and baby daughter. Retrieving the musket, he turned to Margot and said, "Tell Jan I'm going out there and not to shoot me."

Jan hadn't moved. He stood against the wall next to the front door, straining to hear what Margot was saying.

"That's crazy!" he shouted back.

"We've got to try something!" Margot yelled. "They're almost here!"

The back of Jan's head banged against the wall. "O God, help us!" he whispered.

Margot's voice came from the stairway. "He's ready! Are you ready?"

Jan checked his musket, then closed his eyes. "I'm ready!"

"On the count of three!"

Jan took a deep breath as he listened to Margot's count.

"One! Two!"

He stepped away from the wall.

"Three!"

Jan swung the musket out the door and fired.

33

In the upstairs room Matthew mirrored Jan's action. At the count of three he poked his musket through a hole in the glass and fired. Then he jumped to one side for the anticipated response. He wasn't disappointed. A hail of musket balls hit the side of the house and window. Glass shattered and flew everywhere.

He looked to the corner. Rachel and the baby were safely covered by the quilt. Then he checked Margot. She was ducked down in the doorway, her back to him. The momentum of the blast had showered bits of glass at her feet, but she too was unharmed.

She turned and looked at him, giving him a nod. "God be with you," she said.

Matthew took a step back. With a horrific scream he flung himself through the window, rolled across the porch roof, fell off the end, and landed with a thud in the dirt.

Through the shattered window, scattered cheers from the Boers drifted into the room.

After firing, Jan managed to dodge back to safety an instant before a wave of lead balls crashed against the house. Several whistled past him through the open door. The hallway and sitting room walls erupted with splinters. With his back pressed tightly against the outside wall, Jan felt several thuds that would have found their mark in him had it not been for the sturdiness of the house Breyton built.

According to plan, Jan heard Matthew roll across the porch roof. He winced when he heard the thud as the boy hit the ground, then cringed at the scattered cheers from the Boers.

He had to look. Peeking around the door cautiously, he saw Matthew facedown in the dirt. Little swirls of dust still danced around him from the impact. The boy looked dead. Jan bit his lower lip and watched.

"What do you see?" Rachel had thrown off the quilt. Deborah wailed in her arms. Rachel seemed oblivious to the sound.

Margot stood in Matthew's spot near the window. "He's down there," Margot said lamely, but she didn't know what else to say.

"Is he moving?"

"No."

A minute passed. Then another.

"Is anything happening?" Rachel cried again.

Covering her mouth with her hand, Margot stared at the still body in the dust and shook her head.

Jan peeked through the open doorway for the twelfth time. Matthew still hadn't moved. *It was too risky. I shouldn't have let him do it.* He looked for signs of life. Chest rising and falling. The stirring of a foot or arm. But there was nothing. Breyton and the rest of the approaching horde were beginning to arrive. It was too late. Matthew had sacrificed his life for nothing.

Jan looked at Ding and his father. They stared dumbfoundedly at Matthew's body.

"What's that noise?" Rachel asked.

"Breyton and the others. They're here."

"And Matthew?" Her voice was pitched high. Her eyes teemed with terror.

Margot shook her head sadly. "He hasn't moved."

Outside, a cheer went up as Breyton joined the Boers in the orchard. Margot watched them gather around their leader, greeting him with laughter and slaps on the back. They were celebrating as though it were all over.

Rachel buried her head against her baby. She tried her best not to cry. It was a losing effort.

There were no tears for Margot. Just an icy chill dread. Was it really all over? For the first time since Sylvie's death, she knew what it was to love. Why did it have to end so quickly?

A sudden movement caught Margot's eye. It was Matthew! He scrambled to his feet and darted toward the wagon.

"I don't believe it!" Jan whooped. Just as he had given Matthew up for dead, the boy jumped up and ran toward the wagon. The Boers were taken completely by surprise. No one even saw him until he was nearly there.

"It's Matthew!" Margot cried. "He's alive! Run, Matthew! Run! Run!"

Rachel bolted out of the corner. Carrying Deborah, she reached Margot just as the muskets fired.

BLAM! BLAM! BLAM! BLAM!

Rachel and Margot both caught their breaths.

Matthew tumbled in the dirt.

"No!" Rachel cried.

He didn't stop rolling until he was behind the wagon, where he collided with a surprised Pieter and Ding. Then, when he was safely in the shelter of the wagon, he looked up at the window and caught the eye of his wife. He flashed one of his toothy smiles.

"He made it! He made it!" Rachel screamed.

The two women hugged one another in celebration.

Downstairs, Jan shook his head in amazement. "Well, I'll be . . . I'll be . . . I've never seen anything like it in my life!"

Pieter yelled to his son. When he had Jan's eye, he held up Matthew's musket and ammunition pouch triumphantly. Ding pounded Matthew repeatedly on the back.

Jan nodded and clenched his fist to confirm the victory. Their little triumph brought a halt to the Boer celebration.

Then he caught Breyton's eye.

Jan had never really been frightened in his life. There had been the usual heart-stopping childhood scares in the dark, but they were nothing compared to the stark naked fear he felt right now as he looked into his brother's eyes.

The excitement upstairs over the success of Matthew's clever plan could not keep reality at bay for long. Pieter and Ding and Matthew were still caught between the Boers and the house. The next step in Margot's mind was to get them safely inside. Once that was done, they could concentrate on defending the house.

For a while nothing happened. Breyton surrounded himself with men in the orchard. He was discussing something with them. Pieter and Ding and Matthew huddled together against the overturned wagon. They too were discussing something. Margot wanted to go downstairs to be with Jan, but she couldn't leave Rachel and the baby alone. So she waited for someone to make the next move.

With a single command, the storm was unleashed, not at the house but at the wagon. Breyton seemed to have ordered every Boer musket trained on the overturned vehicle. At his shout, concentrated fire chipped away at the wood, sending bits of wagon flying everywhere.

The three men inside hunkered down, bunching together.

Jan stared in horror at the tactic. He ran to the hallway and shouted for all those with guns to return the Boers' fire. Taking up his position by the door once again, he loaded and fired and loaded and fired as rapidly as his fingers would move. The return fire from the house was a pitiful effort. In addition, it placed his father and the others in a crossfire. They could just as easily be killed by an errant shot from the house as they could from one of the Boer guns. But they had to do something to try to back the Boers away.

As Jan fired one shot after another, he tried to think of a better tactic. His thoughts were clouded with rage. He tried to force back his feelings so that he could think more clearly, but he couldn't. And that made him angrier still.

"What are they doing?" Rachel cried. "Matthew! My Matthew!"

The shower of lead was taking its toll on the wagon. Larger bits and pieces of wood flew off. Gaps were beginning to appear in places. The three men jerked this way and that. From fear? Or were the lead balls finding their mark?

From her point on high, Margot could see Breyton standing behind several lines of Boers. Like a general, he was forming them into ranks three deep. While the first row fired, the second two loaded. Once the volley was off, the first row would fall back and the next row move forward to fire. In this way the wagon was showered nonstop with deadly fire.

This was not a typical Boer tactic. This was pure Breyton.

Margot raised the musket to her shoulder. He must be stopped. She aimed down the barrel. A Boer on the front line came into focus. She moved the gun back to the second line, the third line, then on to the man coordinating them. She rested the end of the musket barrel on Breyton's chest. An image from the past flashed into her mind. The *Eagle*. The gun deck. White plumes of smoke billowing from the belly of a pirate ship. Then, as now, there was only one thought. *Stop them. Stop them.*

She held her breath and pulled the trigger.

BLAM!

A chunk of wood flew from the tree near Breyton's head. He ducked instinctively, hands and arms covering his head, his expression one of shock and fear. He looked in the direction of the discharge. When he recognized Margot, his expression changed. He grinned wickedly and laughed.

Below her, from the porch, a voice sounded. It was Jan.

"Breyton! Hold your fire! Hold your fire!"

Jan appeared below, stepping from under the cover of the porch out into the open.

"Jan?" Margot cried. "What are you doing? Jan! Jan!"

She ran to the stairway. Rachel followed close behind, still carrying Deborah.

From the foot of the stairs Margot saw Jan through the frame of the open front door. His hands were held high. They were empty. The handle of a knife was stuck in his belt at the small of his back.

The firing stopped. All was silent.

"Jan!" Margot yelled.

He gave no indication he'd heard her.

She and Rachel ran onto the porch.

All eyes were on Jan van der Kemp. The Boers in the orchard stared at him; many had their muskets leveled at him.

"What are you doing? Go back inside!" his father yelled.

Breyton emerged from the trees and faced his brother.

Just then Rachel screamed, "Matthew!" Before Margot could stop her, she bolted from the porch and ran toward the wagon.

Breyton held up a hand indicating that no one was to fire.

"Rachel!" Jan cried. "No! Get back!"

She didn't listen. Deborah jostled in her mother's arms, complaining loudly the whole way. It was then that Margot saw what had prompted Rachel's action. Blood. All three men bore growing red stains.

Without turning, Jan said to Margot, "Get her back in the house."

Margot nodded. She joined Rachel and the men at the wagon.

Ding had a hole in his arm. He covered it with his hand. Pieter had been hit twice. Once in the hand and once in his leg.

Matthew had been hit the worst. The lower portion of his shirt was soaked with blood. His eyes were half-closed. He was failing. "Go back to the house, Rachel!" he whispered. When she didn't obey him, he turned to Margot. "Take her back to the house! Please!"

Margot made several attempts to pull Rachel away. She wouldn't budge.

"Did you come to surrender?" Breyton asked Jan.

"Yes," Jan replied.

"Why? When you know I'm going to kill you all anyway?"

Jan's hands twitched.

Margot glanced at the hidden knife. She could tell that Pieter saw it too.

Jan said, "This is a family matter, Breyton. We can settle this between us. Send these other people away."

Breyton sneered. "That's a pathetic overture, Jan. You don't really expect me to do that, do you?"

"Jan's right," Pieter said. The elder van der Kemp worked his way to his feet and painfully hobbled toward his two sons. "This is between you and me, Breyton."

Without taking his eyes off his father, Breyton yelled. "But what would I be without my friends?"

A cheer went up behind him.

"And what would they be without me?" he added. "It is I who taught them to raid. I have given them the other farms, and I will give them this one too!"

Another cheer.

Jan spoke up. "When I said this is a family matter, what I meant was that if you want us all dead, you should kill us yourself."

"You don't think I could do that?"

"Could you? I think you could kill Father and me. But could you kill Rachel?"

Breyton looked over at his sister and her baby.

"And Margot?"

Breyton chuckled. Looking back at Jan, he said, "Yes, yes, I think I could—beginning with the old man!" He whipped out his serrated knife and lunged at his father, then swung him around, taking him by the throat with a forearm.

At the sudden movement, Jan reached for the hidden knife.

"Oh, ho!" Breyton cried with delight when he saw the blade. He positioned himself behind his father, using Pieter as a shield. "You surprise me, Jan! You were always the unimaginative one. But I must admit that little trick surprised me!"

In the distance there was a rumbling. It distracted Breyton momentarily.

Jan thought he saw an opening and stepped forward.

Breyton was back instantly.

"Don't worry about me, Jan," Pieter said. "Kill Breyton. Now!"

Breyton swirled the tip of his knife inches from his father's face. "Jan can't do that," he said to Pieter. "He loves you too much. But I don't."

The knife slashed across Pieter's cheek. A ribbon of red appeared.

"Breyton!" Jan cried. "Let him go!"

"You see, Jan? I have all the advantage!"

"Kill him! Don't let him cut me up piece by piece!"

Jan looked from his father to his brother helplessly.

The rumbling in the distance grew even louder.

"What is that?" Breyton cried to the men behind him. When nobody knew, he ordered them to find out.

At the wagon, Rachel held Matthew's head in her lap while she soothed him and the baby.

Margot tended to his wound.

"It's a bad one," Matthew said.

Margot didn't disagree with him.

Looking up at his wife and daughter, he said, "I don't want to leave you like this. But it seems I have no choice. When Deborah is old enough to understand, you'll let her know that I loved her, won't you? That it wasn't my choice to leave her? Tell her that I never loved anyone as much as I loved her and her mother?"

Rachel shushed him. Her tears fell on his forehead.

To Margot he said, "Take care of them for me?"

Margot nodded.

He closed his eyes and took a deep breath. It was a ragged breath, and painful. Opening his eyes again, Margot saw a familiar glint, the kind of look in his eye when he was thinking up an ingenious plan to sell vases to people who never knew they wanted to buy one. He whispered to Margot, "Who better to take a bullet than a person who is already dead?"

Margot's eyes filled with tears. She understood.

Continuing to care for her patient, Margot nonchalantly reached for a musket and moved it next to Matthew's hand.

"Drop the knife!" Breyton said to Jan.

"Kill him!" Pieter yelled.

Jan hesitated.

"Drop the knife!" Breyton stabbed his father in the side.

Pieter's eyes rolled upward, and he groaned.

"That one won't kill him, but the next one will! Drop the knife!"

The knife fell from Jan's hand. It thumped in the dirt.

Breyton laughed wildly. "You are a fool! You should have listened to your father! It's the first time we've agreed on anything!"

From behind them one of the Boers shouted, "Soldiers! Soldiers are coming!"

The orchard came alive. It sounded as though it were infested with bees.

"Then we'll just have to make short work of this!" Breyton yelled to them. A movement from the side caught his eye.

Matthew. With a raised musket.

Breyton whirled to protect himself with his father's body. "Shoot him!" Breyton yelled.

BLAM! BLAM! BLAM!

Matthew spun around. He dropped to his knees.

Breyton rammed the knife into his father's back.

"No!" Jan launched himself forward. Grabbing his father, he pulled him to the ground.

Breyton stood exposed.

Struggling to raise the musket, Matthew aimed it and fired.

BLAM!

Breyton took the full force of the blast in the chest. He flew backward to the ground.

The next thing Jan knew, horses and men were running everywhere. The governor's soldiers from the Castle had arrived.

34

Pieter van der Kemp lay on his bed. Margot did not expect him to live much longer.

He called for his son. "The Boers?" he asked.

"The soldiers chased them back into the hills," Jan answered.

"Breyton?"

"Dead."

"That boy—the Malaysian boy."

"Matthew is also dead."

"Rachel picked a fine man," Pieter said.

"I wish you would tell her that yourself."

"Where is she?"

"She's with Matthew," Margot said.

Pieter nodded. His eyes grew weary. "Jan?"

"Yes, Father?"

"Will you get the family Bible?"

Jan retrieved the Bible from the sitting room.

Pieter instructed him to hand it to Margot.

"Margot, dear," Pieter said, "would you read to me? I'd like the last words I hear in this life to be the words of God."

Margot looked lovingly at Pieter. Then she handed the Bible to Jan.

A puzzled look crossed Pieter's face.

Jan opened the family Bible. He began to read Proverbs 4:1–7.

"'Hear, ye children, the instruction of a father, and attend to know understanding.'"

The expression on Pieter's face at first was one of shock, then it changed to pleasure and pride as he closed his eyes.

"'For I give you good doctrine, forsake ye not my law. For I was my father's son, tender and only beloved in the sight of my mother. He taught me also, and said unto me, Let thine heart retain my words: keep my commandments, and live. Get wisdom, get understanding: forget it not; neither decline from the words of my mouth. Forsake her not, and she shall preserve thee: love her, and she shall keep thee.

Wisdom is the principal thing; therefore get wisdom: and with all thy getting get understanding.'"

Pieter van der Kemp died while listening to his son read to him from the Bible.

Klaarstroom was alive with excitement and festivity. It was a day of celebration. The newly wedded couple stood happily on the porch greeting each of their guests.

"I'm so happy for you!" Rachel said as she hugged Margot. "I liked you the first day I met you. Little did I know you would some-day be family."

"Thank you, Rachel dear," Margot said. "You're the closest thing I've ever had to a sister. And I couldn't have picked a better one if I'd tried."

"Where's Deborah?" Jan asked.

Rachel looked around at the guests. "Last time I saw her, Ding had her. She just loves him! She keeps looking at his skin and rubbing it. I think she thinks his black skin is painted on."

Jan and Margot laughed.

"That was really kind what you did for him," Rachel said. "He is so proud his is one of the first free black families in Cape Town that sometimes I think he's going to bust." She looked at her brother odd-ly. "You know, I always thought you and Father were exactly alike. But you're doing things Father never would have done." To Margot she added, "Keep up the good work—you may make a decent man of him yet!"

Jan spoke softly to Rachel. "In his own way, Father loved you. When you left, a part of him died. He was never the same after that."

Rachel bowed her head. Tears fell. "The day of the raid I came hoping to speak to him—to ask his forgiveness. I didn't expect him to give it, but I had to ask. And now he'll never know how bad I feel about the way I hurt him—disobeyed him. I don't know how I'm going to live with that fact."

Margot touched Rachel's shoulder in comfort. "I'm sure he un-derstands how you feel—better now than if he were still living. Might I make a suggestion?"

Rachel dried a tear and nodded.

"When my Sylvie died, I determined the best thing I could do in her memory was to carry on her legacy of faith. You can do the same for your father and mother. When little Deborah is old enough, tell her about her grandparents, their love for this land, their passion for

God and His Word. Train her to teach *her* children and grandchildren. Do it for your father. And it will make him proud."

With a nod Rachel embraced Margot. She whispered, "As God is my witness, I will make my father proud."

Next, Rachel moved to Jan and hugged him.

"Please reconsider about moving back to Klaarstroom," Jan said.

"Yes," Margot said. "Please come live with us."

Rachel shook her head. "If it was just me, I would. But we all know that Deborah would never be accepted by the other children. She's better off with her own kind. We don't have much, but at least she's accepted."

Margot wished she could argue with Rachel's reasoning, but she couldn't. Deborah was of mixed blood. Many of their neighbors would never accept her.

"Visit us often?" Jan said.

Rachel nodded and gave her brother a bear hug.

When the wedding guests were gone, Jan and Margot van der Kemp took a walk. The late afternoon air was crisp and fresh. The Hottentots-Holland mountain range was especially clear. They walked in silence to a bluff overlooking the house.

The angle of the declining sun hit the house just right. Its fading rays reflected off the windows, making them appear to be made of gold. Overhead, the first of the evening stars began to appear.

Jan took his bride by the hand. He pulled her to him.

With her husband's strong arms around her, Margot looked up at the sky and wondered if Sylvie could see her—if Sylvie knew how happy she was at this moment.